Forty Thousand Years of Separation

A Novel of Possibilities

By

Eric Shulenberger, PhD JD

Publication Information
ISBN 13   978-0692658697
ISBN 10   0692658696
Copyright © 2016 by Eric Shulenberger

Shulenberger Publishing
3912 NE 127th St., Seattle WA 98125
ericshul@hotmail.com

Library of Congress Control Number = 2016905076
Editor #1 = Eric Shulenberger
Editor #2 = Susan C Wessman

Thanks:

My wife, Susan Wessman, has read the manuscript several times, both critically and editorially. A great deal of the structure and content of the story resulted from that help, freely given over the 18 months of writing and re-writing. She quickly taught me enough about using PhotoShop so that I could assemble the cover artwork She has been wonderfully patient with me throughout the entire process.

Others have helped with discussions and comments, or just with general encouragement. Such helpmates include but are certainly not limited to my in-laws (Susan's parents) Jo and Wayne Wessman, Dr Bernie Zahuranec, my nephew Damon Shulenberger, and my siblings Anne, Jeannette and Arthur.

Should the reader encounter something s/he feels is irksomely awry, the fault is mine alone. But do remember, the story is one of **possibilities**, which are not **IMpossibilities**, however improbable they may seem to us at this moment.

****

<u>Pronunciation</u>: readers may, of course, supply their own. Your author hears **"Chys"** thusly **- a hard ch (cheese), long I, ending in a short Z, an overall rhyme with 'eyes'.** Her daughter **"Veejr" is simply VEE, then JER as in jersey. Veejr** derives from the letters VGER found still legible when satellite VOYAGER-1 returned from space in "Star Trek - the Motion Picture" (1979). Voyager-1 was the first man-made object to escape the solar system hence Veejr seems oddly appropriate here.

Table of Contents

(Rev #4)

Chys knew she was dying.

She knew because over the several decades of her life she had seen many people go through what was now happening to her. The concept of death, and the dying process, didn't worry her: besides, what could she do about it? She had no complaints. Her body was worn out, most systems were actively failing now, all except her mind. But the machinery had served her well throughout an adventuresome life. She had experienced and survived things most people could not imagine if they tried. She had single-handedly killed both a Goliath of a man, and a cave bear; led a war party; and produced the Tribe's first blue-eyed baby and artist and Medicine Woman. And her off-spring were legion.

She was happy now, at an age of well over eighty. Way more than twice the average. By far the oldest person in the Tribe, older than any other person was even rumored to have been. Her eldest daughter, blue-eyed Veejr, at over fifty, was already regarded as nearly ancient.

Nobody was certain of Chys's actual age: number of years hadn't yet taken on the mystical aura it would in later times, and no calendar yet existed. Not that the society couldn't count that high, it was simply that there was no need for the number when applied to peoples' ages. Such large numbers could be useful in dividing up resources, yes - discussing or evaluating people's ages, no. Hence nobody kept count. Individuals with good memories could walk audiences backwards through years tied to seasons or events, but two parallel recountings might differ radically - which bothered no-one.

Chys had outlived all her children save Veejr-the-Artist, with whom she had been living now for several years, growing increasingly frail whilst waxing god-like to the rest of the Tribe. Her youthful exploits were the stuff of local legends. "She who kills Monsters and Cave Bears" would live on beyond her death both in story and in her portraits in Veejr's private cave. Chys found that knowledge oddly satisfying. She even found it amusing to wonder who would ever see her portraits. Veejr had assured her that the "younger" portrait - as requested by Chys when faced with a realistic painting of herself as an old, old woman - was almost done now. Chys knew she would never see it in person - but SOMEONE, SOMEDAY, she was certain, would. She hoped those future viewers would like them, would understand the drawings, the stories, and their meanings.

PREFACE

In humanity's deep past, back when Gregor Mendel and the theory of particulate inheritance lay some 40,000 years (over 2000 generations) in the future, in what is now Europe, there occurred two fundamentally different sexual encounters. Their combined effect was, in slow motion, transformative for the Tribe, and echoed forward into the distant future. The second, although not otherwise violent, was clearly a rape. The first was more in the nature of an assault with a friendly weapon. Geographically, the two happened within a few kilometres of one another: temporally they were five human generations apart. Genetic time is measured not in years but generations. Five is a very low number in gene-time. The encounters were independent, unrelated: some of the people involved were not. The events' lack of simultaneity undoubtedly helped with the ultimate consequences, because introduced genes (especially recessives) need time to spread and become more than vanishingly available in the receiving population.

1- GEOLOGY

Some millions of years ago, deep-Earth processes produced stresses that fractured the crust in what eventually became modern France. Locally, Earth's surface consisted of two to five metres of highly productive alluvium, underlain by pure white hard limestone well over a thousand metres thick. Those processes slowly raised one side of a major fracture until it stood as a vertical rampart, a cliff some hundreds of metres tall and nearly 200 kilometres long, trending mostly north-south. The face of the cliff carries numerous deep vertical grooves: from high altitude, it gives the impression of a planetary-scale chimpanzee's upper lip. The fracture captured runoff and eventually generated a wide, permanent, relatively fast stream, which in turn was (and still is) forever busy cutting its own valley Grand-Canyon-like, as the base rock slowly rises during intermittent bursts of tectonic activity. The rising base meant that the river eventually produced a series of flood plains, stepping upwards away from the water. The uppermost plain was against the base of the cliff. The farther up the sequence one went, the less likely became flooding, and the better became the chances of human artifacts being well preserved over significant time periods.

The region's plentiful rain percolated down from the plateau atop the cliff, through minor cracks and fissures in the bulk limestone, dissolving rock as it went. And over the millennia of millennia there was formed a complex ant's-nest maze of caverns. Many of these caves had openings to the outer world, most commonly at the base of the cliff itself. The caves proved highly usable to the early forms of humans who eventually discovered them. Caves plus fire plus water plus an equable climate plus enormous supplies of game: all these together made the area a perfect habitat for _Homo spp_. For thousands of generations human settlements persisted in The Valley, at the base of the cliff: when occasionally one was extinguished for some reason, another soon was founded if not literally in its place, then quite nearby. By human time-standards, human occupation of the region was somewhat spotty. From a more geological point of view, there existed a rough long-term population equilibrium.

In a very long-period time-lapse movie of the cliff face, one might follow the gradual retreat of its vertical surface, perhaps ten to fifteen metres on average over the latest 40,000 years. The thing most notable, however, would be its overall stability in activity and appearance over periods of a few thousand years or so. In such a film, from fairly close, one might occasionally note the blinking open and shut of cave entrances as they were affected by erosion and rock-falls. Large rooms could have an opening the size of a modern house appear in seconds when a big slab sloughed off - a rarity. Other caves, especially those with long, often tortuous entry tunnels leading far back into the deep interior of the limestone, often had openings smaller than a person, but size of cavern bore no relationship to size of entrance. Entrances to most caves cycled into and out of existence. And if the entry passage were long enough, the gradual retreat of the cliff-face meant that the deep inner caves became accessible to invasion by animals including _Homo_, at largely random intervals and for random periods. All this geological activi-

8

ty meant that a great many of the caves were at least intermittently available for human exploration, and even exploitation.

2 - CAVE ART AND ARTIFACTS

Slow geological processes had first produced The Valley's caves, then later ensured that most of them, although formed by solution, went desert-dry and had remained dry for the latest few tens of millennia....through the era of cave art. In some caves, one could find (and still can find) well-preserved art, almost all of it wall-paintings. The art dates to various periods: the subject matter is limited - mostly semi-naturalistic imagery of species that were prey, especially dangerous, or otherwise impressive. There seems to be no obvious reason for that limitation: an artist capable of drawing fine animals on cave walls is certainly capable of doing equally accurate humans, yet we never seem to find such paintings. The reason is undoubtedly cultural and itself left no traces yet found - but it could have done so, and with great good luck one might find them. Subjects of cave-art changed as the environment and its fauna changed over time, and the imagery differed in sophistication - particularly in realism - as societies and individual artists matured. On a societal scale, maturing was a slow and halting process, but eventually produced a few consistent styles each found over a fairly wide area. Seldom does one find art of two distinct styles in a single cave or cave complex. And although occasionally one could tell that a particular painter had done many individual paintings in a given cave - for example, using hand-prints - no modern investigator had ever traced any individual artist from cave to cave.

Beyond wall-paintings, other physical traces of early humans and their activities in and near caves are available to the careful seeker - tools, weaponry, skeletons, gravesites, fire-pits, trash heaps and the like. But at best such materials are patchy, wildly fragmented, difficult to put into temporal sequence, and subject to a huge range of interpretations, almost all of which are guaranteed to be wrong. It does not help that only very rarely are organic materials preserved - much of the most important cultural information has to do with things like food preparation, clothing, and the like. A further problem is that the most critical aspects of culture, and the thinking capabilities behind any culture (e.g., systems of belief about how nature works), are almost unknowable today, save in the most exceptional circumstances. And absent writing, very little indeed of ancient human social behavior remains accessible. It is difficult verging on the impossible to accurately infer social structure or content or language from even the most sophisticated stone blade.

Those difficulties have helped dichotomize anthropologists' views as to when, and how suddenly, the mental capacities of "modern" *Homo sapiens* emerged. Essentially there are two camps - one camp believes in a very recent sudden, massive step-function change in those abilities, occurring between 200,000 and about 40,000 years ago - but the "big steppers" have yet to hypothesize a believable biological driver for that change. The other camp feels that the fragmentation and incompleteness of the record is the problem - that the obvious change in mental capacity over that span (the change being agreed upon by both sides) is simply rapid evolution, driven by fully-understood processes of natural selection - a collection of very rapid steps, each of which is individually unspectacular, but which collectively (mostly because of incompleteness of the record) give the impression of a single spectacular step.

Inferences about mental capabilities depend ultimately on hard evidence, namely physical artifacts. Softer evidence (e.g., organic materials), if found, might give much more accurate windows into social structure and function, and thinking capabilities. What cannot readily be addressed is how well the makers of both our tiny selection of hard artifacts and our nearly nonexistent inventory of softer materials actually thought, relative to our abilities today. Nor can we infer much about the course of cultural evolution - was all progress a matter of slow accumulation of experience, or were there occasional "great thinkers" who individually invented important items such as the spear? The bow-and-arrow? Attaching a hand-held chopper to a stick and so making the first axe? SOMEONE had to be the first for every such forward step. Each step is a great conceptual leap implying something about the person's (hence the species') mental capabilities.

Today's _H. sapiens_ find themselves greatly intrigued by these traces of our ancestors: we spend considerable time and energy seeking out good examples and then trying to interpret and understand them. But even full-time seekers cannot find it all. Although professionals are now involved in the search, and governments too, there is plenty of room for the amateur. And especially for the lucky.

Caves do not last forever. Very little cave art, and few other neolithic artifacts, are being produced these days, and caves do have finite lives, so the inventory is dwindling, slowly but inexorably. Which does not mean there isn't plenty of material yet to discover, just that it is getting rarer. Which in turn means that it is increasingly difficult to tease out the human story either behind any artifact's creation, or contained in cave-art itself. If such a story exists in found art and other artifacts, it can be unraveled only by intense analysis of a broad variety of information, plus the wildest of good luck. Luck always being trump-suit.

In short, it is highly improbable, verging on the impossible, that one might learn any details of human society and life say 40,000 years ago - much less any biographical details of individuals' lives. Success requires a concatenation of events each mundane but collectively not so. However, if merely improbable rather than absolutely impossible, such concatenations should happen occasionally. This is the story of one possible confluence of events.

3 – YESTERDAY - THE TRIBE

The Tribe had resided uninterruptedly in this agreeable place for some thousands of years, well above 100 generations, perhaps over 200. The cliffs were riddled with caves that provided people with winter-time shelter from weather and from most dangerous animals - from all save the big and terrifyingly ferocious cave bears, and occasional even more dangerous humans. Fortunately, bears were increasingly rare because at least locally the Tribe's braver and more foolish men-folk killed them faster than they reproduced. The climate was reasonable: the worst droughts never dried up the river, and it seldom froze across, although mysterious solid water occasionally could be found at its edges during deep winter. The river provided fish and waterfowl of many species in abundances that varied across the seasons - but never went totally lacking. Plus shellfish whenever needed. Four-footed game - all the way up to bison and beyond - was always readily available on the huge grassy plateau atop The Rampart: the problem was not supply, but getting the kills back down the cliff. It was a superb place to live - there was every reason not to leave, and very few ever did so, at least willingly.

The settlement was isolated, yes - but not by any means totally. There could be visitors, even guests. Three tall, strange men appeared one fine day. From their equipment it was obvious to the Tribe that they were hunters, not warriors, which was good. Equally obviously, they were some quite considerable distance from home, for their speech was unintelligible, and their leather clothes were made from species unknown to the Tribe. They arrived mid-afternoon, and from their studiously noisy approach it was clear that they knew where the Tribe's settlement was - and also clear that they did not intend to surprise anyone. A good idea on their part, both courteous and pragmatic. Tribes were rare and widely-spaced even in this benign environment, but murder and occasional warfare were not unknown, hence strangers were always an iffy phenomenon, demanding caution. Caution up to and including pre-emptive manslaughter. The Tribe's Chief instantly sent two men to scout the direction opposite the trio's approach, in case another party of foreigners might be using the distraction as cover. They found nothing.

The trio was welcomed, albeit warily. The wariness increased markedly once they were close enough for detailed examination. All three were several inches taller than the Tribe's tallest. One visitor, clearly the leader, held everyone spellbound, for nobody in the Tribe had ever heard of, much less seen, a blue-eyed human. Bright blue. Otherwise, save his height, he met tribal standards. His two companions had tribal-style black irises, all three had tribal skin tones.

The visitors' behavior had been exemplary - friendly, re-

12

strained. For supper, they had volunteered meat from their day's kill: the generosity nearly eliminated the Tribe's wariness. Because tribes were sparse on the landscape and seldom interacted, every tribe had its own dialect, or even separate language. Despite lack of common speech, communication was easy - basic signing was universal. It transcended those boundaries and met most needs, even for very complex communications.

The Tribal Woman was pretty, young, and unpaired when the trio of strange men showed up. She was fifteen now, although nobody ever kept count - well past the age at which she should have paired off, started a family - but she wasn't ready for that yet. She was much braver and more openly curious than the norm. And much more forward, a very accomplished flirt. Her initial shock and mild fright at being face-to-face with the three aliens quickly dissipated, replaced by gender-driven interest and frank attraction. Blue-Eyes had her totally fascinated, something he perceived instantly and played upon with the subtlest of hand and facial signage. He was an accomplished seducer - he fully understood what initiatives to take, what responses to give, in order to captivate her. Body language was most useful - including Woman's intense reciprocal flirting, focused on Mister Blue-Eyes himself.

He was the Alpha in the three-pack - young but fully mature, heavily muscled, mentally quick, a good signing story-teller, a ready grinner. Overall a genuinely attractive man. Made more so by his foreignness and strange eyes. In this Tribe's developing vocabulary the color 'blue' had no name as yet - neither had the society or its language developed the abstract concept of 'blueness'. But those lacks aside, once she got used to it, she rather liked the new color - it made his expressions much easier to read, which was a good thing for her, probably occasionally bad for him. Throughout supper and into the evening they made increasingly frequent eye contact. Repeatedly, she blushed so intensely it was visible despite her relatively dark coloring. Tribal members politely ignored the developing flirtation - it was simply not their business!

After the communal supper, stories were told by both sides, running on until the last of the skylight was gone and faces were visible only vaguely in the flicker of the dying fire. Eventually the Chief assigned the three a sleeping spot. With a pair of obvious, well-armed guards. Safety first.

As they prepared for the night, Blue-Eyes gestured privately to her, tiny movements of fingers and eyes, pointing with his lips. Winking. Smiling. She should, he signed, come to visit him in the night. But please don't wait too long! Together they would leave the camp, then return - much later! Everything would be okay, he told her - after all, it was plain that no Tribal man had claimed her for himself, so she need not fear raising jealousy in some proprietary male. Come on, Woman!

From across the fire she played coy, teased. An adventure! Of the highest caliber. Maybe she would. Probably not a good idea to go - too dangerous, alone in the dark with a complete stranger! But wait, be patient, maybe. Don't be pushy, don't rush a woman - bad tactics! Maybe. Giggle. Yes... or, perhaps, maybe!

Quiet descended. At home in bed, wide awake and eager, she waited a proper (short!) time, perhaps half an hour, then stirred gently, stood and moved in his direction, in perfect silence. When Blue-Eyes rose to meet her he was clearly unarmed and thoroughly preoccupied, therefore of no concern to the guards, who understood, nudged one another but made no comment. Not their business. And if anyone other than the guards noticed, they likewise didn't show it. Again, not their business!

Paired or not, no Tribal woman her age lacked considerable experience. She soon found, oddly enough, that his having blue eyes seemed to make no difference in what was needed to handle him! Alone together in thick brush a hundred metres from camp, her soundless protestations were utterly pro-forma - fortunately so because he was immensely more powerful than she, and male-urgent. She understood both an urgent man and the parallel deep-seated urgency in herself. The Woman could, and did, provide what both of them wanted and needed, rendering this, the first of two critical sexual events, much more a case of mutual seduction than a classic forcible encounter like the second. The second would follow some generations in the future.

14

She knew the possible consequences of their actions, of course. Most of her small age-group had already been pregnant at least once, her people understood the connection between fucking and pregnancy. The Woman was fertile and had had many trysts: she had failed at conception only by chance. She was slightly worried by that failure, because every pregnancy was positive - a good thing for the Tribe - and certainly no man would consider pairing with a woman who had not yet proven she could bear children. This time, however, her luck either ran out, or changed for the better, depending on one's point of view.

The trio left amicably in the early morning and were never seen again by the Woman or her Tribe.

One month, then two, passed without her period. Three. She was concerned - not about pregnancy - after all, more tribes-people were always needed to replace those accidentally killed by big game, or intentionally eaten by cats and bears. And pregnancy before becoming paired with one man was perfectly normal - the concepts of serious monogamy and women-as-property hadn't yet developed, so 'wedlock' likewise had not yet arisen. In any case, the Tribe was totally matrilineal. No - what concerned her was some basic biology, fully understood by all humans. "Like father like son" and "like mother like daughter". That is, kids look like their parents. She knew who the father was. What, she worried, would happen to her, and especially to her baby, if it had blue eyes? Being an oddity could lead to ostracism, even murder. But it could also be advantageous, if seen as a good omen, signifying the possibility of other special characteristics useful to the Tribe (the concept of 'luck' was better developed than many).

Mendel, were he available, could have reassured her: she needn't have worried. [Although (being a monk), he would likely have tried to convert her [but from what, exactly?] and then to save her soul - 'soul' being another as-yet undeveloped concept.] Simplifying things, he'd have told her that blue eyes in humans are recessive, meaning other varieties of the eye-color gene will overpower or turn off the expression of blue. Simplistically, every person has two genes for eye-color, one from mom, the other from dad. For a person to have blue eyes, each parent must have a blue-gene, and the person must receive blue genes from both parents - having two similar genes is called being homozygous, having two different genes is being heterozygous. If a person is heterozygous, then the non-blue gene -whatever color- will be dominant and mask the blue. In the Tribe, a heterozygous baby would have "tribal normal" eyes with the usual dark, almost black irises. Two black-irised parents could produce a blue-eyed baby, if both parents carried both types of genes.

The Woman came from a lineage having a strong tendency towards identical twins. She was both relieved and disappointed when her (and Blue-Eyes') identical-twin sons had tribal-normal dark eyes - but both carried, hidden, the blue recessive. The twins grew up to be remarkably tall and good-looking. They did what males were supposed to do, namely spread their sperm as widely as possible. They were intelligent, personable, and randy. Each fathered over a dozen children, many of whom were heterozygous for blue, the gene coming from Blue-Eye. Generation by generation, the percentage of Tribe members carrying the blue recessive steadily increased from zero to minuscule.

4 - TODAY

Today, a thriving academic anthropological scene is centered around The Rampart, a strikingly rich source of sites and materials. The Universite de la Pais (aka UP) has a well-established anthro program. A relative newcomer is La Fondation pour Anthropologie (aka La Fond), a privately-funded research institution with an enormous endowment. La Fond has a large operating budget and superb facilities, but is not itself a degree-granting institution - rather, it is strictly a research facility. It has close relationships with many academic institutions, for both research and educational activities. Many graduate students from various universities world-wide come to La Fond from the schools in which they are formally enrolled, to do their actual research. Many spend three to five years in residence at La Fond, doing their dissertation work and taking occasional ad-hoc classes.

The UP has shepherded several decades of steady work at the base of the cliffs, centered on one complex and very large site, half cave and half outside-world. It is at least 40,000 years old, and had been occupied almost continually for at least several thousand years. In Tribal times, the site had been protected from the rear by the cliff, and from stream-ward by a gated palisade of long poles, sharpened, touching side by side, outward-slanted.

Gerard, a modern born-and-bred local boy, had spent much of his early teenage years poking about in the caves. He'd grown up in a town only a few kilometres from the UP's major site. The town was ancient, showing up in tax and property records dating back at least to the Romans. Gerard's mother was an avid and thorough genealogist and had managed to chase the family's history back to the Dark Ages – always in this town – but lost it in the morass of the first wave of bubonic plague.

Gerard eventually decided on cave-based anthropology as a career, and finished his undergraduate work at another nearby school. Accepted into UP's doctoral program, he arrived for his first semester of graduate studies and was immediately thrust into the initial required coursework, an intense program. For some weeks, that kept him far too busy to do any snooping about in the school's anthropological museum, or in the work and prep spaces in its basement. But eventually, having heard in particular about the goings-on surrounding the school's anthropologically famous "Spear-Lady", he and three buddies made the trek to the basement. A couple of more senior students were working on Spear-Lady materials, and invited them in.

Spear-Lady's grave was most intriguing - so much so that a whole new technique had been tried in handling it. The Lady's entire grave had been frozen in situ at the main dig some 80 or 100 kilometres distant. Then it had been excavated whole, and brought here, for painstaking dissection and analysis. Students dubbed it "The world's first portable hole."

Gerard and his friends were far more interested in the skeleton and the huge spear buried with it than in the various other artifacts removed from the grave. As they shifted their viewpoint, Gerard finally looked across the grave at the big slab of calcite that had been laid down atop Lady in her grave. The carefully-shaped slab's very existence was a complete anomaly. It was as if the grave had a huge subterranean stone lid - like for a sepulcher, but without bottom or sides. Just a naked lid. Unique. No such thing had ever been found elsewhere, nor had a second example been found at the UP site.

He came as close to fainting as he ever had: there, big as life, in bright red on the dirty white calcite, was HIS ARTIST'S signature. The triple ess from the entrance, and from every single bit of art inside his personal, secret, cave. Nobody had ever reported, from ANYwhere, finding a signature. No signatures whatever, not even on the best and most formal artworks. But Gerard's very own Artist had gone and signed this gravestone -or whatever it was- as well as the art in Gerard's private cave. And the sites were tens of kilometres apart. There was more: below the SSS, also in red ocher, a five-pointed star painted with one finger. Gerard literally had to lean on the trolley to stay upright - one of his friends even asked if he was okay. He said yes: not completely true - inside he was seriously light-headed, almost nauseous.

"What's going on here?" he asked himself - a simple question but one without an obvious answer. It was many kilometres, a considerable hike, from where Lady had been found to "his" cave. Question: Why would a person, why would his Artist, have signed this slab? He supposed it could be the Artist's own grave, prepared in advance, but that didn't seem very reasonable - that kind of planning worked for Egyptian pharaohs and in some other complex societies say three to five thousand years ago, but surely not back forty thousand, the rough age of Spear-Lady's site. It must indicate, he guessed, a relative - the buried woman, Spear-Lady, was in some way connected to his Artist - perhaps the same tribe, or family? Or even the same profession? Good grief! This strange burial could be anything from an honor to an attempt to keep her spirit locked away for the future. At any rate, she'd certainly gotten unique treatment, whether due to fear or respect.

Now what to do? He was caught in a first-class ethical dilemma: report his cave to the world, or not?

He made what seemed the only possible choice - seek professional help. He needed both advice, and a confessor.

Joan, the lab's Directrix (and, he already hoped, his own eventual major professor), invited him into her office. She looked once at his face, pointed to a chair and said "Sit! Gerard, you're paler than Banquo's Ghost. Are you feeling okay?"

He took a long, deep breath, nodded. "I need to tell you something. Remember the cave I was exploring on my own? The one whose location I wouldn't give to the admissions committee?"

Joan nodded, waited. She remembered perfectly - she'd been quite impressed with his approach to "his" cave. Too bad it seemed to be a dead-end, no-artifact dry hole. Nothing unusual in that, unfortunately.

"Um. I - well, I've been mapping it for four years, and I've never found any traces of human activity. Until a few weeks ago, just before the start of this school-year. "

The hair on Joan's nape rose. She stayed calm: "And it sounds like maybe that's changed. Am I right?"

He nodded, actually gulped, pulled from his backpack a tablet computer, turned it on.

"Here is the best of what I found. There are hundreds more but this one is absolutely the very best."

"Hundreds!?" thought Joan, now distinctly antsy. Hundreds of anything was a big number, potentially a big deal. "Hundreds of what?"

He handed her the tablet, displaying a full-screen view of his Artist's finest work, a three-quarter-view portrait - complete with blue eyes.

Joan's jaw actually dropped. After fully half a minute, she whistled, then said softly "God in heaven. Is it real? Jeezus Mary and Joseph!"

Gerard replied, "Oh, it's real, alright!" Then in a near-whisper, "I've only been able to spend one full day, maybe twelve hours, in the cave since I found the art. Everything about what I've found is a

19

total surprise, especially after three or four years of finding nothing. This art HAS to be important and it's why I'm here right now. See the mark that looks like a triple ess - the SSS?"

Joan nodded, staring hard at the image.

Gerard told her "It's got to be the Artist's signature. The same mark is on every painting in the cave, including a couple dozen charcoal profiles of people. On the wall, but in frames! Charcoal-drawn square frames, all lined up horizontally!"

Joan looked at him in utter mystification, repeated "Portraits? In frames? Lined up?" It didn't compute. But Gerard was no dummy. She knew he wouldn't mis-perceive, or mis-report, something so striking. And there was the Portrait.

He hurried onwards: "Dr Joan, don't you recognize the mark? It's the same as on the calcite slab from Spear-Lady's grave. On her gravestone! The same except for the ocher star on the slab, along with the SSS. There is some big, important connection between Spear-Lady and my cave's Artist!"

In sudden moments of stress, Joan often imitated the speech patterns of her husband Anton - a very smart, articulate man unfortunately given to casual profanity. She nodded, said "Holy fucking shit!" Then, after a pair of deep breaths, "How many works, Gerard? How many individual pictures are we talking about?"

Excitedly, he launched a short, largely random soliloquy: "Hundreds. So many that you can follow the artist's improvement over time. Subjects include anything, everything. Even landscapes - one of them has my favorite mountain in the middle of it, you can see the peak from my family home's back-yard. Birds flying. Geese in a big vee. A vulture landing beside a dead something. Incredible animals. Best horse-heads I have ever seen, old or modern. Profile portraits of people by the dozen, all lined up, one face per charcoal frame. There's even a bear skull, facing away from the art as if to guard it. Someone killed the bear with a spear through the left eye-ball. There's a bark folder on the floor, and in it are five sketches on birch-bark sheets of what amounts to paper, all exactly the same size. Standardized media, forty thousand years ago! I've even found the special paintbrush used for signing smaller works. And I think the Artist's kid came along - a lot! The kid got a whole wall for itself. It's wild! Closest to the entrance, what I call the "kid stuff" starts with a bunch of crude, gobbledygook drawings way down about knee-high above the floor, and they get better and better over time, until they start to be recognizable. And then the KID STUFF starts being signed, too, but with a different signature, that five-pointed star. And the kid-stuff is farther up the wall the farther you go - the kid was growing, and always painting at shoulder-height! Then all of a sudden the kid's signature changes and has both the kid's and the Artist's signature combined! There's a whole wall full of nothing but pictures with the double-signature. I don't know what's going on. It feels complicated. And important. I need HELP, it's way, way beyond ME!"

Joan was stunned. Finally she asked, "How many photos do you have here?"

"Several hundreds."

She thought for a long moment. "Gerard, it's time now for you to tell the world. At least, to tell the local paleo and anthro communities. Agreed?"

"Yes, of course...that's why I'm here - I need advice!"

"First, we really can't take chances with this, it's far too important to lose! So you need to immediately make me a backup copy of everything, before you so much as go home today. Put it in an envelope with detailed instructions for finding the cave."

He nodded, happy that she was taking charge – and that he had already deposited all the information and photos with his parents.

"Second, you pick 100 photos - starting with this mind-boggling blue-eyed portrait. Pick a wide variety. Then, prepare a lecture for the Monday-morning Anthro Symposium - a week from today. I'll advertise it, make all the arrangements. You worry about content and presentation - be simple, direct. And show a broad range of images. That'd be a good place to start. No big mea culpas, either. Be proud of your find and of your Artist's work!"

She smiled and asked, looking like a kid in a candy store, "Any more of those hundreds of pictures stored on this machine? Can I peek? Pretty-please?"

They spent five hours together, more often hyperventilating than not.

A week later, on stage, Gerard stood at the lectern, alone and nervous, waiting to begin his talk. He was in a most unusual position for a graduate student just starting his second semester. The talk he entitled "Some interesting findings from my previous work". He worried that it sounded pretentious coming from such a neophyte, but he'd been reassured by Joan that it did not.

He had done his share of lecturing as an undergraduate teaching assistant, hence facing an audience wasn't a new experience... but facing an audience like THIS nearly floored him. Packed. Every seat and all the standing room. People seated on every step of the amphitheater's stairs. The whole bleeding institution was on hold. For him!

The audience was Joan's doing - she'd made sure that everyone in the institution knew that if they missed Gerard's talk, they would forever beat themselves up for doing so. Everyone seemed to have gotten the word, and everyone including the janitorial staff came. Nobody knew what he was going to talk about - the announcement contained no specifics, no illustrations, no references. Peoples' questions had been answered only with Cheshire-Cat smiles.

She caught his eye, tapped her watch, nodded. Gerard flashed the lights, called for quiet.

"Ladies and gentlemen!"

At least he hadn't choked on his frog. He began in a tight formal voice: "I feel I must begin this presentation with a confession. Most of you do not know me. I was born in and grew up in a small town up on The Rampart Plateau, the town closest to this institution's finest archeological site. As a child I was familiar with the local caves - the whole area is limestone, and riddled with them. Most of them are, I am sure, still undiscovered. Most of the known caves have not been mapped or even very well explored. Those that have been, are forever changing."

"Some years ago, at age fifteen, on an outing by myself, I discovered a cave. I was totally entranced by having "my own" cave, so I told nobody. I spent all my spare time for the next several years very carefully mapping my cave in 3-D. Working, like an idiot amateur, completely alone. I found nothing interesting other than the cave itself, which is large and complex. Nothing until last summer, until the weekend before I arrived here, as a matter of fact! Only that recently did I finally find something. Something both interesting and startling. Something more interesting than mere subterranean geology."

"The confession I must make is that I have been totally selfish - I've never shown the cave or its contents to anyone. I have not yet shared my findings. The site is far beyond my capabilities, and needs a wholly professional team approach. I have been assured by people I trust that my failure to share up to now is not unethical. But from here forward, as a hopeful professional in anthropology, continued failure to share would be in the highest degree unethical. This talk is my opening report and request for help. Here we go."

He pressed the button for his first slide.

Onscreen came The Portrait, blue eyes tightly focused on the viewer.

And instantly he became the stuff of academic legend.

But not simply because his thirty minute talk ran well over three hours, and did so without a person leaving early.

5 – CHYS

Five generations, nearly 100 years since the Woman had delivered her black-eyed twins. Those years passed without any detectable genetic incident involving blue eyes. The Woman had proven unremarkable, and was now long dead and forgotten. There were fireside stories about a probably-mythical blue-eyed man, a giant, visiting the Tribe long ago. Nobody really believed in the stories, much less the man.... blue eyes, indeed!

But the gene was there, submerged, creeping stealthily through the Tribal population.

Tribal woman Chys was a fifth-generation direct lineal descendant of the earlier Woman, by way of the Woman's not-mythical encounter with Mister Blue-Eyes. Although black-eyed, purely by chance Chys carried the recessive blue-eye gene, masked by its dark companion. She was in her early twenties. She had paired off at about fourteen - the usual age - then delivered two healthy boys four years apart, the first when she was fifteen. Two years ago her partner had come home from a winter-time hunt coughing and shaking. Despite Medicine Man's best efforts, within the week he had died and been buried. Chys mourned briefly but found herself in no mood to hurry and seek out a replacement: she was a good provider, and got plenty of help from her older sister. In some important ways, being without a partner was good, not bad. Like her unremembered and unknown ancestor, Chys was more adventurous and braver than the norm: caring for her small brood had irritated her, because it so strongly curtailed her freedom to roam away from the settlement, whether for the pleasure of encountering the new and unexpected, purely for exercise, or for mundane gathering of foodstuffs.

At any rate, Chys had weaned her youngest -now aged four- only a few months ago: her periods had re-started immediately, a phenomenon known and expected by all human societies and women. After weaning, she had given him mostly into the care of his elder brother and her sister, the kids' barren aunt. Then she returned to running, her favorite pastime. She quickly regained her conditioning. In short order, she was as fast as ever, and her endurance also returned. Today she just wanted to run: she handed off her children to their aunt and set out early in the afternoon, unarmed and lightly clad. Alone, of course. She had no particular plan or destination, she was simply re-examining her world, enjoying it as she re-discovered bits and pieces. Perhaps she might find a rabbit, chase it down, re-sharpen her old skills.

6 - CHYS – FEMALE SPEAR-CHUCKER

As a child, Chys had been the ultimate tomboy, jealous of males of all ages and of the things they got to do which females did not. She'd thought the gender-based prohibitions ridiculous and flouted them whenever she could. Her childhood passion was running: she was faster, and had far more endurance, than even much older kids, including almost all the boys regardless of age. She spent hours running alone through the countryside, up and down the series of floodplains.

She was canny, too, and made certain to learn well the 'females-only' things that so concerned all the other girls. This she did only to deflect possible criticism and to avoid restrictions on what she really liked to do. Namely, running! She would chase down rabbits and ground-dwelling birds: Chys brought home enough hand-caught small game to keep the older women mollified when she failed to join them in their gathering efforts. So good was she that against all tradition a few indulgent men occasionally let her come along on their shorter, more local hunts. She could provide small-game for meals, saving precious time for the men to chase bigger prey. When pursuing fleet game such as deer and antelope, the men often had to run steadily for hours on end, ignoring terrain and the screaming of their muscles. They knew, to their amusement and chagrin, that Chys could keep up: to avoid being embarrassed by that, they always cited 'tradition' and excluded her from the really big, long hunts.

"Uncle" and "aunt" were generic Tribal terms for "much-older non-parental blood relative"... with no specific generational over-tones. Then as now, 'aunts' and 'uncles' were often important people in the lives of growing children. Chys had her own very special Uncle.

Although a child, and female, Chys was occasionally present at a kill larger than a rabbit, and therefore Uncle - who found himself endlessly amused by this anomaly in his extended family - at her request taught her to handle a spear, under the not unreasonable logic that it couldn't hurt and just might someday help a little. Using one of his spears, he taught her the basic elements of thrust and parry and slice - even the use of the spear-butt when nothing else was available. However, Uncle's spears were simply too large and awkward for her, and she quickly found that no man would give her a spear of her own, not even a broken-pointed one. After all, it was the SHAFT rather than the point, that was the difficult, time-consuming component. Much less would anyone make one the proper size for her.

Uncle insisted that if she wanted to have a spear, she was going to have to learn to make her own - every hunter did so. But, he warned her, all the adults, male or female, would certainly think it an odd thing for a girl to do. She didn't care.

At first she was puzzled how to go about it - there were three distinct processes to learn - knapping a point, making a shaft, and marrying point to shaft. Uncle made her think about it for herself and figure out how to learn the necessary techniques. Fortunately, Chys had recently discovered that her presence or, even more, her attentions, had odd effects on men and boys. She used that mysterious influence to encourage and persuade one particular older boy to explain the making of stone points and blades, a technique he was learning as part of his entry into adulthood.

Uncle watched from the sidelines. When it became obvious that she was serious about learning to knapp, he took her aside for what amounted to a safety lecture. Eyes were too precious to take chances with, and knapping always produced lots of flying slivers of glass. One unlucky tiny flake could destroy an eye. To prevent such a disaster, she must never, NEVER do any knapping without a special protective device. "Like this!" he said, showing her his own - a flat deer-rib that had been softened and bent to fit his face at eye level. Through it had been drilled four holes - very small holes in front of the pupils, and at the ends, two larger ones for a thong. The rib rested on the bridge of his nose and the thong held it in place. She was impressed. When she tried on Uncle's goggles, naturally they were far too big: he took her to the communal cooking area where they poked about and found a properly-sized rib. He showed her how to use slivers of obsidian to drill holes in the bone. Then, together, they made her a custom-fitted set of goggles. She sweated behind them, but could see perfectly. And unlike many of the boys and men, her eyes were safe. She of course had no idea that her adult version of these goggles would wind up in her grave with her body. And she would have been amused at the furor they caused far in the future, where they so closely resembled Aleut and Inuit snow-goggles that several misguided papers appeared in the literature, purporting to document and explain the close cultural connections between the Tribe and modern high-latitude hunters. More rational analyses eventually correctly identified the goggles' purpose.

Many Tribe members watched in amusement as she struggled, a large pebble of raw flint or obsidian balanced precariously on her knees while she studied it to determine precisely where to strike - at what angle and how hard - using a hammer-stone or a sharp-pointed punch of reindeer antler. She learned fast and was soon better than her teacher, then better than her teacher's teacher. Eventually she learned to knapp a long narrow point, and to put a fine edge on it - dangerously sharp. And then she got the same boy/man to show her how to use leather thongs and pine-pitch to fasten the point securely to a spear-shaft, practicing on junk points and ordinary sticks. Uncle praised her efforts, and explained that she needed two very different spears - one with a long sharp point such as she'd taken such pains to learn to make. And another with a heavier, blunt point.

For her spear-shafts she turned again to Uncle for help. Points were inherently fragile and would inevitably break, to be replaced. But a truly good shaft was a lifetime investment, often buried with the owner after decades of service. Choosing raw material for shafts was a painstaking process. They settled on three-centimetre diameter straight sticks of clear oak -difficult to find and therefore extra-valuable- chosen to be the proper length and weight for her slight frame. It took them two whole days in the woods to find three acceptable sticks. And at that point they were merely raw materials, to be extensively and precisely modified.

Getting a proper balance required first installing the point, then removing weight from the shaft's tail-end by careful shaving with a special flint blade - one with a semi-circular notch in the cutting-edge. Uncle marked the proper place for her hand on the shaft, then showed her how to use the notched blade to shave the butt-end to be perfectly round and smoothly tapered, so as to concentrate weight well forward - only prepared thusly would a spear fly -and land!- correctly. It took quite a bit of time, but she persisted and produced three almost-perfectly balanced spears. Uncle was impressed at how thoroughly she understood everything he explained - and also by her final product. Few male-made shafts would equal hers for quality.

Uncle had explained clearly the need for two different kinds of spears, called 'sharp' and 'blunt'. One wanted to throw the sharp spear as seldom as possible - it was really for thrusting and slicing, a knife-on-a-stick, maneuverable, versatile, dangerous and very effective. But once you threw, you lost control of it, disarmed yourself, and had about a 50-50 chance of the point breaking when it landed. Replacing a broken point was no problem, of course - every hunter carried a small leather bag with extra points and lashings, but having to retrieve and repair a mis-thrown spear was at best a monumental waste of time, and at worst potentially fatal, since spear-sized game were bigger, faster and stronger than yourself - and could be extremely aggressive.

The blunt spear was the small-game killer - thrown well, it would at least stun, and often kill outright. And if the blunt point smacked the ground or a stone or a tree, well, the impact would usually do no harm whatever to the tip. When hunting, she must carry both kinds and use the blunt whenever possible, but always be ready on a fraction of a second's notice to choose the proper spear for the moment.

The sharp version was that era's ultimate close-in offensive and defensive weapon. It was also the premier hunting device - especially when teamed with a throwing stick which doubled both range and power. The bow and arrow which would eventually replace it as the neolithic super-weapon were not yet a gleam in their eventual inventor's eye - some hundreds of generations in the future.

She was eager to learn to actually throw the weapons. Uncle let her practice with a simple stick, then graduated her to the real thing - her own product. He had an ulterior motive in starting her out too quickly, and on the sharp spear. Her very first throw broke the point and wasted the hours of effort she'd invested in it. Just as he'd warned her. Angry at herself, she spent the next few hours making and installing a replacement. She learned quickly - when Uncle asked what she would like to use as a target for further practice she thought for a while, then opted for a thoroughly rotten tree-stump on one of the lower floodplains. Uncle was impressed with the idea - he hadn't hinted at all - and she practiced that day, under his guidance, until her throwing arm was sore. And through a good many sore-arm days thereafter. Right from the start she was remarkably agile and well-coordinated with her spears - a natural.

During her throwing lessons, the most difficult thing to learn was the straight overhand throwing motion - the entire movement had to stay in the saggital plane. Only when thrown with that difficult, almost unnatural motion would the spear fly in a straight line from your hand to the target. Most men, Uncle said, could learn the proper motion, but if one got excited and stopped thinking about the process, any man would revert to a slightly side-handed throw, guaranteed to miss to the left if the thrower were right-handed. And, he grinned, "...men do tend to get excited when it comes time to throw a spear!" She took the lesson to heart, without suspecting that one day such a simple little bit of knowledge would save her life.

From then forward, on her runs, she practiced incessantly with her self-made spears, quickly developing a particularly accurate technique: she could often hit rabbits while both she and the animal were running. And with either blunt or sharp, she was positively deadly on small stationary targets. In remarkably short order, none of the boys would compete with her.

Unlike most Tribal children her age - especially the girls - Chys always sat with the adults at the fireside of an evening, and paid close attention to the men as they regaled everyone with stories of precisely how they wielded these weapons in attacking truly dangerous big game like horses, bears, bison; in defending against the big cats; and, occasionally, in dealing with cantankerous humans too. She was insatiably curious, and whenever a hunter would mention an especially interesting or terrifying encounter, it was she who would demand explanations, then ask for more information. And even more. She would pester, flatter, and cajole mercilessly until ultimately she would egg the teller into staging a recreation of the incident. The men, being inveterate braggarts and showoffs, loved being encouraged. She became a favorite of theirs.

7 - ABOUT HUNTING BEARS

All hunters agreed - cave bears were the most dangerous animal. Rearing up twice as tall as a man, devilishly smart, omnivorous but leaning towards meat, bears were perfectly happy to include humans as a menu item. The few Tribal men who had encountered them up close and survived were adamant - bears were lightning-fast and enormously powerful. Not to mention unpredictable and mean.

One evening, at Chys's insistence, two older men sporting deep bear-claw scars on arms and chest and legs agreed to stage a bear's attack for their eager audience. One man played Bear: he retreated, snarling, into the shadows beyond the ring of firelight. The other played Hunter, and explained the action as he went. When bears were not upset, they went about their business noisily - they often snuffled loudly, or growled or chuffed. That was one way of both finding and avoiding them, and avoiding was greatly preferred. An angry or upset bear, or a bear out hunting, was a silent bear, he told them. Your only chance was to see him first. When you saw him, he almost certainly had seen you or smelled you or heard you first, which meant you were in deep trouble. Going on the offense was simply stupid, usually fatal. There was no choice but to instantly set up a coordinated defense - bears could easily outrun any human, so it wasn't worth trying to scatter and run away, because the bear would just pick one of your party and chase him down.

He then showed his audience the best defense. You had to face the oncoming bear, but the animal was so fast and powerful and heavy that you didn't dare throw your spear. The concepts of kinetic energy and momentum were far off in the future, but instinctively understood: you couldn't throw a spear with enough force to kill a beast like a cave bear - it would most likely just bounce off. Neither could you just hang onto the shaft and stab because you couldn't possibly hold on to the weapon through the shock of it colliding with the bear. Instead, if you wanted to survive, you used the bear's behavior, and the bear's energy, to your advantage.

As the animal bore down on you for the final attack, at the very last moment it would invariably rear upright on its hind legs and

with its forearms spread, while still rushing towards you at an unbelievable speed. At this point the storyteller, now aping the hunter-
turned-hunted, signaled to the shadows. "Bear" moved out into the
light on all fours, charging in slow motion, pantomiming. Storytell-
er/Hunter turned equally slowly to face the charge. As Mister Bear
rose up and spread his arms, the narrator stamped down with exaggerated force to plant his feet, and drove the butt of his spear into
the ground slightly, tilted it towards the onrushing, upright Bear. He
then stepped hard, with all his weight, on the butt-end to secure its
anchorage, whilst gripping the shaft to both guide and steady the
point. As Bear arrived, the storyteller-spearsman lowered the point
to Bear-chest height. Bear caught the spear between chest and arm
to ape being impaled, all necessary force being supplied by the onrushing Bear, not by the human. As Bear impaled himself, Storyteller jumped sideways to avoid being crushed as Bear collapsed on the
ground, dead. Even in slow motion, it happened fast!

The audience applauded and hooted their approval of the performance. The storyteller/spearsman explained that this defense was
so important that the men actually practiced it occasionally. And of
course it would work best if there were say three or four spears involved. In fact, he had once seen a bear stop and back down when
faced by three men together. He joked, with underlying seriousness:
one couldn't expect that result very often, and if you miscalculated,
the BEST result you could hope for was scars such as he wore.
More commonly, if your defense failed, then Mister Bear took you
home for lunch!

Next day saw Chys out alone in the bushes with her spear,
practicing against imaginary bears. The following day, she enlisted
two friends as miniature bears. For this exercise, however, just to be
safe, she wisely cut a new "spear" - a flexible green branch without
a point. The friends though it a wonderful game, at least for a while
(which meant, until the 'bears' got tired of accumulating bruises),
and she got enough practice to understand the need for steely nerves
and serious resolve - not to mention impeccable timing. Display the
anchored spear too soon and the bear had time to react, would just
swat it aside. Ugly!

However, big carnivores are actually quite rare, and except in her dreams Chys had never met face to face a real, live, angry bear. She grew up secretly peeved about that, though in reality she knew she was much better off without such an experience.

8 - CAPTURED

The adult Chys was out running just for the enjoyment of it, some considerable distance from home, but still in well-known territory. She started out running along the very base of the cliffs, a nicely defined trail well used by both Tribe and wildlife, on the uppermost ancient floodplain. After a while she dropped towards the river, going down and over the successive floodplains like gigantic stair-steps - she loved running downhill. On the lowest plain, well populated with shrubs, she trotted over a rise, then veered left, following a game trail towards the riverbank.

As she emerged from the scattered, head-high underbrush onto the riverbank she was running fast, unable to stop quickly enough to avoid detection. She had unluckily placed herself squarely between two pairs of men on the open, sandy bank. The pairs were about a hundred metres apart. Her eyesight was superb: she definitely didn't recognize them. Not from her Tribe. Not only were they strangers, but they were BIG - all four of them much too tall to be of her Tribe. Not likely to be a hunting party, she guessed - each man carried two spears, and they were all pointed - not a blunt to be seen. And she was well within both spear and rock range of all four men.

Their eyesight was equally good, and they saw her instantly.

For any woman, this was danger in the extreme. Conversely, finding a solitary woman in the field was unheard-of good luck for the men: any woman of breeding age was an extraordinarily valuable item. Finders, keepers was the rule. If they could catch her. As to their catching her, well, four on one was terrible odds against her. The four sensed immediately that she was alone, got the message from her hesitation, and from her posture after she stopped. They moved as one organism to surround her.

Chys knew what would happen if she ran - at best, they would chase her down and kidnap her, take her back to wherever they came from. And if she somehow managed to run at their pace, they would eventually in frustration heave their spears at her, rather than let her escape. She could make life more difficult for the throwers by zig-zagging, but that would seriously slow her down. In any case, she might dodge one spear, perhaps two, but certainly not eight, all thrown by experts. Her only escape route would be across the river - but swimming was an almost unknown skill in her Tribe - a skill she did not have.

A piece of her mind seemed to detach itself, then float above her head, as if it were an impartial observer broadcasting the overall scenario to her conscious. She had only a few seconds left. The two encircling men were out of sight in the brush now, but she could hear them: retreat that direction was already impossible. The other two were trotting her way along the riverbank, in a pincers movement. They were not running at all hard - they were quite confident, no hurry. Justifiably so, her out-of-body-observer told her. She really had no way out.

In moments she was surrounded, four spears leveled at her from three metres away. The men really WERE huge, she thought. Much taller than the men of her Tribe. And they all had something she had heard of in old-women's campfire stories, but which nobody living had ever seen - blue eyes! She noted it without letting herself be distracted - spears were important here, eye color not so much. Huge spears - in keeping with the men's own size. She carefully, inconspicuously, studied how they handled their weapons, how they placed their feet, where their gaze focused and for how long. Experts all. Bad news, everything about the situation. Sweat drizzled down her sides.

What to do? It still wasn't clear to her whether this was a hunting party, a war party, or just a group off on some other errand. And that meant she didn't have a clue whether their first response would be to rape her immediately, and then kill her equally quickly to avoid being encumbered by a prisoner. Her mental outside observer was icily analytical - any resistance on her part was almost certain to lead to injury, and any injury would reduce to zero whatever slim chance she might still have for escape...or even survival. Survival

33

was far from being a given, but remaining uninjured probably increased her value immensely - and certainly, whatever this group was doing, they wouldn't need an injured captive slowing them down.

The one thing guaranteed NOT to happen was them setting her free, not even after they'd had their way with her. If this was a war party, then being killed shortly - right here- was the most logical thing to expect. If just a hunting party, as seemed at least plausible, well, then, she was a fertile relatively young female, which made her into unusually fine game - she could be taken home with them (wherever that was) and with luck she would eventually be somewhat integrated into their tribe.

But regardless of the ultimate outcome, live prisoner or dead meat, she would get the same initial treatment. Rape was simply a known, expected part of any woman's being captured. Given Chys's other, larger worries, THAT problem rated a shrug at most.

She spoke, a greeting: they grinned evilly, shook their heads, talked together in some foreign tongue. No relaxation of their guard. Sign language even amongst themselves. This she mostly understood. One man, the tallest by five centimetres, was clearly in absolute command. When he signed to her, she immediately did as he indicated, turned her back to him. He pulled a long leather strap from around his waist, bound her hands snugly. Then a short strap joined her ankles: no running. The leader gestured towards the river and the group set off at Chys's pace, a slow, awkward, shuffling trot.

It wasn't far, perhaps two kilometres, to their campsite on the sand beside the river. They had built their fire up against one of the huge broken rocks, with a large log jammed behind it, a nicely defensible and mostly hidden site. She knew the locale: behind the sand stretched her familiar shrub-land. If she were somehow freed, she could almost run home blindfolded. Not much chance of that!

"Monster" was the mental nickname she gave the leader. He was over thirty centimetres taller than she, perhaps twenty-five centimeters or so taller than her Tribe's tallest man. Hugely powerful: he demonstrated by picking her up bodily by the shoulders and plonking her down against the log. She sat, passive but alert, awaiting developments.

An argument ensued - mostly carried on orally, but there were enough signs involved so that she could get the drift. Not a hunting party. Chance for survival dropped precipitously - impediments such as herself definitely not wanted- too dangerous, troublesome. Three voices together carrying the same message - kill her here, yes she was valuable but not enough to mess up their mission. Monster felt differently - he made it clear that Chys was HIS personal property, not the group's... and he had decided that the group was going to keep her for HIS use when they returned home. The argument got loud, louder, then ended abruptly as Monster gave what was obviously the final word. The win went to the Alpha, as is usual in male groups. The other three men went slightly sullen, shrugged, and turned away, saving face by ignoring the outcome.

Relief flooded her - she would survive the day, at least. Of course, Monster could readily change his mind. She would have to see if she could prevent that. Somehow.

9 – RAPE

A few minutes later, as the three betas began preparing dinner. Monster stepped over to her, picked her up effortlessly, carried her around the log and a few metres into the brush, threw her down on her chest and knees. It took him perhaps five seconds to strip her from the waist down, and five more to do the same for himself.

Sex - she could use that as a tool, if she could figure out how. Men were forever and always susceptible to it: properly deployed it could be a weapon both offensive and defensive. Her floating brain-bit gave her explicit instructions: put up no resistance. Make Monster happy if possible. She wasn't likely to actually be physically injured by a rape, so long as Monster behaved: thus far, the signs were vaguely favorable... at least he hadn't yet actually hit her, just handled her roughly. The best she could do now was relax if possible, at least not fight, purely to avoid injury and appease her captor. If the three damned betas hadn't already started cooking, perhaps she could have made herself useful that way, too. Or tomorrow morning, assuming survival through the onrushing night. She would

35

use anything at all -especially sex and being seen as docile and use-ful- to keep herself worth more alive than dead.

Monster squatted behind her: his sudden dry entry was uncom-fortable, but mostly from his size, not violence. She could tell at once - physical discomfort and mental outrage, but no injury. That was good. And so far he hadn't even threatened to hit her: acquies-cence was working. As she lay awkwardly beneath him, her float-ing observer coolly pointed out, almost in a snicker, that some of her previous partners, all of whom she had most willingly enter-tained, had been rougher and less caring, even, than was Monster. In any event, he lasted only through a half-dozen thrusts, spasmed, then collapsed atop her with a loud, satisfied groan that brought hoots of laughter and ribald commentary from the jealous but cowed betas.

Monster caught his breath and stood, appearing quite pleased with himself.

"Good!" she thought, correctly. "He has to keep me alive if he wants more - which he will! After all, he's MALE!"

Monster pulled her to her feet, handed her the leather skirt he had just removed. The gesture was almost polite. She looked at him blankly, worked up the effort to smile, shrugged: her hands were still tied behind her back. He grinned: a handsome bastard, and al-most human she thought, all the while being careful to control both her outer neutral expression, and her boiling inner feelings. With a great deal of luck, there might be a time for releasing both later. Sometime, somewhere. Not now. Self control was the immediate need. Concentrate.

Monster understood the skirt problem, and shrugged himself, then wrapped the thing around her hips and tied it more or less in place. More politeness! Weird! He carried her back around the log, sat her on the sand, and tied her ankle-thong to a longer strap, which he fastened to the log.

The betas cut cookable strips from a haunch of deer and roasted them over their fire. Chys's mouth watered, but she expected noth-ing. The men chattered loudly, ignoring her entirely. Until, as night came on and a brilliant three-quarter moon rose, Monster suddenly stood and walked over to her, with a long strip of cooked meat hanging from his knife-point. Despite her best efforts, her hunger showed in both expression and body-language. He grinned down at her, master-slave, owner-chattel, not exactly polite now. Gloating. He lowered the end of the strip to where she could get her teeth into it. Whereupon he released it: the meat dangled down her chest. If she wanted it enough, she could figure out how to handle it. He laughed at her first attempts, then turned and went back to the fire.

She did manage to eat it... simultaneously biting, chewing and swallowing wasn't easy. Three times she dropped it into the sand and had to retrieve it by scooting about on her belly. Grit in food was normal and the excess here didn't really bother. This was just another of Monster's ways of establishing ownership and control. And whenever, wherever food appeared, one always ate it. Especially now. The out-of-body bit of herself was happy that Monster had taken such a strong proprietary shine to her - she was sure that his interest and authority were the only things preventing three quick repeats of Monster's own attentions, something she was happy to do without. Not to mention that it was quite likely that his interest was the only thing keeping her alive. Three to one against her, but this was no democracy... "her" Monster-man was in charge.

10 - ESCAPE

She watched the moon slowly climb the sky: it lit the landscape brightly enough so that she could make out some colors. Good for running fast, but terrible for stealth and secrecy and hiding. Her captors posted no guard. "Cocky bastards!" she thought, "...big and sort of handsome, but a bit dumb!"

She listened intently to the small noises from the fireside. Careful now, sort out the sounds, ignore the owls and cricket-frogs and other normal night singers. Everyone breathes and mumbles in their own personal style while sleeping. After half an hour she had the sound-tracks separated. Four men, all sleep-breathing. The important facts were (a) asleep and (b) four. Another half-hour to confirm the analysis. She could afford no mistake in this. A final re-check. Yes, four. One. Two. Three. Four.

37

Meanwhile, behind her back, she had worked steadily at loosening the bindings on her wrists. Monster wasn't especially good with his knots, and he hadn't really noticed just how small her hands were, much less did he know how narrow and pointy she could make them. After all, THEIR big-male hands weren't capable of such a maneuver. Plus, she'd had the presence of mind to tighten her hands and wrist muscles while being tied up - something she'd learned as a child playing 'tie-them-up' games. Now, with the straps fully softened by her body-heat, with her hand and arm and wrist muscles relaxed, with her fingers pointed together, she had some wiggle room.

"Some" quickly became "quite a bit", and abruptly one hand was free. Which meant that the other one was free as well. Carefully, silently, she untied the ankle-strap, then unfastened and removed her skirt. She was going to have to literally run for her life and wanted nothing - absolutely NOTHING- to impede her. The last thing she was going to worry about was either midnight nudity or bramble-scratches.

She stood up silently, tested her legs and arms. Nothing had gone to sleep, everything felt good. She had full control. She would need it. Adrenalin was now sloshing wildly through her, making quiet breathing difficult. She carefully calmed herself, took the first silent, sliding step: she would have to work her way around the log to get into the scrub she knew so well. One hundred metres of head-start and she would be free, barring accident. Even fifty might suffice. With great good luck there would be no pursuit at all.

She was a good hunter, she could be utterly quiet. Until, at the end of the trunk, while making the turn into the brush, something buried invisibly in the sand cracked underfoot. She looked back over her shoulder to see Monster stand up in the brilliant moonlight and shake his head to clear it of sleep, then look right at her. She didn't watch his whole wake-up sequence, but launched herself down the path: at last glimpse, he was starting towards her with two very large spears in one hand. She did hear the roars of laughter from the rousing betas, and it sounded rather like they were not going to help their leader - it was HIS property that was running away.

He had tied her up, she'd gotten loose, it was all his own bloody fault, so he could chase her by himself.

One on one! She had a chance now, one chance, slender, but real. In the intense moonlight, the landscape was a surreal jack-straws mixture of silver light and jet black shadows, all sharp-edged and tangled and brutally difficult to interpret. No foot-grabbing rocks or roots, please! Speed was the key. She was on maximum overdrive at full throttle. Monster was much taller, should be able to catch her easily. But who could tell until the race was run? After all, property loss and imminent death were very different incentives. She could turn sharper, seemed to understand this sort of terrain better than he did. She veered, ran up the scarp onto the next-higher floodplain. Thirty seconds later, she did it again. Then a third time - she hoped Monster wasn't as used to short sharp hills as she was!

A whole minute passed: no stealth here, both bodies smashing through the brush now, visibility was fine, he could see her occasionally, fifty metres ahead. She was good, Monster realized - he wasn't gaining. Two, then three minutes: her breathing was heavy and ragged now. She daren't turn to look, kept track of him by sound alone. Plenty accurate enough.

Abruptly, his crashing stopped: the only possible reason he would stop would be to throw a spear. She had to choose, ducked right - all due to her Uncle's explanations years ago --- most men were right-handed, and when excited threw a spear slightly skewed to the left. This was because with excitement their throw instinctively changed from a proper full overhand to a more sideways motion. Presumably Monster was excited just now.

She won the bet, the first of three - Monster's spear hissed past her left shoulder and stuck solidly in the sandy dirt some distance ahead of her. His brush-crashing re-started before the spear hit the ground.

11 - COMEUPPANCE

One more chance - the spear. If she stopped running, she was totally committed. If she didn't stop, well, her pursuer still had his #2 spear - and so far, she wasn't gaining on him, which probably

39

meant he would shortly be in much easier range. Problem - when mistreated, stone spear-points often broke, and mistreatment certainly included driving them into the ground. She flashed on her very first throw with her own spear, years ago, with Uncle at her side. The point had snapped when it stuck in the dirt.

Nonetheless, she committed to the spear, trusting that such a robust device would have survived intact. She stopped, yanked on the shaft: it was stuck. The spear was huge, four times the weight of her own, and nearly twice as long. Far beyond anything she'd ever handled. A second, then a third desperate tug, and it came free, the point undamaged. She'd won the second bet.

Her eye and hand found the balance, and she spun about to face back in Monster's direction. Five seconds, perhaps ten - that was all she had. Adrenalin turned it into an hour. Clarity, amazing clarity. Slow motion. At the moment she couldn't see him through the brush - so he couldn't see her, either. Good! She took one step to the left, off the path that was Monster's necessary and only route through the brush. Moving to the left gave control of the spear to her right hand, stronger and better coordinated than her left. She then dropped into a spring-loaded deep squat behind a head-high shrub. As if in a dream, she pointed the spear in the direction of the charging Monster, laid it down inconspicuously on the ground at the very edge of the path, her right hand half-way down the shaft, holding it in a death-grip at the balance. In her slow-motion mode of perception, she noticed the unusual roughness of the spear-shaft as she clutched it - he'd done something to the surface that yielded a superb grip. Interesting. Undoubtedly useful. But she forced herself back to the immediate problem - details of spear construction would be moot if this didn't work. A third and final bet - one chance, and only one. But she had an enormous advantage of which she was utterly unaware - no man would ever expect aggression from a woman, and especially he would never expect any woman to handle a spear in any context.

Ready now, she peered through the foliage as the thrashing Monster bore down on her. At ten metres she saw him through the branches, running full-tilt, his second spear held high in perfect throwing alignment: apparently he'd realized why his first throw had missed - he wouldn't make that mistake twice.

Too much adrenaline pumping now for her to be frightened! She took a deep breath and held it, waiting. At three metres she stood, raised and aimed the spear-point, stamped her right foot down hard on the butt to anchor it in the sand.

Despite no practice for well over a decade, she timed it perfectly. Her playmates and Storyteller would have been immensely proud.

Monster saw the motion but never apprehended the danger. In any case, he could have done nothing, neither slow down nor dodge, for at his speed it was under half a second between being able to see the spear, and impact. His momentum drove the spear - his own best spear - through his sternum, through his chest cavity, and out his back. Enroute to cleaving his spinal cord, the point ripped a ten centimetre long hole in his heart. The only sound he made was a single coughing grunt. Chys stepped to her left at impact and the spray of blood fairly drenched her right side. Monster was dead before he hit the ground. As he fell, the shaft twisted, bent under the force of his hundred kilos of galloping biomass. The long glass point snapped where it met the wood, leaving twenty five centimetres of obsidian transfixing his chest.

She yanked his second spear from his dead hand, and ran. There were still the three betas loose somewhere behind her - she was sure she could outrun any one of them, but having to dodge three wouldn't do. That is, IF they chose to pursue. She juggled the huge spear as she went. Running thus encumbered was awkward but she wasn't going to disarm herself now. Two minutes at speed, over several small hillocks that broke the view, gave good concealment. Then several minutes at stealth pace, slower and super-quiet. Finally, a pause: breath control. She listened for a chase, heard only distant plaintive calls, no commotion in the underbrush. The betas were looking for Monster back towards their camp, and were clearly not concerned with her at all.

12 - LEADING THE WAR PARTY

As she trotted homeward, her mind quickly calmed. Amazing how the moon's lighting had shifted from being dangerously misleading to wonderful for running! Home was nearly an hour away at this easy pace. She took time to study Monster's #2 spear as she loped. Like the first spear, this one was huge, appropriate to Monster's size. A trophy! She felt the edges of the point - a fine job of knapping - she wondered if he'd done it himself? The binding of point to shaft was excellent, made her wonder why he had done such a poor job of tying her hands. He'd been youngish - so maybe he'd never tied up a human before? She surprised herself by finding a tinge of regret in her thoughts. If only he had been of her Tribe - or even merely friendly - such babies they might have produced. Maybe even those mythical Blue-Eyed babies! He was a Monster, yes - but he <u>hadn't</u> hit her, he <u>had</u> fed her. And he'd also defended her against the three betas, in his own way and for his own reasons. Not entirely a monster, the man.

She shook her head - silly, stupid thoughts: his blood was getting sticky now on her bare skin and remaining clothes. The blood was the reality! Better to remember things the way they really had been, than to indulge in stupid "what ifs".

The three betas found Monster a few minutes later, and quickly figured out what had occurred. It was far too late to pursue the woman - besides, they hadn't wanted her in the first place, and were now impressed at the very idea of such a small young woman killing a brute like Monster. They were aware, too, that Monster's other spear had gone missing, and they correctly suspected just where. That made the idea of pursuit into a very iffy proposition - after all, anything she could do once, she could most likely repeat. At any rate, this was an unheard of event! Ridiculous, too - Alpha's family would not be happy with this story. Perhaps it would be better if they said he'd been killed and eaten by a bear? That was, at least, a respectable reason to be dead! Killed by that little woman, with his own spear!? Disgraceful! Poppycock! Tell his family the truth and be suspected of murdering him!? The Bear it would be!

They argued briefly about whether to give him a proper burial, decided against it. Burial would use up too much time, and they might very well have only a small amount of it. They thought, too, of stripping the corpse, but his important gear was back at camp waiting for them, and the skimpy clothing on his body was soaked with blood. They gave a collective shrug. The man had been unforgivably arrogant - not at all well-liked. So by consensus they left Monster's cooling corpse to its own devices, returned to break camp, and went back to their original plan. Long before dawn they were gone, heading upriver, moving fast and leaving no spoor - who knew what kind of hell the woman's story would raise in her home tribe? Or how soon! Three was a small number to pit against an entire, aroused tribe. Best to be gone quickly and far.

Chys ran nonstop, and arrived at the settlement at first light, hallooing from several hundred metres to identify herself. She was greeted by an enthusiastic, almost disbelieving throng - anyone who went missing overnight was generally never found, usually written off accurately as having become bear food.

She related her adventure in detail, answering questions as she went. The huge spear, and her coating of clotted drying blood, quelled all disbelief. The news of the three betas on the loose disturbed the elders mightily. Within minutes a war-expedition was assembled - half the able-bodied men would accompany Chys back to the scene. Twenty against three sounded like reasonable odds. The other men would remain at home to guard the settlement, just in case.

This war-expedition was unique in Tribal history. It was led, of necessity, by Chys. Nobody had ever known a woman to go warring, much less as leader. Not even in the oldest and most outlandish legends. The Chief, a sensible and intelligent man, had realized at once that Chys must at least be the guide. Rather than invite confusion by having her instructions relayed through himself, he simply put her in charge of getting the group to the target, as he would have with any male. After all, only she knew exactly where things had happened, where the expedition must go. A few of the men grumbled and looked displeased, but here the Chief was the Alpha, and what he said, went. Pleased and flabbergasted at the responsibility and honor, Chys took half a minute to get her own properly-sized weapon, and to consign Monster's spear to friends for storage and care. She also used up her family's small store of drinking water rinsing herself down. No point in attracting some carnivore!

An hour after dawn, the expedition was within a kilometre or so of the enemy's campsite -for 'enemies' is how they now thought of the betas- and creeping silently down the main game trail, the trail Chys had run so recently. She led, explaining silently with signs that were passed rapidly to all. Then, around a short curve, there lay Monster, in a heap, just as he had dropped. There was an enormous pool of thick, coagulated blood under his face and chest: footprints of the betas were everywhere, but they had obviously simply abandoned their leader. Chys then led her group to where she'd been held: there was no sign at all that anyone had ever camped there. A brief pow-wow rendered a decision: the betas would leave precious little trail, and it would be both dumb and un-productive to follow them. Pursuit would be a complete waste of Tribal time and effort. Forget it. But Chys did retrieve her skirt from her spot beside the log.

Back at Monster's body, Chys explained her actions, demon-strated, basked in the men's astonishment and admiration, grudging-ly admitted to though it might be. When she told them about Mon-ster's bright blue eyes, there was utter disbelief, so strong that against taboo several men rolled the body over, pulled open the eye-lids, and proved her correct. All were amazed.

Nobody asked the reasonably obvious question - had she been raped? If so, nothing could be done, and besides, it wasn't their business. And if she had been, well, her revenge lay at their feet, didn't it?!

13 - HONORIFIC RENAMING

A Tribal tradition dating back to time before memory was to give a special "hunting-name" to any man who outdid himself in bravery or cunning or strength, whether in battle or hunting. A name not exactly secret, but private - to be used only amongst the Tribe's hunters and warriors, or in telling stories in the settlement. Chys had

44

never heard of a woman being given such a name, and was utterly nonplussed when the Chief called for quiet and announced -right there in the brush beside Monster's body- that such a feat as hers required a hunter's name regardless of her gender. Again a few men grumbled, but the Chief stared them into silence, then asked who among them would like to try repeating her feat himself. The men took another long collective look at Monster, and dropped the protest.

Chys became "Woman who kills Monsters" forevermore.

14 - BURYING MONSTER

After considerable discussion, it was agreed that despite Monster's being a foreigner and an enemy, his being left unburied by his comrades was understandable but uncouth at best, positively uncivilized at worst. Nobody of any tribe wanted to die and simply be left for the wolves and cats and bears. They decided to bury him then and there. It was an hour's work to excavate a barely-adequate grave: four men it took to manhandle Monster into the little pit, get him oriented head to the east, in fetal position. Rigor mortis had set in with a vengeance, and they had to cut his arm and leg tendons in order to fold the body. That rough treatment left knife-blade scratches on long bones, at the joints. Far in the future, those marks would one day be noticed and lead to considerable speculation about an interrupted cannibal feast.

They cut his spear into thirds so that it could fit in the pit with him, shoveled in all the bloody sand, filled the grave, packed it down. Then they built a simple cairn, two rocks high, made of four-man and five-man boulders, adequate to foil scavengers. Had he been one of their own, or had he fallen in some sort of honorable combat, they might have built something a bit more impressive.

After which, led again by Chys, they returned home. There her exploit, like Gerard's lecture, quickly became the stuff of legends, and she became an unofficial apprentice to the best Storyteller in the Tribe.

45

15 - PREGNANT

Two months later, Chys knew she was pregnant again - and Monster had been the only possibility, something known to everyone in the Tribe. They all knew of the man's blue eyes. Few spoke openly of it, but all wondered and waited - what would Chys's and Monster's baby look like?

It was an easy pregnancy - she vomited only every other day, and that only early on, before developing a big belly - a belly that suggested to many onlookers (especially men) an unusually large baby. Something commensurate with the reports about Monster. The women who acted as midwives tried to explain that size of belly, or even size of the father, didn't necessarily correlate with size of baby, but they were ignored. It was much more fun to speculate!

General personal cleanliness was prized in the Tribe, the necessary effort greatly aided by the river's proximity and the ancient discovery that certain aquatic tubers could be heated and mashed to make an effective scrubber laden with mild soap. Birthing was always done in a specially-built willow hut at river's edge, away from the settlement itself. Water was special stuff, and it was routinely poured liberally over mother, child, and afterbirth alike -primitive un-knowing sanitation, but far better than nothing. In addition, there was repeated washing for both mother and attendants, before, during and after the birth. The mess of childbirth was treated as special, but perfectly understandable. It required thorough cleaning-up. The resulting cleanliness was far from asepsis, but good enough to result in the Tribe's remarkably low loss-rate for both mothers and newborn. Lucky women gave birth in deep wintertime, when the river water was icy cold and would also dull sensations - a bit of an anesthetic. Not to mention encouraging the newborn to cry lustily.

16 – VEEJR WITH BLUE EYES

Chys delivered this baby, her third, easily and quickly. The afterbirth came away cleanly: one of the midwives bit through the umbilicus in traditional fashion -no knife allowed-, then ran off into the underbrush some hundreds of metres to bury the intact placenta in a deep hole she had prepared in advance. Nobody knew WHY the biting and burial, only that they were traditional and important.

The child was female. And notably long, the midwives told Chys immediately - quite unusually so. She would be a tall person if she lived to adulthood, as did only about three of five babies.

It took some minutes before the baby quit squalling long enough to open her eyes.

Blue. Brilliant, clear, pure bright blue.

Word of the blue eyes spread instantly, fueled by the anticipation and curiosity that had built throughout the baby's gestation. The recessive blue gene inserted into the genome of the Tribe five generations earlier, and hidden since then, had finally reared its head in public. And to some tribal members, it was an ugly head indeed. The circumstances of the child's conception and birth, and especially its eye color, were the subjects of intense discussion by the entire Tribe, less Chys and baby. The discussion turned into an uproar, quickly stanched by the Chief, who declared that the Tribe would have an all-members meeting some few days hence to discuss the child, her meaning, and her future. The meeting would be deadly serious - every Tribe reserved the right to select, or reject, members. Explicitly including newborns.

Chys and baby would attend: Chys would do the normal thing - display the child, naked, for all to see. This was to be the official "initial viewing" – and the very idea made most mothers smile secretly, for as with any ordinary birth, each and every one of them would have already visited Chys, well before the meeting. Which was mostly a men's meeting, and men were ignoramuses when it came to anything baby.

By the time of the meeting, almost every adult Tribal woman had held the baby herself - passing a newborn around to all the women was a rite of welcome and acceptance, unique to women who had given birth. Men, unable to conceive and carry, had no clue, and sincerely believed they were going to decide the infant's fate. But in reality, the women had decided the non-issue long before the men began trotting out their opinions. Of course, there remained the necessary formalities - chief among which was the slow-motion day-long meeting, now secretly regarded by most as strictly pro-forma.

As in most societies, on almost any question, there were in the Tribe several groups, including positives, negatives and neutrals. Or, perhaps, conservative, neutral, and liberal. On the question of the baby's fate, the few hard-line conservatives were all men, and largely older. They were rabidly against anything new being allowed to exist at all, much less countenanced and encouraged. Any and all new things were automatically to be shunned at best, actively sought out and destroyed at worst. In the communal discussions around the central fire during the formal meeting, the "Nothing New" brigade held forth loudly. Their agenda was simple - new equals dangerous, therefore kill the oddity before it could bring down disaster. Best to do it NOW! A few felt so strongly that they refused even to look into the infant's face for fear of causing something evil but utterly undefined.

They were counterbalanced by a more numerous "liberal" group, which felt that any whole, healthy child was too valuable to waste, there being so few of them and there being also a steady need for replacement people. Luck probably ran from mother to child, so likely this child would inherit some of Mother Chys's incredible good luck - not a bad thing at all. Plus they made the point that the kid had already spent her first nine months amongst them - albeit out of sight - plus a week fully visible. Presumably, they argued, if the kid were going to raise hell for the Tribe, that hell should already have begun. And it had not. Also, every person who had actually examined the child, including many men, said it was extraordinarily active and attractive. The 'liberals' felt that having blue eyes, although certainly both odd and new, was no more unnatural than any other human characteristic - after all, every characteristic one could name about a human came in variations. Why not eye-color too? Should the Tribe perhaps decide to kill babies that were over a certain length, just for that reason? No, of course not. Nonsense! Besides, if the child were to affect tribal luck, then they should at least wait to see which way that effect went - if they were to kill the infant now, the Tribe might be throwing away GOOD luck. The idiot old-fogey nay-sayers could not possibly know which it would be - if either!

A third group existed, almost subterranean - vociferous and unyieldingly in favor of the baby. The Tribe's children, who to a person were utterly fascinated with, and completely unafraid of, the child. An unacknowledged force, their experiences with and curiosity about the baby carried an amazing - although well hidden - weight.

And in the middle of the argument stood the fourth group – a majority of the Tribe, quietly led by the mothers. This large group's opinion was laissez-faire, and leavened by the collective maternal instincts of its women, who had all seen and held the child. They thought of the baby in maternal terms, and managed to convey to the men their overall intense dismay at the idea of genuinely arbitrary infanticide. As in a much later Greek play, the men got the message.

The meeting had convened in late-afternoon. Chys and baby were seated at the far eastern point of the circle, a locus not necessarily of honor, but at least signifying the sitter's momentary importance. Chys had been fully briefed by her women-friends - she knew who was in what camp. After the prolonged round-robin discussion, she stood at the Chief's gesture, opened the blanket, and with head held high presented the child. She worked steadily around the circle, making hard, defiant eye contact with each man she knew was in the NAY camp. Some of them refused to meet her eyes at all. For those who would, always she held their gaze until it was they whose eyes dropped away, yielded. Through the entire circuit the baby smiled, waved its limbs, acted perfectly normal and attentive. And she stared with her blue eyes directly into any inquisitive face nearby.

When Chys finished her tour, she sat, re-wrapped the baby, and put her to nursing. Settled, she looked up and said in a remarkably strong, well-carrying voice: "Most of you have no problem with my daughter. Most of the women and children have already held her. To those old men who would destroy my child I would say just this. I have noticed that not very many of you have earned hunting names." Her voice dropped an octave as she continued, speaking slowly and forcefully: **"I remind you few who think we should kill my baby that my HUNTING NAME is Woman who kills Monsters. Everyone here should remember that!"**

She paused and defiantly scanned the assembly. "This baby, my child, is normal. I think her blue eyes will be lucky. They are the color of the bee's favorite flowers, and the bee is certainly our friend! If there is anyone who disagrees, I, Woman who kills Monsters, remind them what I did to this baby's father. I remind you also that I still have Monster's second spear. I will gladly argue with you one by one, if you insist." She grinned tightly at the entire group. "Maybe I could persuade you to change your ideas!?"

She stopped, looked at the Chief, who stood and silently scanned the entire Tribe one face at a time. When he was done, he announced: "The baby is normal except for its eyes. We know where the eyes came from, there is no magic in that. Everyone here is forever forbidden to harm Chys's daughter in any way. She may bring us luck: we must wait to see if it is good or bad."

A fine politician after fifteen years as Chief, he then declared "We will stay up this evening and tell stories while dinner is cooked. Then we will eat together. ALL of us. Including Chys and her daughter. The child's naming ceremony will be at the usual time. Right now, the women should prepare the dinner we all need. GO!"

Shortly there was a line of children waiting to stare at and touch the infant whilst the women set about making dinner.

17 - NAMING

Some weeks later came the child's formal naming ceremony. Naming was critically important, and was done twice: the first time in private, immediately after birth, as soon as the baby was known to be alive and healthy. Then a lunar month later, in a public ceremony around the central fire. Mothers always chose the names for their own babies, especially the girls. After all, the mother had done all the hard work of producing the new person. If she were tightly paired, a mother might let her man weigh in on the name for a boy-child, but never on a girl! What did men know of such things? Nothing whatever. The very idea was stupid!

Because this baby carried something brand new in Tribal history, Chys felt compelled to invent an entirely new name. She made it short, sharp, unusual. A good name, an unnatural sound, distinctive, you could say it accurately either loudly or quietly. Clear. Unique, without history, therefore leaving the child's future entirely open, unconstrained. A good thing, being unencumbered.

She would be Veejr.

18 - MONSTER'S GRAVE DISCOVERED

Forty thousand years later, a class of anthropology students from La Fond fortuitously discovered the grave containing Monster's skeleton, complete and properly oriented, head towards the east. During their careful excavation, they'd encountered the femurs and pelvis first. It was quickly apparent that they had a big skeleton - instantly assumed to be male and, therefore, nicknamed 'Goliath'. They marveled at the long spear-point of beautifully-knapped obsidian which had entered from the front, cut through the sternum, traversed the chest, then finally cut so deeply into two adjacent upper thoracic vertebra that they remained impaled on the point, one on each cutting edge. The point itself was still exquisitely sharp to the touch.

A very attentive student excavator had noticed a pinhole opening into what had to be a cavity in the packed dirt beside the skeleton: something had been buried with Goliath, and had decayed away leaving a hollow, a mold. With great care, they had mapped the cavity using high-frequency acoustics but no physical probing: then they mixed up a thin slurry of plaster of Paris and filled the mold gently, pouring into its uppermost point. Two hours was overkill on setting time, but they waited. You only got one chance at something like this. Their painstaking work was well rewarded: they got a perfect casting of Monster's spear, broken into three parts so long ago. The casting was so good that it came free of the sandy earth with the butt-end of the broken-off spear point perfectly held in a plaster replica of the binding, on a plaster shaft. Nothing quite like this had ever been reported. The excavators were stoked. The skeleton and spear-casting were removed to the institution's facilities for study.

51

One of Goliath's discoverers actually developed a good picture of what had happened. The spear had entered from the front, going upwards: it had penetrated –and still held onto- the sternum, and it had also sliced his heart nearly in half, enroute to the spine - which it had completely severed. A truly killing blow. Clearly no other strikes had been needed. Except for some odd knife-scratches on the long-bone joints, there were no other marks on the skeleton. Some at first thought the scratches indicative of cannibalism, others pooh-poohed the idea - the body had been laid down whole, that was easy to see, and furthermore, none of the long bones had been cracked for their marrow. Much less charred. And cracked-open human long bones were never found properly buried anyhow. The pro-cannibalism forces conceded without a big fight.

The group's main wonderment was about the person who'd done the deed - serious, large-scale force was required to drive even a sharp edge through so much resistance - which implied a big man as spear-wielder. Had the spearsman survived? What had the dispute been about? Were any other people involved? The same scientist who did the speculation laughed ruefully once the shin and thigh bones were fully exposed - this man had been a large fellow even by modern standards, absolutely huge for his own era. The scientist readily admitted to deep fright, approaching panic, at the idea of taking on such a specimen while armed only with a glass-pointed spear.

In fact, his speculations got everything right save the spear-wielder's gender and his vague idea that there must have been some sort of hand-to-hand combat involved. Errors he would not remember when eventually they were corrected by better knowledge.

Goliath's bones still contained a goodly amount of DNA - enough so that eventually -considerably later- investigators got his complete genome. But even the immediate unsophisticated preliminary DNA analyses showed that he had had blue eyes. Radiocarbon dating on his long bones made him by far the earliest blue-eye found to date.

19 - GERARD'S CAVE

A modern small town, a geological youngster merely several hundred years old, sits on the plateau some two kilometres from the edge. It is situated atop the most thoroughly fractured Rampart limestone, hence is underlain by a bewildering 3-D collection of caverns. The citizenry are blasé about caverns. A few decades earlier, two adjacent houses and their outbuildings had disappeared into the gaping maw of a huge sinkhole. It took only fifteen minutes from first rumble to final disappearance, slow enough so that everyone got out safely, too fast to save anything substantial. Careful explorations showed that the sinkhole appeared to be an isolated cavern, which fact for some unknown reason reassured the town's residents.

Behold Gerard, a modern early-teenage example of _H. sapiens_ and citizen of said town. Bright and almost hyper-inquisitive, his goal already is to become a scientist. But he's not entirely sure what that means - he is just now becoming aware of the existence of species and sub-species of both science and its practitioners. Luckily for him, he has a fine teacher for general science, with whom he is beginning to explore the nooks and crannies of various fields of knowledge. He is interested in EVERYthing.

Gerard lives within easy bicycling range of the top of The Rampart. Aged fourteen, he is a good deal of a loner - plays well with others, certainly, but frequently chooses to do his own thing, and often by himself. Last year he'd been given a good off-road bicycle. His favorite use for it did not involve The Plateau, but rather The Rampart itself. Before the bike, he had explored the cliff on foot despite being told not to do so - just like generations of boys before him - the horror of a 200 metre fall being vividly imprinted in all local parents' imaginations. The parents of course know of the area's caves, and have likewise forbidden any childish attempts to explore the known ones nearby: "Stay away from the cliff and out of the caves!" But once or twice per year, an expedition has to be mounted to explore the obvious cavities seeking missing kids, who are almost always found before long. Almost. Not so terribly long ago, perhaps 300 or 400 generations at most, cave bears had roamed the region: back then, kids still missing by nightfall were presumed eaten by bears - an assumption seldom proven wrong.

Before getting the bike, he'd already found three not-overly-arduous foot routes from the upper edge down to the base of the cliff, thence to the riverbank. Unknown to him, those routes had all been traversed by a great many generations of people bringing game caught on The Plateau down to the Tribe's settlement at the foot of the cliffs. For the strong and sure-footed it was a relatively easy trip either up or down, if you were empty-handed - but always a difficult and dangerous downward journey when laden with, say, one complete leg of a full-grown horse. But living was so otherwise easy, down at the base, that the effort was worthwhile - and stayed so for thousands of years.

Six months after getting the bike, Gerard made himself a promise - he would find a bike route down The Rampart, and back up, too. He would be the first person ever - EVER!! - to make that trip. Smallish and wiry, he had a strength-to-weight ratio, and agility, that made the idea at least semi-feasible. He scouted the possibilities every weekend through the summer, and quickly decided that going down might just barely be doable, but a return up the face was going to be utterly impossible no matter what gear ratio his (or anyone's!) bike might have. An intelligent being, he adjusted his goals accordingly. Down the cliff-face he would go, but as for going back up, well, he would take the path along base of the cliff: a few kilometres upstream there was a lateral valley big enough, and of shallow enough slope, so that four-wheel-drive vehicles could navigate from Plateau to riverbank - as could his one-wheel-drive vehicle.

He made it down safely on his first try, using the best (meaning easiest) trail, over in one of the small laterals, a large crack complete with game-engineered switchbacks just barely navigable by his machine. He did have the requisite number of heroic close calls, nearly pitching over the handlebars multiple times, but somehow he arrived safely at the bottom in a semi-controlled sideways slide amidst a shower of small and not-so-small rocks. And with his brake pads half gone: he could smell the stink of overheated hard rubber when he finally arrived and stopped, nearly exhausted and dripping sweat in the flat-calm hot air.

Panting and ecstatic, wondering how he was going to success-fully brag to anyone about this feat without getting grounded imme-diately, he stopped and leaned against a small tree, looked back up - he couldn't even see the edge. The base of The Rampart was re-markably clean, with only an occasional small scree-pile. For most of its extent the cliff base was nearly vertical and met the underlying terrain quite sharply. He set off homeward, walking along the well-developed path at the base, pushing the bike, and glowing internally with kid-pride. After a few hundred metres, he stopped, set the bike against a large slab of limestone, part of a pile of such slabs. The pile was a huge and apparently very old rockfall: an enormous chunk of the cliff had failed an extremely long time ago. He stood there breathing deeply as the adrenaline continued to slowly burn itself out.

Resting, he peered about, now much more aware of his sur-roundings. He was a good observer, and knew how to see and inter-pret small details - his observations could drive parents and friends, not to mention teachers, batty. It was an ability that should stand him in good stead, if he ever achieved his goal of becoming a scien-tist. Something about the pile of slabs -he couldn't figure out just what- made him feel as if it must have recently shifted. But it could have been only slightly, because co-weathered edges where adjacent slabs butted together showed no break in patina. At least, that was so down where he stood, at the base of the pile. Something else.

Gerard possessed an extraordinary sense of smell, and lived in a very different olfactory universe from his family and friends - something it had taken his parents many months to discover while they tried to figure out what the HELL their baby boy would eat. Eventually they understood and accommodated - all the crucifers were a no-no due to their sulfur content. Boiled eggs were agony. And so forth.

Standing by the pile of slabs, he wondered why he felt uneasy, sniffed the air. Burnt rubber, of course - the overused brake pads. And his own sweat. Pine aromas from some nearby trees. Hot rocks in bright sunshine, smelling like concrete but softer. Dust. And that

55

odd undertone, the 'something else'.

Having caught his breath, and since there was plenty of his Saturday afternoon remaining, he took the time to try to parse the unknown smell. It was intriguing, very, very faint. Musty? Mushrooms, perhaps? He walked around the pile, sniffing. Yes here, not here, no, no, yes, no, yes yes yes. He felt like a dog, a bloodhound. The scent seemed to strengthen upwards on the pile. He climbed slowly: the odor grew steadily stronger.

He squatted, put his face down close to the rocks. And felt the tiniest breath of coolness on his cheek. A touch of cooler air just barely in motion. Air tinged with that odd, elusive odor. Tinged, not laden: delicate. But from where? Totally absorbed by this puzzle, he thought for a second, then picked up a big handful of powder-fine dust from between two slabs and tossed it at the rocks in front of him. Nothing at first - the dust hung in the air. But not motionless. Another handful, then another, more precisely placed. The current was coming from behind the topmost big slab, still well above him. The airborne dust drifted slowly downwards. That made sense - if the air was cool, it had to be denser than the surrounding warm air, so it **should** be flowing downwards. He was pleased with himself for the deduction - getting weight differentiated from density had taken a long session with his science teacher a few weeks back - and here he was, using the knowledge already!

He scrambled farther up the pile, did the dust thing twice more. And found the hole. His unease had been correct; up near the top of the heap, a metre-thick slab bigger than a sheet of plywood had recently slid a few tens of centimetres - the scuff marks in the dirt were plain. Everything looked stable, the slab's movement at least arrested for the nonce. Gerard studied the hole. He could probably get his head through -barely- but certainly not his shoulders.

And who knew what would be inside?

That question, of course, was precisely the point of the whole exercise! Who, indeed! The "who" was going to be himself. Grinning and humming tunelessly, he thought "This is going to be MINE!! I'm numero uno in this cave!" And it had to be a cave, not just a hollow in the pile - otherwise there wouldn't be this steady stream of exhaled air.

He studied the entire scene - close beside him there were three pines, the largest well over a half-metre in diameter. Not much water up here, on the topmost floodplain, and pines in The Valley grew slowly anyhow, hence a tree that big meant this pile had been here without major disturbance for several hundred years at least. He would bet the cave's entrance had been sealed for at least that long. Perhaps much, much longer. This was a very old rockfall. Whatever cavern was providing the cool air, it had probably been sealed up for thousands of years. Hooray!

A quick trip to the nearest pine got him a thick, stout dead branch. With it he levered and dug and prodded at the edges of the hole - all the dirt he dislodged disappeared, vanishing traceless into the growing aperture. This was more work than coming down the hill, he thought. Especially with the wrong tools! Ten minutes, and he judged the hole might accommodate his shoulders. He checked - they barely fit. He enlarged it by a few centimetres, just to be certain. Getting stuck was such a monstrously bad idea!

Then he started talking to himself out loud - a habit he'd developed for good reason - namely personal safety. "Careful! It might be a vertical drop, who knows how high. Keep your balance, dig in with your knees. Don't do anything really stupid - if you get stuck you can easily die right here before anyone finds you. BE CERTAIN that you can always back up!" Part of his brain also screamed "Not alone, dummy!" and "What about LIGHT, stupid? You've got no flashlight, and your body is going to plug the hole. You won't be able to see! Go home, get a friend or two, get a ball of string and flashlights, THEN go inside."

The advice he actually took from his alter-ego was to go slowly and feel his way carefully. His shoulders fit. Wiggles. Hips narrower than shoulders, they slid right through: a gently-sloping floor, dry, firm. He reached up from his kneeling position: no ceiling. The walls swept away from him on either side. He was in a chamber, not a passageway. He felt to both sides, fondling the floor, making sure there were no holes to drop into. Then he shifted sideways, to let in whatever light could make it. He understood dark-adaption, sat patiently waiting. Having just come in from the brilliant sunshine, it would take at least five minutes, maybe even fifteen, before his full night-vision would be available.

Shortly, he could sense more than actually see that he was at the edge of a large room, entirely walled and floored with white calcite - that was good, helped bounce the light around. Near him, within a few metres, there was enough light so he could see the walls - on both sides they quickly dimmed out to invisibility - the space could be infinite for all he could tell. In front of him, headed deeper into the cliff, a slight halo of illumination with a dead-black center: distances were difficult to guess - the view went to total darkness in that direction within maybe ten metres. This was NOT a baby cave! And there was no sign whatever that any other human had ever been here!

His very own cave.

Wunderbar!

Finally he yielded to his inner warnings, took a last long look around, and exited headfirst, blinking in the sunlight. Five minutes of heaving small slabs, and he had the opening nicely blocked and camouflaged. He carefully memorized the precise location.

Enroute home, he was already planning his investigations. He was actually using the word, mentally. He couldn't possibly get back to the cave before next weekend, but that was good - the cave wouldn't be going anywhere, and he could use the time to study and get ready to do things right. And he was NOT going to let anyone else know about this! He would be super-careful, take no chances at all, but this was going to be HIS cave - no sharing, no telling. At least, no telling until he was ready to share. Someday. Just like his bicycle descent!

The high-school library yielded little. Queries to his teachers and the librarian got Gerard pointed to several books in the municipal library, where he checked out three -one specifically on caves and techniques for their exploration, the other two more general geological sciences. He devoured them in a sitting. The books' authors wrote serious no-nonsense prose: regardless, it filled Gerard's head with self-generated romanticized fantasies that certainly spurred his interest. Caves weren't just intriguing holes in the ground - they could contain important human artifacts, traces of long-dead communities and societies, paintings on the walls done unimaginably long ago. Man-made tools. Ancient camp-sites. Human burials, too. You never, ever knew what you might encounter, either in today's cave or in the next one. Or in your hundredth. If a cave had ready access to the outer world, one might find almost any kind of wild animal living inside, from pigs and raccoons to bears, so one had to be alert for dangers other than just structural features of the cave itself. Reality overlaid with his daydreams made for exciting stuff. He, the whole town in fact, was sitting atop a potential gold-mine of geology and human prehistory - and nobody but he seemed to care. Well, fine - that meant more for himself.

As a result of his reading, he set a very specific goal. He would turn himself into a cave scientist, a speleologist. Not a spelunker - that term just meant a fun-oriented explorer. He was going to be serious about this. He would both explore and map the cave. As a scout, he'd done a good bit of hiking, had learned to read maps and could use a compass well. His folks had encouraged such activities, and he had both his own personal good compass and several flashlights - plus he could commandeer the white-gas lantern that the family had owned for years "for emergencies" - and had never ever used. Batteries were expensive and flashlights didn't really illuminate volumes well - the gas lantern was the ticket - bright, simple and cheap. He took money from his jar of miscellaneous change and got himself a good clipboard, and some ridiculously expensive –and completely unnecessary- waterproof paper. At the local hardware store he got four liters of white gas, extra lantern mantles, a box of kitchen matches, and (most important, probably) a huge ball of strong polypropylene twine, five kilos, the label said 250 metres per kilo. That should be adequate to provide permanent guidance, a lifeline, from anywhere he could reach in the cave, back to the entrance.

It had become his habit to spend Saturdays by himself, riding the bike and exploring widely - his folks were comfortable with him being gone all day. Early the next Saturday he strapped his gear on the bike and ferried everything to the cave, traveling via the 4-wheeler trail. Inside the cave, he arranged his equipment in the entry-chamber. Eager to see how big that chamber might be, he filled and lit the lantern immediately. And was totally awed - the room was huge.

Gerard tried to emulate the authors of his 'cave exploration' book. No hurry, ever. That way lay injury, even death. Do things right both scientifically and ethically. Mark nothing permanently. Lay down string trails, semi-permanent trails from rock to rock. Import the rocks if needed. In the strings, put knot-patterns every ten metres, patterns that told which way to go to the exit... be able to get out in the dark if all lights failed. For all features, get compass directions, distances, plot them, make notes and little drawings. He was quietly grateful to M. Bailey, his eighth-grade geometry teacher, for the field exercises in mapping - in teams of three the students had actually surveyed the entire ten-hectare school grounds. In detail, to a professional level of accuracy.

Gerard worked slowly and carefully. Very slowly and very carefully, rechecking, improving his maps, gradually extending his string-line deeper, making arbitrary choices of direction as options arose. By about his tenth visit, he'd mapped in near photographic detail the antechamber and the first fifty or so metres of oddly-connected passageways headed deeper into the limestone. The cave was thoroughly dry - not a hint of moisture. All walls and ceilings and floors of glistening white calcite, sometimes rough and convoluted, often-times smooth and nearly flat. Not many stalagmites and stalactites, but plentiful vertical sheets, traces of long-ago seepage through cracks. No signs of any animal activity so far -about that he was perfectly happy. He had, of course, hoped for paintings, or at least marks of some sort showing that humans had once been here, but no such luck. Perhaps deeper?

20 - DISCOVERIES

On one early visit he went about 60m into the cave, through several short passages and around three or four sharp corners. From there he had undertaken to find his way to the exit in perfect darkness, testing his knot-trail. It had worked perfectly. When he got to the antechamber's outer entrance, he stopped in the extremely dim light trickling through the entrance-hole, and relit the gas lantern. This was a new vantage point from which to view the entrance itself. He tilted the big lantern to shine it somewhat upwards.

Instantly the hair stood up on his arms and neck. How had he missed this? Too much focus on getting through the entrance, most likely. In plain sight on a particularly smooth bit of white calcite wall, well above his standing line of sight, there was a mark. A completely unnatural mark. Sometime long past, someone (a quite tall someone, in fact), had stretched upwards and made a mark using three fingers dipped in red ocher. He knew instantly what the coloring material was despite never having seen it outside of photographs. The person unknown had made a three-mark ess -SSS- as long as a human hand. All three fingertips as a brush, moved together as a unit. Someone. A human, therefore a relative. He could hardly breathe. He was probably the first to see this since it had been painted. (When? When? When? And what for?) What an enormous, mind-boggling honor and privilege. And mystery.

He left for the day shortly thereafter, having copied and plotted and measured appropriately - preoccupied enroute home by thoughts of cameras and flashes and the wonderful insensitivity of ocher to light, an insensitivity that he would use to justify the extensive photography he was planning.

He hoped the entry-sign meant that there was more to see, more art, somewhere deeper in the cave, but he forced himself to remain methodical. He continued to explore and map, but so far, nothing more had surfaced. Just that single SSS. Maddening, suggestive, even seductive - with its promise unfulfilled. Meanwhile, the need to really investigate, to understand, was becoming a living flame - he was rapidly firming up his determination to major in anthropology in college. Cave anthropology, specifically.

College? He would be the first from his family to go so far, but everyone (especially himself) expected it of him - family and teachers alike. Anthropology for an undergraduate major field. There were several universities with good anthropology curricula within a couple of hundred kilometres. Ultimately, of course, there would be graduate school for advanced degrees - so that he could do this 'work' as a profession, be paid eventually to do his hobby. Skipping about on a scientific playground at someone else's expense, his job being to have fun developing new knowledge and presenting it to the world- knowledge about his own species' early history.

The extensive time he spent on the cave work eventually forced him to confess to his parents. Much to his surprise, once he'd explained to them what he'd been up to and just how carefully he was proceeding, they weren't upset - in fact, they seemed fascinated and encouraged his work. 'Anthropology' they could, and did, develop at least a superficial interest in, both self-protective, and supportive of their son. Privately his folks agreed it was good that at his age he should have a consuming interest in something scientific, as opposed to pursuing most of the other handy possibilities.

By the time Gerard left home for college, he'd mapped the cave to a depth of over 100 m, and had even built a papier-mâché 3-D scale model of it. On his final visit before heading off for his freshman year, Gerard moved his equipment deeper into the cave, unstrung the near-exit part of the twine, then carefully double-sealed and camouflaged the entrance.

21 – GERARD'S RETURN

He didn't return for four years, being immersed full time (including summers) in his undergraduate work, becoming an honest-to-god certified professional anthropologist. As he matured, he could watch his self-centeredness fading, being replaced by a sense of being duty-bound to finally tell the world -or at least his budding colleagues- about "HIS" cave. Even if he'd so far found nothing of scientific worth in it, save the entry-way SSS. When he thought about his cave now, he was much more mellow and less selfish. He just hoped that someday he and a group could complete his mapping project. Someday. Meanwhile, he'd done well in his classes and fieldwork. In his senior year, he applied to a graduate program at the nearby Universite de la Pais, a good school having solid connections with a very up-and-coming private research institution formally titled La Fondation pour Anthropologie - widely nicknamed La Fond.

La Fond had just hired a new director - directrix, to be more accurate - named Joan, a youngish researcher already well on her way to becoming a powerhouse in local-area anthro. She and her team had made some amazing discoveries at sites near The Rampart. One of the most exciting developments had been discovering that two widely-separated sites, being investigated by rival institutions La Fond and UP, were closely linked in some extraordinarily intimate ways not yet understood. In fact, Joan and her husband Anton (not an anthropologist, but rather, a world-class solver of jigsaw puzzles, and academic student of murder mysteries) had made the initial connections between the two sites. From that connection had come the first-ever cooperative investigations by the two institutions.

Joan had a deserved reputation for knowledge, interpersonal skills and boundless energy. La Fond's benefactor understood that it was she and her husband who had precipitated the successful initial collaboration - for which bravo! He had hinted broadly, more than once, that she should focus significant energy on similar cooperative ventures.

As Directrix, Joan had immediately received seats on the graduate-student admissions committees of several universities (including UP) that sent students to La Fond to do their research. One year early in Joan's reign, the only highly-qualified well-recommended student from the immediately surrounding area was Gerard. He had made a difficult decision when he applied. Knowing that competition would be tough, he had provided to the admissions committee the existence, maps and model of his personal cave. Part of his sales-pitch. But he'd not given away the cave's location, and he hadn't mentioned the SSS at the entrance. Overall, it was a fine strategic choice. Those materials and an explanation of his activities, plus Joan's support, had sealed it - he was admitted to the UP graduate program, and would be doing his actual doctoral research at La Fond. At their important site at the base of The Rampart - within easy hiking distance of his own cave, his bicycle path, his family home. And Goliath's grave.

It was after his admission, late in the summer between his senior year and the start of graduate school, before he finally revisited his cave. Nothing had changed outside. Inside, he found and reinstalled the outermost flight of twine, took a long, very pleased stare at the entryway SSS, wondered why the gods of anthropology were teasing him with this entry-way mark, then headed deeper, picking up the twine ball and lantern. Deep inside, at the end of his already-laid twine, he faced a well-remembered tee intersection, and chose to go left so as to give himself a special treat - opening up a known but completely unexplored passageway. It could be a kilometre long - or a five metre dead-end. Only one way to find out.

Three steps around the first angle, and he stopped short. At eyeball height, a scattering of stick-figure humans, several very crude animals, drawn in charcoal, apparently a hunting scene. Crude, crude, crude! But real!

For over four years he'd often been within five metres of these paintings! Amazing. Such occurrences were, he knew, part of the overall "romance" of caving, of research underground. He looked about - high ceiling as usual, and no smoke-smudge traces of torches. No litter of 'art' materials on the floor. Just the wall pictures. With some imagination he could make out a deer and (he thought) a horse. Maybe. The humans were much less well done, mere stick figures. But still! Art, at last, in his personal cave. Hooray!

Out came his digital camera. He justified extensive photography as a preventive measure, intended as insurance against some catastrophic loss. A cheap rationalization, but sufficient for the moment. He moved to his left, unrolling twine. A two metre break without art, then something completely different - a single horse, in profile, this one definitely recognizable as to species. Not just done in lines, but having some large body-areas filled in with shading. The artist hadn't attempted hooves - the legs ended in midair- but the beast's mane was handled reasonably, the ear and eye were properly sized and located.

He shifted left again, holding the lantern high, barely breathing. More animals: this time overlapping. More photography. Three horses. And a two-horned animal, the horns on its snout, the body squat and heavy and evil - a rhinoceros. The horses overlapping one another and facing left, the rhino facing the other way. No more human figures, though.

He moved still farther left, and new images kept appearing at the edge of his puddle of light. Now a single horse, full height, with recognizable hooves and streaming mane, tail upright, right front foot raised, a proper arch to the neck. "For damn sure better than I can do!" he told himself aloud, admiring the work. Above the horse, three stick-figure men with stick penises, spears and spear-throwing sticks. One obese abstract "Venus-fertility goddess", almost a requisite for any cave having even a touch of art.

"Why are the animals done so much better than the humans?" he wondered. It was always so. Did all primitive cultures share some taboo about accurate human images? "NOT PRIMITIVE!" he scolded himself – "...let's just say "EARLY"!

Three metres of blank wall which even non-artist Gerard could tell was too rough to be a good canvas.

And then, magnificence, gape-worthy. A metre-tall rhino in left-facing profile, two metres long. Anatomically correct: long, tapered, pointed horns midline on the snout, the front one longer than the rear. A properly located and sized tail. Tiny eyes and ears, massive wrinkles in the armor-plate skin, splayed feet on realistic-looking legs. Shading to emphasize the shoulder and haunch muscles. A clear depiction of the creature's pointed, prehensile upper lip, raised as if testing the air - the artist must have gotten bloody close to the living beast to notice such a detail because most certainly you wouldn't notice it in a dead animal! A nicely-done small bird - a symbiotic parasite-picker, standing on the beast's butt. The picture was done entirely in charcoal, but the lines were of varying widths - the artist had either had several sizes of charcoal, or a fine knowledge of how to vary line width and texture from a single charcoal-stick "brush". Very different from anything else so far. Sophisticated work, this.

And down in the lower right, a splash of red that made him catch his breath - the same SSS as in the entryway. He peered and looked closer - the symbol had been laid down atop the drawing.

It screamed a simple message: "I made this picture."

"I. ME! Yes, I'm talking to YOU!"

Self-awareness, language, communication to others distant from one's-self in time and space. All were contained in that set of three red wiggles.

Inferences to be drawn, Professor? Well, claiming authorship for one - that seems a rather advanced concept. Then, the location of SSS's drawing on the wall implied other things: it was partly atop, hence newer than, a couple of small lower-quality drawings. The painter was definitely not whoever had done the earliest images. Even Gerard could see the differences in 'hand'. In fact, up to here, the images formed a progression, possibly showing the slow improvement of one artist, but possibly, too, a series of artists probably separated by time. Perhaps both? Is there, Professor, a difference between 'drawing an inference' and 'speculating'?

Gerard abruptly realized that he'd subconsciously given a name to his unknown artist - "Esses". Having done so changed his perception. Interesting. There was suddenly a human-recognizable, knowable person behind this work. Not just some anonymous far-back semi-human ancestor diddling with a burnt stick, but a complete person with highly developed observational and mechanical skills, and artists' tools. In one blinding moment his attitude towards his objects of study metamorphosed completely. No feeble intellect had produced these works.

Almost fearfully, he looked farther left. More paintings. Four horses side by side, overlapping, in step. And three half-height men, standing together, facing left, holding spears - FINALLY! he thought - some realistic human figures, drawn, as he would come to call it, "in the round", meaning quite accurate, sculptural, naturalistic. Several species of deer-like critters, unknown to him but surely identifiable by any mammalogist. Birds on the ground feeding, flying, singly and in small flocks. He'd never seen birds in cave art.

More photos.

Esses had a fabulously accurate eye - one superb horse-head displayed jaw musculature, lolling tongue, forward-focused ears, flared nostrils, wide-open frightened or angry eyes - the whites

66

shown by leaving bits of wall untouched by charcoal. Another death-of-prey scene with three men in chase, the prey - a horse, a stallion complete with scrotum - down on its knees, several spears in the animal, more coming shortly, one shown in flight. Realism! Red ocher for blood - one spear through the horse's chest, blood dripping from the entry wound, and also from the mouth and nose. "Whoever painted this..." he thought out loud, "...really understands in detail how an animal dies from a chest wound." Namely bleeding copiously from the mouth due to lung damage. He pondered, thinking, "...to get such accuracy and detail, the artist is almost certainly a hunter, too. As well as a very close-up observer of LIVE rhinos."

Esses, he realized, was quite the multi-talented person. Funny indeed how his thoughts now put the artist in the present tense.

The consistent signatures and steadily improving technique, plus a feeling of coherent style, told Gerard he was looking at one person's work over time. The signed paintings made a definite one-artist progression, getting better and better, more and more complex, as he moved deeper into the cave. An artist with a highly developed aesthetic plus the technique to support it, and improving steadily. Such a display by a modern artist would be a 'retrospective', a study spanning the artist's career. Esses had obviously returned many times to add to the collection, showing improvement with every consecutive image. Surely that meant that Esses must have practiced outside, in between wall-painting sessions - how else to get better between adjacent images?

He pondered: most radiocarbon dates for human materials from The Valley clustered around 40k years. Query - who, in a neolithic society 40,000 years ago, would have had the spare time for such development? Hunting/gathering in today's world was almost always a full-time occupation, sunup to sundown and no vacations. Learning to draw took time and practice and material resources- lots of all three. So this body of work spoke of an artist with considerable 'leisure' time. Gerard knew about all the time and effort involved in becoming an artist, and had long ago given up on himself. No talent. SSS was in fact light years above his level, artistically - forty thousand years ago!

He could again hear Dr Joan, his favorite professor, challenging the class, challenging him personally. "Draw some inferences, please, Mister Grad Student. Impress us with your savvy. Extract some MEANING from your observations."

Today he could answer, "Very well, Doctor - Here are some social-structure speculations." That structure being the holy grail, at least for many students. "Maybe SSS could have been something like a protégé, supported, not needing to do life's time-consuming routines? Might there have been a 'patron of the arts' in 38k BC?"

Speculation was such fun! He could visualize Dr Joan's face as he rattled on.

"If not an individual 'patron', then how about public support for the arts? And surely, 'patronage' in turn could suggest a leisure class, perhaps an upper or wealthy class, or else some form of long-term ongoing societal support for this artist's work."

What a wonderful, spine-tingling bundle of concepts to play with.

Fifteen, seventeen, now over twenty Esses-signed wall images of animals. His mind reeled. Thank god for digital memory and its nearly infinite capacity for photos.

Around another corner he went. Fading away into the penumbra of his lantern, a double horizontal row of twenty-centimetre charcoal-drawn squares at chest and face height. Precisely aligned both horizontally and vertically, number three of the top row exactly above number three in the lower. First impression was just of pattern regularity - that, plus a blob of darkness inside each heavy black outline.

He was befuddled - squares are abstract geometrical figures, regular and precise. Cave art is about animals out in nature, and neither animals nor their environment have much in the way of right angles or straight lines. There was no precedent for this: his mind scrabbled for traction. This was surreal. Brighter light might have made things move faster, but not any more effectively. There had to be at least two dozen squares. The wall area inside each square was darker than the surround, but textured.

Frames.

Two dozen bloody picture frames! His Artist had done a series of some sort, and had figured out the need for, or just the use of, frames.

And had figured out how to align them. They were done as neatly as if with a straight-edge. No charcoal marks sticking out beyond the corners. The frames weren't merely sketched, they'd been DRAFTED! All the top and bottom edges were in two pairs of straight lines, interrupted but parallel and dead level. As if laid down using a string - which, he guessed, was probably exactly how it had been done. Now THERE was an unexpected tool! String was easy – so, what had the artist used for a level? And the width of the frames was absolutely consistent, about five centimeters, tops, bottoms, all sides – doing that layout had been a non-trivial exercise! How?

Just before the first pair of frames, protruding from a deep crack in the calcite, the end of a large bone. It distracted him for a moment – he guessed the tibia or femur of some man-sized or even horse-sized mammal. The visible end was neatly sawn off, squarely. A man-made artifact – which term almost always signified a tool. But for what? He touched it, expecting it to be firmly cemented in place but no, it moved. Pictures to show its original position. Then, gingerly, he extracted it from what was obviously its storage-spot. A long bone, about fifty centimetres. Polished, and with one side flattened. The knobs of its articulation remained on the other end. On the flattened pure-white surface, crosswise scratches, deep, anything but accidental – they had been filled with soot, scrimshaw-style. Strikingly visible even in poor light. Straight black marks permanently set into white bone. What the hell? He studied the device – there was a mark as close as possible to the cut end. Then five centimeters along, a second mark. Blank space for twenty centimeters, then another pair of marks also five centimeters apart. The knobbed far end of the bone made a perfect handle. He stared, turned the object around in his headlight, considering. Then, abruptly, all the hairs of his arms and neck erected: he held the bone horizontally, laid it under the line of frames. It was a ruler – a template, a layout device. The marks matched the width of the frames and width of the

69

enclosed "canvases" perfectly. He was awed, replaced the bone into its spot carefully.

No dummy this Artist!

This place, his cave, the Artist's cave, was a serious neolithic art gallery. Not only that, but a technological museum of sorts! A one-person show and gallery, for god's own sake, from forty thousand years ago!

He shivered, returned his attention to the twin lines of frames - he could only imagine one topic that could rate such a series, and it would not be horses or rhinos or phases of the moon. With a deep breath he confronted the first pair of frames: he knew before leaning in and stepping close to examine the first stacked pair. The hairs on his nape and arms went vertical.

Faces.

He'd wondered where the people were in cave art? Well, here they came! In spades.

Profiles in two matching horizontal rows. Drawn in thin charcoal lines. Not up to modern portrait or even caricature standards, but clearly of different people. At last, for the very first time, anthropologists had a few faces of individuals making up the nearly anonymous collectivity with which they were usually constrained to deal. Real people, individuals, actual faces from forty thousand years ago... not forensic reconstructions from a quarter of some badly-shattered skull. These looked for all the world like people he'd encounter today, on any street in France. How many times had he, or a friend, or a professor, wished out loud to know what these ancient ancestors actually looked like? Look in your mirrors!

It appeared that all of the top row were women, the lower row men. Why stacked pairs? Couples? Relatives? No reason except the pleasing geometry of two lines of squares? Portraits of an entire village, a tribe? The world's first census? First yearbook? Esses's relatives, friends, enemies, neighbors? What the hell!?

Gerard shrugged to himself. This was a GOOD artist by any standards, clearly enthusiastic about drawing. Of COURSE such a person would do human profiles and faces - Esses had really gone deeply into it. Why didn't other cave artists do likewise? Some sort of taboo, perhaps? If a taboo existed, why did it apparently NOT apply to Esses?

Gerard sidestepped ever so slowly down the line. Again, the pictures improved as he moved: the final pair was quite significantly better than the first - definitely a man and a woman, and with radically different nose-shapes. Both with some sort of marking on their faces - personal decoration, zigzags and squiggles. The man with short hair, the woman with a bun. Individualized, personal hairdos. And makeup - none of the others had face paint. Plus, he realized, not a Neanderthal brow ridge in sight - not a trace.

"Interpret what you see, student!"

Chief and number one wife? He laughed at himself as he corrected the thought, trying consciously not to be sexist - perhaps Chief and number one husband! Who could say? Lots of early-stage societies were matrilineal, and some were even matriarchal.

In the lower right quadrant of every picture, a small red SSS. Much too small to have been done with the fingertips - and identical from picture to picture. Mechanically perfect signatures. Unreal. How? Printing? Egad. This gallery had to be years, decades of work by one artist. Persistence. Skill. Why? An internal voice whispered to him but he succeeded in ignoring it: "Perhaps this artist just liked to draw and paint!? You don't need to postulate any other rationale, at least, not before some new finding suggests a different reason."

The series ended with a pair of king-sized portraits, in non-square frames. The penultimate was a completed drawing of a woman, the first person in the gallery shown in full face. A good portrait of an old woman - perhaps very, VERY old? Heavily wrinkled face and throat. Her eyes were slitted, almost closed, the mouth sunken from loss of teeth. She wore a massive necklace, precisely drawn, and as detailed as the face itself. On the necklace, the central item was a good-sized lower jawbone. a mandible. A carnivore's mandible. It hung as a vee with its top nearly at her collarbones, the thong shown going right through the heavy hinges. There were teeth and claws strung on the thong on both sides of the mandible. He counted: symmetrical (of course!), ten claws and one tooth on each side. There were also two of the small SSS signatures, one on either side of the head at ear level. What had been so special about this ancient woman? Tribal shaman, perhaps? Or even the actual chief herself? Some relative of the Artist? The Artist's mother or grandmother seemed a reasonable possibility. Certainly an important someone, carefully singled out for special treatment.

For all his concentration on the images, Gerard knew that the important thing was the frames. The portraits were good, perhaps great, but they were just a pair among many. No – it was the frames that told something brand-new and important. Old Woman's frame was a perfect circle of dense black charcoal – the frame itself was absolutely uniform in width, the curvature perfectly smooth, not a squiggle out of place anywhere. Imagination coupled with a finger as a center-pivot, a bit of string, and one could easily lay out two concentric circles, then carefully fill between them. Obvious and easy the second time, perhaps, but NOT so the first time! Again this was unique, and bespoke volumes about mental capabilities. Practical geometry and tool-making.

But it was the frame of Ms Unfinished that broke the bank. Like its neighbor, perfect curves, perfectly uniform width.

An OVAL.

Seeking to fully understand the difference between a circle and an oval had required the services of humans the stature of Euclid, Newton, Hypatia, eventually even Einstein. And it had taken millennia.

Circles are easy – ovals are not. It takes an utterly monumental leap to visualizing the perfect oval – and even more of a leap to figure out how to make such a thing. Gerard understood the mental leap involved here – thanks again to his geometry teacher. Even the mechanics are a stunning mental feat. Ovals have two foci, and drawing one requires TWO "pivots" connected by a cord, properly manipulated. It was utterly beyond Gerard how the hell this Artist got TWO pivot-points, two foci, singlehandedly, on this wall, and held them perfect through the layout of two concentric ovals. Much less what fertile imaginings had led to the attempt! The very idea left him gasping.

More. Two larger, 50 centimetre tall drawings accompanied

Old Woman, one above and one below the circular portrait. Both drawings were in lightly-charcoaled frames, and each frame shared an edge with Old Lady's frame. Gerard understood, without analyzing any further, that these extensions of the portrait applied specifically to Old Woman. They were attached to her, in the most graphically literal sense, and were definitely not part of the overall Gallery milieu. The extensions were detailed drawings. The upper attempted - quite successfully - to depict motion. It showed a hunting party: three breast-less hence presumably male figures, in the round, standing together shoulder to shoulder with spears upraised, facing a bear twice their height... and all three spears were broken! Off to one side stood a smaller figure, obviously female - she was complete with breasts. She had three right arms, showing motion - one raised and pulled far back, holding a spear at the ready: a second half-way through her throw, the arm horizontal and pointed at the bear, spear shown in mid-air. A final arm was pointed down, end of follow-through. And the final spear was embedded in the bear's left eye, painted complete with blood. Gerard was flabbergasted. There were so many unique aspects of just this one scene... a woman not just hunting with men but apparently killing this bear by herself and thereby (presumably) saving the three men. Who could the female savior be except Old Woman herself? Motion pictures, good grief! The Lumiere Brothers were going to lose their place in the encyclopedia as inventors of movies! An <u>activity</u>, rather than static figures, as the central theme of the picture. Humans in the round. Yee gods.

The second attached drawing, below the portrait, was of another female figure, this time holding a very large, seriously outsized spear at an upwards diagonal, the butt on the ground, her foot squarely on the butt to hold it in place. Impaled through the chest on the big spear, spraying ocher-blood, was a male figure, much larger than the woman. The man's right arm was straight above his head in 'ready to throw' position, holding another big spear - the same size as the one held by the woman, and appropriate for the man's physique – but wildly inappropriate for hers!

Gob-smacked again, utterly flabbergasted, Gerard came out of his brief daze, studied the two ancillary pictures, instantly realized there was only one interpretation of these two amazing drawings: the events depicted were REAL EVENTS in the life of Old Woman herself. Biographical studies, events from a life! Biographical motion pictures! Mind in a whirl, he couldn't yet integrate everything he was seeing. He once again shifted his attention leftwards.

To the left of Old Woman and her 'attached events' was the other large frame, the oval, last frame in the portrait lineup, with the unfinished charcoal outlines of a face - female again, with the same look and shapes and proportions as on Old Woman beside her. Unfinished. The forehead, eyes, cheekbones and part of the lower face had been given a good bit of work, and entirely lacked old-age lines. This woman would have been a great deal younger than Old Woman next door. Interesting... it certainly looked as if Esses had intended to do another version of Old Woman - but younger? Why? More and more mysteries.

Esses had never finished the second big picture, the oval. Why? All individual works, so far, had been finished and signed - all save this one. The unfinished picture made the whole scene smell of interruption. Probably, he thought, the entrance had collapsed or closed while this portrait was in process. He shuddered - if Esses had been inside, there was a very high probability that the Artist's body was somewhere quite nearby. He hoped not, shivering at the thought. He really didn't want to confront anyone's shade, or even a skeleton. That would make things far, far too personal. This was all hard enough already.

Gerard sat down on the floor and stared at the portraits, trying not to think, just to saturate himself with the moment. After ten minutes or so, he stood up, prepared to continue. There was something much larger on the wall to the left, looming in the edges of his light-puddle.

He sidled towards it, found that he was too close to take it all in, took a step backwards.

"Jeezuz Keerist Almighty!" He was certain that no such imagery had ever been found in a cave, anywhere. Landscape, two metres wide, well over one tall. With a horizon. Outlines of a distant mountain range, charcoal outlines of peaks, charcoal fill for the bottoms of mountains but the tops had been left white, done in outline only. Snow-caps. One distinctive mountain was far bigger than the others surrounding it. No perspective, but showing hints - some animals painted large to seem close - tiny "far-away" images halfway to the horizon, and of at least four species of big animals. Also trees both near and far. Two very distinct species of tree. Gerard wondered - would he be able to identify all those species? Did they still live up there on the plateau, somewhere? A cluster of small human figures, in pairs, in the lower left. So much detail!

Gerard's attention wasn't on internal details of the picture. Because in the first second of studying the landscape, he had identified the mountains - the big central peak had been part of his back-yard home skyline since birth. The artist had painted Gerard's own personal favorite mountain!

Too much new stuff all at once. Gerard was in visual and mental hyperdrive, a classic overload for both data input and processing. Due to his preoccupation with the depiction of the backyard scenery from his own house, he'd missed many details in that big landscape.

Feeling as if he'd accidentally wandered into the Martian Louvre alone and in the dark and as the first human ever to see the contained treasures, he picked up his lantern, checked the twine, and continued left. The art stopped. Five, ten, fifteen metres of blank wall, rough-textured, lousy canvas. He breathed a sigh of relief to be off overload. He kept on, slowly following the bend to the left. Still a high ceiling. Then, a ledge sticking out into his path, a calcite shape projecting out at right angles to the wall, waist-high and flat-topped, looking quite like a podium or an altar. Gerard almost jumped when he finally got close enough, and the proper angle, to identify the lumpiness atop the ledge.

22 - BEAR SKULL

A bear skull! And beside it on the calcite, two long, slender light-weight bones - with holes in them. First animal remains he'd ever seen in his cave. Bears and birds. What a way to start!

The skull was completely clean and starkly white, sitting nonchalantly on the "altar", facing away from the main wall, guard-like.

He peered closer. No mandible, just the skull. JUST?! Hell's Bells! It was HUGE! He got out a flashlight, set down the lantern, studied the skull more closely, not touching. Lots of photos.

On the otherwise-perfect skull, the left orbit had been shattered- but because of his ongoing mental overload, the penny failed to drop and he missed the connections. He did wonder, though: shattered before or after death? The skull was eerily white, too perfectly so... the only naturally really white-white skulls were sun-bleached and weathered, emphatically not the case here, hundreds of metres underground! A wicked set of teeth on the beast - but no canine teeth. The canines were the only teeth missing - probably, he thought, taken by the hunter as trophies or souvenirs, or by the finder of the skull if the beast had died naturally. However, the more he looked, the more unlikely "natural death" seemed - the shattered orbit was mighty peculiar. Diagnostic, actually. Such damage had to have been done by something small and sharp and speedy. He knew that local ancient societies hadn't yet developed the bow and arrow - without arrows, the only candidate was a spear. Someone way back then had had balls or been both stupid and lucky. Not to mention GOOD with a spear. Or all of the above.

Someone.

The two long, slender bones next to the skull were the size of modern snare-drumsticks but hollow, pipe-like. He recognized them from pictures. Bird-wing-bone flutes. He could play the recorder, although not at all well. He bet himself that he could get music out of those bones - if he dared to try. Which pleasure he denied himself, feeling slightly righteous about behaving properly.

Again, what the hell!? Was this an altar to the bear god? To the god of bird-flight, too, perhaps? He carefully touched nothing, held up his lantern, turned it slowly, scanning. He had to admit to himself that he was getting a bit superstitiously hyper. If he had believed in ghosts and spirits, this was certainly the place for them to manifest! But nothing supernatural hove into view.

To the side of the 'altar' there was a five-metre tall vertical wall, convoluted, with one narrow vertical slit in it, rather like a set of stage curtains almost but not quite closed. Behind the slit there was obviously open space, and another white wall.

The lantern's shade made it too wide to pass through the opening. He took his best flashlight, and stepped up to the slit. A medium squeeze: he studied his body, the various clearances. It would do. Not easy, but at least no chance of getting stuck on the other side. Not for the first time in his cave, he was glad to be skinny.

23- PORTRAIT OF TALL BLUE

Gerard sidled himself into the narrow vertical opening. Doing so took all of his attention for some seconds. Then he was through, standing free, powerful flashlight in hand. The completely enclosed room was about 3 x 4 metres, and nearly 4 metres high. Wholly of highly-reflective pure white calcite. Its entire volume lit up brightly as he shined his light about.

For the first time ever in his life, including all of today's discoveries, he found himself emotionally stunned into immobility both physical and mental.

Across the room, at slightly above his own face level, a portrait.

Not a profile - and not a quick, easy sketch. Nothing at all like the gallery of work he'd just seen.

A classic three-quarters frontal view, almost three dimensional, honest-to-god portrait, a head-neck-upper torso study. And such details! The subject was a strikingly attractive, high-cheekboned young woman. A narrow, aquiline nose. Heavy, strongly-arched eyebrows. Slightly flared nostrils. Prominent collar bones. Real lips, full and dark, not just skimpy lines. The face alone established the model's gender, but it was emphasized by accurately-done breasts. Faint superficial traces of ribs. Her facial features were exquisitely presented, brilliantly displayed. The visible ear with its complex topography. She was in a genuine POSE, too. Her hair was pulled back into two braids - one hung forward over a shoulder, not quite reaching her breast. Areolas and nipples, even. No bloated simplistic, faceless, big-butted big-boobed Earth-mother, this woman! The tip of the braid was held by a cord or thong tied in a perfectly recognizable simple bow-knot. Gerard's mother and two sisters had long hair, which he had braided for them many times - and always finished with a bow-tied ribbon - no rubber bands allowed, ever. Her eyes were tightly focused on the viewer. He shivered again: things were getting far too close, too personal.

Wonder of wonders, this portrait was most emphatically NOT a generic face, certainly not some blank planar expressionless primitivo. The progression was mind-boggling - first stick-figures, then two dozen steadily improving profiles, then the two big full-face portraits. And now, what was to all intents and purposes a post-renaissance-quality three-quarters-view formal portrait.

She was clearly a real person, not an idealized concept. An artist's model, from 40,000 years ago. Across that time-gulf, Gerard almost said "Hello" out loud. Impossible. Nothing like this had ever been found, never, nowhere. The impossible was staring straight at him. A rendition so far beyond any cave or rock art he'd ever seen in real life, or in books, or in lectures, as to be momentarily incomprehensible. Stupefying. Again he thought to himself, "Well, we all wanted to know what you folks actually looked like!"

Gerard realized that for this moment, he was unique among all people through all of human history - this entire event, the portrait, the joy of discovery, the explosive emotion of understanding what the picture must mean - all that was his and his alone. A moment to savor, probably a once-in-ten-billion lifetimes happening. Of course, it couldn't remain "his" for long - the portrait and its meaning belonged to the whole of *Homo sapiens*. He would report the portrait, the entire unbelievable gallery, properly and immediately, although with a tinge of sadness at losing exclusivity of knowledge about "his" magnificent collection. But he couldn't really regret anything - after all, eventually revealing this "Gallery" had been inevitable since the moment he'd realized he was going to become a professional in the field. He also knew that as soon as he reported this find, he would himself be forever famous, merely due to the accident of having discovered Her - Gerard felt that the pronoun MUST be capitalized, until somehow a formal name could be settled upon for Her. At any rate, he couldn't have cared less about the prospect of fame. The find was the thing - it would transcend his own existence and accomplishments-to-come, whatever they might be. He chuckled - not yet done with his doctorate, he could already retire as famous as Schliemann, discoverer of Troy

He gasped to re-start his breathing, then finally took a step forward, then another, to close the distance.

Done in charcoal - the partially-charred twigs that had served as both brushes and paint littered the floor in front of the portrait. The underlying texture and shape of the wall itself, and its color, had been used to conscious advantage. The whites of Her eyes were exposed bits of wall-surface. The whole face was on an outwards bulge in the wall, yielding a distinct real three-dimensionality. Marvelous!

Then the chill hit him, erected every tiny hair on his body.

The eyes.

Blue. Bright, clear blue.

How the HELL did a painter get BLUE, permanent BLUE, forty thousand years ago? Red, yellow, white, black - sure, commonplace in cave-art the world 'round. But this portrait had the whites of the eyes properly shown, and BLUE irises. With black pupils. And wonder of wonders, her eyes were tightly focused on the viewer.

On Gerard. Blue-eyed Gerard.

They were related, so said the eyes. More than merely conspecifics.

He was Her first company for forty thousand years.

Holy crap.

He peered more closely: the irises were two carefully-matched bits of turquoise, inset into sockets drilled into the very limestone itself. Not mere pebbles but manufactured beads, with the stringing-holes used for pupils, holes filled with something black, surely charcoal. The smudging over cheekbones and forehead wasn't just charcoal. There were actual skin tones, highlights, subtle traces of red in the skin, most likely ocher mixed with charcoal? The whole picture seemed more impossible the closer one looked. A modern fake? He dismissed that idea - no way, because no modern person except Gerard himself had been inside this cave. What to think? Anything you clearly observe is *ipso facto* not "impossible" howev-

79

er unlikely it may seem. Just say monumentally unlikely, not impossible - and begin searching for an explanation, however odd.

Forty thousand years - widely held modern theory hypothesized "them" to have had fully modern brain capabilities back then. The believers were probably correct, Gerald thought... his own civilization hadn't produced portraiture this realistic, this accurate, until the middle fifteenth century.

He abruptly checked himself, again corrected his thinking - he was doing a lot of that today, a symptom of being on a vertical learning curve. Correctly stated the thought must NOT be "**They** were thought to have had..." but rather "**WE ARE THOUGHT** to have had..." The important thing was the pronoun and who it included: **not "them" but "we, us!"** For without a doubt, this Artist was his own equal, and was clearly the finest mental representative yet discovered of 'we humans' from back then. An emissary across the time-gulf, driving home a critical point. Here, the "equality of brain power" hypothesis was confirmed in spades!

Gerard took another step, and as he got close had to look slightly upwards - the artist had been taller than he. Or else had stood on something no longer in the room... but Gerard knew that no ladder-like object could be fitted through the door-slit. No, this artist had been tall - way, WAY out on the cave-art people's bell curve for height.

In the top left corner of the Portrait were two of the now-familiar full-sized triple-ess-squiggles he'd seen so many times already. He stared at the marks, so obviously made with three adjacent fingertips dipped in pigment and stroked together in unison, not laid down with three individual strokes. Surely it was what he had surmised already, in the Gallery – namely, the signature of the Artist. Esses's signature. He wondered - was it just a mark, the Artist's "X", or was it part of a larger symbology? Equality of brain-power - they could have had an alphabet, or pictographology back then - it was a huge stretch, but why not? If they had had one, what bits of it might survive as evidence, survive for 40k years? What to look for, how to think about it if found? A wonderful essay question for a final exam someday.

He pondered the Portrait. Something was tickling: he waited for his brain to sort things out and present its analysis. In all paintings leading up to here - be they faces, animals, or landscape- the signature SSS had always been in the lower right portion of the image. Not so, here. The Portrait flaunted three signatures, none of which was lower-right. One, the smallest and neatest, was centered on the woman's forehead, and was the same size as the signature SSS in the little gallery portraits.

The hair stood up on his neck again as he continued to study the work. Not just the signatures' placement - something else was different, too. Details, the Devil's own playground. He examined the two full-sized SSS's which lay close together. A double signature, another first. Laid atop and partially obscuring one SSS was the edge of a black braid. Beside that signature, nearly touching it, was the second SSS. With the signature atop the hair. One SSS had been laid down before the hair was painted, another done afterwards. It had to be intentional. Before and after, raw canvas and finished product?

Gerard stared hard. His real job was to extract human meaning from physical artifacts. He tried. Then suddenly, blindingly, he understood.

Here, the only possible -the only even <u>conceivable</u>- meaning was straightforward:

<u>THIS IS ME - BEHOLD MY IMAGE AND KNOW ME, YOUR ARTIST.</u>

<u>I DID THIS WORK.</u>

<u>I WILL NOT BE ANONYMOUS, I WILL BE KNOWN.</u>

<u>I AM AN INDIVIDUAL, AND BECAUSE YOU SEE ME I STILL EXIST.</u>

This was, without a shadow of a doubt, a self-portrait. The signature on the forehead could mean nothing else: "This image is of ME!"

The painter, the Artist, the model, his artist now named Esses, was a woman. Not just any woman, but THIS woman, right here, on the wall. And SHE had known EXACTLY what she was doing. She had composed this painting with exquisite care, to be sure the message was forever available and unmistakably clear. Had differentiated it by signature from all her other works in the cave. This painting was a message into the unknowable future, sent by this individual, not by some anonymous *H. sapiens of variety X*, but this individual, this person.

Someone who clearly understood time and future and memory.

Someone, Gerard realized with a shock, whom he would now recognize at once were he to pass her in the street tomorrow. But nobody else on a crowded street would find her other than an attractive, rather tall, woman. With bright blue eyes. Anthropology made personal and immediate.

Two, three, four minutes passed. Normally he was supremely stoic and unflappable, but just now Gerard's eyes were tearing badly - he had to squeegee them with his fingers to clear his vision.

Finally he was able to breathe deeply again. He grinned at himself internally: intermittently going short on oxygen seemed to be the order of the day! He swept the room with his light. Nothing on the walls save the Portrait, nestled inside its perfect little room, totally protected. Utterly timeless. And in this extended, exquisite moment, from now until whenever he would tell the world, She was all his!

And there was so much more to see, to understand.

Propped in one corner was a long multiply-forked stick. At its base was a neat stack of a half dozen large clamshells, each with a soot-mark at the hinge. Oil- or grease-fueled lamps, he supposed, their wicks and fuel long gone, the soot-marks laid down by the wicks. The smaller forks in the stick could have readily held two or three or four shells - a multi-light floor lamp! In another corner, a small dark object on the floor, with other smaller items beside it, neatly piled. Forty thousand year old personal property - of the Artist? Who else!? Some loose twigs with ends charred, which he would have to call 'brushes'. A separate, thong-bound bundle of twigs of various species and diameters, all charred at one end. Two fist-sized balls of moss, partly compacted, one filled with charcoal paste, the other with powdered red ocher. Probably 40,000-year-old artist's smudging sponges - and now far too fragile to touch. Several thumb-sized bits of charcoal of different textures, perhaps made from different species, all with worn-smooth ends. He photographed the materials from many angles.

Amongst the loose brushes lay a carefully-shaped stick 30 centimetres long and three centimetres wide, whittled flat. It ended in what looked like a capital letter E, also three centimetres wide, with the very tip of each of its three arms finely shredded: together the three made a triple-brush-like affair. He picked it up gingerly: the entire "E" was caked with ocher. One penny dropped: this was Her signature brush for the small works, where using fingertips would have obscured too much of the picture. He'd seen the mini-SSS several dozen times only minutes ago! And now again, on Her forehead. He shivered violently at the idea of actually holding something She had not only touched, but owned, undoubtedly had made for herself, and used. Used right HERE! Reverently he returned it to its place. If he didn't stop finding such impossible stuff, his brain was going to short-circuit.

It didn't stop, and Gerard's brain didn't explode.

Not quite - next came a flat object which, incredulous, he identified almost instantaneously, now that he had accepted the personhood of the Artist. It was quite obviously a folder, well-used. He knelt, studied it carefully without touching. Made of bark, darkish off-white. Surely bark from the birches that even today covered the banks of the river and all its tributaries.

Why had she left all these materials here, when the rest of the gallery had been swept clean? Was she perhaps not finished with her portrait? If so, what might she have intended to do? Start another? Unknowable. Too bad.

He studied the folder more closely. It didn't look fragile, and wasn't attached to anything. It could be safely lifted. He photographed it in place first, then, carefully, picked it up, the act of an untrained anthropological idiot, never allowable, and excusable only *in extremis*. Like now.

It was well-used, too - and just like his own school folders, the maximum of finger-dirt was midway down the spine, where one's hand settled in carrying it about. A perfect, small artist's folder made of a goodly sheet of nicely-flattened bark, held closed with a feather quill. It could have come straight from any modern office-supply store, except for the materials. A line from Shakespeare floated past: "There are more things in heaven and Earth, Horatio, than are dreamt of in your philosophy!" Indeed, Mr. Shakespeare had gotten THAT right! This closet-sized underground room contained several careers'-worth of questions and work.

He wiggled the quill: it came out easily. Gingerly, utterly over-taken by the need to know, he once more set his training aside, pried the folder open just wide enough to let the contents slide out into his hand. Five pieces of flattened bark, each about 20x20 centimetres. Neatly squared, almost identical in size. "Standard paper!?" Gerard was again staggered. Sometimes it was the smallest details that con-veyed the most information. This woman had drawn on standard-ized material forty thousand years ago!

 Good god, the speculations that concept could open up!

He wondered if she'd cut the paper herself. If not, then there had quite likely been a trade in paper 40k years ago! What traces of such a trade might have survived 40,000 years? None, most likely. Just as with 99 percent or more of cultural artifacts (excepting bone and flint), in general the probability of any item surviving closely approached zero. Especially bio-reactive materials like this. Any survival of such materials was to be treasured. "How the blazes are we supposed to find out what happened back then?" - he asked him-self for the Nth time.

He turned one sheet over: the back was clearly just the inside of the bark, far too rough and dark for drawing - but the paper-cutter had solved a manufacturing problem. A series of fine, shallow slashes across the grain of the inner bark had severed the fibers that would have made the sheet curl up, go back into its original cylin-drical shape. A simple but probably not obvious solution.

He was impressed - again. This woman, his Artist, had been a professional, there was nothing at all amateurish or beginner here. Nothing. Pigments, brushes, charcoal sticks. She probably went out and cut her own bark-paper. And undoubtedly She did for herself everything else connected with the enterprise. He came back to two details which for reasons unclear had really gotten to him - She'd even had PAPER, for god's own sake - and art in a folder! From forty thousand years ago. Inferences? The folder implied carrying art about, transport, preservation, probably display to other people.

Gerard consciously reined himself in. So many un-investigable implications! Certainly it was trivially easy to over-read one's data, see far more in it than was truly warranted - but one should beware of the inverse, namely reading too little. "Be generous in the face of so much unknown..." he told himself. "Give credit rather than deny-ing it" seemed the best approach - humans are quick, inventive crea-tures. Have been for a long, long time. If you found and were certain of Fact X, then you were entitled to add supporting speculative sug-gestions out at least one, perhaps several inferential steps. A diffi-cult and delicate balance between interpreting real data, and specu-lation.

Two of the five sheets held portraits of the same size and style as the extensive gallery just outside - the topmost two were the same two images as the gallery pair closest to this portrait room. He guessed that the bark pictures were preliminary studies that the Art-ist had brought along, then copied into the gallery. In fact, he real-ized, these identically-sized, identically-shaped pieces of bark-paper were also the same size and shape as the portraits in the gallery. Perhaps the artist had initially marked out on the wall a square the same size as these sketches - it might make copying them easier. Then, he could imagine, his Artist might have liked the effect of the black outlines and chosen to emphasize it. Accurately lining up se-quential portraits seemed intuitively a good thing to do, whereas the concept of framing was not at all intuitive - at least to Gerard the non-artist.

The other three were also charcoal pictures - simple, quick sketches, just lines and a tiny bit of smudging for shading. All three were rough, one full-face view, one slightly left, one slightly right.

All were clearly, absolutely, of the Blue-Eyed woman on the wall, the Artist herself. She had found a mirror surface somewhere, done these sketches to prepare for the self-portrait in this chamber. These were undoubtedly tests and memory aids. She had wanted to get this RIGHT. And why not!? - after all, she'd been painting for the ages and seemed to know it.

24 - COMMUNICATION

Gerard returned his attention to the portrait.

"Art is pure message!", he thought, with his eyes firmly locked with Hers.

Messages.

Across huge amounts of time, despite evolutionary changes, intentional communication was perfectly possible, at least in one direction. There was even a subtext, perhaps invented wholly in Gerard's whirling brain but defensible nonetheless. Across the gap She spoke - Gerard could hear Her plainly:

*"Yes, now you know. It was I who did all those animals that so fascinated you outside, over which you exclaimed. And that was before you found out what I could really do! Those head-shot portraits of my people, outside in the gallery? Those I did for others to see, to appease their needs and tastes. And for practice. But I am so much more than those pictures, so much better than those pictures can ever tell. For their own purposes, to meet their own needs, other people required and received my pictures of prey animals and my hunting scenes - of course I did such work. But so what? You, whoever sees this in the future, you should not concern yourself about those works. What you have right HERE is so much more important! You **must** understand me. I am eons beyond those herds of horses and fighting rhinos, beyond stick-men with huge penises, beyond faceless, obesely-droopy, impersonal Venuses. See, here, on this wall, what I can truly do, see what WE can do, my people. Your people. OUR people! I know you are out there somewhere! Let us talk to one another across this silliness called time."*

Totally incongruously, Gerard giggled. He was holding five preliminary sketches made by this woman forty thousand years ago, an artist determined to let the world know just how good She really had been. Gerard self-corrected once more - it should not be "had been" - rather, "How good She IS!" Because any artist whose work is still being viewed is, in a very real sense, still alive at that moment. He would bet (just for fun) that if one were to try to set an open-market cash value on these five bits of bark, the number would far outstrip that of any five known renaissance grand masters' canvases combined.

Gerard faced the Portrait again. Perhaps he was thinking too much? Or not enough! With more unaccustomed tears in his eyes, adrenalin pumping, completely breathless, he muttered "My god, how I wish I knew your name!"

Then he did something utterly out of character both scientifically and personally. He, Gerard, the self-acknowledged ultimate Mister "self-control", Mister "staid and unemotional", reached out and touched the charcoal image, the outermost edge of a braid. One fingertip only, the tiniest contact. He withdrew the finger, studied carefully the skin that had touched the image - no charcoal. He leaned in to study where his fingertip had alighted, found no effect, no desecration by smudging or smearing. He stretched upwards on tiptoe, wiped his sleeve across his forehead, nose and mouth. With both hands carefully planted on the unpainted wall he leaned in and let his lips touch Hers - the tiniest of butterfly kisses, a few milliseconds, just enough so that the touch registered as real, not imaginary.

Then, embarrassed even in this underground solitude, he pulled back, calmed himself emotionally, and resumed photographing. Many dozens of pictures -hundreds- because in the near future the inevitable curators and security people would in the name of preservation disallow most photography. But right now he would document the portrait, document Her, thoroughly. And Her work. For the whole world.

25 – RELATIVES!

For all the image's emotional impact, the direct human-to-human connection between them, between Gerard and Her, between the ancient human Artist and the "modern" man, hadn't yet dawned on him. But it soon would- and it would again render him briefly wobbly-kneed. He knew more than basic genetics, knew that the recessive blue-eye gene had arisen exactly once in humans, as a single-point mutation in ONE individual, then slowly spread through the species. That meant that every single blue-eyed person on planet Earth could trace his or her ancestry back to that one UR-person, to the UR-mutation in that gene. The mutation had happened between 3000 and 5000 generations back. It probably had some as-yet-undiscovered survival value - at any rate it had become fixed in several high-northern populations.

The single-pointedness of the mutation meant that he, Gerard of the bright-blue eyes, and his Artist were absolutely, positively, directly related. Related genetically, in some convoluted but unbroken line. They MUST have had a common ancestor somewhere, sometime. Family. His 3245th-great grandmother, perhaps? More likely something much more tangential, say 42nd-cousin twelfth removed? Silly thinking? Maybe. No, probably! But it made him feel less stupid about wanting so badly to say things out loud to the Portrait, to his shirt-tail relative the Artist - and about his tears. And about the kiss - his secret for life.

It truly is unfortunate that what we can detect and understand of our history is so intensely and randomly fragmented. He didn't know, and unfortunately no-one would ever find out, that the point mutation was the result of an over-long stay by Gerard's and the Artist's forebears, hundreds of generations earlier, atop a pitch-blende outcrop nearly a thousand kilometres away, in modern Czechoslovakia. The same outcrop from which a later-generation woman with a deeply embedded curiosity about the world would extract an interesting new substance... a substance that was the direct proximal cause of that point mutation, and which would also eventually kill her.

It had taken over one hundred generations post-mutation before the world's first blue-eyed human baby arrived.

26 - VEEJR'S CHILDHOOD

Needless to say, Veejr, by virtue of being the first-ever blue-eyed member of the Tribe, stood out amongst the few Tribal kids her age. Or any age. At three, however, she was fully integrated into the child-pack, and also more than fully accepted by all the adults - and nothing bad had happened as a result of her presence. The nay-sayers of her first appearance had all been mollified or won over - she was an extremely personable tyke. In fact, the adults took occasional pride in showing her off to visitors, always claiming that her eyes brought the Tribe good luck. And she was no longer unique - two of the sneaky recessive blue genes now available in the Tribal gene pool managed to find themselves together in a fertilized egg, and one memorable day nine months thereafter the Tribe was astounded when two perfectly ordinary dark-eyed parents produced the second blue-eyed baby. Blue-Eye#2. The man of that couple would figure prominently in Veejr's future. The new pair of blue eyes occasioned much speculation (Mendel not being available) and amazement - but with familiarity breeding acceptance, this time no suggestions of infanticide arose. Veejr was briefly fascinated when told that the new baby had eyes just like her own - which she had never really seen, having no mirror. At any rate, Veejr's specialness took a significant hit that reduced how thoroughly she was spoiled.

Veejr's 'family' contained only Mama, Brother, and herself. For various reasons Mama Chys had not permanently paired with another man to replace her first, hence the family had no adult male. To begin with, she was fiercely independent, and enjoyed it. Second, she had demonstrated her power and prowess by killing her gigantic rapist single-handedly. Hence in terms of combat success, she out-ranked all males in the Tribe except possibly the Chief, who had long ago killed several enemy men. That rank, in a nominally "man's" field of work, made it nearly impossible for her to find an appropriate male with whom to pair. The only real possibility might have been the current Chief, but that wouldn't work - he already had two "wives" and a goodly family. Mama had also produced the Tribe's first-ever blue-eyed baby, and was therefore regarded by all - especially by the men - with superstitious reverence bordering on awe. The concept of gods and goddesses was in its very early gestation, but Chys in many ways fit it for the moment, and this scared men away. But not entirely - she was by most standards quite an attractive woman, and plenty of men were eager to disappear into the shrubbery with her late in the evening, to partake of her special powers - but the disquieting idea of full-time exposure to her, of permanent pairing with such strength, certainly helped keep her single. Chys did not complain, realizing that in many ways she had the best of all possible worlds. The extra freedom of "no resident father" further enabled Veejr's natural tendency towards independence, to exploring on her own, and in general to being comfortable with being as different from other kids as her interests required.

Veejr was only four when Chys began to teach her the basics of knapping. That knowledge had been extremely useful and important in her own life, and she was determined that, gender be damned, her daughter was eventually going to know everything her Mama knew. How to make a spear-point, how to choose a stick for the haft, how to properly fasten the point to it. How to get the proper balance in the completed spear. And then how to use it. How to track and kill large animals. Uncle, her own teacher, was still alive and active and willing to undertake teaching the kid - after all, his first attempt at teaching a woman had produced some good results! Mama Chys had been the first woman in Tribal memory to learn these things, formerly the exclusive province of men. When it came to actual use of the spear, Veejr was never able to match Mama's skill at hitting small targets such as running rabbits, but by age seven she was nonetheless good - better than many men, in fact. But that would not be the direction life would take her.

27 - ARTISTIC STARTUP

By age five, Veejr either stuck like a leech to Mama - not fearfully, but to see what the big folks were up to - or went off entirely on her own. One warm day, she'd gone with Chys and a gaggle of women down to the riverbank to collect shellfish. That required wading in adult-thigh-deep cold water, feeling around on the bottom with your feet for clams. Neither the women nor Veejr could swim, and in clamming-depth water, Veejr couldn't stand on the bottom and still breathe, so she spent the time alone on-shore, amusing herself. The clamming grounds were mostly sandy, but at their edges, just millimetres above the water level, there were often flat, shiny-damp deposits of clay - many square metres of paper-smooth putty-like surface, with a few random footprints at the edges only - everyone except Veejr preferred to walk on easy-to-remove sand rather than across a sheet of glue-like clay.

For her own reasons Veejr liked and greatly preferred the clay. She had taught herself to draw - at least, to make marks - nothing representational. Unlike in sand, she could draw a sharp, precise line in the clay with a fingertip and its nail, and the line would stay put until and unless she erased it. Creator and Destroyer both, she was! Powerful doings. Magically the lines would disappear completely with application of a little water and rubbing with her palm. The world's original Etch-a-Sketch. It quickly became endlessly amusing to draw patterns, do finger-painting... tic-tac-toe diagrams were nifty, as were crosses. Long rows of slashes and linked loops appeared and vanished at her command. It was fun. And it also made Mama happy for it kept Veejr out of trouble and in a known location.

The clay was unusually stiff one day, and her drawing-finger soon got sore. Veejr picked up a willow twig and tried making lines with it. That didn't work well - the twig was far too flexible. She puzzled over the problem for a few moments, then trotted to where she had set down her little leather shoulder-bag. In it, she had her very own small knife/scraper/all-purpose edge of obsidian, carefully wrapped in leather. A small roll of leather binding-cord. Some bits of dried meat and cooked tuber: the group would eat a few clams raw at lunchtime, but she liked other foods better.

She knew how to use the knife - and she'd made it herself. No other kids her age had knives of their own. This blade was a diminutive version, a "travel" tool, an early Swiss Army Knife. It sported a razor-sharp double-edged serrated blade capable -in skilled hands- of skinning a whole deer without losing any of its sharpness. Better performance than its far-distant stainless steel cousins would yield. Mama had shown her how to hold it and cut (not chop) with it, and then let her practice on small game and bits of finished leather. Veejr had of course cut herself several times while learning - just enough to make her very wary and careful. Now, kneeling alone at the edge of the clay, she erased everything, then took the butt-end of the willow twig, the thick end, and snapped it off at a length about twice her hand's breadth. She skinned off the bark, wiped the slippery naked stick with dry sand, and then studiously sharpened the narrow end to a chisel shape. She jabbed the twig into the solid sand beside her sheet of clay - at this short length, the stick was quite stiff, all that annoying initial flexibility was gone. Small child the toolmaker.

Veejr leaned over the clay sheet, held the twig as one would a fencing foil, and made marks - but her initial grip was obviously wrong for what she wanted to do, all she could manage was to poke holes. Not much fun. In a second, she changed to what would some-day be called a "writing" grip, the tips of thumb + index + middle fingers only, a uniquely-human grip familiar even to a five-year-old forty thousand years ago - familiar from using small tools at home for domestic tasks.

She laughed, quite pleased with herself... now it was EASY to make marks. And because the tip was asymmetrical - practically a calligraphy pen - she could vary the line widths as she went. The lines were MUCH finer and more regular than those made by her finger. Prettier by far. She was especially taken by how the slash in the clay changed in width and angle as she guided the twig -call it a stylus- around curves. She made a row of figures very like integral signs. Then X's strung together. Linked loops were especially pretty. Rows of circles, lines of parallel slashes. Circles were difficult - very hard to make them truly round, and it was very, very difficult to make two that were reasonably alike.

28 - SIGNATURE

Then a large squiggle, an ess. A row of them, nestled together. One by itself, then a pair, then a trio. Four, she realized, was too many - the eye somehow liked one and two and three of them to-gether, but balked at four. Four always became two twos. Interest-

92

ing. She got the same feeling about fours of any shape she tried. Initial experiments in the optical-processing characteristics of the human brain. The trio of squiggles, she decided, was both the prettiest and the easiest. She did triplets both left and right handed, laughed at her left hand's uncontrollability - just like in throwing. Weird. Left was a mere helper, right was the worker, in charge. The leader. There was no reason she could think of why such a difference should exist, but Mama and Uncle had the same problem.

The women finished their clamming - they had plenty for dinner. They opened a few using fist-sized cobbles as hammers, eagerly ate the sweet, cool meat raw. Veejr ate one clam, then finished her private rations. Clams were slimy unless cooked in the fire. Raw, she thought them pure ick, and said so loudly. Two of the women shook their heads meaningfully at one another - what could one expect, anyhow, from a kid with blue eyes?

After lunch, Veejr joined the women for a bath. Baths were important - any dirtiness of body was discouraged from earliest childhood. With water and plenty of soap-root always at hand, cleanliness was both easy and fun, and baths had long ago become important unisex community-and-bonding affairs, often taken several times per week in good weather, less often but not entirely neglected during winter. Veejr and Chys washed and rinsed and then braided one another's long black hair. Veejr loved the closeness and ritual.

Before leaving the riverbank, Veejr proudly showed her day's final edition to Chys, who patted her gently on the head and made the usual preoccupied-parent noises of vague approval and praise. The praise wasn't very important to Veejr - she'd had fun. The gaggle trooped home.

Veejr was hooked. From that day forward, she made at least twice-weekly pilgrimages to her riverbank, to the horizontal clay blackboard, for practice. Over time, she manufactured a wide assortment of marking tools for different effects. Making marks for the sake of making marks. It was almost like the "sounds-for-sounds'-sake" produced by the flutes some of the men played, flutes made of the long, delicate, hollow bones of a big bird's wing. Mother Chys could play the flute well and many times tried to teach Veejr, but the girl simply wasn't interested in making music - listening to it around the fire was fine, but making it herself? Nonsense!

It was the difficulty of making a perfect circle freehand that led her to experiment with twigs and cord. A stout twig stuck vertically in the mud provided an axis. 'Play-with-a-goal' led to putting a loop of cord over the vertical, and mere seconds later her stylus-twig, caught in the loop, stretched the loop into a line. By keeping the radius-cord taut and moving the stylus, she could make perfectly smooth arcs in the clay. A compass. Her very first attempt yielded a perfect circle. She was amazed and quite pleased with herself. She decided to keep this magical device as her personal secret – after all, the adults didn't seem to care about her markings in general, so phooey on them. Weeks later, continuing to play, she discovered the oval – a far more complex proposition than a mere circle, the oval required two widely-separated verticals and a loose loop enclosing both. But once she'd figured it out, the mechanics were simple. Again, she decided to keep this discovery to herself.

She was peeved whenever the river failed to cooperate, either flooding or drying her blackboards. On cold or rainy days she would take from the fire partly-burnt twigs, even finger-sized chunk of charcoal, and make her markings on local walls and boulders and slabs. She didn't really like the rocks' surfaces: they were too rough, it was hard to make consistent marks, and they ate her brushes and charcoal at a furious rate. The smooth clay was infinitely better, but of course it couldn't take charcoal. There was a frustrating mismatch between reality and her needs, namely something that would take charcoal the way clay took marks from her twig styli. That would be ideal. But there seemed to be no 'ideal' medium for charcoal.

29 - LACK OF MIRRORS

Veejr was intelligent, active and curious about everything in her personal world. Far in the future, she would have made a fine scientist. During one long afternoon at the riverbank, making her usual marks on the clay, she got tired of that exercise, and began to re-explore the riverbank. The river had gone down a few centimetres the night before, which had both renewed her blackboards, and left behind several metre-wide puddles of clear water. Each puddle was only a centimetre or two deep and had a smooth clay bottom.

It was a hot afternoon and windless. In her boredom, she tossed a few small pebbles into the stream, then into one of the puddles. Each made an oddly satisfying splash. The river flowed smoothly: the still air made no ripples on either the puddles or the river itself. She picked up a fist-sized rock and chunked it into the river, enjoying the big splash, and watching the circle of ripples expand, move, reach the shore and die there.

She turned back to the puddle, tossed in a rock the size of her thumb. The puddle's ripples were not at all the same as the river's. They didn't get nearly as tall, and they moved differently: they died out much faster. She was intrigued - the same process - rock plus water - yielded similar but not identical results in stream and puddle. After a stone landed in the river, she could watch the ripples for several seconds. But in the puddle they disappeared almost instantly, quickly leaving a completely renewed, perfectly flat surface on the water.

Curious, she knelt beside the puddle, peered into it. And gasped: the light plus a perfectly still surface over a smooth clay bottom made a fine mirror. She knew without thinking that the image in the water was of HER. Ten seconds of gazing spellbound, then she touched her nose with a finger, watched her reflection do the same thing. She moved slightly and the image disappeared: anxiously she moved about until she caught it again. The sun had to be just right for this to work. She smiled: her image returned the favor. Ten more seconds mugging herself, and she splashed the puddle with her hand - the ripples distorted and fragmented her image, but in two or three seconds all was well again.

The actual breaking-up of the image was scary - she thought she should feel something, probably pain, since this fragmentation was happening to HER, and was mystified that she didn't. The image was of herself, but wasn't actually HER, or even part of herself - if it were, surely she would feel something when it broke up. Wouldn't she? A very curious thing, that reflection.

Then she leaned in close and studied her face. For the first time, she knew what she looked like. And she could study her eyes, those blue oddities that everyone seemed to love, hate, or at least comment on. She was used to her eyes getting attention, but had not really understood why they did. Even when Chys showed her some springtime flowers that were, she insisted, very nearly the same color as her eyes, Veejr hadn't really understood.

Now, an epiphany - she got it. And she quite frankly thought her eyes were a great improvement over the blah uniform black owned by all other members of the Tribe. All except that one other kid. Blue-Eye #2 just seemed like an alien, hence nothing about #2 necessarily applied to herself. At any rate, she had now -finally!- seen her own blue-eyes, which made her feel quite special.

Driven by a burst of inspiration, she dug up a fingerful of soft clay and painted lightning strikes on her cheeks. It was weird - in her mirror, the image moved backwards! It took some time to get used to that, and the phenomenon certainly got in the way of doing a good job of makeup. Once she was satisfied with the markings, she immediately trotted uphill to the settlement, where she tried to explain her new knowledge to Mother. Of course Chys knew about reflections - everyone had seen reflections in still water. What was Veejr so excited about? Come have dinner, girl!

Finding mirrors and studying herself in them became a significant, although decidedly secondary, passion - second to drawing.

Her drawing control improved steadily, as she both grew physically and accumulated practice. Patterns got more complex, more fun to produce - especially she enjoyed getting a startled rise out of an adult. Eventually she was spending most of her free time drawing. Fortunately, Chys was indulgent: between the women and Brother, collecting enough food was no problem, and lack of a father/disciplinarian also helped Veejr get drawing time.

There **was** a problem, however, in her charcoal practice - logistics. She quickly ran out of surface to work on. There was only so much drawable stone surface within her ambit. She even went so far as to carry a skinfull of clay back up to the settlement, where she smeared it on rocks stucco-style, seeking to make a drawing surface.

But it wouldn't stick well and dried out fast, at which point it always shattered and fell off in chunks. Frustrating. Likewise, the lack of good substrate for her favorite charcoal work drove her over and over again to her second choice, scratching on the clay-slates of the river. The underlying need for a better surface was driven by a rapidly developing desire to be more representational. But doing representational work on the river's clay surfaces was difficult indeed - it was almost impossible to control the stylus, any stylus, with the degree of precision she wanted. Doing her art on that ephemeral clay surface, inherently non-portable and always far from her subject matter, was both a pain in the tush, and an interesting process. Especially interesting was handling distant, out-of-sight subjects, working by memory rather than either pure imagination or direct viewing. She was slowly discovering something about how her own personal brain worked. Of course, she couldn't tell from the inside that hers worked differently from most others. And without knowing about, or at least suspecting, a difference, there was no reason to do any sort of comparison.

30 - JIG-SAW MASTER

Regional finals - next stop for today's winner would be the National. The two dozen contestants sat quietly at their well-separated individual card-tables, all eyes glued on the regional Honorable Grand Puzzle-Master. The HGPM himself unsealed and opened the big carton, extracted two dozen identical white boxes containing identical puzzles: each puzzle had been carefully disassembled at the factory, the pieces thoroughly mixed before being boxed. Acolytes delivered one to each contestant: nobody touched their box. Rules. There was nothing on each contestant's table save a large-screen digital timer and, now, a plain box stamped in large black type: "A-800".

Anton studied his personal box: an A-level puzzle for regional? Impressive. The "A" meant top-of-the-line for difficulty. The fees from the multitude of now-eliminated players probably didn't even cover the cost of today's two-dozen identical puzzles. Not just any old A, either - the 800 meant 800 small pieces, each would fit on a one-Euro coin. Jigsaw puzzles difficult enough for upper-level competition were expensive items, produced to special order only, in very small quantities, by only two companies in the world. Archival paperboard, lithographed, laser-cut without any repetitive cutting pattern whatever, all in extreme secrecy. "A" level also meant no straight-edge borders - the puzzle had been laid out and cut so the outermost rows, the frame, were missing. Solving an "A" was made considerably more difficult that way. Appropriate. For those wishing to keep their puzzle, the missing border pieces were included, sealed in a plain brown envelope.

Of the 24 players today, about six stood a real chance. Anton was one of them - after all, three years ago he had won the national title, and the A-1200 from that competition was framed and hanging in his study - an aerial view of the Allegheny Mountains in full riotous fall foliage. A $500 puzzle at retail, a real bitch to solve! He'd then gone to the World Cup, only to finish second, thirty seconds behind an unknown Aussie. Anton really, REALLY wanted another shot at World. Uncharacteristically, his palms were damp.

First to complete their puzzle would win. First prize was an all-expenses-paid trip to the National. "Ready?!" asked the HGPM. Twenty-four hands went up indicating readiness. Each acolyte made sure his four contestants were ready, all clocks at zero, then nodded to the Honorable.

"Go!"

The Honorable's switch started the master clock and the 24 individuals' timers. Aides checked all clocks, gave thumbs-ups to the Honorable. Clean start.

Anton opened his personal puzzle: the 1200 pieces had been randomized, but they were always packed the same way for a competition, with the pattern-face of all pieces upwards. One skill required in this level of competition was simply getting the pieces out of the box all still facing up, to save time - most contestants tore the corners of the box, slid the heap sideways from box to tabletop. Anton didn't move - he instantly recognized the complexities of the print - a moiré pattern for god's sake, a complex bird's-nest-cum-fishing-reel-snarl of black curves on white background, repetitive but minutely changing with each cycle. Interference patterns, the surface of the wind-blown ocean. This race was going to be won by shape-recognition, not pattern-matching. Goody!

He turned the box upside down to show only the back-sides of the pieces, then slipped the pile out. Pure shape, all pieces now a uniform gray. Spatially reversed, of course, but that was no problem for his brain, whose machinery got the new instructions, dropped color and pattern from the search-and-grouping criteria. Things were simpler now, but not at all easy. A hemi-semi-demi bitch, not the whole nine yards. Anton spread the pieces out: two minutes gone. He stopped and stared long at the board. He had a strangely-wired brain. He didn't have a photographic memory, not at all. What his brain did superbly was detect and classify and remember and manipulate patterns and shapes, either planar or 3-D, but 3-D jig-saws were vanishingly rare. The ability worked in lots of modalities, not just jigsaws. His brain could simultaneously handle shapes of any kind, by the thousands. The most fun were shapes he could mentally rotate, invert, reverse, move about, all at will - like today's jigsaw. And Anton was fast. Other vaguely similar brain wiring re-sulted in 7-second solutions to the Rubik's Cube.

So he stared as others began trying to fit bits together whilst looking at the seasick-inducing front faces. He knew that his initial inactivity freaked out some players, but that was just too bad for them. He sat stock-still for over ten minutes - until, in his mind, pieces began to move, rotate, slide. His fingers suddenly flew, bits came together into random-shaped larger patches. Each conglomera-tion was turned over before getting too big to handle.

Anton flipped and placed the last small aggregate. Done! He studied his puzzle with its dizzying op-art, patted and stroked it to be sure everything was flat and properly in place, then reached for his timer.

DING! First place! Anton pushed himself away from his table - no more hands allowed on the table after ringing off. His timer read 2h02m57s - exactly the current world record for the men's mar-athon. Appropriate! Twenty-three heads came up for a moment, re-turned to work. There were lesser but worthwhile prizes for second and third places, so nobody stopped. Even fourth was worth having, just in case of a higher-level disqualification.

Ten minutes passed, then twelve. Twenty. A resounding, convincing win!

Bing. Bing. Numbers two and three rang in. Finally the fourth bell, at which the Honorable announced "STOP". Numbers 5 through 24 sighed, pushed themselves away, did a huge collective stretch. Tradition - numbers one through four met, did a quick tour of their four puzzles. Any one of them could protest any of the four completed puzzles, but as usual there was no protest. Number four shrugged, congratulated Anton. Gold-plated four-inch bronze jigsaw pieces, engraved, went to the top three, and then the meeting quickly broke up.

Happy with the results, thinking mostly about the upcoming National, Anton jogged the mile and a half home. He was an advanced English Lit grad student, and university was in session, but he had promised to take the next few days off to do a bit of campus- and department-touring with his roommate/fiancé Joan, an anthropology post-doctoral researcher interested in human cultural evolution, especially the difficult-to-document time when _Homo neanderthalis_ was being rapidly replaced (some thought assimilated, she thought out-competed and perhaps even actively killed off) by _Homo sap_. She was going to make what she called an "artifact tour", looking at collections of human and other bones, stone tools, various bits and pieces with possible biological or cultural significance. Those tiny scattered fragments from which mankind tries to assemble a coherent history of our species. The tour was at her mentor's behest, intended to give her a broader overview of the local region, whence so much significant material seemed to be coming these days.

Too bad, Joan thought, that there wasn't just one single repository for all artifacts. Such a thing would make it so much easier to do the comparisons which everyone needed in order to advance the field. But anthros were stingier than art museums about making loans. Happy to show off their stuff to the world, so long as the world beat a path to the owner's door in person. But no shipping artifacts about! And rivalries? The general public thought rivalries in sports, or say the Israeli-Arab thing, were serious. Hah! Laypeople had no concept of the level of competition between rival academics, both institutional and individual. Especially in anything having to do with human origins or evolution. Even though there was no Nobel Prize in the field.

Joan's trip was partly to try laying groundwork for eventual inter-institutional cooperation where today there was little to none. Joan had invitations (from grad students and administrators, not faculty!) to visit two relatively nearby institutions both of which were doing research in the same remote rural valley - one, Universite de la Pays, aka "UP", had a fine anthro department many decades old. UP personnel had been excavating a major cave site in The Valley for some years, regularly producing lovely important material. The other institution, formally named "La Fondation pour Anthropologie" and generally nicknamed "La Fond" was private, funded only a few years ago by a retired airline industry tycoon - an up-front endowment of a third of a billion Euros from a highly knowledgeable and well-published "amateur", who like Joan was particularly curious about the transition to *H. sapiens* - the interface of Neanderthals and other varieties with modern humans.

La Fond's scientists, resident and visiting, were roundly envied - they had the best and most modern of everything, both personnel and instruments. However, despite some gentle browbeating from La Fond's benefactor, there had been as yet only nominal, really insignificant, cooperation between the institutions, although they were less than one hour's drive apart and working in the same valley. La Fond had recently laid out a new plan for an aggressive program of studies in a geographical area that butted up against UP's "territory" in the Rampart Valley. The very idea had, of course, incensed the UP folks. But the governmental ministry in charge thought it would be good for all to have teams of rivals at work, and issued the necessary permits to La Fond, over UP's strident protests, duly noted.

La Fond's efforts in "The Valley" were still getting spun up. So far, they had made only one serious strike, and that accidental - the skeleton of a huge man, *Homo sapiens* for sure, obviously killed by humans and buried in an odd location some twenty kilometres or so from UP's main site.

Joan and Anton planned two days at La Fond, and then the short trip to UP. Two more days there, and home again. It would be a nice change from working on his own dissertation, thought Anton. A much-needed sanity break. He could be interested in Joan's work if he tried, but it simply wasn't his bag so there was no depth to the interest. And he thought the various internecine rivalries, as described by Joan, were simply infantile - something to be expected in English Lit departments (or, maybe, amongst fifth graders?), not in the sciences! At any rate, he would try hard not to be bored: she insisted that he would undoubtedly find some aspects of her work fascinating, given his jigsaw abilities... after all, in physical anthro there was a lot of 3-D jigsaw-puzzle work - even some 4-D. Bones and pottery and other artifacts were almost never found intact, had to be reassembled, even when thoroughly smashed. Difficult, painstaking work. Three-D jigsaws with randomly missing pieces. He grunted, pretended to agree - sort of.

The basement of La Fond's lovely new building (a mere €128M, complete with initial major equipment that would have done a research hospital proud) was dominated by one huge room full of wheeled work-tables, and several smaller rooms for long-term specialized projects. Plus the unheard-of luxury of individual private offices for grad students! In one corner several of Joan's student acquaintances clustered around a large flat table draped in black cloth. They had laid out a skeleton - a more local item, not from The Valley. Good training material. The long-bones were quite intact, but the critical skull was represented by three silver-dollar sized pieces and two teacupfuls of smaller fragments, now strewn across the cloth where a skull belonged. The students were poking delicately, dispiritedly, through the fragments.

Joan knew most of these students from various meetings and symposia: it was their invitation to come visit that had precipitated the entire junket. Anton was introduced, then stood looking down at the skull-chips whilst Joan and friends gabbed. This was nothing but a semi-3-D jigsaw, he realized. "Interesting", he thought, contrary to his expectations. He let his mind slip into puzzle mode: the pieces became outlines, began to move. He grinned. Easy pickings, no sweat!

He tapped one of the worker-students on the shoulder and pointed, one at a time, to five fingernail-sized bits scattered randomly amongst the hundreds of fragments. "These five go together."

The student looked up at him, uncertain as to Anton's status, and said "I don't see it!" Then he handed Anton a set of forceps: "Show me! I'll take all the help I can get!" He grinned - it was a blatant dare.

Anton said "Sure. Happy to help" and laid the five in a small circle, moved them about and then rotated each. He then flipped one over, and suddenly they DID fit. Perfectly.

"Jesus!" said the visibly-impressed student, notifying his compadres, who clustered close to watch. "We've been working on this thing for a week and gotten nowhere. What else do you see?"

In ten minutes Anton had over half of the bits engaged with one or more other bits, and a couple of rebuilt silver-dollars matching edges with one another.

Bored, Anton quit then, despite the students' urgings to continue. He wandered, opening specimen cabinets and drawers, snooping, poking. In a corner he encountered a small glass case inside of which was a good-sized flint core, the prepared raw material for stone-age blade-making. It was a fine, carefully done exhibit, almost an exploded view... long flakes were held in place with plastic putty and fishing monofilament so that one could see how precisely the flakes matched both one another and the remaining core. There were also hundreds upon hundreds of small flakes, all fitted nicely together. Most of them had come from the sharpening process - usually pressure-flaking the edge using a deer antler- that turned a long thick flake into a spear point or an arrowhead, or an axe.

To himself, Anton muttered "More damn jigsaw puzzles! - but genuinely 3-D for a change. And guaranteed to have plenty of missing pieces just to make things more difficult. Cute!"

Aloud, he called out "Hey, guys ... what's with this exploded rock?" and was told by the most senior student "One of La Fond's first bunch of senior investigators once upon a time, in a land far, far away, found a heap of flakes buried near the mouth of a cave, then found that core in the pile. He realized he'd stumbled on a neolithic workshop, and he re-assembled the core to prove it. Took him a couple of years. The thing is famous, its picture is in all anthro and paleo texts. We get to stare at it if we're bored or discouraged. It's an anthropological icon. Three thousand and some bits, he put back together. Fucking monomaniac he was. And a goddamned first-class showoff. I just barely knew him. He's dead now."

Shortly thereafter, another student, Jorge, took pity on him during a coffee break, said "Hey, Anton, I'm sorry - I know this stuff can be a bit boring for the non-specialist. Come with me for a sec. I'll show you something supercool. Our newest big find, our first from the limestone cliffs area where we're scouting - just getting set up. It's a whole skeleton, an adult male, and complete - you very seldom ever find whole skeletons. We even found the hyoid bone!" He paused, got no reaction, explained: "That's a bone deep in the throat, part of the human vocal apparatus. It's tiny and not attached to any other bones, so it's almost never found. Important in the evolution of speech, probably, but we're not sure yet. Anyhow, in this case we got it."

Anton nodded that he understood, and Jorge went on. "He was buried on the uppermost level of a multi-level floodplain, pretty much in the middle of nowhere. Strange place for a grave. My guess is he was buried where he died - he's a big guy and hauling him back to wherever he came from for burial would have been one hell of a task."

Jorge pointed to a large topographic map on the wall: it showed perhaps sixty kilometres of the steep-walled river valley, with the towering cliff paralleling it, and a multi-level stepped floodplain. A red X marked the burial site. "We're going to publish on it early next year, but special for you, today only, you get an advance peek. Because you're Joan's guest." Jorge actually giggled: "We're going to steal a big march on UP with this one - they've been working in The Valley for quite a few years now and haven't found anything like

104

this - and BOY are they pissed! They think the whole damn Valley is their private preserve! WRONG!"

Some considerable distance away on the map, at the base of the cliff, was another X - colored blue this time. Jorge pointed to it: "This one is the main settlement site, the biggest that anyone has found so far: it's UP's cave site. It's magnificent - been totally dry forever which means things are preserved so well it's sometimes eerie. They even get some good organic stuff once in a while. Site's been human-occupied for the very long term, and it's one HUGE site. They even think they may have found a real graveyard! Bits of the site are located both in the caves and just outside them. For those lucky UP clowns, everything is nice and concentrated, and they've found some really interesting graves and artifacts." He laughed: "Now that you've been HERE, I'm sure when you get to UP on this tour of yours, they'll show off for you! They've got lots of great stuff. We're a little jealous, you know." Grinning widely he continued: "And THEY are a bit selfish! Fortunately, those adult emotions go both ways – everything in balance!"

31 - GOLIATH

Jorge paused, waved his hand towards one of the side-room doors. "This guy you'll see in here was just an oddball lucky discovery... we've not yet found anything else in his area, and ohboy have we scoured it. He died about twenty kilometres from UP's settlement. He's way, way bigger -meaning way the hell and gone taller-than anyone else we've seen from the area, or from anywhere else in Europe, for that matter. So he probably isn't a local yokel. We call him "Goliath". Altogether weird. My own guess is he was wandering through the UP Tribal area and got himself murdered."

Anton perked up- his forte was historical development of the crime novel as an independent genre - more specifically, the murder mystery. "Murdered?" he said.

Jorge grinned, opened the swinging door, and said "Draw your own conclusions from the evidence!"

In the small prep room, laid out on a table, again on black cloth, was a complete skeleton. Big. He was only a few centimetres short of matching the two-metre-stick next to his right side, as if to say loudly "Yes, I'm as big as I look!"

"Shit!" said Anton after a first glance - "This dude was lots taller than I am! I didn't think Neanderthals came this big!"

Jorge snorted: "He's not a fucking Neanderthal, Anton... look at the forehead! Pure *Homo SAP*, no brow ridges!"

Then "Behold, evidence of the crime. Look what killed him!" Jorge pointed to the obvious cause of death - the twenty-five centimetre long spear-point, still exquisitely sharp, fully five centimetres wide and two centimetres thick where it had snapped at the spear-shaft. It had entered from the front and sliced through the sternum, which remained impaled on one edge of the blade. The long, tapered point was stuck firmly in two adjacent upper-thoracic vertebra.

"Jeez!" said Anton, impressed, "Looks like an elephant spear or something!" He leaned over to study the point, cocked his head, changed his point of view. "Damn! The spear cut his spinal cord clean in two, didn't it!?"

His guide nodded, grinned, and said "Not only that, it had to have gone right through his heart, too. After puncturing the sternum. This guy was dead when he hit the ground. Then somebody buried him, probably hunting buddies, or his troop if he was on some sort of war-party. We're lucky he got buried on the uppermost flood-plain. It was a quick, sloppy burial. Family would have constructed a better grave, I'm sure. And NOT on a floodplain."

Anton studied the spear point closely for some seconds, shook his head. "Wow! Whooda thunkit! Wonder if it was murder, or some kind of combat? Self-defense?" He grinned at Jorge: "Of course, if it was self-defense, then there's no murder mystery because there's no murder! I'd rather keep the mystery going, myself."

Jorge just shrugged and said "Me too, but I guess we'll never know about that!" Then "Look at this." He pointed at a large white plaster-of-Paris object on a cart. "That's obviously the spear that killed Goliath" he said. "The blade with the bones stuck on it matches the snapped-off bit that's still lashed to the spear-shaft. We think his burial buddies cut the shaft into three pieces and bundled it up so it would fit in the grave with him." Jorge grinned: "I helped with that item - I found a little hole, figured out that something had been buried and rotted away and might have left a mold. We mapped it with ultra-sonics, then made that cast. Plaster of Paris is wonderful stuff... make it soupy-thin and it'll preserve even micro-scopic details." He tapped the casting: "Not my invention, though. They did exactly the same thing with human bodies in Pompeii."

Anton stared at the casting, impressed: "Great job, man! You guys even got the actual butt-end of the broken point! Supercool indeed! Look at the binding that holds the point to the shaft - looks like modern string." Then, "So somebody killed this dude, and the spear point broke. Then someone - my guess it was probably not the killer - decided to bury him and chopped up the spear so it would fit in the grave. Wonder if it was his own spear that killed him? It's certainly big enough to fit him! But man oh man, who the devil could take it away from him? And then kill him with his own weap-on!? He was an honest-to-god giant for his time - hell, he's huge even for today!"

It was late morning by that point: Joan and several students trooped into the prep area and clustered around the grave, jabbering about lunch.

Anton thought for a moment, then said "Maybe the poor bas-tard was ambushed! This is truly nifty. I do love a good mystery!"

Jorge agreed, "Yeah, me too - especially when it's forty thou-sand years old!" Then he paused, grinned, reached under the draped black cloth to a low shelf, extracted a cardboard box. From it he lift-ed a two-foot long plastic model of the human skeleton. "Here's my own contribution. I like model-making."

A properly-scaled spear was embedded in the skeleton's chest. "This is our guy, Goliath, before the spear point broke off. The spear's the right size, and the angle of the wound is correct. Nasty business! Model makes it easier for us non-jigsaw-whizzes to visu-alize."

Anton accepted the model, studied it for a second, muttered "Great job!", stared silently down at the actual bones for another minute, then said to Jorge "My academic specialty is murder mys-teries. Mind if I try analyzing the scene and the evidence? This could be a hoot. You people know all of this pretty well and you can keep me honest. It won't delay lunch much."

Jorge grinned: "That would be fun." Then to the new arrivals, "Hey, folks! Let's hold up lunch for five minutes. Anton is a specialist in murder mysteries and he's going to give us an instant analysis of the information -the evidence- about Goliath's death. Listen up - he wants to be corrected if anyone sees something screwy with his story."

Jorge grinned again, pointed at the model. "Here, Anton - my toy makes a good demo, a good teaching prop."

Anton launched. "Okay then. We are not going to discuss motive - that's immaterial for the moment. We want an explanation of exactly HOW - not WHY - Goliath wound up suddenly dead. We need to consider three things - forces, angles, and implements."

He held up the model for all to follow his analysis.

"Implements first - pretty obviously the spear. But there are peculiarities. Think of angles... the spear entered from the front, going UPWARDS. That's obvious from the damage to the sternum, and the fact that those two upper thoracic vertebrae are still, even today, stuck on the spear point. Like in this model. Now, it's hard to imagine getting that angle of entry on a standing man - you could get it if he was lying supine and you were straddling him, striking downwards, but that's about the only way. If you were standing and threw a spear at him, it would probably be on a downward arc when it hit. That's how spears work when they're thrown. From really close range you might get it into him horizontally. But a thrown spear isn't a boomerang, it won't suddenly decide to go UPWARDS. And that's the injury-path. Namely, upwards. Odd." He demonstrated, using the model: his point was clear.

"And on top of that, there are the required forces. Goliath was BIG, and it took a boatload of energy, kinetic energy, to drive a spear that size through a body his size, especially since it hit bone twice enroute. It would take a powerful man to do it. And there are more forces involved - from somewhere there came forces strong enough to snap the spear point... and that's one thick, heavy, strong chunk of glass! Plus it broke AFTER doing all the damage - it didn't snap while traversing the body, but rather after it had done so. That means some considerable force continued to act, at least momentarily, after the spear went through him. The most reasonable way of applying enough force to snap the point where it broke, namely precisely at the end of the shaft, would be a sideways force on the spear-shaft. Like if the spear was driven home and then he fell on it. At any rate, a pair of goodly forces was needed to penetrate the body, and then to snap the point."

He paused, looked at Jorge, asked "So far so good?" Jorge nodded.

Anton started again. "SO! We need a source of enough kinetic energy to drive that spear all the way through Goliath, and then after that to snap the point. My guess is that the energy came not from whoever wielded the spear, but rather from Goliath himself. I bet he was running full-tilt boogie and somehow his attacker, his opponent, got him to impale himself on that spear. Like Jorge, here, suggested, an ambush. And when he fell, the shaft caught on something, and that snapped the point. And there's one more angle to consider - if I am right and Goliath was running at speed, then he was upright when he was struck. To produce the injury-path in his torso, the spear must have come UP towards his chest - like, from ground level maybe?" He held up the model again. "I think the spear-wielder must have lain in wait for him, then nailed Mister Goliath using his own spear and momentum. There's your ambush! But how the killer got possession of Goliath's spear, now THERE is a question! Assuming that the killing-spear actually belonged to the victim. Which seems entirely reasonable. Unless he was killed by another Goliath with that killer's appropriately-sized spear."

Jorge looked inordinately pleased. "Sounds at least plausible! The details fit. That's a fine potential solution to the mystery. Of course, we still don't know if it was self-defense or murder. But a good solution nonetheless. I vote in favor of it. Too bad we'll never really know!"

The entire group murmured assent, several raised, again, the concept of lunch, and the flock exited the room together.

That evening, for Joan's benefit, Anton reviewed his day's experience. To him, the high point of the visit to La Fond was Goliath: so much so, in fact, that when Joan told him she had a full morning of meetings next day, after which they could head for UP, he decided to go back and spend the morning just studying him. He was deeply intrigued - a first for Anton and anthropology in any form. Joan was happy and, although she had not spent much time herself with Goliath, encouraged him to speculate, which he did, and which whomped up his enthusiasm even more.

Anton spent four hours with Goliath next day, in the company of Jorge, who was thoroughly enjoying showing off. Together, with Jorge jabbering away, they inspected everything they could see, every bone, every bit of the man, the three-piece spear, and the spear point. Except for a few minor scratches at the hips and knees - apparently made by blades - the skeleton showed no signs whatever of any other damage from weapons or accidents. No knitted fractures, no signs of any illness or other influences that affect bones. The teeth were not badly worn, almost free of caries, and remarkably free of plaque. Muscle insertions on the bones were very well developed - Goliath had been heavy in proportion to his height, undoubtedly over 100 kilos, and massively muscled. Truly an impressive individual.

They examined the spear point using flashlights, mirrors, and magnifying glasses. Anton's cell-phone camera was in steady operation. Then they did the same with the shaft. In the middle piece of the shaft there was a foot-long area that had been roughened, probably to give a better gripping surface. The roughening consisted of regularly-spaced grooves, with swirls and curves and lots of pattern-overlap. It was altogether impressive, the workmanship on this spear - particularly the roughening of the grip-area, and likewise the binding that held point to shaft.

Joan joined them with the students and two senior researchers, for an informal lunch at which Joan was given a strong although unofficial mandate to suggest cooperative works with UP - preferably minor to begin. "If you can get UP's attention!" grinned one of the senior scientists, knowingly. A challenge.

32 - BOUQUETS

The drive to UP took just about an hour, leaving them free to find dinner at their own pace. Sushi. They arose in easy time for their first full day on UP's campus.

"In here" the UP student guide said, leading them into a good-sized prep room. He gave them a thumbnail sketch of the work and progress.

"The site is huge and complex. In this lab, we're working on two graves that were side-by-side, with even a tiny overlap, so we can tell which was dug first. Everyone knows about the Lady. We found Spear-Lady's grave first, and it's the older of the two. It's so interesting we froze it in place, dug up the entire grave and brought her in here to do the detail work. Then we did the same with the second grave - mostly because we already had the equipment and expertise on-site and hey, two for the price of one, why not? The second grave is proving to be at least as interesting as Spear-Lady's, just without any single artifact quite so spectacular as Lady's big spear. We got lucky!"

In the workroom dedicated to the two transported graves, there was a deep cluster of students around Spear-Lady's materials, so the guide stepped Joan and Anton over to the second grave, muttering about gawkers getting in the way of progress.

Anton had visited lots of anthropological exhibits as "accompanying other", and seen excavations in the field, but this was unique. The second grave's skeleton had yet to be much exposed, but other work was proceeding around the remains. A middle-aged woman was seated on a stool next to the grave, peering awkwardly down into it with a binocular microscope on a swing-arm, studiously picking out tiny fragments of what looked like floor-sweepings. She placed each tiny bit carefully on a black wax tablet, in a growing row of similar tiny bits. As Anton and Joan arrived, she sighed, stretched and stood up. She introduced herself as "Helena, our team's certified plant paleontologist."

Anton peered into the grave, looking at the area Helena was picking over, and said "I don't see what you're doing. But then, I'm not an anthropologist, or a plant person. What gives?"

Helena explained. "This is a screwy grave in lots of ways. There's so MUCH to it, even though it looks simple at the start. The so-called "Spear-Lady" is over there..." she said, gesturing. "And of course she gets everyone's attention, but the smaller and more frag-ile stuff is equally interesting. Harder to deal with, though. Anyhow, when we were first opening this grave, which is the younger grave of the pair, one of the brighter anthro students noticed that there was this funny discontinuity in the fill dirt."

Helena pointed to where it was visible on a vertical cut surface of the excavation.

"She opened up a couple of centimetres of the interface and de-cided it was caused by a layer of plant material that was put into the grave when it had been partly filled. Then she stopped and got me. The plants of course decomposed and are long gone, but this fill-dirt is a nice mix of clay and sand, and we still have good impressions of the plant parts, if you dissect carefully. We've already identified several species. They were put into the grave in little bundles, bou-quets, each tied with a cord. The cords are also gone, but the im-pressions are clear. Fun work... just slow and a pain in the tush as far as care and delicacy go. We've never found identifiable plants in a grave before, although occasionally we've seen a few stem-impressions. Nothing at all like this - there were lots of bouquets. There are a couple of peculiarities I haven't figured out - first, there are no mixed-species bouquets. None. There are no species with more than one bouquet. And a few species are represented by bun-dles of lower stems and roots only - no foliage. It's like a collection, or a sampler! Genuinely strange."

Anton asked the obvious: "So, what does it all mean?"

Helena shrugged and laughed. "Maybe she was a florist? Kid-ding, there! Maybe she was a gardener and just liked flowers... gar-dening is probably a pretty routine form of early agricultural devel-opment, in any long-term settlement. At least, we shouldn't pass over the idea. These could also be simple grave offerings from fami-ly and friends. But they were NOT just tossed into the hole - they were laid down perfectly regularly, with the tops of plants alternat-ing left-to-right. And they are in a horizontal layer about five centimetres above the body itself - the grave was partly filled, the plants were placed, then the final fill was done. Pretty complex! I wonder if there was a formal ceremony of some kind involved? The species and the arrangement must mean something, but I haven't a clue yet what it would be. Right now I'm just building a list of species and maybe from developmental stages of flowers and leaves we can get time-of-year for the burial. Who knows?"

Joan thanked her: Helena went back to work, Anton left shaking his head - first shattered skulls, then exploded and re-assembled flint cores... and now the investigation had devolved into microscopic plant jigsaws! The crowd from Lady's grave was herded out to view other materials and projects, leaving guide, Anton and Joan in peace at Lady's grave, where they were immediately joined by a gaggle of interested, relatively senior students. Polite introductions all around: the students respected both seniority and priority, formed a penumbra of interested low-volume kibitzers.

Spear-Lady's skeleton had been given a careful but preliminary excavation and cleaning in-situ, before the entire grave-site had been excavated en-bloc. Just for her grave, a chunk of dirt and rocks one metre wide and deep, three metres long, had been frozen with copious liquid nitrogen, then cut free and moved bodily to this room. Lots of hard physical work. Anton wondered what the shipping had cost? Lots. What kind of vehicles would you need to do the retrieval and transport? Could you even buy insurance for such a load, for such a move?

Detailed excavations inside the grave were still ongoing and would likely take months stretching into years. Spear-Lady's grave wasn't yet empty, and had already yielded a wide variety of burial goods, many of which had been carefully removed and laid out on an adjacent table - several nice intact knives, a hatchet, a pile of pierced fish-vertebrae apparently used as beads, three spare spear-points, five variously-sized bone needles, a flint-knapping tool made from a deer antler. A curiously-bent rib from a large mammal, with pinholes above a notch - probably primitive goggles of some sort.

113

33 - CLAY PANCAKES

Some other goods remained in the grave - in particular, a good-ly heap of mostly-shattered flatish clay objects, pancake-like and palm-sized. They were made of apparently intentionally-fired clay, a wild anomaly in this region, which was entirely pre-pottery. The heap was a mess, a 20-liter-bucket full of well-mixed shards - an interlocking jumble glued together with a sandy-silt matrix, semi-consolidated but friable. The two or three unbroken pancakes that had been cleaned in-situ were covered with incised patterns, no two pancakes alike.

The guide had heard, via the student grapevine, about Anton's magic-like reconstructive abilities: he grinned at him, pointing to the pile of fragments, and said loudly, for the entire group to hear, "Say, Anton, you're already famous for your jigsaw ability. Here's a good puzzle for you, sometime when you have nothing else to do for a week. Nobody in our group has had the guts to try to recon-struct however many tablets there may be in that mess. Someday soon, we hope. But OHBOY, have the intact ones given people fits: nobody's ever found anything else this old, here or elsewhere, that looks so much like writing. I personally think the marks look like doodling, but there have been a couple of serious attempts to inter-pret them as writing, or perhaps proto-writing. If so, what a find! At any rate, there's a hell of a debate over them - it would help a lot if we could reconstruct all the tablets. Bigger sample! There has al-ready been a lot of analysis and scholarly discussion, just over the three or four intact tablets we've partially uncovered. Discussion complete with faculty temper-tantrums, and several refereed articles in good journals. Makes for good fun. And oh by the way, we found another heap just like this one, in the #2 grave immediately adjacent to Lady's. Just as much of a busted-up mess as this one - too bad! Interesting that both graves have these heaps of ceramic. Probably means there's some relationship between the two, don't yet know what it is, and with our usual anthropological luck, we'll probably never know."

The guide then gave a sweep of his arm, very impressario-like, and said "Voila! Anton, please meet our famous Spear-Lady!" He grinned: "The rest of us have been introduced already."

In the open, stabilized grave lay a smallish, fully disarticulated skeleton: the body had been laid down on its left side in a fetal position. Even as separated bones, it looked rather shrunken. Their guide said "She's female, almost certainly over eighty at the time of death. Bloody miracle, living that long back then... nobody's ever seen the like, believe me. Fifty was antique for her era. They must have thought she was a goddess by the time she died! Natural causes, best we can figure. That's a weasel way of saying we don't yet know what finally killed her. Disease, simple old-age, who can say?"

He pointed to the bones of Lady's hands and wrists, and to her knees: "Serious, far-advanced arthritis, and she had spinal and hip osteoporosis, too. I doubt she could walk when she died. Only three teeth left - she couldn't chew, so her people must have taken really good care of her in her old age. She was small even when she was a young adult - we think about 145 centimetres, that's five feet or a bit less. Forty-five or fifty kilos, tops."

Then "Look at her left ribs and arm."

They peered. Anton's jigsaw sense helped him to a 3-D reassembled view of the now planar skeleton. The injury was spectacular. Five ribs had been stove in together by the impact of some massive blunt object. Each rib had snapped in two places about fifteen centimetres apart, making a huge depressed fracture, leaving almost an imprint of the object. The bones had all healed nicely, but she for sure hadn't used the left lung much until the healing was well underway.

Joan said to the group at large, "Good grief! She really got walloped! She was one tough cookie. How long did she live afterwards? Everything seems to have healed completely so she didn't die from this... which is pretty much another miracle."

The guide agreed: "You're right about the miracle! She lived a long time after this injury - our best guess is this happened when she was maybe twenty-five or thirty, which was late middle-age for them. She died about fifty plus years later. UP's very own female Methuselah!"

Anton nodded, still studying the skeleton and playing anthropologist despite his lack of formal training: "The fact she survived at all says a lot about how physically strong they were, and also about the level of medical care they were able to provide. I don't think most modern folk would survive a hit like that. Something broke her left humerus too. Same impact, I bet."

The guide pointed to the healed arm-fracture: "Can't really tell if the two injuries were simultaneous, but it seems likely. Maybe she saw it coming, whatever hit her, and got her arm up. Who can say for sure? Maybe it was a falling rock - there are plenty of them anywhere near The Rampart. At any rate, the impact had to have displaced the broken ends of the humerus, but they are almost perfectly re-aligned, missed perfection by about two millimetres. Which means somebody reduced the fracture - pulled the bones back to where the broken ends met properly. I couldn't do that - could you? And they must have kept the bones immobilized for a while, because they healed so nicely - which suggests they put her in a sling and splint. Which in turn means they took care of her through her convalescence. And all of that implies extensive knowledge about human internal anatomy! More than I know, probably. No dummies, these people."

He paused, thought, then said "Your "falling rock" theory is reasonable, Anton. Probable, in fact. I don't know what else it could have been. A fall? An animal attack? Personally, I doubt it was caused by a fall - in bad falls, a person usually breaks limbs, not a half-order of ribs! And I also doubt it was an animal, that she got injured on a hunt. Even before the osteoporosis she was pretty small to be a hunter, and besides, we don't think women went hunting. No known cave art shows a woman hunting, and any hunter-figures that have genitalia always have cocks, not boobs."

Anton snorted gently, muttered about not concocting stories, avoiding empty theorizing, and about just using the actual evidence unadorned with speculation.

Joan pointed at the three perfectly-preserved spears in the actual grave with Lady: they seemed of quite an appropriate size for her, back when she was a young adult. One with a long sharp obsidian tip, another with a heavier and intentionally blunt tip. Two very different tools. And a third, with the blade gone, snapped off short at the shaft.

Sensing a teaching moment, Joan said to the whole group of students, who had not responded to Anton's comments: "Like Anton said - what's the actual evidence? If she was NOT a hunter, then why did they bury those three ordinary spears with her? They look like the perfect size for her to use. Even though one has a broken tip its shaft matches the intact spears. The oddball probably was broken before she died, and I'd almost be willing to bet on its having been broken while hunting... it just feels that way. Maybe it had sentimental value or something. Anyhow, folks, any spear is a great weapon, as La Fond's so-called Goliath found out! Suppose you're barefoot and wearing skins, and unarmed, and you encounter a potentially unfriendly person - do you really care at all whether it's a small woman with one of these spears, or a larger man with a bigger spear?"

Then, a bit peeved, she asked the group rhetorically "Where is it written in letters of brass that women couldn't and didn't hunt way back then? A spear, just like a gun, is a great leveler of physical differences! Every autumn, I go hunting with my male relatives, looking for deer and boar. Two thousand years from now, what anthropological evidence could we find of THAT female activity? Bullets through or stuck in a skeleton, brass cartridges on the ground, neither will tell you what gender fired the damn gun! Or invented it, either. There's no reason at all that women couldn't have hunted with a spear. Maybe they wouldn't hunt if some cultural taboo was involved, but it sure wouldn't be PHYSICS getting in the way!"

The student guide nodded, red-faced: "Sorry. Of course, you're right. And I get the point, really I do. Those do look like her hunting spears. Which does make you wonder why she was wearing this necklace." He led them to a small specimen case on another worktable. "It's a cave-bear mandible, with holes for a cord drilled through the hinges. For wearing as a necklace, we think. The two big teeth are cave-bear upper canines, also with thong-holes. Part of the necklace. New thong, though. My old bootlace."

He watched their reactions, then said quietly "On a bear, upper

117

and lower canines slide against one another. They make matching wear patterns like what you see on a bullet after being fired through a gun-barrel. I've looked at these teeth under a microscope. The loose upper canines have wear-marks matching those on the lower canines. Same animal. There's your next bit of 'hard evidence' - but what it's supposed to mean, I haven't a clue. We're wondering where the skull went. Not into her grave, for sure! It'd be larger than a half-squashed basketball. Hard to miss if it'd been buried with her."

Then, "Hey, maybe she got whomped by a cave bear! You don't suppose that just maybe she was hunting a bear!" He laughed at the apparent absurdity, debunked his own idea. "RIGHT! And lived through it! A forty-five kilo woman, fifty max, against say a ton of bear? There's a classic flyweight-versus-heavyweight mis-match for you!"

Anton looked at him sourly and said "I really do believe Mister Goliath over at La Fond might have something to say about spears as equalizers. The Colt revolver of the stone age!" Then, "Visibly matching wear patterns on the teeth - that's what I like, real evidence rather than opinion. Someone took the fierce teeth, the canines, and probably just threw away the rest of the skull. And there I go my-self, over-reaching the data! Maybe it was too big, or they already had a dozen, or it was used for some religious gobbledygook. Or perhaps they buried it, maybe to propitiate the bear gods? Who knows? I have to agree in doubting that she attacked a cave bear - talk about a dumb idea! But nothing's impossible. After all, the first two laws of the universe and anthropology must be 'Shit does hap-pen!' and 'Murphy was an optimist.'"

They turned to the grave-block: the student pointed to the long narrow 'auxiliary' trench that transected, lengthwise, the actual bathtub-sized hole of the grave itself. In the trench was an enormous spear, intact, fiber-twine lashings and traces of bone-dry, amber-like pine resin still holding the point in place. The huge spear was the reason for the size of the excavated grave-block. It was nearly three times as long as this woman had been tall, and obviously far too heavy for someone of her stature to ever wield effectively. Never-theless, when buried her right hand had probably been wrapped

118

around the shaft - at the very least, her arm had been draped over it, for all the hand-bones were found in a heap on one side of the shaft, the farther side from the skeleton. The ulna and radius lay together on the body-side of the shaft. And actually in the grave proper, beside her, were her three much smaller, slender spears, all of them much more reasonably sized. All four spears were intact only because the grave site had been well into the cave, weather-protected and perfectly dry for its entire existence - a real rarity.

"It's easy to see why we call her 'Spear-Lady' said the guide. "This big spear is the confoundedest thing! Not only is it the biggest spear any of us have ever seen - by a huge margin! - but NOBODY seems to have ever heard of a spear being buried with a woman before. So of course, she has to have four! Talk about a puzzle." Then, to Joan he said, "I agree with you. Being careful, as Anton says, to use just the evidence, my own bet now would be that the trio of small spears are her own. And that she really used them. Nothing about them or their placement says 'ceremonial burial object'. In fact, the one with the tip broken suggests USE, not 'ceremony'."

He took a deep breath, hurried on: "Which if true means we have to re-do our ideas on gender roles in neolithic hunting. We've never before had weaponry tied to gender, like we do here with Spear-Lady. The ASSUMPTION, going back ages in anthro, is that males did all the hunting. At least, the heavy-duty hunting. It does seem to be that way in most remaining hunter-gather societies, but today's ubiquity isn't necessarily yesterday's!"

Mollified, Joan said "I totally agree. At least you're one male who is trying to think intelligently about gender, which is both rare and much appreciated. Honestly, given the high-technology of the spear, there's nothing whatever to prevent women from hunting, except for cultural restraints. The mere fact that a few stick-figure 'hunters' in cave art are provided with penises instead of boobs proves nothing except that probably the artist was male. What we have here is an obsidian ceiling, and it's being imposed by people who are supposed to be objective modern scientists."

Anton looked puzzled: she poked him in the chest with an index finger, said "Obsidian. Volcanic glass. Glass ceiling for women.

Assuming that only men hunt. A 40,000 year old glass ceiling! Get it yet?"

He got it.

The guide grinned: "She had at least one characteristic of to-day's modern woman, you know."

Joan eyed him quizzically, said "Better you not go all sexist on me now! You've handled the gender business pretty well so far - pity to spoil your record. Careful! Tell us - just what might that characteristic be?" She felt secretly good at his mild discomfort.

The student went pink, shrugged: "Nothing sexist, just observa-tions. She loved her jewelry. Not just the big jawbone necklace, but around her left wrist she had a bracelet of shells. They're in the little cup in the case with the necklace. Still nice and shiny after all these years. Twenty-two of them."

Anton took one glance into the cup, did a double-take, sput-tered "How the hell far are we from the ocean? Five hundred kilo-metres in a straight line, twice that afoot? Doesn't anyone in this group have a background in general biology? Those are COW-RIES! Salt-water snails. No species of cowry lives in fresh water! They didn't CRAWL here on their own. Therefore, either Spear-Lady went to the ocean and got them, or someone brought them here!"

There was a prolonged silence whilst all digested the revela-tion.

Seeking to jump-start the conversation again, the student spoke up - "There's plenty of weirdness to go around. A great first-order question is, why the devil is the King-Kong spear here in Lady's grave? That sucker is simply HUGE. It can't be hers - at least, not for her to actually use, like in hunting or defense. Maybe it's just a ceremonial item? Maybe she was a tribal chief? Or medicine-woman? It could be ceremonial and intentionally made oversize to serve as an exaggerated power symbol or some such. But actually, we haven't a clue what's going on. Sure would be nice to know!"

Then "Even weirder is the way the grave was protected. Com-pletely unique. Hell, everything about Spear-Lady seems to be unique!" He pointed to a badly-fractured but cleanly re-assembled

120

slab of white calcite propped up on a bench on the far side of the grave. "Never seen anything like this, either. It covered the whole body, under almost fifty centimetres of dirt, like a headstone laid down flat. About 350 kilos of pure calcite, in one carefully shaped piece. Under it were those six big pebbles, holding it up so it didn't crush the body. When you think about building this grave, it was unique, and obviously well-planned – a complicated thing to do, requiring a lot of forethought and advance planning, and probably previous experience too. Lots of detailed communication, both operational and theoretical. The hole has multiple levels, cut to provide good footings for the big supporting pebbles. The pebbles are actually flint nodules, raw material for knife blades and arrowheads and spearheads - the stuff doesn't occur locally, so those six rocks must have been quite valuable, given they had to be brought here from a long way off. Maybe they are both structural and a grave offering, or supplies for the next world. The fact of those flints and the cowries being here says something pretty strong and important about either the local folks' ability to travel, or the state of transcontinental commerce in BCE 38,000. Or both. For sure there seems to be a heck of a lot more to early commerce than meets the eyeball. Anyhow, someone thought that Spear-Lady was worthy of valuable gifts in death. Plus - the grave-cover has that doo-hickey painted on it. I personally think it's the world's first gravestone. Others disagree but I like the idea - Ockham's Razor and all that."

He pointed to the mark: it was a simple triple-striped ess-shape, an "SSS" some 20 centimetres tall, done in red ocher. Below it was another mark, also in red ocher - a single five-pointed star. One big crack had transected both marks, but the reconstruction was good. "Looks like someone used three fingers to make the SSS mark, and only one to make the star. Those marks are certainly not accidental, but whether they're a blessing, a curse on her or on anyone disturbing the grave, her name, the tribal name, some god or goddess, a greeting, who can say? This grave is really intriguing, in so many ways at once!"

34 - THE OHMYGOD MOMENT

Anton stopped looking at the slab, shifted his attention to the point of the big spear. "Can I touch the tip?" he asked. Joan poked him in the ribs, but the guide nodded: "Sure, but don't grab or push or wiggle it. Touching is really a huge NO-NO, but you can do it. Just be delicate, even if the artifact itself isn't. Touch away!"

Anton did so. He studied carefully the exposed spear-point, under which had been laid a mirror so both sides could be seen. He briefly went oddly dreamy-eyed, almost as if in a trance. Joan watched him: she knew exactly what was happening. Anton had just dropped into his separate universe for pattern-recognition. A tiny chill went down her back. She waited, wondering what had triggered him this time.

Anton had made a momentous discovery and knew it, but as a mere guest he found himself worrying about how to diplomatically disclose it. Joan watched his face for a few more seconds, wondering why he was hesitating to speak – most unlike his normal mode. Finally she shrugged and said to him, "You look like the canary-eating cat. Come on, OUT WITH IT! What do you suddenly know that the rest of us don't? Give!"

Anton glanced at her for reconfirmation, then addressed the entire little group. "Joan told me that it's been a bit hard to get UP and La Fond to work well together…" He stopped: there were murmurs of agreement. He took a long deep breath: "Well, I've just noticed something that I think you will all find interesting. AND it's almost certain to force the two institutions to work together. Closely. No choice at all."

The students looked uniformly puzzled: Joan's spine-tingle was intense now. Anton was having entirely too much fun and was almost giggling - for certain, he'd noticed something significant, something nobody else had yet detected, but which would be readily visible to a total amateur – once it had been properly pointed out.

He took yet another deep breath and said "Let me recheck some basic facts. Each of these two institutions has a huge spear. They were found in separate burial sites twenty-five kilometres apart, right?"

Nods all around.

"Well, folks, BOTH of your King-Kong spear-points were struck from the SAME DAMNED CORE!"

They gawped in total silence.

"Just from the spears' sizes alone, I personally think both big spears were Goliath's property" continued Anton. "After all, if Lady didn't need and couldn't use ONE such spear, she certainly wouldn't be likely to have TWO of them! If they were hers to begin with, then what the hell was she doing out there in the middle of nowhere with a pair of such huge, awkward things? They just HAD to belong to Goliath. Nonetheless, our Lady of the Celestial Spears somehow wound up with one of them. Stolen? Won in combat? A gift? Some discard found in a prehistoric dumpster? Payment for favors received? I dunno. But HE, Mister Goliath, originally owned BOTH of the big spears, of that I'm certain. Ockham's razor - they fit HIM, but not HER. Then Mister Goliath wound up in a lonely grave with his own broken spear through his chest, and SHE was buried in her very old age with an intact twin of Goliath's death-spear. Interesting, to say the least."

Silence. Complete bewilderment and disbelief on the students' faces. But not on Joan's - she knew Anton didn't make mistakes in pattern analysis. Never. Bits and pieces either fit together, or didn't. And he was the whiz-kid.

Anton shrugged. "The broken point stuck in Goliath's chest over at La Fond, and this point right here, came off the same block. Side by side. Sister flakes. Adjacent flakes. Just like the flakes on the world-famous exploded core in La Fond's little glass case down in their basement." To a person, his audience held a gob-smacked silence. He laughed gently, asked "Want me to show you, prove it? Let's do a quick check - put my photos of Goliath's spear point on-screen, right beside my pictures of Lady's king-sized point. I'll prove it. The two points' long edges will match perfectly."

Continued silence. Shell-shocked disbelief all around. Joan's chill turned into a full-scale hair-on-end event. Anton really, truly, did NOT make errors in pattern recognition. "Oh my god!" she thought to herself.

Still nobody said anything.

Finally, feeling a bit peeved, Anton said firmly "Goddamn it, seeing how broken bits fit together is MY THING. I've been both national champion and runner up world-champion at jigsaw puzzles. Can anyone here put my phone pictures on thumb drives and into a couple of projectors? I've got a bunch of pix of each of the big points. Let's all see, together and right now, whether I'm crazy! I'll take all bets offered, and give you five to one odds! Any amount you name. C'mon! Step right up, try me out! Call my bluff."

Nobody bet, which pleased him. Three students volunteered, and shortly two projectors were online, the room was darkened, and all hands were watching intently as pictures from many angles flipped by on-screen, the two series side by side.

In five minutes there was no longer any doubt... none of the pictures paired up perfectly, but the cumulative imagery left no uncertainty. Struck from the same core, literally side by side.

Lights back on and projectors off, the group sat quietly for a minute, until Joan said "Wow and double wow! Putting these two finds together like this will make us all famous. Plus I believe we have here a real paradigm-breaker." Then, to the students, "SO? What are you-all going to do now?"

One student piped up, tentatively: "I guess we'd better go tell our mucky-mucks." Joan said nothing, waited. "Nope." said another student..."Bad idea. Joan's here because our faculty have longstanding problems working with other institutions. Any good, thorough analysis of all this will require close cooperation." She paused, thought for a second: "Especially NOW, what with the two spear-points and skeletons being at different institutions. Goliath and Spear-Lady are closely tied to one another and it's our job to figure it out. That'll take all of us."

Joan nodded, trying to look old and wise, but managing something between Alice's Cheshire and the famous canary-eating cat. She kept quiet. This was an absolute career-maker. She'd better not screw it up - after all, she was both the leader of the moment, and also odd man out because her own institution was a non-participant.

A third student said "That's right, it's up to us students to do something useful." She snickered in amusement – then, speaking mostly to Joan, "Might be fun if we could scoop the elders, don't you think?"

Anton shrugged, said "I'm an outsider here, but it seems to me you need to put these two big points physically side by side so there's no doubt whatever that they match. Then you can all have my kind of fun - solving a murder mystery mixed up with a jigsaw puzzle! Not to mention embarrassing the old fogies of both institutions."

Silence in the room. Anton grinned broadly: "Any of you got balls enough to go kidnap the point from La Fond, bring it back here and photograph the two side by side? Bet you could enlist a couple of their grad students - some of the folks we just met over there seemed to be independent and have some cojones! Even the ladies."

Howls of protest, mixed with several variations on "Great idea, but guaranteed to get us all kicked out of school forever!"

Joan turned to the group: "Have you guys made a mold of the point of Spear-Lady's big spear?"

Making such a thing was routine. Two students said, together, "Yeah, sure!"

Joan spoke again: "Then how about this as a plan. You two get cracking and mix some clear black resin, find that mold, and we'll make our own replica of Spear-Lady's point. Then we all get into a couple of cars and together take the replica of UP's point to visit La Fond's point. A reunion-date, after 40,000 years! Making the replica shouldn't take an hour - while you're doing that I'll call the students at La Fond and warn them we're coming and why. We'll have a secret "students-only" meeting in their basement and compare the points side by side. And THEN, after we're done and have a preliminary write-up, we'll let the oldsters know about it. Real scientific cloak-and-dagger stuff. Okay?"

It was okay.

Joan made her calls, got serious enthusiasm at the receiving end. The La Fond students would meet the little convoy upon arrival, in say two hours max, cell phones for coordination.

Excited and deep into high-intensity anticipation, Joan went

125

back to visit Spear-Lady as the replica was being made. While she was contemplating, her eyes were roving. Something was nagging at her - she understood her own mind, kept out of its way while her analytical demons wrestled. Then, after a couple of minutes, both her eyes and her demons stopped moving: she stared at the specimens, then grinned to herself. Anton had scooped them all – but now it was HER turn! Insider status would be hers in a moment - she was about to become a serious, full-fledged member of the 'Spear-Lady et al.' research team.

She stood up, stuck her head through the doorway and called out "Hey! Anyone who's not busy with the replica, trot your buns over here. I think I've found something else."

Anton and several students clustered with her at Lady's graveside.

Joan said "Um... hey, guys and gals, we're all completely fixated on the points. Look elsewhere. Does anyone else see what I see?"

Necks craned. Nobody said anything.

She turned to Anton: "I know you have a lot of other photos from Goliath. Like, pictures of that cut-up spear he was buried with. Could you get them up on your phone for me, please and thanks very much."

Anton did so, handed her the phone: she flipped through pictures until she found a clear full-frame shot of the three-part casting. She held it up, then passed the phone around so everyone could see. Bemused shrugs all around - a big, collective "So What!?" The phone came back to her. She zoomed in on one part: the casting was all white, no colors or gray tones whatever, which made it hard to get fine details with a cell-phone camera and flash, but one could see a patterned roughness encircling the middle piece of the big shaft for a couple of hands'-breadth. She passed the phone again. Still nothing, no reaction, no light-bulbs overhead.

"Look here, you students!" she exclaimed: "If you're going to work in this field you have to keep good mental images of important stuff. And unimportant stuff, too! Data tends to morph from unimportant to important pretty often. You can't afford to ignore or forget or overlook ANYTHING!"

She held up the phone with its enlarged photo, as she also pointed to the grave. The students looked at her, then followed her point to the spear-trench. Both Goliath's and Lady's big spears had a foot or more of the mid-shaft roughened with dozens of criss-crossing shallow grooves, done in an intricate interlacing pattern. She said quietly, "Back when whoever buried Spear-Lady, her hand was carefully laid squarely on the roughened part of her big spear - exactly where she would grip it. I personally do not believe in that sort of thing being merely a lucky coincidence." Then, quietly for emphasis, "My Dad and brother are both hunters and they like their guns. On a steel hand-tool that roughening is called "knurling" and it's done to give you a better grip. Like when your hands are sweaty or damp or cold. Gun enthusiasts pay a lot of money to have the same thing done on wooden gunstocks. On a firearm it's called checkering, and can be done in very fancy patterns. Medieval pikes and spears had it, too. Just exactly like this! It's hand-work and takes skill and time - lots of time. At today's prices, I'll bet this chopped-up spear has several hundred Euros' worth of checkering!"

Even with the suboptimal photography, all could see that the knurling was going to turn out to be identical on the spears - location, style, quantity, depth, pattern.

"That settles it for me. The big spears are both his for sure!" said one student - "Anton and Joan win this round, big time." Then, with a sigh, "Where the devil are Agatha Christie and the forensics squad when you need them!? Help! I want to know what the hell happened between these two! It must have been a classic something or other - confrontation I guess."

Nobody had a good hypothesis yet.

Another silence: it lasted for more than a full minute - an eternity - until the oldest student muttered "Jeez, we're in the soup now... this is another truly interesting find, maybe really important, so we're going to have to tell the department. About both the points matching, and the checkering. Which means confessing that we played with specimens without either an approved work-plan or any authorization. Ugh."

Then Joan sighed and spoke, her enthusiasm obvious: "They'll forgive you, trust me. In fact, you can use me if you need a goat. Rules like those are usually meant to keep the dummies under control: not a problem here. Anyhow, to hell with rules and politics – for the moment, the interesting question is 'What happened?' How are these two sites, and especially these two people, connected?" She paused, took a deep breath. "At La Fond yesterday, after looking at Goliath and his injuries, Anton gave us a good short analysis of the forces, angles and implements involved in Goliath's death. It would be very helpful if he would go through it again, because none of you folks from UP heard it - but he could expand on it, now that we know the relationship of the two spears to one another."

She turned to Anton - "Would you update and recap your crime-scene analysis for us all?"

Anton was a good extemporaneous analyst and lecturer, and was happy to do it.

"Ok folks, in a nutshell. Goliath seems to have been killed by a single spear-wound. The spear entered from the front, going UPWARDS. You can't throw a spear so that on a standing man it enters going upwards. The only common-sensical way to make that direction of injury would be for Goliath to have been lying supine, and the assailant to straddle him. I think the most likely assailant is your Spear-Lady, but now that I've seen how small she was, I doubt that she could have thrown the killing spear at all. And if she COULD, she certainly couldn't have made it fly UPWARDS so as to cause Goliath's wound. I also doubt that she could have straddled him and driven a hand-held spear with the needed force. Common sense doesn't seem correct just now, does it?"

He paused: all attention was riveted on him.

"So we have a puzzle about angles. We also have a puzzle about energy. You need a LOT of kinetic energy to drive a spear that big through a body like Goliath's, while cutting through bones twice enroute. Loads of energy. I doubt Spear-Lady could have generated it - she's just not that BIG! There's a second forces-problem. The point went all the way through Goliath's sternum and chest and spine. And then AFTER doing all that, some major force snapped the point, right where the shaft ends. That is one honking tough BIG piece of glass! The only way I can see it snapping AFTER lodging in Herr Goliath's chest, is if some major force was applied to the spear shaft but not until AFTER the point had done its work. Like for instance, if Goliath had been running fast and was ambushed, he would have had enough kinetic energy to impale himself, then fall on the shaft and break the point. That, by the way, is a classic tactic used by foot-soldiers to defend against a cavalry charge or even a chariot attack - stand firm with long spears: anchor the spear-butts in the dirt and let the enemy impale themselves. We have written and pictorial evidence that the tactic worked for the Assyrians, Egyptians, Romans, and throughout most medieval European wars. Could have worked here. At least, it's a tactic that could readily yield the observed wound. How the hell this woman got one of Mister G's spears in the first place, I have no clue!"

He raised a quizzical eyebrow: "Actually, you know, she got BOTH of his spears, didn't she! Killed him with one, took the other home as a souvenir. What a woman! Whizzer!"

One male student piped up: "Where the dickens would a woman learn about such a thing, such a tactic? I can't imagine her inventing it ad hoc, extemporaneously, under pressure! She would have had to know about it in advance. But WHY would her society NEED such a tactic? They didn't have domesticated horses yet, so no cavalry. For sure no chariots!"

None of the modern humans present thought about the need for a defense against cave-bears - the students and faculty were at too many removes from such worries. But some of them did try to think outside their personal shoeboxes. One female student shrugged, grinned, and said "Admit it you males! It's Amazons! Better still, Viking shield-maidens - they'd provide an even better explanation. She's a member of a warrior caste of women. Very well trained - she took this giant's spear away from him and killed him with it. What more do you need?"

The student tittered briefly, but Joan said "Why not? Maybe she just fought lots smarter than he did! Neolithic spear jujitsu. In modern martial arts, plenty of women can beat lots of men. Barehanded, too." Joan shook her head and almost got to the truth:

129

"You're correct that they had no cavalry to worry about back then, but maybe a similar tactic was used for other purposes, say in hunting? But then, she'd have had to be an experienced hunter, wouldn't she? We're not supposed to believe that about ancient women. All this is pretty speculative and murky." Then to the entire group at large, "Any other ideas?"

When it was clear that the discussion was done for the moment, Joan took the floor, after composing her thoughts. "There are two parts to any analysis, folks - data collection and manipulation and argument and drawing of conclusions - that's one part, the formal part. It's what we all spend our time learning in classes. It's what Anton just did for us. But people forget about the other part, which is speculating about the humans and events and causes behind the data - and which is the whole reason I'm in this field. For me, that's where the fun lies. So, here I go - this is Analysis Part 2, my version. Everyone feel free to interrupt."

She launched: "It's my belief that even in her PRIME, our petite Spear-Lady couldn't begin to throw that big spear effectively. No way. For her, the spear is probably completely useless as a throwing weapon. But it IS the right size for Goliath over there at La Fond, and everything says he owned them both. Maybe he even MADE them both! Now... I'm going to make a guess. Goliath had two spears, these two. Somehow she got hold of one and somehow, miraculously, she managed to kill him with it. Anton has outlined a plausible scenario for the kill itself. A first question for ME to ask is, 'What was her reason to be so upset with Goliath?' She didn't kill him accidentally, that's for sure! Nor did she bury him by herself after the kill. Whatever it was that happened between them, whatever she did to fix it, it occurred when she was young - she was arthritic a long, long time and you don't do squat physically when you have bad arthritis and that humongous batch of healed rib-fractures. Especially you don't do anything physical against some giant of a man! I suggest that she must have killed Goliath before she sustained the big chest injury – I'll just bet she never fully recovered from that."

"Why do I think it was Lady who actually killed Goliath? I

think it had to have been her that did it, did the killing, else why would she have kept his other spear, and why would her people have buried it with her... fifty or so years later? She kept the spear her whole life, folks! And it ended up in the grave with her - in her weird, very specially constructed grave which took a lot of extra work - and most of the extra labor was because of that spear. It was special, somehow. Her grave-diggers were in no hurry, they didn't have to or want to chop up her þig spear, like somebody did with Goliath's toy. Only powerful stuff gets buried with bodies, so the big spear must have been a powerful item."

She paused, then continued: "Are there more reasons to think Spear-Lady did the deed? Well, consider - it probably WASN'T that she had a male Prince Galahad-the-Protector with her out in the woods that day, some man who did the actual killing. Because IF there had been any such MAN involved, HE would have been the one to keep the spear as a memento, a trophy." She shook her head. "So, accepting for argument the hypothesis that Lady is the killer, what was her motive? Almost certainly it was self-preservation - this whole scenario smells of desperation, a "last stand" sort of odor. I'd bet you dollars to doughnuts that Goliath kidnapped Lady, or found her alone for some reason and captured her. Then she managed to do this while escaping, God only knows how! Or maybe I'm completely off base, looking for a heroic woman forty thousand years ago. I do wish I knew what really happened. Welcome to the "Ultimate Mystery Club", students. No contemporaneous witnesses are available to be interviewed. Too bad!"

Nobody else proposed a better theory, much less one that was either more interesting or less provable.

35 - JIGSAW GENOMICS

Monday morning, 0700, more than a year later. Anton and Joan pulled into La Fond's parking lot. Anton pointed out to her the four UP vehicles parked side by side. "Hmmm..." he said: "Signs of co-operation, perhaps?"

Joan had completed her post-doc and become junior faculty at a third institution, where she was doing superbly well. She and Anton had finally gotten married, and with his new PhD he'd found an academic position where he could do his research and teach to his heart's content, mostly about his specialty, the murder mystery novel.

Last week they had received an invitation from La Fond's Director: "Dear Joan and Anton - please bring four to eight of your brightest grad students, come spend the day with us. We have something to show you that will - we think - blow your minds. Anton's presence is REQUIRED, since you two were the ringleaders who got our institutions to work together. What we have to show you is output from our collaborations on the Goliath/Spear-Lady problem. Such a lovely, intricate problem. Free lunch, too!"

Both had maintained an active interest in the Spear-Lady and Goliath research. It was no problem for either of them to quickly arrange a bit of free time, so of course they went, with half a dozen of Joan's students.

They were greeted in the big basement lab by the Director, two brand-new junior faculty from La Fond, ditto two from UP, plus a swarm of grad students from both institutions. After the requisite introductions, coffee, OJ, and croissants, they trooped upstairs to a small, exquisite 150-seat auditorium. A cloth curtain entirely covered the blackboard wall.

The Director motioned everyone to sit in the far forward seats. "Welcome, all! What I want to show you is behind the curtain. It is a direct output of our first ever real collaboration, La Fondation plus UP." He grinned at Joan and Anton, pointed them out: "Caused entirely by these two gadflies, who got some of you folks to break some silly rules about handling and loaning valuable specimens."

Scattered applause from the students who had actually participated.

He paused for effect, then said "So why are you here? Well, behind the curtain is a puzzle for the group. We have just this past weekend finished mapping the complete genomes of our collective three most famous specimens - La Fond's "Goliath", UP's Spear-Lady, and the body UP found in the so-called #2 grave touching, but later than, that of Spear-Lady."

The Director continued: "Many moons ago, Anton and Joan here forced us to work together by conspiring with students, behind the faculty's back, to "borrow" the Spear-Lady's spear-point - actually a resin replica of it - and by proving that Lady's intact point and the broken point that killed Goliath were adjacent pieces struck from the same core. Obviously there is some interesting back-story, given that the points were found over twenty-five kilometres apart. We've all wondered what that story might be."

"To recap things: Spear-Lady was found first, and her entire burial site was moved from The Valley to our lab, intact. While excavating her grave en-bloc, we encountered the very edge of another grave, number two. The way they overlapped showed that the second grave was younger than Spear-Lady's. In number two we have another complete skeleton -amazingly undisturbed- and some odd-ball grave goods... but no spears this time! However, there are some extremely interesting plant materials in the second grave, which are slowing down other work on it." The audience almost all knew the story to this point - only brand-new students didn't. "Just for the record, we all know about the strange heap of baked-clay fragments and incised tablets found at Spear-Lady's feet. We at first thought that that was a unique occurrence - but now we've found the same thing in the second grave! So, that's yet another mystery. Perhaps we can enlist Anton's help again - the tablets are an unholy mess of fragments. But that mystery is also for another day. Let me bring everyone completely up to date, then we will move on into today's activity!"

He was thoroughly enjoying himself.

"The second skeleton, in grave number two, is also female. She stood about 185 centimetres - that's six feet. Which is about ten or twelve centimetres short of UP's Goliath, and 30 centimetres taller than Spear-Lady. In fact, she's definitely the tallest female we've ever encountered - from this vicinity we have a dozen female skeletons now, and the next tallest, the runner up to our tall lady here, stood only 150 centimetres. No contest."

"Plus, instead of spears and suchlike, the tall woman's burial goods -what we'd exposed up until last week- were obviously personal decorations. No advanced weaponry. A couple of simple bear-claw necklaces, plus a pair of knives. But we've known all along from X-rays that there's plenty of other stuff with the skeleton. Including the layer of plant materials that has slowed us down a bit. We are by no means done working the grave, although much of the skeleton is now clean. She's lying on her left side, and so far we haven't unearthed the left arm or leg."

"However.... some interesting artifacts have surfaced. First of all, there is the thin layer of plant materials, in bundles yet, over all of the grave's contents, but above the skeleton-level. The grave had to have been filled in two steps - layers. That's an oddity. Plus, we've known from the X-rays and acoustics that just beside the tall woman's chest there were four good-sized clamshells - which is totally new. Clamshells belong in kitchen middens, not in formal graves. So we excavated around them and got them out, matrix-free. They aren't half-shells, they are complete shells, and they'd each been held shut with a cord or thong. Just like pill-boxes. When the cords decayed, the grave's fill-dirt held them shut. Good sized shells, too, about like an adult hand. Of a species that still lives in the river. The contents are intact. Care to guess what's in them?"

Nobody ventured a guess.

The Director shrugged, said with a laugh, "Cowards! Number one, the largest, was chock full of ground charcoal, all nicely solidified into a block. We're going to get a precise C-14 date for a change! We already know it'll be 40k years, plus or minus a couple of kay. The second was half-full of yellow ocher. Shell number three was full of red ocher. And number four wins the "oddness" prize. Inside it was a second clamshell. Inside THAT was yet another smaller shell. Of course, at first we thought we'd discovered the original version of the famous Russian "nesting dolls", but inside the third were several small pieces of turquoise, all round-cut and pierced for use as beads. We've done some nondestructive spectroscopy on them, and identified the source - in Afghanistan, more than three thousand kilometres away - more transcontinental trade! Beside the shells was a pile of pieces of charcoal, some with smooth, worn-down ends. All the contents of the various shells are inorganic

134

minerals, which is why the stuff was still present. Our tall lady was obviously an artist. I think this may be a first – firm assignment of a trade or talent to a specific neolithic *Homo* individual. That's cool in itself!"

He finished with another wide grin: "Not even to mention that the blue beads are nearly identical with the pair used as irises in the famous portrait found by Gerard!"

Joan's neck hair stood, but she said nothing.

"Plus, just one more teaser. Our resident plaster-caster, Jorge, found another concealed cavity in the artist's grave and we got a fine full cast of the hollow. It looks for all the world like a book about two inches thick, complete with deckle edges and thong ties. There's nothing left of the original materials, but it was obviously a stack or bundle of something like sheets of thin cardboard. We're calling it a book: my writing friends are frantic - they think it was an actual book - with pages and writing. Of course, they have no evidence, just opinions, because none of the original materials survived. I personally feel that because the woman was an artist, and the grave is loaded with artist's supplies, it was most likely a bundle of "drawing paper" - probably tree-bark. Now, even THAT would be an interesting find. With lots of inferences to be drawn. Let's be clear - that's pure speculation. My next guess is that this discussion will go on for some time. Should be fun!"

He scanned the audience, then resumed: "But neither the baked-clay fragments, nor analysis of clamshells full of pigments, nor the so-called book, is today's topic. Not even close, as a matter of fact. You all know that materials from The Valley sites, especially the UP site, tend to be ridiculously well preserved. Well, we've gotten plenty of DNA from all three individuals. We're doing the genetic analyses here, at La Fond, for both us and UP - another little instance of collaboration that goes back to Joan and Anton."

"Now for some results! Mister Goliath was homozygous for blue eyes. He must have been a spectacular specimen, especially for the time. Almost two full metres of human muscle-mountain with bright blue eyes. He would have been an amazing sight."

He paused. "We're now sure that the tall woman, the artist bur-

135

ied in grave #2, right beside Spear-Lady's grave, was also homozygous for blue. We've nicknamed her Tall Blue. Spear-Lady's genetics show both blue and dark - she's heterozygous, so "blue-eye" was present but hidden - she was dark-eyed in life."

"Which details finally bring us to today, to this meeting."

Now the Director had everyone's closest attention. "The main genes for human eye-color are on chromosome 15. Behind the curtain are the complete DNA blot-plots for C-15 of Goliath, Tall Blue, and Spear-Lady. As I said, we have the complete genomic data for each, but C-15's data will serve our purposes here. Besides, there isn't enough wall space to display even a single complete genome."

He looked around, grinned, and said "I understand that Anton recently finished his dissertation on murder mysteries as a genre. If what I intuit is correct, this whole confusing business should be right up his alley."

Murmurs, eyes towards Anton, who tried to ignore the attention. Unsuccessfully.

The Director continued: "You will recall that once one has the DNA blot-plot, the data are then analyzed for patterns. In this case the analysis will be done on our resident mini-super computer, using updated protocols that originated in the old Human Genome Project. Ours is a good, powerful machine, but even so it'll take several hours to run the analyses. We will do that tomorrow or next day. But no pattern analyses have been done yet, and there's a reason. I want you all to have first crack. Before the computers get to it."

He looked squarely at Anton and said, pointing, "In particular, I wanted Anton to have a shot. We know he's got an amazing ability in pattern perception, and he did get this whole project rolling because of that ability, so he certainly deserves to be part of the analytical team."

Anton blushed at being so singled out.

"Here we go. I'm not going to tell you yet which is which."

He drew back the curtain. Posted on the wall side by side were three enormous blot-plots, labeled A, B, and C. Each was a one metre by two metre sheet of paper covered with elongated dots, in rows. Row after row after row, tens of thousands of short fuzzy blue lines of variable intensity and length, arranged like maize kernels on their cob. A blur, each bit of which corresponded to some tiny chunk of chromosomal DNA.

"Here's the challenge, folks. It's called "find the pattern". I think there has to be one, and I think I know what it is - or should be. I have an advantage over most of you, my training is heavy on genetics. But I haven't examined these plots, so right here and now is the first analysis. Virgin grade-A data, everyone - we all start together. Even. Nobody say anything at all until you have some idea what's going on here, and are ready to explain your thoughts to us all. I'm in this race myself. Go!"

Joan poked Anton in the ribs, muttered "You're getting a hell of a lot of credit, M'sieur. I hope you realize that!"

Anton muttered "Yeah, thanks. Let me study this for a minute."

Nobody said word one for five minutes.

Ten minutes.

Twelve.

Then, Anton issued a gentle "Um..." and all eyes swung his direction.

He coughed and said, low, "Three individuals, right?"

The Director nodded.

"If I remember correctly" said Anton, "You just told us that Spear-Lady was black-eyed with a recessive for blue; Tall Blue was blue-eyed; and Goliath was also blue-eyed. Is that right? And blue is definitely recessive."

Several people nodded: he had it correct.

The Director understood immediately where Anton was going, began to squirm silently, like a five year old needing to go Number One. He truly hadn't done any analysis, not even looking closely at the plots, and he was pleased.

Anton pointed to the plots and said, softly, "I see part of A in B, and part of C in B. And nothing at all the other way 'round."

From one corner came a sotto voce comment - "Bullshit!"

Anton bridled, kept cool, replied "Wrongo! Not bullshit. Don't forget that my brain is wired funny. Jigsaw puzzles aren't the same as this, and they aren't the same as those two spear points - but to my brain visual pattern is just pattern. Here, in these plots, B contains part of A and also part of C. Period. Let me show you..."

He stood, strode to the plots, and outlined areas with his hands, indicating what could be moved where, to make a match. One or two people in the audience, plus the Director, nodded as he spoke. Anton hoped it wasn't just casual agreement, that they could actually see some of what he was seeing.

He turned to face the audience and said quite firmly "I never went beyond advanced bio in high-school, but the only way I know of to get some of both A's DNA and C's DNA into B's DNA is if A and C were the parents of B. That's got to be what's going on here. Tall Blue is Spear-Lady and Goliath's kid. The eyes and these plots prove it - TB's height being in between those of Goliath and Spear-Lady just helps nail it down."

Stunned silence, broken by applause from the Director only.

The Director finished clapping and faced the audience. "Congratulations to Anton. It will probably take two days of computer time to do the complete analysis, and of course we'll get lots of details, but Anton has, I believe, gotten over ninety percent of the critical results already. In under twenty minutes. Isn't the human brain an amazing analytical engine? The point of all this education is to teach you how to use perhaps 20% of its capacity. That goes for me, too!"

The audience finally applauded. The Director beckoned Anton to the lectern and asked him "How about updating your analysis of all this? Mysteries are, after all, your personal specialty, and you've been along for most of the ride on this project."

Anton at first looked thoroughly embarrassed, but then faced the audience squarely and took command. "I said back when all we had were the two matching spear-points, that I love a good murder mystery, especially if it's forty thousand years old. You folks do the science, I will do the mystery analysis. I'm going to speculate. And to give proper credit, I got a lot of these ideas from Joan and Jorge and others, last time we were here, stealing specimens. Or borrowing their replicas."

"The B plot belongs to Tall Blue. She is the daughter of Spear-

Lady and Goliath, who are the A and C plots. Her Daddy is our Goliath, so no wonder Tall Blue's so damn tall! Goliath is no way part of Spear-Lady's Tribe - he's a blue-eyed man-mountain, a stranger. A perfect "mysterious stranger". Goliath obviously had sex with Spear-Lady - after all, she had his kid. Because he's a stranger, and died so violently and so far from Spear-Lady's settlement, she most likely wasn't with him willingly... meaning she wasn't a runaway or a volunteer or a bought bride. That means probably a kidnapping and rape, in my opinion. Goliath originally had two spears the right size for himself. After the rape, Spear-Lady got hold of one of those spears and managed to kill him right where you all found him. After that, she probably grabbed the second spear for protection and lit out for home - which is where she was buried decades later with her souvenir. Bet you nobody would have believed her story, except that the king-sized spear was good evidence. I would also bet that she and a bunch of tribal men went back to the site of the action, immediately. She was the only one who knew where to go, so she must have led. Why go visit the site en-masse? Her people would at least want to be sure there weren't more giants in the bushes nearby! Plus, they needed to check out the details. After all, the headline "One hundred fifty centimetre woman, 45 kilos, kills her rapist, a two-metre man, 100+ kilos - and does it with his own spear!" wouldn't be common back then. Or even today! And she didn't have any male help, either - no male who killed Goliath would fail to keep the man's big spear for himself as a trophy - but SHE has it - even unto this very day! To me, that means she did the deed. She kept the spear as a good-luck charm, or a power-symbol, or some such, and they eventually buried it with her. And without chopping it up - the spear was quite a special item."

He smiled at his audience. "End of speculation, but I do wish we could have watched the encounter, just to see whatever maneuvers she used to bring him down. She must have been one scary warrior. The ultimate Viking shield-maiden indeed. Now - if you scientificos can get some more details, we can write a better story! Let me know. Please!"

36 - ROMANCE AND SLAUGHTER AT THE CAIRN

As Gerard walked his bike homeward along the base of The Rampart, he passed within sight of an oddly incongruous heap of large boulders. He paid it no attention whatever - he was still in his adrenaline high and deep-breathing phase after his bike descent of The Rampart. Unknown to him, sixteen years earlier a couple had come down today's four-wheel-drive road, on foot. A romantically-inclined young couple, the man carrying a small backpack with blanket and water bottle, plus some excellent chocolate. And no contraception. The day was warm, the wind calm, the entire area utterly deserted. Fifteen minutes or so of wandering about over the uppermost flood plain had led them entirely by accident to Goliath's cairn. And there, some five feet above Goliath's earthly remains, in the open air and warm sunshine, Gerard had been conceived. He would eventually get acquainted with the pile, and would return to the site repeatedly over the years, but he never knew. The closest he came to finding out was the time he brought his parents down to the main site. Although the conception cairn itself had been leveled to gain access to Goliath's grave, his folks recognized the site. Busy driving and being tour-guide, Gerard didn't notice that they were both of them red-faced and tongue-tied as he drove slowly past the place, jabbering away about Goliath.

Quite a while after Gerard's bicycle walk-by, the pile was visited again, this time more or less incidentally by a small group of faculty and students from the recently-established La Fondation. They were doing some preliminary scouting of The Valley, seeking sites that might yield good anthropological materials. They stopped at the pile merely for lunch. One of the more observant students felt there was something odd about the pile, and studied it from a few yards away... growing steadily more convinced about its being distinctly weird.

He walked around it once, then again. The others ignored him, were busy with sandwiches and candy bars and fruit.

The pile was essentially two layers of good-sized boulders. He clambered up atop it, surveyed the scene. Suspicions confirmed. He clapped his hands loudly for attention.

"Hey, everybody! Listen up! I have a question for you all. What's queer about this pile of rocks? And the environment around us?"

No comments from other students. The professor in the lead looked around, and instantly figured out what it must be that concerned the speaker, but let the student proceed. "Let's see if this kid is as good as he seems..." thought the prof.

"Look around!" said the student. "This place is pretty unnatural. Especially this rock-pile. There aren't two other rocks one atop the other anywhere nearby!" Everyone gawked, looked about, nodded. The student shrugged and said "Not only that, but if you climb up here for an aerial view, rocks this size..." he pointed to the pile "...are pretty much randomly distributed over the immediate landscape. But there's not a single one on the surface within about fifty metres of us. They didn't pile themselves up this way. Somebody gathered them and piled them right here. A long, long time ago. These are big rocks - it took a bunch of people to do it."

The prof ahemed and said "Good job of observation and analysis. Much better than we have any right to expect from a new student on his first outing! Bravo!" The student went pink again, basked in the praise. The professor asked the group "Why, anthropologically speaking, would people build this pile. It took considerable effort!"

Several students answered simultaneously: "Grave marker!"

"Right! - and out here in the wide-open. This is a prime strange locus for a grave. Everyone get out your topo maps and chart this boulder pile. Scour and map the area for 200 metres in every direction. Then we're going back to La Fond and think about this. Get lots of photos."

Having mapped and thought, they came back a week later in force, well equipped, and with a plan. Rocks that had been four- or five-man rocks for the cairn-builders had magically become ten-man rocks today, despite a considerable increase in mean body size of the workers - but the group had plenty of warm bodies.

Goliath began his return to the land of the living that very afternoon.

37 - SELECTIVE EIDETIC MEMORY

Veejr had, and was using in her art, a sort of semi-eidetic memory. Nearly photographic, but only for selected materials. In particular, she could take one good solid look at an object of interest and have enormously detailed permanent memories, recallable upon command. It had to be more than a passing glance, and had to be actively intended to render a permanent memory. Casual glances, ordinary activities, did not trigger the ability. Later, having brought up the memory, she could zoom in and out, too, and the level of detail didn't seem to vary. If she walked slowly around an object, studying it, she could replay the entire movie at will. With zoom.

From long experience, Mama Chys certainly knew that her kid had a peculiar memory, but the ability didn't manifest itself in ways either startlingly good, or obviously bad. The rest of the Tribe only very rarely noticed anything related to it - and an occasional person with a good memory was not something inherently frightening. Even if female, with blue eyes.

For Veejr, however, her oddball memory made easier the job of trying to draw an object: she needed to see it but once to have forever all the details she needed. If she had many different views, so much the better. What she was developing was not so much hand-eye coordination as memory-hand coordination, which is a function partly of repetitive practice and partly of nervous system maturity. The maturity portion she could not control but it would inevitably arrive. The practice part she doted on.

38 - FIRED-CLAY PANCAKES

Veejr's explorations and experiments, driven by a need for more and better work-surfaces, produced some interesting results. On one all-day food-gathering expedition the women had built a fire on one of her riverbank clay "slates." It had been drying for some days due to the river dropping and now the clay provided a convenient smooth, dry place to work. After the fire had died, Veejr was poking through the remains looking for usable bits of charcoal, when she noticed that the clay surface under the central part of the fire, its hottest part, had broken into palm-sized flat pieces with

142

curled edges, almost asking to be picked up. She obliged: except at the very edges, the pieces were nearly flat, and about five or six millimetres thick. They were all baked hard as rocks. Permanently fired into their burnt upper surfaces were various scratches caused by sticks in the fire.

Thinking about the fire and clay later that evening, she had an idea.

Next day she went to the river for a skinfull of wet clay, brought it home. She smeared handfuls on a flat rock surface hot from the sun. She smoothed it nicely with her hands, and then wrote her marks on the flat clay surfaces. She waited impatiently for the clay to dry. When it began to crack and flake off, she encouraged it, and wound up with a small handful of nearly flat, partly dry mud-flakes, each bearing her marks. She knew from studying the riverbank fire that only the dry clay would become stone in a fire, so she waited -an incredibly difficult wait- for her flakes to dry well in the sun, until they had a texture like that of the original, unbaked clay from beneath yesterday's fire.

While waiting, she collected a good bundle of firewood. When asked by Chys what she was doing, Veejr told her it would be a surprise, to please wait until maybe sundown. Meanwhile, she was going to build her own fire beside the regular family hearth. She hollowed out a bowl-shaped depression in the dirt, put her air-dried pancakes in it, then built a small, very hot fire atop the bowl. Shortly, to her great glee, she could see through the flames that the flakes were glowing red hot, just like ordinary wood embers. They didn't seem to be falling apart, either. She let the fire burn down on its own - that was what had happened at the riverside - and again waited patiently. The riverbank-fire clay flakes had been only warm to the touch when she first handled them. She could wait.

Mother was only vaguely curious, didn't push for an explanation - after all, Veejr was famous for doing odd things - not totally crazy, just distinctly odd. The child's mind, everyone knew, worked differently from most peoples'. And often, the kid's being "different" turned out to mean "better".

Her fire pit cooled, and Veejr finally retrieved the still-hot pancakes. She chortled - they were hard as stones - even harder, she thought, than the riverbank pieces. One had exploded, two had cracked but not quite across, and three were perfectly intact. All had her markings permanently baked into their surfaces. Not even soaking in water would erase these marks! She showed the hard pancakes to Chys, who didn't understand the fuss her daughter was making. Everyone who had ever built fires knew that sometimes the dirt or mud under the fire would bake into stone. Veejr tried to explain that she had created something brand new - a way to make permanent her marks in clay. Nobody, nothing could wash away her new marks! What she was trying to say, and lacked both the words and concept for it, was "I can be immortal!" Chys was generally good at abstractions, but didn't understand.

Both pleased and frustrated, Veejr made a great many more pancakes over the next few months, in an extended burst of experimentation through which she learned about thicknesses and curvature and flatness and moisture and time and temperature. But the step to a useful fired object, say a simple cup, forever eluded her.

She baked many batches marked with her incised patterns. She also baked several with her fingerprints pressed into the clay, and even a few with her entire hand-print. Because her hands were so important to her, the full-handprint flakes, and no others, got her triple-S mark as well, that mark being her overall favorite regardless of the medium. She accumulated dozens of cakes and, like children everywhere and throughout time, she didn't want to discard them. So she got Chys's okay to store them in a pile far back in the main cave, out of the way, alongside Monster's spear.

Shortly thereafter Veejr lost interest in the clay project, and for many years she forgot all about her stash - nevertheless, she eventually found a use for them.

The reason for the loss of interest was that all her work with clay didn't help solve the problem of a lack of good practical surfaces for her art. But something else did.

39 - PAPER?

One hot summertime afternoon, on a trip to the riverbank,

alone, she found the river had risen enough to cover her favorite clay surfaces. Chagrined, she hiked slowly along the water's edge, hoping to find another un-flooded clay slate. She carried with her, as always, a small leather pack with her knife, a couple of pieces of leather thong, a meal's-worth of food. And just in case she might encounter a smooth bit of fresh white limestone, she carried several lumps of charcoal, and several different-diameter stubs of twigs with their ends charcoaled.

After working her way perhaps six hundred metres upstream, she hadn't yet found another usable clay surface. She was pushing through a dense tangle of small trunks of a water-loving tree - a white species she'd seen all her life and been taught to ignore. It was too soft for making hut-ribs or tool handles or spear shafts. It burnt poorly, too. The Tribe called it the "useless-tree". In this thicket, the trunks ranged from thumb- to thigh-thickness, and even larger. Just where she pushed her way out of the copse, a big chunk of riverbank had been undermined and then broken off. The process had snapped several useless-trees. Dangling from a twisted and broken end, practically in her face, was a small flap of white bark the size of her hand, gradually peeling free of the underlying wood as the current tugged on the tree's partly-submerged crown. She stopped and poked at the bark. A thought stirred. Flexible, reasonably smooth, and white! Her breath caught. She tugged on the flap: more of it peeled from the trunk, then it tore off, leaving her holding a slowly-re-curling sheet of useless-tree bark, dry and smooth and white on one side, wet and rough and greenish-yellow on the other.

Thirty seconds later she had her charcoal sticks unwrapped and was sitting cross-legged on the bank, trying simultaneously to keep the sheet from curling up again, and to draw on the white side. The dry, white, outer surface took the charcoal beautifully - marks could even be erased easily, so that a mistake needn't ruin the work.

She looked around - just in this local grove there was a nearly infinite supply. And useless-trees covered the riverbank densely for many kilometres in both directions.

Experiment time: once more, the child as tool-maker and inventor. The dratted curling was a pain - having grown up cylindrical, the bark really wanted to return to that shape. Frustrating. Bending and flexing it the other way, briefly reversing its natural curl, didn't really fix the problem, but did make the stuff more tractable. Slicing it into pieces lengthwise to the trunk helped a lot. Cutting half- circumference slices into short pieces helped, too. But what REALLY made a difference was cutting deep scratches with her knife on the inside surface, the cuts going parallel to the original long axis of the parent cylindrical branch and cutting the circumferential fibers that were causing the curl. After discovering that, she flattened one palm-sized rectangle against a hot smooth rock surface, thinking that since animal hides got stiff when they dried in the sun, maybe this bark might behave the same way. After all, the bark was very like an animal's skin, just on a plant! Tree-skin. She placed a small, warm flat rock on the rapidly-drying sheet, then walked into the grove of more mature trees farther from the water.

Bark on dry-dead trees was useless, because it stuck tight to the trunk or branch, would not come off in one sheet. Pieces from bigger branches were less sharply curled, hence easier to flatten... so she looked about for the biggest tree. It was over a foot in diameter. On the smoothest part of the trunk she carefully incised a square twice as big as both her hands combined. Square because squares had all straight lines and would therefore be an easy shape to cut. She could feel when the knife was through the bark and encountering the tougher, denser underlying wood. Carefully she pried up one corner. The process of loosening the sheet from its substratum was very like skinning an animal - proper gentle application of the knife at the moving seam where bark and the underlayment met, plus a gentle lifting and pulling. No problem for her - the bark was much tougher than say a rabbit skin, and she could field-strip a rabbit without making an unwanted nick.

In two more minutes she had a lovely, almost-flat, square piece of white bark. Gleeful, she returned to her ironing board and flattened the big sheet with several small, warm flat rocks.

It would take a while for the new material to dry. Meanwhile, she began really testing the drawing properties of the bark still on trees. It was delightful. So much better than rough rock! Not to even mention how much nicer than clay. The bark squares were PORT-ABLE! And easy to prepare. In the two hours it took to thoroughly dry the first sheets, she had used up her drawing-sticks, and moved on to harvesting fresh squares from the biggest trees. She got eight more nicely-sized sheets, bundled them carefully for drying later, retrieved her dried pieces, and headed home to show off.

Showing off was a disappointment: Mama and Brother didn't really understand the fascination of making curly or squiggly or linear marks on bark - certainly not when dinner was only half ready!

40 - VEEJR'S ARTISTIC GROWTH

Her invention of bark-as-paper changed things radically. With an unlimited supply of good surface, Veejr abruptly promoted herself from drawing mere patterns and half-hearted tries at representational art on clay, to serious attempts to draw identifiable objects on bark. This new exercise was much more difficult: it required among other things the ability to turn almost any visual image into a deeply abstract representation. Still-life drawing was what she tried at first-- beginning with objects that were easy and whose abstractions resembled her pattern work. Such as a tree branch. Six or seven roundish rocks in a pile. A fallen tree with now-vertical branches.

After several weeks and many sheets of bark, her final attempt at a complete standing dead tree, skeletal and leafless, was a major triumph. The oddly-shaped model tree was at the very edge of the settlement, known to all. When Chys saw the drawing, she grinned widely, said "I can see now. This is that tree over there!" - pointing.

Veejr had a deep sense of having won some important battle, a battle with herself. Being able to produce at will an accurate picture of an object made her feel almost as if she had taken control of the thing itself. Quite a heady sensation.

'Models' were easy to find. Mushrooms. Leaves. Individual rocks. And then there were rabbits - she quickly became a bit bored with drawing rabbits, but there was a permanent good supply of them in camp -dead ones awaiting dinnertime. The dislike stemmed from a disconnect - there were no hard edges on the critters, but the charcoal sticks made hard, sharp lines. Nothing either linear or regularly curved on the animals, either. And they were gray, with white bellies. White was easy, she would just put no pigment on the white areas, using the bark as if it were paint… but that meant the eventual white areas -the entire picture really- had to be thought out in advance, before her charcoal touched the bark. She couldn't just launch and start making marks, she really had to PLAN. To plan carefully, way out ahead in the process. Half the work was merely sitting still and thinking. Sometimes it made her head hurt. Hard work, but internal. Other Tribal folk thought this behavior very odd - but as usual, not their business. Nobody understood, so she let them stare their fill while she ignored them and worked.

If you got the white right, what to do about the gray? Gray she finally solved in two ways - first with ashes from the campfire, and second by smudging light charcoal lines with her thumb. The mere "drawing" of patterns in river-clay was now far behind her. It took fifty some attempts at a rabbit, using up several day's supply of bark, before she was satisfied she had gotten the core of rabbitness - really long hind legs, bent twice; big, prominent eyes, long floppy ears; whiskers on a small pointy head. Gray with white belly, check! She showed this to Chys, who was one of the few people who seemed to always figure out what a picture was all about, and who seemed also to genuinely enjoy looking at her art-work.

Next day, Mama Chys proudly showed the rabbit drawing to all her close women friends, one at a time. Over half of them recognized it at once, the rest understood after a bit of explanation. Only one woman bothered to ask "What is it for, this thing? Why is Veejr doing all this silly stuff?" Chys just said that if Veejr wanted to do this with her spare time, it was okay.

41 - THE MEN'S-CAVE: A PROBLEM LOOMS

Later, Veejr herself showed the rabbit to the men, who had seen only her simple repetitive-pattern art so far. They, like everyone else, had watched with amusement as she worked away at her drawings. Their thoughts as they watched had been simple; first, "Stupid activity for a kid!", and second, that Veejr's new "paper" if properly dried and shredded might be useful as tinder for starting a campfire, but the finished drawings were of no known value or utility. Nonetheless, every one of the men was or had been a hunter, and every one recognized the rabbit instantly.

Uncle and Medicine Man were thoroughly and openly startled by the rabbit drawing. One got the impression that their old feeling that her drawings were utterly useless might have changed when faced with the rabbit. It was unclear why such a change of attitude would occur: Veejr didn't even notice and if she had, she wouldn't have cared.

The change had to do with what had been found on the walls of a nearby cave. The men were cogitating: Veejr's artistic abilities might be of some help. But unfortunately she was female. A big, serious problem.

Veejr was clueless that she and her art had just presented the men with both a new problem and a possible solution to an older one. She was having too much fun, kept right on cutting bark, making paper, and drawing, experimenting nonstop with kinds of charcoal and widths of twig-brushes. She even invented a real brush - a finger-diameter twig with one end very finely shredded. She used it to apply another invention - paint. Ashes mixed in a big clamshell with a little water or even some animal fat. For covering a large area, paint - especially the fatty kind- made the job much easier than it was when just using chunks of charcoal. And the paint really soaked into or stuck to her "canvas", be it limestone or bark - a very useful property.

42 - CHYS'S BEAR PROBLEM

For some considerable time, life simply coasted. Veejr spent her free time getting better at still-life drawing, Brother matured and was initiated into adulthood, began to go on hunting parties. Chys went on the occasional hunt, even a couple of times with Brother - who didn't know whether he should be embarrassed by, or overtly proud of, Mama's company. Chys simply ignored Brother's potential 'problem' completely.

One day when Veejr was eight, Chys volunteered to go on a long hunt for bigger game up on The Plateau: it was time to start

149

drying and storing meat for the winter. Planning and getting ready took the hunting party a couple of days. Brother had twisted an ankle, and to his disgust had to remain at home.

One never knew just how long a hunting party might be gone - it depended utterly on luck. But two weeks plus or minus a few days was commonplace. On day ten, an excited runner arrived at the settlement with the sketchy news that Chys had been seriously injured by a cave bear - which she had helped to kill. Runner had been at the rear of the hunting group, but had seen all the action from a distance. He said that the incident had been the most marvelous thing to watch - precisely what the Tribe should expect from Woman who kills Monsters!

Unfortunately, Chys had been sideswiped by the bear as it collapsed and fell to Earth in a furious death-flurry. The blow had missed her head - she was alive and could talk, all her faculties seemed okay, but she had several obviously-broken ribs and couldn't walk. And a broken left arm, too. She was being brought home on a litter made of spears and the fresh bearskin. The skin alone weighed more than any one man could carry! Chys's kids and Aunt and Uncle should get ready to take care of her. The party would arrive about dusk. The Tribe's Bonesetter should be ready to work on her arm.

Medicine Man and Bonesetter queried the messenger: Yes, Chys was having considerable pain just from breathing, but no, she was not coughing up frothy blood, and there was no break in the skin on her chest or on the broken arm. Runner knew this for sure because he had personally seen the injuries up close. Bonesetter relaxed at the news. He turned to Veejr and Brother, reassured them, and sent them off to set up a recuperation hut and bed for the patient. Chys would be in great pain, she would need a soft bed in a warm, private place where she could lie without moving much, and rolled skins to use as cushions to make her as comfortable as possible. She would be able to do nothing more than the simplest of movements for at least half a moon, and not much more than that for another three, perhaps four complete moon-cycles.

Meanwhile, as they waited, Medicine Man would prepare infu-

sions of several plants that would help with the pain. He and Bonesetter would do what they could to fix the arm, but the most important thing would be to keep her still, so that the broken ends of
ribs didn't do damage deep inside her body. She must be kept warm,
well fed, and almost motionless for a considerable time, with most
care to be provided by Veejr and Brother. After the hut was ready, a
mere couple of hours' work, the kids should go to their Aunt and
help her to prepare a warm soup, rich with starchy tubers and
mashed fatty meat. Chys might or might not be hungry at the moment, but she would have to eat a lot and regularly if she was going
to heal quickly.

On arrival, Chys was greeted by Bonesetter and Medicine Man.
They had seen many injuries and wounds, and Chys welcomed their
examination and help. They quickly checked the damage and agreed
- yes, she was badly hurt, but she would survive. The most important thing was that her skin was unbroken - people with injuries
involving broken bones that had poked through the skin almost always died of their injuries, slowly and in ugly, painful ways. Broken
bones that didn't poke through usually healed reasonably well - especially if the break was simple and could be readily set. That was
Bonesetter's specialty.

Before they went to work on the injuries, Medicine Man gave
her a dried gourd cupful of warm water murky with plant extracts
that were both sedative and anesthetic. In a very few minutes Chys
was incoherent, almost unconscious and limp as a rag-doll. It would
be almost forty thousand years before better anesthesia was anywhere available.

The very first concern was getting her chest quite snugly band-
aged, to hold the ribs in place. A large piece of thin, strong gazelle
leather served, wrapped tightly and held with pins made of bone.
Her breathing eased instantly.

Then came the arm's turn. Three men held her while Bonesetter
manipulated the bones. It was an easy set - ten seconds of powerful
traction to stretch the contracted muscles, a little wriggling, and he
felt the broken ends meet properly. Chys made not a sound. They
splinted the arm with sticks and wide straps, then tied it immovably

to her chest. Only then did they install her in her brand-new quarters - the children's new purpose-built small hut of hides over a framework of green branches, well sheltered, with its own hearth and leather buckets for water and sanitation.

Between them, Veejr and Brother could handle most of Mama's needs. They spelled one another, taking turns hunting and housekeeping/nursing on alternate days. While Chys slept, the stay-at-home "nurse" mostly helped Aunt cook. And right from the start, they had extra help from Uncle, the man who had taught Chys to knapp and to both make and use a spear. And to hunt with the men.

Chys healed remarkably well: in under two weeks she could breathe without much pain and was anxious to get up and about - but she had seen Bonesetter's and Medicine Man's miracle-working all her life, and heeded their advice to stay quietly in her hut for a few days more.

43 - CAVE-BEAR PROBLEM CLARIFIED

Much later, as a grown adult, Veejr had heard Chys's "Bear Story" so often, from so many people, in so many slightly different versions, that she no longer knew her own "real" memories from other peoples' memories or inventions. But the outline was clear: the core never changed.

Chys had volunteered to join a hunt - THAT, Veejr recalled perfectly because she had wanted to go as well, and been denied. The absolute novelty of Chys as "THE" female hunter had quickly worn off, and such offers were by then routinely issued and accepted – partly because Chys's presence was held to be lucky, but mostly because she was a genuinely good hunter. Plus, her diminutive size could be advantageous occasionally - like climbing far up into a slender tree to scout. She was also adept at fixing small wounds, an inevitable part of every hunting enterprise. Using her own long hair as suture material, she had even used her 'women's training' in sewing to close up several deep flesh-wounds, all of which had healed nicely. The injured men bore the stitching perfectly well - it was a minor irritation compared to being tattooed, which every man had undergone. In fact, it was a mark of distinction (although a minor one) to wear the scar of a repair made by Chys.

Veejr was already not just aware of, but proud of, the fact that of all the females in the Tribe, only Mama was allowed to go with the adult men on serious hunts. And when it was time for storytelling around the fire, Mama was a favorite. Veejr knew that Mama's special treatment had something to do with the huge spear that she kept far back in the cave with other valuable things like hides and leather bags full of dried meat and edible plants.

But Veejr still didn't understand why there had to be so many differences in how the sexes were treated, and in what they could or could not do. No, that wasn't quite what she meant. It wasn't a matter of 'could' versus 'couldn't', it was a matter of being 'allowed' versus 'prohibited.' And nobody could explain it to her in a way that made sense. She knew, of course, that just due to size alone, strong full-grown men differed from boys in what they could do, and differed from females of any age, but she had no idea why some of the societal gender-differences existed. How about hunting? Both she and her Mama could keep up with the boys and men. Certainly men were in general physically bigger, and usually stronger, than most women - but if you needed some stabbing or slicing done with a spear, who cared about the gender of the operator? Chys versus Monster should have settled that once and for all. If you had a four-man rock that needed lifting, and did the lifting with five or six women instead, what was the difference? The rock got moved in either case. There were plenty of other things that were different, too - things where size and strength weren't particularly important - and that included almost all hunting. A puzzlement. But at least Mama had gotten around that taboo.

Chys's hunting trip would take about a week, perhaps even two, up on The Plateau topping The Rampart, up where game swarmed this time of year. She explained the trip to her kids: Brother had hurt himself in some minor way, and couldn't go. However, he was now old enough to be nominally head of household while Mama was gone, but real authority (and food!) would be in the hands of Chys's elder sister, with whom the kids would sleep and eat. Veejr already knew how to prepare most foods, so she would help Auntie cook.

Brother she considered an ignoramus because he did not know about and was not interested in food preparation - just in eating. At which he was an acknowledged expert! Auntie thought Veejr's umbrage at Brother not sharing the work but getting fed anyhow was silly - that gender-based division of work was normal, wasn't it?

44 - BEAR DETAILS: PROBLEM AND SOLUTION

Ten days later in mid-afternoon, a lone runner from the hunt arrived home breathless: that memory was Veejr's own and crystal clear. The news - Chys had been hurt, badly, during the return trip. By a bear. She was being brought home by stretcher, would arrive in a few hours. It had happened yesterday, late, not too far off, at the bottom of The Rampart. The hunt had gone well. They had killed a horse and a youngish bison, which when butchered and smoked on the spot were all the group could carry. The prepared meat had been distributed, and everyone had safely packed their load down The Rampart's trails, arriving on the floodplain about a day's steady walk from home. The party had been traveling as two groups a hundred metres or so apart. The front group was three men plus Chys, all well burdened with strong-smelling meat. And the entire party was marching downwind. It was moving downwind that caused the problem - the scent of the meat preceded the party and overwhelmed the human-scent. The meat had attracted a cave bear. A big one. And he didn't expect the humans who came with the meat.

A surprised bear was the most dangerous animal of all, except an upset rhino.

Chys's quartet came around a rockfall, and they and the bear had sighted one another simultaneously, at dangerously close range. Mister Bear, they were certain, had been following the meat-scent to find the source. This bear had been, as bears usually were, instantly both curious and aggressive - maybe he was hungry? At any rate, Mister Bear had spotted them, sniffed loudly, risen to his full height to get a better view. Then he'd dropped to all fours and charged - more of an inquisitive than an angry charge, but nonetheless a full ton of bear coming their way at high speed and with bad intentions openly displayed.

Mister Bear paused in his charge, instinctively stood upright again to look about, which had given the leading group time to form the standard anti-bear defense, but not time to do the very best thing, namely discard the bear-attractant and skeedaddle. As the bear reared up for its final charge and lunge, Chys realized that her sharp spear was so much smaller and lighter than the three men's weapons that her standing with them would hinder rather than help the defense, so she took two giant steps backwards and to her right to get out of everyone's way. That move gave her a fine, clear view of Mister Bear's head.

The impact of the charging bear snapped the shafts of two of the men's spears. Although both points ended up solidly planted in his chest, neither penetrated deeply. The third spear skittered off his ribcage under the skin and was yanked from its owner's hands. Bear was still standing, reared up on his hind legs, injured and stunned, momentarily motionless, but retaining all of his infinite capacity for doing damage - probably fatal - to the humans.

At that moment, the odds were poor indeed - three disarmed men and one small woman with a rabbit-spear, versus a ton of angry, wounded bear.

For a long moment Mister Bear was fixated on the three-man defense, looking straight at them. This was unfortunate for Chys, because the only tender spot on the beast's body was the eyes – and bears, like humans, have forward-facing eyes for superb binocular vision. With Bear focused on the men, Chys couldn't even see his eyes – at best she was at the edge of his peripheral vision. In the pause after being injured, Bear seemed to be studying the men. Chys dropped her blunt, cocked her right arm with the sharp. And waved her left arm frantically.

Bears and rabbits have something other than warm-bloodedness in common. Like a rabbit's, Mister Bear's instinct was to get a good view of whatever was moving in his peripheral vision. Distracted from the men, he turned his head to face Chys squarely, then focused on her. With his head held perfectly still.

A cave bear's head is a large and massive thing, made of extra-thick, extra-dense bones protecting a not-very-large brain. Even modern rifle bullets would glance off it more often than not, rather like shooting a bowling-ball. The only access to that brain is via the eye-sockets. From four metres away, with Bear's attention entirely on herself, Chys very deliberately set her feet properly, coolly took the half-second she needed for careful aim, and threw her spear.

It was intentionally not an especially forceful throw - she knew for certain that what was needed here was accuracy, not power.

The messenger was lavish in his praise - Chys was famous for her abilities with what the men jokingly called her "child's toy" spears. This particular child's toy took Mister Bear squarely in the left eye, drove through the eggshell-thin bone of the orbit behind the eyeball, and tore through his brain. The spear was too light to penetrate the skull itself, but the slender obsidian tip dug a long gouge as it shattered on the inner surface. With such a strike, size and weight of spear were immaterial. The hit dropped the beast instantly, stone dead enroute to the ground.

The astounded men, suddenly reprieved from near-certain death, all had time to back-step and get clear of the collapsing bear. But in his death flurry, through purely bad luck, Mister Bear had given Chys a powerful backhand blow -the messenger demonstrated- to the left side of her chest. No claws, but lots of force from a very heavy object. At least the object was semi-flexible and well padded - less damaging than a stone. The blow had also broken Chys's arm - nothing to worry about, the Tribe's Bonesetter would fix that - but much more importantly she obviously had several badly broken ribs and could barely breathe. Or walk. So they were carrying her home.

Runner grinned at Veejr and Brother, who were now pale and shaking. He told them "Don't worry. Your Mama is strong, tough. You two will have to take care of her for a while, but I'm sure she'll be okay. Takes more than a big old bear to get rid of Woman who kills Monsters! Even if those men had completely missed, her spear would have killed Mister Bear all by itself."

He chuckled, partly from glee, partly to help calm the children a bit. "The three men she was with have decided she will get the head. They agree she saved their lives, and that their own spears

156

didn't do enough damage to Mister Bear to stop him. They were dead men, and now they're alive again! Your mother's gift to them!" He laughed, then provided a bit of spin for the story - spin that would do a modern PR person proud. "If those three men tried to take credit for the kill, they'd be lying and look stupid. All the rest of us saw everything. Much better for their pride if they can brag truthfully about being with Woman who kills Monsters when she added a cave-bear to her list! She will be more famous than ever, and they can get a little of that instead of feeling foolish for not killing the bear themselves. Everybody wins!"

Then he told them "You should be proud of her!! She's killed the two most dangerous animals in the world, a cave bear, and a big, hostile man. Now she just needs to kill a rhino all by herself. No wonder she has no man of her own! Every man is afraid of her power." The kids understood the tone, but not the details.

Regardless of Chys's injuries, a work-party of over a dozen was formed and sent to the site of the bear-killing - properly butchered, a thousand kilos of intact bear would yield several hundred kilos of delicious bear meat, certainly smokeable and definitely something not to be wasted. Runner gave detailed orders, then led the work-party back down the trail towards the carcass.

Chys was laid up for almost six weeks with her five doubly-broken ribs, but she healed fast and by the end of week two she was antsy to move about. By week three, she was largely taking care of herself - her kids had become blasé about Mama's injuries now that it was clear she was in no mortal danger. Chys largely released them from any extended nursing duty. The ribs would heal more slowly than the arm, and Bonesetter refused to let her try the arm until a full two moons had passed – that time being needed for solid first-order healing of broken bones. Only then, when all the primary healing was finished, should she begin all of her normal camp activities. As to a return to running and throwing, another two moons of healing were needed. She was NOT to start early just because she might feel like it. And both men said that after such a significant injury to her chest - not to mention that at twenty-eight or so she was well into middle age - she should probably expect never to return to the physical condition she had been in when the bad-luck bear-hunt began. She took the advice and warning stoically, her internal attitude one of 'wait and see'. In the event, she had to admit they'd been correct.

Chys's boredom was alleviated in week five by a ceremony in her honor. The hunters were simultaneously proud of Chys, and embarrassed for themselves, spin notwithstanding. But the pride (being ever so much more fun) eventually won out. The party had taken the bear's feet, plus the complete head, as trophies for her. More particularly, the properly prepared skull was to be a thank-you gift from the three men whose lives she had saved with her perfect spear-throw. Each man had gotten his own spear into the beast, which normally would entitle him to partial credit for the kill, but the men all admitted that they had, collectively, failed to stop Mister Bear - and that they had thought themselves dead for a moment, until Chys had done the killing. She didn't do it entirely unaided - after all, the men had sort of slowed him down! - but largely so. It would be ungracious to claim otherwise… especially with two thirds of the hunting party as eyewitnesses.

45 - MISTER BEAR'S HEAD

A cave-bear's entire head is no trivial item: fresh, it weighs perhaps twenty kilos, and either side's jaw muscles far outweigh the entire brain. The skull alone, denuded of all flesh and other soft tissues, is dense, hard bone up to three centimetres thick, and weighs about eight or ten kilos. The three men wanted to make a presentation, and cleaned the skull as best they could using scrapers and knives. They carefully tied the mandible to the skull: they wanted the entire assembly, and it would come apart into two subgroups - mandible and skull proper- when all the jaw ligaments were gone. Then they boiled it to get it cleaner yet. As a final step they staked it to the bottom of the river, near the clam beds, and within days it had been microscopically cleaned by insects and their larvae. Another boiling with herbs from Medicine Man gave them what they wanted - naked, bright white bone. The teeth were fearsome - Mister Bear had been a big, fully adult male. His canines were longer than a man's thumb – and where they met their sockets, were thicker than that thumb. Serious killing machinery. Whilst the three men were polishing the bones with sand, one of them re-articulated the jaw onto the skull, and won his bet that the bear's mouth, fully open, would easily accommodate a man's head.

During the cleaning required to empty the braincase, nobody noticed the gouge on the inside of the skull, a ditch five millimetres wide, five deep, and thirty long, made by Chys's spear-point, which had shattered upon impact with the interior surface. There was no outside sign of that gouge. In handling the carcass, her spear had been rudely yanked from the head: the point was gone, of course. Inside the brain-case remained the shattered bits of point: they eventually came out with the brain matter and were discarded without comment, as were the bits of skull from the shattered orbital bones and the gouge. The man who found and discarded the wreckage knew what the bits were, but so what? The point had done its duty well, and the bits were useless. The spear-shaft had been tossed aside in the general hubbub of dealing with the carcass and Chys's injuries, but one of the lucky men retrieved it for her, mostly on general principles of not wasting a good shaft.

In considering what they might do to thank Chys, the three hunters decided on presenting the skull as one item, a fairly traditional 'thanks', but also on doing something unusual with the jaw and the twenty long, curved claws. They carefully bored a five millimetre hole through each condyle of the jaw - the smooth knobs at the open ends of the mandible which articulate it to the skull proper. Plenty of room for the holes - each condyle was the size of a modern golf-ball, and drilling through hard bone using splinters of obsidian was routine for making needles, hooks, and pegs. Then they extracted the upper canines, which were very firmly mounted in their sockets - it took extended gentle tapping on each tooth with an antler-hammer to loosen them, but eventually they dropped free without any damage to the skull. The skull looked a bit less ferocious absent the big teeth. A bit.

Teeth were much harder than simple bone - it took time to drill holes through the roots of the extracted upper canines. While that was being done by one man, the other two men drilled holes through the bases of the twenty claws. The claws being keratin instead of calcium phosphate, that was a much easier task.

The end product was a wonderful necklace, stunning and quite heavy. It had the mandible - with the big canines still in place - as its centerpiece. It hung pointing down, and was flanked on each side by an upper canine and ten bear-claws, the claws with their convex curves facing the viewer. It was a thoroughly impressive item. And the men managed to make it in secret.

The entire Tribe -all ninety plus souls- attended the presentation ceremony, held in the evening during the fullest of the full moon. Hunters had brought in three deer for the accompanying feast. While the meat cooked, the group demanded that Chys tell once again the well-used story of her conquest of Monster. She agreed, apologizing for the weakness of her voice and slowness of her movements. Regardless, the audience was spellbound, listening in perfect silence until they greeted the impalement and death of Monster with a concerted cheer and loud applause.

Then the three hunters brought in the skull, wrapped in a sheet of hide, and gave a very detailed recounting of the bear incident. Just at the climax they dramatically uncovered the skull and held it up in the eerie mix of moonlight and firelight, a thoroughly evil and frightening object. One hunter had brought Chys's salvaged spear, broken point and all, which he thrust through the eye-socket into the brain cavity. He left it there while the skull was carried on a circuit of the fire, so that all could admire the skill involved in the throw. While exhibiting the gleaming skull, they announced their decision to present it to Chys - but something must happen first. They were sorry, they knew she wasn't perfectly recovered, but would she please, as both Tribal Storyteller and heroine of the story, explain in pantomime what had happened.

Egged on by demands from the audience, reluctant and moving slowly, with her arm still in its sling, Chys did so, purely extemporaneously. To great applause. Careful of her ribs, she then gingerly sat down in the place of honor reserved for her. The three men brought the skull over and set it at her feet: Chys looked infinitely pleased. She already knew that someday she would give this skull, and the wonderfully good luck it contained, to Veejr. It could then go to Veejr's own daughter, if and when. A legacy gift, something few people ever received from a parent.

Then came the men's real surprise, when the oldest of the three magically produced the necklace, carried it around the fire for inspection, then announced that it was the three men's personal gift for Chys. They were sure it was chock-full of good luck, she must wear it whenever an appropriate occasion might arise. Together the three draped it around her neck, properly arranged all the bits, and retired to their places. Nobody had ever seen such a thing - the jawbone at first sight boded well to overwhelm her small frame - but in minutes it seemed an integral part of her, physically and emotionally, as if it had always been there.

That night, Chys told Veejr about her plans for eventually giving her the skull as her own good-luck piece. Chys enlisted her aid in wrapping and storing the skull with Monster's huge spear. They would bring the skull out for public display whenever it seemed like a good idea: on such occasions Veejr would be the skull-keeper, to unwrap, display, and re-wrap it. Along with it they stored Chys's bear-killing "rabbit spear", complete with the merest butt-end of a point.

46 - A SKULL AND TWO STUDENTS

During the first visit of a scientific party to the Gallery, at Anton's and Gerard's suggestion, the huge bear-skull found posted like a sentinel outside the Portrait's door had been carefully documented in-situ, then taken back to the lab for detailed studies. There it had a place of honor on a side-cart. For the moment it was mainly there as a curiosity, properly tagged and identified, waiting patiently for the furor over other more overtly human discoveries to die down.

Gerard and Jorge eventually conspired to dedicate a two-man weekend to the skull. Gerard was the more aggressive investigator: as they wrestled with the specimen he asked Jorge "What do you want to bet the mandible from the necklace will be a perfect fit?" To which the response was "No bets. Sorry! Because I agree with you."

Because the skull and mandible were solid bone and intact, anything but fragile, Gerard and Jorge were quite cavalier in how they handled them. Shortly they had the skull positioned upside-down on sandbags. Moments later, they had the necklace disassembled and were checking the match of the mandible's condyles to the sockets in the skull. The letter-perfect fit surprised neither of them - the mandible actually 'popped' slightly as it went into place, and thereafter stayed nicely in position unaided. The upper and lower rows of teeth meshed well. As Jorge noted, "Damn bear had a better bite than mine!"

Gerard cycled the mandible to open and close the mouth: It was painfully obvious just how dangerous a beast this had been - the jaws would easily open wide enough to handle either man's upper thigh. The enormous jaw muscles - size inferred from their massive attachment scars on the bone - would have enabled the parallel rows of heavy-duty cutting teeth to shear right through a human leg without slowing at the bone. Jorge placed his forearm in the mouth, closed the mandible on it, gingerly, gently. "Damn! His teeth are still sharp enough to do damage!" he informed Gerard, then respectfully disengaged.

Jorge picked up the skull, righted it, peered closely at it from the side, and observed "You know, even if we didn't have such a nice fit between skull and mandible, we'd still be able to prove they go together. Look at the pattern of scratches near the hinge. To get this thing clean, someone had to scrape like crazy - looks like scratch-marks from a knife or scraper. The marks start on the skull and go right on down onto the mandible. A perfect match. Just like bullet-fingerprints."

He paused. "Let's make a prediction we can actually test - I'll bet you that the upper canines from Spear-Lady's grave, the ones that are part of the necklace, will fit exactly into the sockets on this skull. Shall we take a look?"

Indeed, the two upper canines did nestle perfectly into the sockets: not only did they fit without a rattle, not only did the tartar lines on the teeth perfectly match the edges of the sockets, but the teeth occluded perfectly as the jaws closed. The mutual wear-patterns on uppers and lowers were clearly visible to the eye, and matched nicely.

Jorge then flipped the skull over so he could look straight into the destroyed left orbit. "I just had an idea..." he said. "Hand me a flashlight from the toolkit."

Gerard did so, wondering. Jorge shined the light into the brain cavity through the big spinal-cord foramen at the base of the skull, applied his eye to the orbit to peer inside.

"AHA! Just like I hoped!"

"What's so exciting?" asked Gerard.

"Look for yourself!"

Gerard took the skull, imitated Jorge. Clearly visible on the interior was the gouge made by Chys's spear-point. He whistled gently in admiration. "That has to be a notch cut by a spear. They didn't have bows and arrows. What a throw our hunter made!"

The men looked at one another silently for a second. Jorge shrugged and asked: "So tell me, Gerard - can you come up with any rationale at all why Spear-Lady would have the jawbone and canines, and probably the claws too, of this particular animal, if she didn't kill it herself?" He waited until Gerard shook his head. He went on: "I mean, someone made for her that necklace of mandible plus incisors plus all twenty claws. Why else would they do that, other than to honor her for having killed this beast?"

Gerard suddenly went completely quiet, perfectly still. Jorge looked at his face - it had gone bright red and he was grinning broadly. "What's wrong?" asked Jorge.

"Nothing. In fact, I think something just went perfectly, absolutely right for a change. I think we are about to become even more famous! Let's go get my laptop. We need to take a good look at one of my slides from the Gallery. NOW!"

Jorge, utterly at sea, muttered "What the hell? " but followed Gerard to his little office. They returned with the computer: Gerard turned it on, humming happily to himself. Jorge just watched. In seconds Gerard was stepping through slides, looking for a particular image.

He stopped with the Old Woman's portrait on-screen.

"LOOK!" he said to Jorge. "Look here! I'd totally forgotten this scene until just now - we have so damned many images to deal with."

Jorge goggled - he had never seen the complete suite of several hundred images,, and this particular picture was new to him. But instantly he understood Gerard's excitement.

The displayed drawing was the small but exquisitely clear scene painted above Old Woman's portrait, and attached to the circular portrait via a shared bit of frame. It showed three men side by side, their three clearly-broken spears helplessly raised in parallel, facing a charging, rearing bear. Off to the side was a female figure in the act of throwing a spear. Her spear was shown three times, as was her throwing arm. The spear in her hand raised for throwing, then in flight, and, finally, driven squarely through the bear's left eye. With blood spurting.

Abruptly, Jorge went completely silent and stayed so for a few seconds, long enough that Gerard noticed, waited, then asked "What is it, Jorge? You've obviously just thought of something interesting. Otherwise you never go quiet!"

"Gerard...." Jorge said very softly, "...we are all in love with Spear-Lady and her giant spear, and with what all that might mean about her and Goliath. And we've all looked at the two smaller spears, the intact ones, sharp and blunt, that are the proper size for her. We've used them to support the idea she might have been a hunter. But nobody has paid any attention to the third small spear. The one with the point broken off. Nobody seems to have even asked why such a useless object was buried with her. I think that any apparently useless object in a grave must have had some special significance to the deceased or her tribe. Useless in OUR ignorant eyes, maybe, but not insignificant to whoever did the burying. I think I just figured out what that significance is for the busted spear."

Graphically, he stuck his finger through the open orbit, stared – wide-eyed and questioning - at Gerard. Gerard stood speechless for some seconds, then whooped loudly and said "Where do we store that broken spear?"

The business-end of the spear fit perfectly into the hole in the orbit.

The two men looked at one another, unbelieving. They revisited the picture of the bear-killing. Finally Gerard managed to speak. "I don't believe it... we have a painting showing our Spear-Lady actually killing the bear whose skull we have in our hands! A picture painted by her daughter, Tall Blue the Artist! Here, Spear-Lady's out hunting with three men, they got attacked by a huge bear, and all three men have broken their spears! **Our little woman saved all three of the men's butts!** Talk about a blow to the male ego of the day! No fucking wonder she got that fancy bear-jaw necklace. I wonder - was it from her whole tribe, or just from those three lucky bastards?"

Then, softly, "How much luckier a pair of grad students could there ever be?"

After a few moments of quiet self-congratulatory back-slapping, Jorge again stuck his index finger through the spear-hole in the orbit, wiggled it and said "What a throw, man! And she got a perfect hit, in the only place she could have done real damage. Anywhere else on the whole damned head and her spear would have bounced off like it hit a rock. I wonder how far back she was when she chucked it? How far away can you or I stand and still hit something smaller than a tennis ball, with a spear? And under that sort of performance pressure, too, a full-grown bear coming at you, and all your compadres having only broken spears!? Spear-Lady was good! Hell, she was GREAT! Her spear went all the way through the animal's brain, with enough force to take out that big chip on the inside of the skull itself."

He reached for the computer, scrolled the imagery: the drawing attached to the bottom of the portrait's frame came into view. He stared, then sighed, snorted: "Look here! A woman killing a man who is much larger than herself. These two events, the two killing-drawings, are so similar, they're almost repeat encounters. Both opponents were speared at point-blank range, and both were dead before they hit the ground. It's a goddamned neolithic female Jack-

165

the-Giant-Killer we have on our hands, brother. No way was either contest a fair physical matchup - it was pure guts and skill against brawn. Twice. My guess is that she probably had exactly one chance against each of them. And she won, both times. We should be proud to be part of her lineage! At least, I call dibs on choosing her for MY team! And I don't give a damn what the event is. She's MINE!"

Gerard agreed, then muttered with a visible shiver, "Can you even IMAGINE standing there and taking aim at the eyeball of a thousand-kilo bear? Probably with him up on his hind legs exactly like in the drawing, with all those teeth showing. Sucker would stand 10 feet tall! And there you are, you with nothing for a weapon but a glass-pointed stick? And your backups are all kaput!? I'd simply shit my pants and die of fright on the spot. Which she did not! Man, oh man, whatever the female version of 'cojones' is, she had them!"

Looking down at the skeleton, Jorge said "You know, Gerard, we've all wondered what it was that caused her chest and arm injuries. I think we can figure it out. Let's the two of us play 'Anton the Murder Detective'."

Gerard eyed him skeptically, waited.

Jorge grinned: "So - just exactly what do we know? That she killed Goliath when she was relatively young, and that she must have done so before the chest injury. Why 'before'? Everyone agrees that after the injury she most likely never did anything requiring very much physical effort. Such as killing a giant man. So whatever she was doing when she got hurt, it happened after Goliath. After Goliath she went on about her business - and had their kid. Then some time later she both killed this bear, and got injured. She killed the bear BEFORE she got injured. Doesn't mean the killing and injury couldn't be close together, just means that the two events had to occur in a particular order. So - we know that both Goliath and this bear were killed by an as-yet uninjured Spear-Lady."

"My guess is that she killed the bear and got injured in the process. For sure, if you're involved with a cave bear, an injury is either reasonably to be expected, or even likely. Consider the injury to her chest. How big is a bear's paw, anyhow? They are NOT small animals! I think cave bears and polar bears are about the same size, and I've seen a photo of three men, kneeling side by side, all together holding one front leg of a polar bear. Those suckers are HUGE!"

A long thoughtful pause, one index finger tapping on the bear's cranium: "Now, suppose I'm right, and she got hurt by this bear. How could that happen and she still kills the beastie? IF the damned bear hit her, caved in her chest and broke her arm, it must have been AFTER she threw the spear! Because she sure as hell didn't throw it this accurately AFTER being hit - not with five newly-busted ribs and an arm too. This is like Anton's analysis of sequential forces acting on Goliath's spear. And this bear sure didn't live long after the spear hit him. So, guessing again - if she threw her spear and THEN was hit, she must have gotten clobbered by the animal as it died. Because this animal was dead from the instant the spear arrived."

He grinned again, widely. "God but I love to speculate! Any holes in that one?"

Gerard shook his head: "I don't think so. It's all speculation laid on over a foundation of some data, and it's the best we're likely to come up with. I like it and would like to believe it, but she could still have been hit by a rock after the bear incident. Nonetheless, THIS WOMAN obviously killed THIS BEAR, and apparently did so single-handedly. And who's to say exactly when and where and how she got the chest wound!"

Gerard shrugged, then went lost-in-thought for so long that Jorge snapped his fingers theatrically in front of his face to bring him back. Gerard took a deep breath, then said, with his fingers drumming on the skull, "In most hunting or hunt-and-gather societies today, a person gets nicknamed if they do something spectacular. So far, we've figured out that our Spear-Lady killed a giant man, and now we think she also killed this bear. Hell's bells, man! Really, we KNOW she did in this critter! No jury in the world would decide otherwise."

"Therefore I think we ought to stop calling her 'Spear-Lady' and come up with something more appropriate. 'Spear-Lady' isn't much of a name. It's just descriptive of her grave-goods, really. She needs a good 'Tribal Heroine' name, dammit!" Like 'Woman Who Kills Giants and Bears' - at least that refers to specific acts that we can actually associate with this particular person. I believe that association is a first, you know - first ever for someone this old."

Jorge nodded, then laughed: "I agree completely, and I can't do better than what you just suggested. Let's just declare her re-named in recognition of her deeds. I suspect the others will agree." He grinned. "Hmmm - 'Woman Who Kills Giants and Bears' - I like it!"

The others thought it a fine idea. And if one were either superstitious or a believer in the persistence of souls, one might have heard the gentlest whisper of appreciation hanging in the air. Might have.

47 - FIRST SMILEY-FACE

Quite late in Chys's convalescence from the bear encounter, when she was nearly fully healed, an apparently trivial incident occurred that would shape Veejr's world forevermore. And also the lives of a good many anthropologists in the far-distant future.

Sitting beside Chys's personal cook-fire at noon one hot day, with Mama sound asleep, Brother and Uncle almost drowsing, Veejr was thoroughly bored. Since the bear attack on Mom she hadn't touched her charcoal and bundle of sheet-bark. No art.

At the moment, she was playing idly with a partly-charred twig whilst considering lunch. She tested the burnt end with her thumb, then studied the mark left by the char. She took the twig in hand like a pencil, and drew a circle on her thigh. Nothing odd about putting charcoal designs on skin instead of her paper - charcoal was regularly used on faces, always applied by another person due to lack of portable mirrors for self-inspection. She tilted her head in thought, then abruptly had a flash of inspiration. She made three marks inside the circle: then a fourth. Two dots for eyes, two dashes as nose and mouth. The far-future's sober "smiley face" but without a smile-curve in the mouth. About the most abstract human face possible.

Excitedly, she tapped Brother on the shoulder, pointed to her leg. He didn't react: nothing weird about that, he NEVER reacted to "little sister" any more, had even stubbornly refused to recognize the rabbit picture. But this drawing was something genuinely new. She had a second inspiration - the picture, the FACE she had just drawn, was upside down for him. No wonder he didn't react. She tugged on his hand, brought him around to where the face was right-side-up. He stared at it, shrugged, sat back down. His whole body continued to say "So What!?" Evidently he had perceived nothing interesting. Neither of them knew that the wiring in Brother's brain would need considerable re-education and training to be able to see meaning in such an abstract image. For people with the wrong brain-wiring, getting it re-trained could take months or years. Sometimes never.

She was astonished - couldn't he SEE what it was she'd drawn? She was so excited by her invention - he should be, too! It was something brand new. She looked at her companions, then at her leg, then up at Uncle's suddenly-attentive face: she had eventually noticed that ever since the men saw the rabbit drawing, Uncle had paid a lot more attention to her, even coming over to look at some of her work occasionally. Twice he brought Medicine Man with him, embarrassing her with the attention. At this moment Uncle was watching her intently.

Uncle was widely regarded as either ugly or handsome, but not ordinary - take your pick. He certainly had unusually strong features - a big nose and prominent ears. And huge, bushy black eyebrows. She studied him, thought a moment and added two simple ears to the drawing, just little hooked lines: she smiled to herself - the addition was a major improvement, and so simple a change! Then, enthusiastically, she added an awkward mop of black hair, again just like Uncle's. And moments later, his unusually heavy black eyebrows went in as simple thick lines above the eye-dots. The eye-dots weren't correct - real eyes were bigger than just dots - in fact, eyes were very, very complicated. Puzzled how to improve the eyes, she left them alone for the moment.

She paused, studied the overall result. Amazing! Although it really didn't look at all like Uncle, somehow the process resembled capturing a rabbit in a snare: here, she'd caught a bit of Uncle in these few lines of charcoal. Without even touching him, she almost OWNED some part of him. Shivers ran down her spine.

Uncle, who had just become the world's first-ever artist's model, had seen the light come on in Veejr's face. Having taught many things to many kids, including her, he knew a student's "AHA!" moment when he saw it. Uncle also knew Veejr as one of the quickest and brightest kids he had ever taught. She learned so FAST it could be scary. Hence anything she did on her own was *ipso facto* of possible interest to him.

She drew furiously.

Uncle was watching her even more closely now, but she didn't notice. She kept working: some parts of the drawing were better than others. She was too busy, too focused, to go get a sheet of her bark and start over. The parts that didn't work irritated her, she knew not exactly why. She checked the details. First of all, his face wasn't really round at all! It was much closer to square than round. She had started all wrong by using her best circle, which had made everything not quite work. She would have to fix that, but doing so properly would mean erasing the entire picture, which she didn't want to do. With spit and a thumb she erased the worst bits, dried the skin-canvas, and then modified the image.

Why wouldn't her hand and this burnt twig produce a better representation of what she was looking at? The twig almost had a mind of its own: it was ridiculously hard to control at the desired level of detail, and especially with her intense inner excitement. Not at all like her long-ago willow-stick in the riverbank's clay. Here it was dab with the charcoal, stroke, erase, try again. She bit her tongue, looked at Uncle once more to compare her drawing with reality, noticed him studying her, and ignored the attention. Concentration. She was more tightly focused on this drawing than she had ever been on any game animal, or on anything Mama Chys had taught her. For the nonce, her universe had shrunk to her thigh and Uncle's face - nothing else existed. She made more changes, got more frustrated. Damn charcoal anyhow!

By now seriously curious, Uncle stirred, intending to stand up and step over to her. His first movement was met instantly with an order: "Sit still! Don't move! Wait until I'm done!" Uncle was the first artist's model ever to receive that order: nothing has changed much since then. Veejr didn't even realize she was giving orders to this very senior, adult man - and didn't notice his amusement as he complied and settled back to resume his original pose.

A minute or two later, when her drawing-hand stopped moving, he stepped over beside her, said "Let me see!" It was the same authoritative tone he used when teaching boys how to knapp. It snapped her out of her focus. Now she became aware of his interest - it was a good sign, she thought, that he was open about it: as an elder, his interest totally counteracted Brother having been nonchalant and uninterested to the point of active rudeness. (Or maybe, Veejr thought to herself, Brother's just even stupider than I thought!)

Uncle studied the no-longer-simple drawing for some time. At first, the tangle of marks made no sense, looked purely random. His brain had never been calibrated for this new form of imagery, it was hard to get a grip on it. Her rabbit he had understood at once, that animal was familiar territory - this was not. But after a few seconds, and quite suddenly, the lines resolved. He abruptly recognized the drawing as a face - an extremely abstract human face - something neither he nor any other person had ever had to contend with. He almost jumped when the face appeared out of the chaos of lines. It was like suddenly realizing that there is a full-grown lion in plain sight, motionless, contemplating you from the bushes five metres away. Veejr saw the startle in his body language as he exclaimed "A face!" His being so surprised pleased her enormously.

Forty thousand years hence, in a very different human world, a man named Pablo would be publicly reviled for doing another version of what Veejr had just done - reviled until he became ridiculously famous and wealthy from his work. But M'sieur Pablo would never have to make an intellectual leap even approximating the one she and Uncle had just made together.

After nearly a minute of study, he caught her gaze, pointed to the drawing and asked "Is this ME?" The simple question silently spoke volumes – it was a profound mental feat, requiring recognizing an abstract face, at all, then as being of one's self – a clear un-

171

derstanding of "self", something utterly unique to humans.

Veejr nodded, "Yes, that's you." She was immensely pleased with herself - she'd succeeded! Uncle GOT IT!

Uncle patted her shoulder and stood silently beside her for another minute or two, examining the drawing, pondering. The question uppermost in his mind had been percolating for over a year now - ever since he first noticed her drawings, and especially their increasing realism. The question was whether or not to show her something private and very secret, something known only to male elders of the Tribe. Something not for all men to see, and certainly not for women. Quandary - reveal or not? What factors weighed in favor of the idea? She was different from her mother, but must surely possess much of Chys's powers by virtue of inheritance. Mother Chys, Killer of Monster, and now also killer of cave bears, Tribal legend and heroine squared - SHE would certainly rate being brought in on the secret if any woman did. And her daughter had just invented something, this business of a picture of a human face. Something closely related to the secret. Veejr also had those amazing blue eyes, which must give her special powers of her own, in addition to anything she got from Chys - even if those powers had yet to reveal themselves. Surely Veejr, like Chys, could be cleared to know the secret?

But "men only" was a strong interdiction. He shrugged to himself - he needed help with this. He looked down at Veejr and said "I have to go talk with Medicine Man. Do not go away, stay right here." He left her puzzled, staring at his departing back.

48 – THE MEN'S-CAVE PROBLEM

Uncle and Medicine Man went a hundred metres into the brush for private discussion. After considerable debate, they agreed: Veejr should be shown the secret if for no other reason than to enable her luck to finally manifest itself, either good or bad. Her today's invention, the drawn face, was an omen demanding almost in a shout that she be told. And if they told Veejr, it was foregone that they must also bring in Chys. If they didn't include Chys, they were certain, it would mean no access to Veejr. And so they decided - a decision the two of them were making for the entire Tribe, without the Tribe's explicit permission. Medicine Man was adamant about one thing - Veejr and Chys must understand the concept of absolute secrecy, and agree to it. Other Tribal men might well get angry if they knew the secret had been compromised. Other men could not be counted on to be as coolly logical as themselves! Uncle was sure the two women could keep quiet. They were both very smart people whom he knew intimately. He would make sure of secrecy.

Uncle returned with Medicine Man to Chys's recovery hut, motioned for Veejr and Chys to come with them, and for Brother to remain where he was. The women stood and walked into the brush, leaving Brother behind, mildly hurt and wondering at being left out. Once out of sight in the underbrush, Uncle pointed out to Medicine Man and Chys the drawing on Veejr's leg. Veejr watched as yet another pair of human brains could not, at first, unravel the mystery. But Medicine Man was used to encountering strange things, and after only a few seconds he grunted his surprise as the drawing gathered itself together and leapt out at him, chaos becoming instant order. He stared at the picture, then into Veejr's eyes. He stood, took Uncle aside for another brief discussion. Moments later, Chys got it as well, grinned at Veejr, and said "Strange. Uncle's face on your leg! Nice!"

The two men returned to the women with the oddest expressions on their faces. Uncle remained silent, watching Veejr closely. She was nervous - she'd never had such intense, serious personal attention from adult men. She and Chys waited. Medicine Man finally spoke: "We are all four of us going for a short walk. We will show you women a secret. This will be the most important secret you will ever learn. You cannot ever tell anyone. Nobody. It is supposed to be for men only - you two will be the first women ever to see it. You must never tell anyone, man or woman or child, about it. Understood? Promise to keep the secret, from everyone, forever?"

Veejr was both smart and quick - in a flash she understood the significance of what was happening. Suddenly, she - "still-a-female-child-Veejr" - had been promoted from girl to "woman" - and she was about to be shown important secrets supposedly for men only. Things which, apparently, no woman had ever seen. She'd just been put on the same level as Killer of Monsters! In two seconds flat, she was no longer a child. Goosebumps - bumper crop. Uncle's and Medicine Man's eyes were boring holes into her. After a second, she realized that a response was required. She nodded, whispered "I promise!" Beside her, Chys said "So do I."

49 - WOMEN'S SOLUTION TO MEN'S PROBLEM

As soon as both women had agreed, Uncle told Veejr, "Very good. You should go get fire to take with us. We will need it."

That made Veejr intensely curious - a person needed fire for cooking, for light at night, sometimes to discourage prowling nocturnal animals. For making charcoal too, she grinned to herself: charcoal was certainly important! But those didn't seem like sensible reasons for carrying fire just now. It was bright daylight, and would remain so for many hours. No daylight-active animals needed scaring off with a blazing torch; and she had plenty of charcoal. Fire for cooking? No - what in the world would she and these three adults cook? And where? Carrying and having to care for fire made no sense right now, in daytime - but, sensible or not, she trotted back to Chys's hearth, extracted a good, travel-size nicely-burning stick.

She soon discovered that despite her doubts, fire was going to be really important, because the group stopped off at the big cave and picked up a bundle of good torches - pine limbs with knots and dripping resin, valuable items, very useful, collected by all and stored communally for use as needed. They also picked up a small leather bag with a half-dozen oil lamps. The Tribe had long ago figured out how to catch in clamshells the fat dripping from roasting meat, how to make a wick. Rather than waste any fat or oil, they made and stored away large numbers of lamps. Each lamp was both a potential source of light, and equally a source of dietary calories should the need arise for emergency rations - which it did, every few years.

After just a minute of pondering, Veejr was certain she understood the "fire and torch" business - they were going to a cave! She was certain of that, it was the only logical thing - otherwise, why so much fire? Lots of torches, many clamshell lamps. It was now broad daylight, and the lights could only mean they must be going into serious darkness. Which meant a cave. The torch was just an easy way of carrying fire - the clam-lamps were for providing light, they were useful for nothing else. Interesting! Almost scary, too.

Veejr squelched her curiosity and remained silent, mimicking the men. Moving at Chys's pace, they traveled along the base of The Rampart for more than a kilometre, eventually stopping at the bottom of a large ancient rock-fall. Uncle led, clambering awkwardly up and over several gigantic slabs, rather like a huge staircase. Veejr paid more attention to the fire she was carrying than to his precise route. Everyone helped Chys over difficult spots. Then, suddenly, Uncle turned left, stooped under an overhang, dropped to all fours, and disappeared down a man-sized hole. Veejr was pleased with her analysis. Holes meant caves. A shivery, exciting idea - she had always been forbidden to go into caves. Easy to get lost inside any cave, even small ones, she had been warned by Chys, and they were the preferred home of cave bears. Frightening stuff. But at least Chys was with her right now, along with the two men - that presumably made everything doubly okay.

Medicine Man pointed to the hole down which Uncle had vanished. He told Veejr "Give me the torch and follow Uncle. You, too, Chys. Go! But go slowly! Veejr, you help Chys if she needs it."

Uncle was waiting underground - the one-person entry-hole expanded immediately into a huge, almost totally black cave - the only light was the trickle from the entrance. It was cool and musty-smelling, Veejr thought, and scary-dark. The intense darkness was frightening, almost palpable. She squashed the urge to voice her fright. She thought quickly - and reasoned that, Mama's warnings aside, this business couldn't be too dangerous, since the two men had obviously been here before today and had survived! The men knew what they were doing, even if neither Veejr nor Chys did. She scooted sideways, out of the way. Even the trickle of light was blotted out for a moment as Medicine Man wriggled in, then paused to

175

retrieve the torch and bundle of extra faggots, plus the bag of lamps. He stood, held the torch upside down for a moment to make it flare brightly, then raised it high overhead and said "Look!"

Veejr's eyes were quickly adapting to the dark: far above her was a ceiling, with stone icicles hanging down. The walls, the ceiling, the floor - all were a brilliant white. She had seen snow and even small icicles once, in deep winter. She remembered their coldness, reached out to the wall, touched it - cool yes, but not icy. Dry and rough. She was fascinated: there was a whole different, new world underground!

Uncle pointed to the floor: there were several chips of calcite laid out in a line. "Those stones show the path for getting out - it's easy to get lost, so we've marked the way. To get out, you always go from one to two to three chips in a row." He pointed out the pattern. "This is a big cave - very big! Be really careful - If your light goes out, you will probably die in here. Even with the stone trail you'll probably never get out and you'll starve. What we want to show you is about 200 steps ahead. We'll all stand here while we light three more torches so we can each have one, and each of us needs three or four extras. Remember this - to be safe, at the latest, we will all start back together when the first of us lights his last torch! Nobody leaves the group for any reason."

It made Veejr feel much more comfortable to have all this explained, and to be led by such obviously experienced people.

The path was well defined - there were always at least two or three marker stones visible in the moving pool of torchlight. Veejr marveled at the height of the room - it was quite variable, some places it was low enough to force them all to stoop, other places the ceiling was out of the light entirely - overhead could have been the midnight sky, except there was neither moon nor stars to relieve the blackness. And the quiet when they would stop was spectacular. She was positive she could actually hear her own heart: certainly she could hear the men's breathing. The men had been here many times before, she was sure, because they kept stopping to show the women odd shapes of melted-looking, flowing rock, or to give them "show-off" instructions such as "Just past the bump, look to the right and

176

up!" Everything about the cave was glistening white. And bone dry. Even if a surface looked for all the world like it was dripping wet, a touch told you otherwise.

They squeezed through a narrow door-like opening, and then stopped. They were facing a relatively smooth wall about three metres high, which disappeared into the gloom on their left. Uncle handed a lamp to each person, lit the wicks. The several lamps provided quite a bit of light, but without the smoke and annoying flicker of the torch. When each had a lit lamp, Uncle said "Here is the secret." and he pointed to the wall, raised his torch.

50 - MEN'S-CAVE ART

From floor to low ceiling, the lighted section of wall was covered with crude drawings. Chys and Veejr goggled. Veejr caught her breath, then swept her eyes across the entire wall, soaking it in. Chys did likewise, but an order of magnitude more slowly. Crude stick figures throwing spears, pictures of recognizable prey species and dangerous animals - bison, horses, rhinos and the like. Animals were always shown in profile, nary a full-frontal view, nor a quarter-view, to be found. Positive and negative imprints of hands, sometimes singly, other times like flocks of birds. There were animals both as individuals and in small groups. And some were shown impaled on spears.

The men watched the women, not the wall, studying their initial reactions. Veejr found the various pictures interesting but certainly not enthralling - most of the drawings were much larger than her bark drawings, but she was instantly confident that even her early drawings, long ago discarded, had been much better than this stuff. Some of this work, especially the handprints, she found laughable - not at all interesting since no talent seemed to be involved. Any five-year-old could dream up and execute a mere handprint! She herself certainly had made such prints, back when she was playing with baked clay. Funny how that now seemed so far away and so long ago.

Chys had been far more impressed by the cave than by the art in it. Her reaction to the art was very low-key - especially to the initial stick figures and outlines of hands, all seen through a veil of Veejr explaining excitedly, showing off and not being shushed for it, a first! It had taken Chys only seconds to understand what the first, crudest drawings represented. Whereupon she harrumphed, said nothing, shifted her attention to the adjacent higher-quality drawings, amongst which she was able to identify a horse and a rhino. The men watched her nervously as she studied the work. If for any reason she didn't like their idea, it would not fly. Finally she said firmly "Veejr can already do better than these stick-animals" and patted the girl on the shoulder.

The two men were relieved: no outright rejection or upset. They immediately went off into a half-discussion, half-argument about the meaning of the drawings. Veejr listened with a fraction of her brain whilst the men debated unknowables, but 90% of both Chys's and Veejr's attention was on the drawings themselves.

Curiosity about the drawings was intense, outspoken. There was no question in anyone's mind about the art having been made by humans, sometime long ago – certainly far outside of living memory - and with 'who, how, why, when?' all forgotten. The lack of knowledge allowed for – even encouraged – wild speculations and argument. For Veejr, the most important thing was that SOMEONE ELSE had also figured out how to do this! She was not alone, art was not exclusively hers. That was a shock. But it helped that Chys whispered to her again, privately, "You can do lots better than this."

Going deeper into the cave, the works got more and more realistic, and were soon beyond Veejr's capabilities. That realization triggered Veejr's first twinges of professional jealousy - the quality was a challenge. The rhinos and horses in particular showed striking improvement, getting steadily more realistic. At least, so said the two men: they had actually seen, killed, and butchered such animals, hence had personal knowledge from which to make judgments about realism. Being both a child and female, Veejr had never seen any large game herself, except as cookable bits after extensive butchery. Certainly she had never seen up close the actual head of any big-game animal. Very little of a head was edible except the brain and tongue, hence lugging it home would generally be stupid, when one could dedicate that load-carrying capacity to pure meat. The heads of really large animals were far too heavy to carry home from a kill site, unless of trophy quality and killed near home, like Chys's cave-bear. So Veejr had no basis for an opinion of her own.

Veejr watched the pictures change -clearly improve- as the group went deeper. The artist had certainly gotten better, if it was one person... which she doubted because she could readily see at least three different categories of pictures, different hands. But while the animal pictures changed radically, never was there any improvement in the depiction of humans. THAT, at least, she could judge for herself, from extensive personal experience with the species. The humans were far and away the worst-portrayed beasts. Plus, although most of the stick-figure-humans had no genitals, if genitalia were shown they were always male. Always. Why was that? Maybe because the paintings were all about hunting, and women didn't hunt? Except, of course, that Mom DID hunt! Confusing. She really didn't know, and didn't feel she could ask. And besides, why should she expect the men to know? After all, they hadn't done these paintings - in fact, they knew less about them than SHE did, herself! She felt a sudden lovely inner glow. She might still be a child, but she already knew much more about these pictures than did all the Tribe's adults combined!

The men eventually admitted to the women that they had always been, and still were, uncertain what the drawings meant. In their extensive discussions, it never occurred to either man to wonder if, perhaps, the Men's-Cave drawings were the work of someone who just wanted to draw - like Veejr. No, the questions they posed, and the answers they imagined, were more complex – much more. Were the drawings a plea for help? If so, then to whom? Or perhaps a bit of bragging about successes? Again, if so then to whom? Who could say? If they were appeals, then, importantly, had they worked? If the appeals had worked, should they try it for themselves? Should they just charge ahead and try blindly, to see what happened?

Medicine Man explained that after lots of thought and discussion the two men had agreed on a guess as to the art's function. The drawings were probably intended to promote luck in the hunt, they opined, although they had no theory as to why a drawing might work so. The concept of external, appeasable forces (aka bribable gods) driving human affairs hadn't yet developed. They also felt that better drawings would likely be more effective than poor ones - and there was no doubt in any of their four minds as to which were better and which poorer.

51 - MEN'S-CAVE TODAY

Tuesday midmorning. A gaggle of five graduate students descended on La Fond's Director Joan, unannounced and unexpected. She knew them all well - three from UP, two from other institutions, all five working together out of La Fond's facilities. Working on extending the big UP site.

These were her prime students, the cream, all thoroughly experienced, broadly knowledgeable, all intimately familiar with the various sites in The Valley, and all close to finishing their doctorates. They had been out in the field for a week, but were supposed to be there through this week too. Their sudden unannounced return was a considerable anomaly.

Joan took one look at the expressions on their faces and knew they'd found something. Something significant, or they wouldn't have driven the hundred-plus kilometres and arrived en masse.

Her office had two couches - there was room for everyone. She settled them in, sat on the edge of her desk. Cool and calm, arms folded, she waited a few seconds, then said "Ball's in your court, folks."

Finally Sarah, the most senior of the group, spoke up. "We found something. Last Friday. All of us, working together."

Joan nodded, smiled at the group. "That's what you're SUPPOSED to do. You even get paid to do it. I'm happy for us all that you've made a discovery... but of what, exactly? Why is it worth abandoning the dig and driving home mid-week?"

Sarah was, apparently, the group's chosen voice: "A cave. A whole new cave. Big one. About three kilometres from the main site, the other direction from the Gallery. James found it - when we were hiking as a group, scouting, last Friday. We scared up a rabbit and James chased it, being silly. He saw it disappear under a pile of boulders at the base of The Rampart. He showed us the hole, we got suspicious and widened it using branches as shovels and pry-bars. It was easy: in ten minutes we had a crawl-in entryway. But we only had one flashlight among us."

Joan tilted her head, waiting. The story came tumbling out.

"Joan... it's a whole brand-new cave full of art. I mean FULL! Like the Gallery. But it's got a very different feel, a different theme. Seems to be all hunting scenes. We just did a quick-scan tour on Friday, remember we had only one light, then we got our gear and went back this weekend - about 20 hours each day. We did a rapid survey, with photos. You are never, EVER going to guess what we found! I have the pictures on a thumb-drive - let's put them up on your monitor so we can show you."

Doing the setup took two breathless minutes - Joan was convinced that she was about to be shown something at the least profoundly interesting, and at best, who could say? These were GOOD anthropologists all, just young. For sure they could tell gold from dross, and they were excited. Contagiously.

Sarah continued: "Here's the entry. Nothing inside at first, then about a hundred metres in, there's this..."

A photo of ultra-primitive art, just stick figures, both of animals and a few penis-laden men.

"As you go inwards, the art gets better real fast - just like what we found in the Gallery - it's as if you are watching an individual artist mature in time-lapse. That goes on for a few tens of metres, several dozen images. Then it all changes, blooey, between two successive pictures!"

Joan felt goosebumps rise on her arms, an absolutely lovely feeling for any scientist. Electricity.

"The change is dramatic and instantaneous. Look at this... the pictures on the right are what we're calling "Old Pix" - showing the individual artist's increasing skill. Then THIS happens! A completely different style, we call it "New Style" --- it's much, MUCH better!

And look - the very first big animal done in the New Style is this one - and it's completely X-ed out! Joan, the artist CANCELLED her first drawing! And then she repeated it right alongside, but a whole lot better!"

The female pronouns weren't lost on Joan.

Nor were the expressions of the five, who unanimously focused their Cheshire-Cat gazes on her face, a bank of lasers, waiting.

Joan could hardly swallow. She looked at the projected image, then back at her students, and managed to croak "Her? She?"

The students grinned together as if choreographed, a silent but clear "gotcha!"

Sarah spoke again: "You go past about ten animals, each better than the last, several species, and then you get THIS!"

Joan's hair tried hard to stand up: more goosebumps appeared.

A magnificent bison, three-quarters front view, heavily shaded and done totally in the round, the anatomy correct in every detail. A style with which she was so intimately familiar that she didn't need to look in the lower right corner to check for the SSS in red. Of course it was there... how could it not be?!

Stunned, she sat almost open-mouthed for some seconds. Sarah giggled, said "These were done by Tall Blue. For sure. Hundreds of signed paintings can't all be forgeries!" Then, softly, "Joan, correct me if I'm wrong but I believe we have a first here - one positively-identified artist doing work in TWO caves some tens of kilometres apart."

Then, before Joan could state her agreement, Sarah said "Even farther inside the cave, look at this - TWO signatures again. The same as in the Gallery - triple-ess and five-pointed star!" She took a deep breath, then coasted to a stop with a final image. "Here's the last of the two-signature works. From here on, it's nothing but single-signatures, always the five-star. Not a single more triple-ess. Not one. It's like she just fell off the edge of the world."

Almost reverently, Claude, one of the male students, said "I think they were working together, and then Tall Blue, Ms SSS herself, died. That's why her signature disappears. Tall Blue's protégé carried on, and did a fine job - but with a different hand." Then, "I wonder - was it one of her own kids who succeeded Tall Blue? Or did she find some outside talent to encourage? Would be nice to know."

The group watched Joan. She shook herself, grinned broadly and said "My compliments to you all. Not too shabby for one weekend's work!"

Claude looked like he was about to burst - something clearly remained to be told. Joan looked at him, silently raised one questioning eyebrow, very Mifune-esque.

"There's something else, Joan. Something your husband is going to like - a lot! I learned from him what to look for, even if my brain isn't wired like his. Let me show you a couple of photos."

"Number one - this is taken just a little way down a side-passage, say ten metres, where there isn't any wall-art. Then number two, taken a few more metres inside, just at the start of a big chamber." He pointed to a pair of raggedly-broken calcite stumps, one pointed up from the floor, the other down from the ceiling, resembling a bad set of teeth. He went on: "This used to be a free-hanging smooth wall of calcite. Like a big white curtain. But look at how it's just snapped off --- there are all those big chunks and chips on the floor, the bottom edge of the top part, and the top of the bottom, are battered, broken. I've never seen rough edges like that on a natural formation… nor a whole pile of what looks like stone-cutting debris except beside something that was this obviously cut by humans. Besides - the big chunk that was removed is nowhere to be found. It's just gone."

He paused, let Joan stare and mull, then said "Does this make you think of anything?"

Joan nodded. Her hair came back to attention.

Claude said "I thought it might! Look at these three photos side by side."

A composite view: bottom stump, top stump, and the repaired calcite cover from Spear-Lady's grave. "Look at the pattern of vertical stripes in the calcite itself!"

There wasn't the faintest doubt - the lid had been cut from the missing section of the free-hanging tapestry.

Claude smiled, shrugged his shoulders. "Not only do we have the same artist in the two caves, but by god they cut a chunk of our new cave's calcite to use in Woman Who Kills' interment in the main settlement area. They carried that damned rock all that distance. By hand! After all the work of cutting it. What a job! Guess maybe they couldn't find anything quite right any closer to home. Not to mention they must have thought she was pretty special to do all that extra work!"

Joan turned her gaze on the group and coolly made a half-second's firm eye-contact with each student. Finished with her survey, she crossed her arms, leaned back and said "This is great, folks. I hope it's everything you think it is. In any case, here's the drill. Because you found it, you five own this cave for the next year. We need preliminary maps and an inventory of the readily-accessible art by next weekend. Also an outline of a research plan. With defined roles for each of you- and each will get a first-year grad student as personal assistant for this work. By next Monday I want a five-page write-up over all five signatures - it should summarize what you've found, and also how you think this new material fits into the overall picture we're getting of the people back then - relationships, activities, everything."

Then she laughed. "I would also like you to collectively plan an article at the educated-layman level, explaining what we actually know so far, and with a clearly-labeled section of speculation, all of which has to be firmly grounded in the known materials. For the widest popular consumption. After all, an important part of our job is to educate and inform the public. And also, don't forget that public enthusiasm means more research money! So, do the article in whatever format you want - but it has to have all five of you as co-authors."

The group spent several seconds inventorying one another's faces. Finally Sarah turned to Joan and said "We'd really like to add two co-authors - you and Anton. After all, you've led years of work leading up to this. Besides, we're still students and could undoubtedly use a few more months of leadership."

Joan smiled: "Gracious of you. I agree this far - I'll take the

184

god's-eye view, write an introduction. But you five have to figure out things like group goals and leadership. You're collectively in charge through the next year. Learning to evaluate, plan, direct and report are all parts of what you're supposed to do to earn your paychecks."

52 - PROBLEMS WITH GAME: A PROPOSITION

The Tribe faced a problem. In recent times game had thinned on the upper plateau, said the men to Chys and Veejr, standing in the Men's-Cave - not drastically but significantly. That was worrisome - it would be wonderful if something could be done to stop or reverse that trend. Veejr's unique propensity -not to call it a mania- for drawing had given them an idea. They were, in effect, proposing an experiment. If Veejr could teach herself to draw important game animals, to do so really well, even better than this cave's most accomplished images, then perhaps a few of her best, painted alongside these existing drawings, might help remedy that developing scarcity. It couldn't hurt, so they thought.

Veejr was skeptical of the men's speculations, which made little sense to her. She thought that their oh-so-serious discussions of what the art might be for were purely silly. To begin with, for instance, if they didn't KNOW what the art was for, how could they KNOW that it should be kept for male eyes only? That was nonsense! And she knew for sure what HER OWN art was for – namely to satisfy herself! She wouldn't argue with these two men, but certainly she was not going to attribute a different motive to THIS artist! Not without a good reason. She said nothing aloud.

After the women had closely inspected several large good drawings, the men finally advanced a proposition for Veejr - and for Chys, since the two women were both going to be affected if they agreed. Would Veejr like to help? She (and Chys, of course) would be doing the whole Tribe a favor, and even if it didn't work it was worth trying. They had watched Veejr for a year now, making her rough but recognizable drawings of things, even of human faces, and were sure she could do it. The men weren't dumb - they knew it was going to take dedication and lots of her time to get good at

185

painting. But that was no different in principle from becoming good at knapping or tracking or spear throwing or sewing or even cookery. All of which were valuable skills. It wouldn't just happen overnight! Teaching herself to draw really well would be time-consuming, and would take her away from the family's food-chores, the men understood that. And any such change would surely upset Chys's routines. Because the idea was to benefit the whole Tribe, the Tribe would make up, to Chys, the decrease in support due to Veejr's being otherwise occupied.

The men gave the women time to think, as the whole group toured the rest of the artwork, which ended with several horses and bison each a metre tall and accurately done. The string of images ended abruptly half-way down a long flat wall. There they stopped to talk again. Veejr was doing the typical young-kid's anxiety-and-anticipation squirm, hoping for a favorable outcome - she really wanted Mother to okay this project.

Chys opined, "I don't see why these pictures could help in the hunt! All you need in hunting is knowledge of how the animals behave, an ability to track them, and a good spear. Not this." Although that sounded like the start of a "no", she surprised them all when that opinion was followed quickly by "But it would be interesting to try." Veejr's hopes rose, as did the men's. Chys paused, thought, then told the men, "I will propose a bargain with you. The Tribe accepted my daughter, with her blue eyes, but there were some who thought she would bring us all bad luck. Now, she is the only person who might be able to help us try your idea, so even if the idea doesn't work, that's already good luck for the Tribe, just being able to try. And if it does work, then that would be really good luck!" Another pause, then her patented grin: "We will help. Veejr can practice all she wants, until she's really good, and then we can try your idea. But you have to tell the whole Tribe, tomorrow, that you know Veejr is bringing at least a little good luck to us, and maybe a lot of it. But you don't have to tell them exactly what it is, so you can keep this cave a secret. And, if Veejr does not want to do it, she does not have to!"

Chys's body language brooked no debate - she was very sure of herself and her position in the Tribe. The two very senior men were totally at sea in negotiating a contract with a woman. Especially a she-bear of a woman who was busy protecting her cub. They took the easy route - and agreed to her terms. Veejr loved the idea, and hugged Chys hard, muttered her thanks. Unlimited freedom to do her art, for at least a whole year!

53 - FIRST ARTIST-IN-RESIDENCE

Veejr thus became the world's first subsidized artist, functionally the first ever National Artist in Residence. The title, however, would have to wait.

Mother and daughter discussed the whole idea on the way home, and agreed that it was the most interesting project they had ever encountered - so much more interesting than, say, tanning leather. Or clamming! Of course they would do it! Which really meant that Veejr would do the work - become the required artist. Mama would be supportive however she could.

Veejr practiced enthusiastically, to the verge of becoming the official Tribal Pest. She did sketches of almost everyone in the Tribe - and likewise of everything the Tribe owned. She even dreamed up and executed the idea of pictures of events as contrasted with pictures of things. And she didn't take herself too seriously - that winter during a brief but very heavy snowstorm, a serious white-out, perhaps twenty people had clustered around the main fire amidst the swirling snow. Veejr coughed for attention, held up an obviously blank sheet of dead-white bark and asked "How do you like my picture of the storm?"

In fairly short order the whole Tribe, including idiot Brother, could understand her drawings at a glance. But within the Tribe, drawing was, and remained, exclusively HER skill. Veejr had no competition, and liked it that way. Potential copycats were intimidated by her proprietary attitude, her steadily increasing height, her blue eyes, and -of course- Mama Chys's reputation.

54 - CLOSE ENCOUNTERS

Nearly a year later, after months of intense practice and growth both physically and artistically, there arrived a problem long fore-seen but finally needing to be faced squarely. Veejr had worked hard and improved enormously. However, down on the uppermost flood plain where the Tribe lived, there was no big game for her to study. That was a problem, because the goal was to do new art that would be much better than the existing art, art especially of the important big game animals.

She could draw a good tree, now, and a rabbit of course. She had done respectable squirrels, marmots, even a spider. And a gorgeous long-tailed pheasant-like bird that made her wish she had in her kit lots of colors instead of merely black and white, and occasionally some red or yellow ocher. The men understood that to do a good job, Veejr would need ochers and time to learn to use them well. The ochers were obtained for her, under Medicine Man's orders, by hunting parties whenever they encountered a properly-stocked trader. She had even done a simple, primitive landscape, with several trees and crows. She was still puzzled about how to deal with relative perceived sizes - in a picture with a crow drawn large enough to be recognized, she was hard put to add a tree that didn't make the whole arrangement somehow ludicrous. On paper the tree and crow were the same general size, but they were certainly not so in real life. She could do respectable profiles of peoples' faces, much to general amusement, and with considerable work she could produce reasonable planar, expressionless frontal views of human faces. Most of her recent works could be recognized as individuals and correctly referred to the model. She was prolific: almost everyone in the Tribe eventually had at least one picture of him or herself, an original "Veejr". Both fragile and biodegradable, no example survived a half-dozen generations.

That was all well and good, but now, if she were to advance towards the tribal goal, she really needed to see, to study up close, the animals she intended to portray.

Hearsay just wouldn't work. Men could describe the species until their breath ran out, but that didn't really help. After all, they might be trying, for example, to describe in words the differences between the faces of a horse and a gazelle, and to succeed they needed to do it well enough so that a person, an artist, who had never seen either, could accurately portray both. And of course none of the men could draw a circle, much less a recognizable whole animal.

The problem, then, was simple and straightforward: no personal knowledge of the critters she was expected to draw. The solution seemed simple, too - make use of her now well-developed semi-eidetic memory. Just two or three good close-up views of each kind of animal should serve her for a lifetime of drawing. The key was getting really close. Preferably, of course, without also getting killed.

Being both female and young, Veejr had never been on any expeditions to the big animals' habitat on The Plateau. She would need permission from the men to go with them on a big-game hunt, and that posed difficulties. Her presence, however theoretically important to the Tribe, would drastically slow a hunting party - or so the men all argued. Without any evidence, of course. Plus, in their view, taking the time to help her get close to animals, but without intending to kill them, was the purest idiocy. And men on the hunt were supreme short-term pragmatists - for them, the only possible point of a hunting trip was the kill!

In short, the hunters' answer was not only no, but HELL NO!!!

Had Chys fully recovered her strength and running form after the bear-wallop to her chest a couple of years earlier, she would have been able to force the issue by joining a hunting party herself and bringing Veejr - thus allowing Mama to handle the "unwanted girl-child along for no good reason" problem. But no: full recovery to her old hunting form had not happened, and obviously would not. That being admitted, she wasn't mobility impaired, just not up to hunting-party standards.

The difficulty of evaluating short term costs versus long-term societal benefits reared its ugly head for neither the first nor last time in Tribal history. Unlike the male hunters, Chys understood the larger context, and agreed that provided one didn't starve enroute, the long-term goal was more important to Tribal survival. Veejr of course thought the whole idea of such a trip simply marvelous.

Luckily, the Tribe's need for Veejr to see in person the big-game species also coincided nicely with an agenda of Chys's own, giving her extra incentive to push ahead. She wanted Veejr to have the same expanded world-view as did Chys herself. Much of that view came from her experiences as a hunter on the vast plains of The Plateau. Just in terms of physical space alone, the difference between being tucked into The Valley and exposed naked on the huge plains was well worth experiencing. Two radically different worlds whose rules were very different. Veejr should know both. The experience had certainly changed how Chys thought - for one thing, people were much less significant once you had seen them and dealt with them on the enormous Plateau! When you thought about humans and their size relative to that nearly infinite land-scape, people were so PUNY as to be almost invisible.

55 - WOMEN ON THEIR OWN

So, having been emphatically rejected by the all-male hunting team, and after a night's thought, Chys proposed something unique. She and Veejr would undertake their own expedition, independently of the male hunters. This would take the entire burden off the men. It would avoid interfering with an important hunt, and undoubtedly do a better job of providing for Veejr's artistic needs. That plan was carried by Uncle to the other men. Male agreement and relief were unanimous and immediate.

The women would make more than one trip, if needed - exactly how many would depend on their luck and skill. Like the men, they would be hunting big game, but in a very different way. Seeking not meat, but something immaterial, to wit purely visual knowledge. They would go together, at Chys's speed, up to The Plateau. Once topside, there should be no problems. Chys was an experienced hunter and a fine tracker - a superb stalker, well known for her abil-ity to get within jabbing distance of suspicious, wary game animals. Years ago, purely showing off, she had collected a huge long-lasting bruise on her thigh when she got within kicking range of a wild colt before it noticed her. That sort of closeness was exactly what Veejr needed.

In a trip lasting half a moon or so, thought Chys, they could probably get Veejr up-close views of many (and with luck, perhaps most) of the major game species. It would be fun: they would travel very light. Either she or Veejr, alone, could easily provide all the small game they needed to eat well. It would be exciting, teaching her daughter about all the strange plants and animals common on The Plateau but unknown in The Valley.

Some days later, the pair set off on what may have been mankind's first hiking vacation - they were off-duty and doing something utterly unnecessary for the survival of anyone. Regardless of the 'official rationale' for the trip, they were going essentially for the fun of it: pure luxury consumption of time and resources. They carried between them the basics for such a trip, in two well-designed and constructed rucksacks, complete with shoulder-straps that left their hands and arms completely free. Two well-furred small hides as blankets, tinder, spark-making rocks, a small amount of food, several knives, their hunting spears, spare parts, a small stone hatchet, twenty metres of thong, a bone awl for sewing leather. Veejr carried several sheets of her paper, and a few carefully-wrapped charsticks. Just in case there was time to actually draw something rather than merely do tracking and viewing. Chys also carried the dried anal scent glands of a male beaver, wrapped in a deer's bladder - a standard bit of hunting equipment. She explained to Veejr that the pungent oil from the glands, when rubbed freely over their bodies, would hide their human-scent and make it easier to closely approach even very wary animals - most of the large game-animals had learned long ago that humans were to be strictly avoided.

They departed via the trail along the base of The Rampart, headed for the side-rift up which Gerard would ride his bicycle homeward some 40,000 years in the future, after making the first bicycle descent of The Rampart. As they walked to that rift, Chys and Veejr passed within spear-throw of the closed and hidden entrance to the cave that would become Veejr's private gallery, and which would someday link Gerard and Veejr across the millennia. Farther on, Chys made a small detour past the cairn marking Monster's grave. She explained the cairn, made it clear that Veejr's father

191

was buried here: that was why she'd grown up without a father in the family. Veejr understood the concepts of dead, gone, and burial. Details beyond that were unimportant, at least right now. They continued on.

56 - THE PLATEAU

Veejr's first view of The Plateau, as they topped the final slope, was breathtaking. A plain dotted with individual trees and small groves spread out for tens of kilometres - the horizon at the end of the plain was actually below them. For the first time ever, she had an unimpeded view of the far horizon. Behind them the world dropped spectacularly away: down in their home valley every horizon Veejr had ever seen had been above the viewer -well above. The new sense of huge distances was both enthralling and verging on terrifying. Also deeply disturbing was the very different perspective - scattered trees went from huge (because close) to mere dots, with every intervening size. But the most impressive thing was the mountains, looming up from beyond the horizon line, perhaps 90 or 100 kilometres away. Impossibly far. Both the plain and the mountains were too big for instant belief. Although the plain was green, as were the bottom halves of the mountains, the mountain-tops were glistening white. And their edges were so very, very clear and sharp against the sky! She stared at the skyline with intent to remember. Nothing, she was sure, could ever equal this view. Certainly this new world-view outclassed the mere animals that were what the trip was all about. Future artists would coin the term "The Sublime" for both such a view, and the emotion evoked by it.

Chys remembered her own first reaction to this very same view, and she understood her daughter's just standing stock-still, staring. Finally, she began gently to explain. Yes, it was a huge distance to the white-topped mountains. Nobody from the Tribe had ever gone that far, but there were other people who lived over there - it was from them that the Tribe got flint nodules and obsidian and Veejr's ochers, trading mostly for dried fish - the Tribe's river had an endless supply of fresh water and fish, the other Tribes did not. One might occasionally encounter foreign hunters and traders up here -

but they were always friendly, not like the blue-eyed Monster who was Veejr's father.

A traveling stranger had told her that the spectacular mountain-tops were white because they were permanently covered with frozen water, the white kind that had twice last winter fallen from the sky at home, and which had lasted on the ground for less than a day each time. It seemed odd that such cold, hard, white water should stay on the ground all year in the mountains! Veejr thought for a minute, then said "It must be really cold there, all the time. It would be a bad place to live!" It was a deduction Chys had never made for herself, and she was impressed. She agreed.

Chys explained that most of the smaller objects in view were big trees far away. She pointed out a cluster of tiny dots of a differ-ent shape from the trees beside them. "One day's walk from here to there." she said. Veejr goggled. She was finally beginning to get a sense of scale. "But the right-hand dots, the tiny round ones, those are bison. Each one is taller than a man. You've eaten parts of such animals. They are very hard to kill --- they form a circle with their heads outwards and work together to protect one another. They put all the babies in the center - very hard to kill those bison, they're too smart!"

Then she pointed out a faint game-trail nearby, and suggested they take it. If game could walk there, so could people, and game would invariably proceed from one water-hole to another, so water was a certainty even if they found no animals immediately.

They made a good team. Chys was very pleased: Veejr under-stood silent movement, and vocal silence too. Chys pointed out and explained various signs of large animals as they walked the trail. A small group of gazelle-deer had preceded them by perhaps half an hour, moving the same direction as the women. Veejr had eaten this animal her whole life, but had never seen a live one. The first "new species" for her life-list, if they could find them. Chys knew where the animals were headed - to a watering hole she had often stopped at herself. Waterhole number three of the dozens occurring near the crest of The Rampart.

They traveled steadily: the trail eventually curved away from the lip of The Rampart, heading in the general direction of the distant mountains, out across the infinite-seeming plains. For Veejr there were many things about the plateau countryside that were new, intriguing, sometimes a bit frightening. It took almost an hour of steady travel towards the mountains before she suddenly realized what the most disquieting aspect of the environment was - NO STONES! In her entire life, she had never been anywhere that rocks (big, little, huge, tiny) didn't litter the landscape near and far. Here, there were literally no rocks at all visible in any direction - none save the very mountains themselves. When she explained her observation and the nervousness it caused, Mother just laughed, patted her on the shoulder, and said "There are lots of new things up here, daughter. Tigers instead of bears to worry about, and other things like that. But you'll get used to most of them. I did."

As the women came over a small rise, they simultaneously spotted the deer - six females, one male - at the water-hole several hundred metres ahead. The women squatted to remain undetected: Chys had taken in the entire layout and its possibilities in one glance. Now she described the situation to Veejr, explained how they must proceed. These were not dangerous beasts - too small. Very nervous animals - flighty, and speedy once spooked. The little group would probably stay at the water only for a few hours because big predators, wolves, cats, would come in the evening to drink. To survive, the herd by then must be long gone. This was a very good size of group to hunt, if one needed meat. But during some times of the year a massive herd of these animals might number far beyond any counting, paving the plain shoulder-to-shoulder for a distance equal to many minutes' run.

At the moment, Chys pointed out, the wind was favorable, blowing from the little herd towards themselves. No need this time for the beaver-gland. But the animals weren't dumb, they knew they were vulnerable from downwind and they would be keeping an especially sharp eye in that direction. Which meant Chys and Veejr would have to be extra careful to avoid being seen. The women would use the tall grass and occasional bush as cover, while also taking advantage of tiny irregularities in the terrain which Chys

194

pointed out to her amazed and very attentive daughter. Clearly, chasing quail and rabbits back home was a whole different universe from the process of stalking big game!

"We will leave our packs and spears here" said Chys. "Follow right behind me - stick to the ground, and not a sound no matter what!"

Down now on her belly like Chys, following precisely in her path, Veejr composed herself, studying every inch of the terrain immediately at hand, over which she would have to crawl silently despite the brittleness of most of the plants. The opportunities for making noise were endless. But she was determined not to disappoint Mama - or herself!

Ninety minutes later, having moved at a third of Chys's normal stalking pace specifically to accommodate Veejr's inexperience, they were hidden behind a tiny, twenty centimetre bump in the ground, covered with half-metre grasses and two short bushes. They hadn't had even a glimpse of their quarry for over half an hour, but Chys knew exactly where the animals would be. Veejr had lost situational awareness and was just following Mama carefully. Chys motioned her to come forward, to lie beside her with the breeze in their faces. Veejr could now detect the herd's warm-animal smell, but could see nothing of them. She was practically shivering with anticipation. Mama smiled, covered Veejr's mouth with her hand - absolute silence! Then she carefully parted the lowest branches of the bush. She had done far better than she'd thought: a fine view, a great start!

Veejr goggled - suddenly, her whole world was full of deer. Two hornless females lying on their sides, one facing her and one facing away, both within ten metres. She could see their breathing, see ribs moving under skin. Another was cleaning herself, a ridiculously long tongue washing back and forth. Two more females standing, grazing, one within five metres, almost touching distance! "How in the world," thought Veejr, "...did Mama know? How did she get us this close!?"

She mentally photographed the whole scene, especially the cleaner's actions, which might make a very interesting picture.

The buck, in his prime, was standing watch, showing them his full profile, head up, displaying his magnificent set of long, slender, straight horns. He was alertly sniffing the wind, and scanning the horizon - and failing to spot the humans so close by. He actually did remind Veejr of one Men's-Cave drawing. She snorted silently to herself as she studied the animals, putting them forever into her memory-banks. She was sure that she could already do better than that other artist, her unknown rival! These animals were MAGNIF-ICENT - they deserved better artistry! She studied the animals until Chys touched her on the shoulder. Eye to eye, Chys grinned at the girl's near-paralysis, signed with her eyes and lips - was Veejr done studying for the moment?

Yes, she supposed so. Why?

Chys raised her hands, made a silent clapping motion, signed for Veejr to watch the animals. One handclap and the entire group levitated - Veejr was convinced they literally went straight up. In five seconds they were out of sight, leaving a smell in the air and tiny hanging puffs of dust where feet met ground. Indelibly in her memory were the images of panicked animals floating weightless in midair, eyes wide in surprise and fear, ears rigidly vertical, every erect tail flashing its white underside in warning. Airborne, and ready to dash as soon as they returned to Earth.

The women stood, Chys pointed to the fleeing herd, already two hundred metres off. "See!? It isn't hard to get close. That was easy distance for spearing! But with some animals it can be VERY hard to get away again once you get close. Retreating before you are too close is something every hunter has to learn. You do NOT want to have to run from a rhino - that's what happened to your oldest brother, and he lost the race and is buried out here somewhere. So always plan at least two escape routes before you start approaching a big animal. Even one of those 'harmless-looking' little gazelles can kill a human with a lucky kick!" Then she asked "So, daughter, was that close enough so that you could see everything you needed? Can you draw that animal now?"

Veejr hugged Mama again, assured her that indeed it had been plenty close enough. Then, giggling half-seriously she said "Maybe we won't need to get THAT close to the big dangerous animals!?" Mama just laughed: she was sure from Veejr's behavior so far that getting close to really dangerous animals was something they could manage just fine.

Hours later, having made real headway on the long trek towards the herds of animals between them and the mountains, they found a good sleeping-spot. They had killed three rabbits mid-afternoon. Now Chys and Veejr took the rabbits a full 200 metres from the campsite for butchering. Chys explained that this would separate themselves from the smells and remains that would surely bring scavengers or predators.

Back at the campsite they built a tiny cooking fire, using Chys's special spark-making rocks, plus fluff from a dried cat-tail for tinder. It was a time-consuming process - the rocks produced only a very few long-lasting sparks and the fire-maker always got plenty of exercise. But eventually the tinder would catch.

Three rabbits made not a large meal, but adequate. They took the remains back to the butchery-spot. Enroute they gathered enough wood to feed the fire overnight, then had a discussion of possible night-time predators, the need for fire, and for standing watches - especially the need for the watcher NOT to go to sleep! Predators that would attack a human in the dark were very rare, but still - caution, always caution. "Nobody has ever died from an excess of watchfulness, Daughter!"

Then, in a reminiscing mood, Chys told Veejr for the first time the detailed story about being captured by Monster, how her captors had made a mistake, they had done Chys a huge favor by not mounting a night-time guard. How that negligence had probably saved Chys's life. Eventually that mistake had resulted in Chys getting control of Monster's huge spear, with which she had killed him. Veejr was impressed both by the story and by being brought into Mama's confidence. The fact they were discussing her own father didn't disturb Veejr in the least - after all, she had never met the man. She was feeling more and more like an adult - very different from the 'child vs. adult' confusion back home. She liked the change.

197

Next morning they started off well before sunrise. Chys was quite pleased by yesterday's exercise, and from half-way up a tree she showed Veejr a pair of grey objects, in the middle distance - objects which she declined to identify. Identification would be Veejr's job. They watched patiently for some minutes: Veejr was sure they were just good-sized rocks, the first she'd seen on The Plateau - until one of them stood up and galloped a few metres sideways. These animals were HUGE! Mother then gave in and told her they were rhinos, and that they were the most dangerous animals: more dangerous even than cave bears because rhinos are so huge. As heavy as sixty men - as heavy as half the entire Tribe combined! - with skin too thick to drive a spear through. They were herbivores, so at least they weren't hunting YOU, but they were bad-tempered and had such poor eyesight that they would on general principles attack any unusual thing seen, smelled or heard. And for all their magnificent bulk, they were blindingly fast.

As the women discussed approaches and escape routes, the wind rose to a mild, steady breeze. They would circle to be down-wind, then sneak up to where they could get into a large tree close to the pair. Chys explained that rhinos never seemed to look upwards, probably because a rhino had nothing to fear from above. So being up high in a good strong tree was almost like being invisible to the beasts.

This time, just as insurance against changes in the wind, they rubbed the beaver-gland oil over every bit of their exposed skin - it wasn't a horribly unpleasant stink, and it certainly did mask their own odor.

Sixty minutes of stealth, and they managed to get themselves up in a large, very sturdy tree at the edge of a small copse that might be the rhinos' home. They climbed silently to a safe, comfortable place to sit, about four metres off the ground. As the sun continued its own climb and the air heated up, the rhinos drifted into the shade of the closest-neighboring tree, adjacent to the women's. There they browsed, bumping shoulders amiably as they went. This allowed the women an extended close-up study of the beasts: Veejr could see such detail! Even eyelashes, and the strange prehensile pointed upper lip. Plus the crazy little bird who walked about on the rhino's backs, pecking at the heavy skin, a most ridiculous sight. The rhinos ignored the bird, and they never looked up. After an hour or more the pair suddenly lifted their heads simultaneously, sniffed the breeze, and trotted off together out of sight, going straight upwind. Chys said she believed they were both youngish males, and that probably they had smelled a female.

She and Veejr beat a silent retreat on a reciprocal course. Chys told her, later, that she'd never been so close to anything so powerful - and they admitted to each other that they'd been seriously frightened. No, frightened was too strong - perhaps 'concerned' would do? Whatever! Their oh-so-careful stalking had worked perfectly, and now rhino images were indelibly stored in Veejr's brain.

Early afternoon, and small-game hunting was good. They spooked and killed two more rabbits, a porcupine and four large quail-like ground birds. They gutted and skinned them where killed - no more predator attractants- then threaded all seven little carcasses onto a cord for easy carrying. The sunshine was warm, and when they found a large rain-puddle beside a shade-tree, they stopped to rest. Veejr got out a sheet of her bark and a fine charcoal stick, thought about what she should draw, settled on doing the head of a rhino - such exciting animals. Chys watched over Veejr's shoulder as the drawing swiftly took shape, Veejr's memory providing every needed detail. She felt it was one of her better drawings to date, so she signed it with her SSS. Chys was openly admiring, and said it was the best ever - and it had taken so little time! Not to mention being of an animal Veejr had met for the first time today. Impressive! Veejr packed it away carefully so it would not get smudged.

After a couple of hours' rest, they set off again. As they topped a gentle rise, they spotted a group of several people in the middle distance. Chys froze: Veejr imitated her. These were the very first non-Tribe humans Veejr had ever seen, so she was intensely curious and somewhat frightened, but copied Mother's sang-froid. Easy to tell from the mix of men, women, and one small girl-child younger than Veejr, that the group was peaceful - not a war party. Not to mention that each of the foreigners carried a knapsack larger by far than the women's.

The alien group's behavior made it very clear that Chys and Veejr had been seen. The leader raised and waved his spear in greeting, then turned its point downwards and stabbed the earth. Chys returned the salute: neutrality and peaceful intentions declared and agreed to. Veejr was surprised - apparently Mother intended to meet with the strangers. Chys relaxed, said "I know these people. We have met before during big hunts."

They stood fast as the aliens approached. Chys said quietly "They are very weak hunters. Study their spears and how they handle them. The spears are poor quality. For killing rabbits maybe, but nothing larger. They are a strange people - they are a family of traders - they carry valuable stuff from one settlement to another, and trade those things for food and skins and whatever else they need. A foolish way of living, not doing your own hunting. But there are several families like this up here on The Plateau. Some of the things they trade are useful." She smiled at Veejr: "It's from people like these that we get the big obsidian pebbles we use to make blades, and also your painting colors. Exchanging smoked fish for special rocks - it sounds sort of stupid, but it isn't. Without these people, our Tribe couldn't make a living hunting because we wouldn't have any spears! There are no knapping pebbles near our home. We'd have to move!" Veejr understood, but made no comment, just filed the information. She was learning so much, so fast! Veejr found Mother's store of knowledge, and her ability to both use it and teach, quite impressive.

As the family arrived, Chys said perhaps four words of greeting in what was clearly the group's language. A perfect ice-breaker. Smiles and nods all around, then intense sign-language. The alien child was bolder than Veejr, and obviously quite used to encountering strangers up close. She strode right up to her fellow-child and from touching range jabbered away in her unintelligible native tongue. Veejr understood only the body language, which, fortunately, was entirely friendly, as was the limited signing they were able to exchange.

The aliens -especially the women- were obviously puzzled by

Veejr and Chys being out on the plain without menfolk. Sign-jabber helped explain the situation. Meanwhile, the men were eyeing the little stringer of small-game - it was obvious the aliens were all hungry. Even Veejr could tell that they had little idea of weaponry - such rinky-dink spears! - hence little chance of providing much real game for themselves. She understood at once, from Mama's comments, that if these people couldn't provide well for themselves, then perhaps they would be interested in trading something for food. Food being a non-problem for herself and Mama.

Trader-Girl was wearing a bracelet made of extraordinarily pretty small snail-shells. Veejr had never seen a shell other than from a fresh-water clam or mussel, and those were not in the least pretty. In fact, river clamshells were a pain - they had to be carried deep into the main cave and discarded into a huge sinkhole where all Tribal trash went. Except for the big shells kept for use as lamps.

These traders' shells were cowries, each about three centimetres long, shiny, multicolored, almost iridescent. Veejr was utterly captivated by the baubles-on-a-string. So was Chys, but she managed a poker-face. As she had just told Veejr, she had met such folks before and knew what to expect. Nonetheless, she was every bit as captivated as Veejr. She was certain that nobody in the Tribe had ever seen, much less owned, anything as pretty as those shells.

One of the men -an experienced trader- had been watching Veejr's eyes, saw them light up at seeing the child's bracelet. Silently, he opened his pack and delved, brought out a leather bag full of cowries, each with holes drilled in it for a string. Jewelry-making supplies. He grinned, showed off the contents -several hundred shells- then re-stowed the bag.

All the while, the two alien women couldn't keep their eyes off the little pile of carcasses. Chys and Veejr had far more than they needed for a single meal, there was no easy way to quickly preserve any excess, so Chys diplomatically volunteered the heap of game for a communal dinner. The generous invitation was accepted instantly. Whilst the alien women cooked, the others all sat around a small fire, sign-talking. As part of the general conversation, the two men unpacked several more small bags: traders, yes, but at the moment they were showing off more than marketing. Red ocher. Small flint nodules. Deer horn. The bag of cowries. A very small double-bag of something the women had never imagined - small bright-blue pebbles and deeper-blue flakes, shiny and glittering, some of them a blue that almost exactly matched Veejr's eyes. Veejr's eyes had attracted brief hard stares but no open comment so far. Now the man laughed and pointed out the similarity of color: everyone took turns comparing stones against eyes, exclaiming. There were no worries raised about bad luck.

Trader-Girl was waxing slightly obnoxious, teasing by waving her braceleted wrist in front of Veejr's face. Finally Veejr became a bit irked and jealous, signed "STOP IT!" and reached for her own pack, extracted the stack of bark sheets. The move got everyone's attention.

Veejr's turn to show off. She untied the stack, pulled out the rhino-head drawing, held it up so the strangers could see it, pointed at it, then herself, made drawing motions until she was reasonably certain that the aliens understood.

The reaction was everything a jealous girl could have wanted. Every one of the alien group, excepting only the child, recognized the image almost immediately. Wide-eyed amazement shone in all their faces. Chys explained in her more accomplished sign language. The drawing was passed almost reverently from hand to hand, until it came full circle. Veejr decided to show definitively that the drawing wasn't simply her property, but rather her product. She pulled out a clean sheet of bark, selected a brush, and did a very quick rabbit - pretty much her stock in trade, she'd practiced so much on the beast. The entire alien family clustered and watched, obviously convinced that they were seeing some sort of deep magic. A bit of tree-bark was somehow being transformed into a living rabbit before their very eyes, by this mere child - a most impressive demonstration of a skill unknown to them.

After dinner, one of the men brought up an interesting subject - and he addressed Veejr directly. He obviously understood that the drawings belonged to Veejr, not to Chys, and in slow, careful signs he asked if she would be willing to part with the rhino drawing. If she would, perhaps she and he could make a trade? He'd noticed that she liked the child's cowrie bracelet.

Hmmmmm....

Veejr didn't fully understand the concept, much less the intricacies, of trading, so she looked over at Chys for guidance. Chys took her aside for a moment of privacy: "Here is how this works - he will offer much less than he thinks the drawing is worth. Say 'no' and he will raise the offer, but he may pretend to be angry each time – it's a game, really. You just keep saying no until I nod my head, or until you both agree. Don't say 'yes' too soon – remember, he has some idea in his mind about what to do with your drawing. Remember also that what is of no value to you and me may be very valuable to HIM! Once you agree, once you say 'yes', there's no changing allowed, so don't say YES too quickly. We do this sort of bargaining about our smoked fish every winter but usually we get flint and obsidian and ocher - not pretty shells. I've never seen such beautiful things before... much prettier than the fish vertebrae we use for beads!"

The man clearly was smitten with the drawing, and also both amused and a bit aggravated by Veejr's adamant 'NO' as he kept increasing the offer. Finally, Veejr turned to Chys and said - knowing the aliens would not understand - "This is fun. I want two bracelets like the girl's, one for you and one for me. And I really want some of the blue beads. Would that be okay?"

Mom sighed, nodded, muttered "If you can get it. You are doing very well so far."

Clearly the trader had some idea in mind, some plan to which the rhino drawing could be profitably bent. The bargaining lasted over half an hour. She got what she wanted. Bargaining, she discovered, was FUN!

The value of the cowries being entirely abstract, they qualified as money - and this particular transaction was the first-ever cash sale of a work of art.

The man used his hand to measure Chys's wrist, spoke to his child, who immediately extracted from her own pack a carefully-rolled hank of very long black human hair. She selected several

203

strands and in short order had two bracelet-strings of braided hair - a material that for all its apparent softness and weakness would eventually provide the motive power for the projectiles from Roman catapults. She worked quickly and produced two bracelets, each with two eleven-cowrie strands. Chys and Veejr were pleased. Then the man took out his pouch of lapis and turquoise. He spread the stones out on the skin: some were just smooth pebbles, but most were manufactured beads, made to be strung, each about the size of a thumbnail, with one flat side, a central hole for a string, the top side smoothly rounded. The trader held up ten fingers, and gave Veejr her choice. She asked Chys for help. Veejr wanted those stones that were closest to her own eye-color. Chys would have to do the selection as to color match - and the deal was for beads only, no pebbles.

The ten chosen beads got wrapped up in a twist of leather and handed to Veejr. She was so pleased with the whole exchange that she quickly finished the rabbit drawing and simply gave it to the trader, who in turn was both astonished and extremely happy.

Veejr hadn't known it, but in the trading society from which the aliens came, such a gift required reciprocity. For a moment he hesitated, then made a decision, reached into his pack for another small as-yet-unopened sack. Out tumbled three thumb-sized bits of very peculiar-looking silver-gray rock with smooth knobby surfaces. Plus four chunks of black rock shiny with embedded gold-colored flecks. He watched the women's faces, realized that they didn't understand. He picked up one of each type, smacked them together with a hard scraping motion. A huge shower of big, long-lived sparks flew: the women were so startled that the trader laughed, then handed the rocks to Veejr. The gray one was far too heavy for its size, but it lay nicely in the hand. The trader made striking motions: Veejr did it, and sparks flew again. Chys gaped - she understood immediately. Really GOOD fire-making rocks! She'd heard of them but never seen one. With ordinary rocks, you were lucky to get one usable spark every ten whacks – but these magical gray rocks, the heavy ones, were so hard they never broke and never wore out, and always gave plenty of sparks with one stroke. An immensely valuable tool. She practically salivated with instant jealousy and need.

Then the trader did the most amazing thing: he signed "thank-you" for the rabbit picture, and handed Veejr the smallest meteorite, gave Chys a chunk of the iron pyrite, grinned at their shock, and re-packaged his wares.

The groups parted next morning after breakfast. Veejr nearly stumbled several times from eyeing her jewelry instead of the ground. Eventually Chys declared the distraction too much to deal with and put both bracelets away in her pack for safe-keeping, along with the infinitely more valuable fire-rocks.

Midmorning, they spotted a cluster of airborne dots circling over something in the far distance. Chys headed them straight that direction, explaining that the dots were seriously large birds special-izing in eating dead animals. The women would go that direction, but warily - a dead animal usually had been killed by a large preda-tor, and they didn't want to have an argument with such a beast - themselves being armed only against rabbits.

There were no predators on the site, but there was part of a meaty bison skeleton, the vulture-attractant. The women walked up to within a few metres of the vultures - the birds were totally preoc-cupied and utterly unafraid of humans. Veejr got her fill of close-up viewing - the birds were far bigger than any she'd ever seen in The Valley, totally fascinating. Their landings and takeoffs indelibly imprinted visual details - feet and legs outstretched, wings swinging powerfully, big terminal flight-feathers grabbing air like hands try-ing to catch water. Birds and carcasses would ever after grace her art.

In the next few days they managed close encounters with sev-eral more important big-game species. And eventually, after a week, they had circled back to the top of The Rampart. They descended more or less via Gerard's future bicycle route.

Uncle and Medicine Man were anxious that she should start immediately on the additions to the Men's-Cave art, but Veejr con-vinced them that she needed more study and practice first... it would be best to do really good work in the cave right from the start. They agreed to be patient for a few moons - but not too many! Veejr and Chys made three week-long expeditions, and Veejr used up an inordinate amount of bark, before she felt prepared to try.

57 - GRAND OPENING - GERARD'S GALLERY

The week after Gerard's public lecture, he led a small group to his Gallery for an initial visit, a grand opening. In planning for the visit, Joan decided to exploit the find as a perfect opportunity for proposing close cooperation between La Fond and UP - after all, the two institutions were working cheek-by-jowl, on much the same settlement, tribe, and underlying pool of artifacts. Sharing could do nothing but accelerate and improve the work of both parties.

Many felt like they were at the premier of a neolithic-arts version of King Tut's tomb. Joan and Anton came, of course - plus a few of the most senior graduate students and several bright young faculty from both institutions. Also present was the UP's Dean, who had earlier been Joan's personal guest at Gerard's lecture. It was an all-day trip, by 100% professionals, properly equipped. In 4WD vehicles. With box lunches. With a professional videographer to capture everything digitally, using a low-light camera.

Driving along the base of The Rampart, Gerard pointed out the path he'd taken down the cliff on his bike years ago, enroute to discovering what was already being called "Gerard's Gallery". The troops were properly impressed. They also passed close to the site of Goliath's cairn, just a few kilometres from Gerard's Gallery. That site had been worked to death without producing anything except Goliath in his grave. Nada.

At the Gallery, they crawled single-file into the antechamber. Gerard gathered them together, said "Look!" and lit up the entry-way SSS. A collective short gasp as everyone recognized the mark from Spear-Lady's buried calcite gravestone.

Anton stared, added his own flashlight beam. "It sure looks like this mark was made with fingers, not a stick or brush. So - let me try something..." He paused, stretched upwards, couldn't reach the mark. Satisfied, he said " Hah. That answers one question - Tall Blue is the owner of the mark. It's her signature, maybe even her name! Spear-Lady is way too short to have done this without a step-ladder, and Tall Blue is taller than me, so she'd have had no prob-

206

lem. Given that all of Gerard's photos of this art show this same symbol, it's got to mean that Tall Blue is the artist." There was a general murmur of agreement.

"Follow me" said Gerard. He explained the knotted safety-string as they worked their way to the start of the paintings.

Despite Gerard's lecture and slide-show, from the very first painting, the group was uniformly flabbergasted, nearly speechless. After fifteen or twenty increasingly realistic paintings, Joan asked, a bit louder than needed, "How many images, again?"

"Well over five hundred. I don't have an accurate count yet. And what, exactly, constitutes "an image" is anything but clear – for instance, are three overlapping horses one image, or three? Plus they sort of turn into a blur after a few dozen. But it's a NICE blur!" Then, "Right around the corner is the big landscape, with my personal favorite mountain in it. Almost like I see it from my backyard. Forty thousand years, and no detectable change!"

The group clustered to study the picture. Their massed flash-lights lit it up far better than had Gerard's lights on his earlier visit. He was impressed. Again. One of the students leaned in, then pulled back to a better viewing distance, announced "She's good. Hasn't quite got perspective figured out. But hell's bells, she's only forty thousand years ahead of OUR time! And a heck of a lot better than I will ever be. Who'd have believed this? Who'd have believed ANY of this? I still can't really get ahold of it!"

Another student pointed out some details in the big landscape - details which Gerard had missed, and which practically curled Joan's toes. In the middle distance on the far left side were three pairs of small figures, about thirty centimetres tall, very carefully and finely drawn in charcoal only. It was a tight, busy composition. All six figures were facing right, walking in the direction of a small herd of deer. Each pair included a copy of the same figure - a woman with pronounced breasts, carrying a ridiculously outsized spear. In the leftmost pair, the second figure was smaller than the pair's spear-carrier. In the middle pair, the second figure was as tall as the spear-carrier, and appeared to be an adolescent girl, complete with minor breast-bumps. In the rightmost pair, the unchanged mega-spear carrier was shown walking in second place, being led by another full-busted woman drawn considerably taller than the spear-carrier.

Nobody said anything for a minute, and then Joan managed to get going. "Is there any doubt at all about these being women? The one figure has bigger boobs than anyone in this cave today! Even more importantly --- is there any possible doubt about the identity of the woman carrying the big spear?"

A quiet, unanimous chorus of "no".

Joan spoke again: "So here we go on a time-line from left to right – anyone, please correct me if I do something stupid. Leftmost pair - Mother Spear-Lady and young daughter, out hunting. They have to be hunting - one figure in each pair is carrying a rationally-sized spear. For certain they are on an expedition - they have backpacks! The middle pair is Mother with her adolescent daughter, who is already as tall as Mom. The final pair, on the right, is going to choke me up - the kid is now a full-grown woman with her Mom's busty figure, much taller than Mommy, and the kid is in the lead - the monster spear is being carried by the short woman, who is bringing up the rear now."

She had to stop for a moment.

"I believe what we have here is an autobiographical sketch from forty thousand years ago. And just in case there was any conceivable possibility of us not getting the artist's message, look here..."

She pointed to a tiny SSS under the foot of the 'child' in all three pairs. Then she pointed at Veejr's signature on the landscape, as usual in the lower right. Nods of agreement all around.

"Tall Blue is both Spear-Lady's daughter by Goliath, and the artist responsible for this cave - for this entire Gallery. Damn, but she liked to paint! She made sure we would know who both she and her mother were in this short-story, and also that we'd understand that she painted all these." A sniffle: "Good god! What a find."

"You're right," said Anton. "The artist wanted to be sure a viewer could correctly identify the two figures. Which suggests that someone other than the artist herself was expected to see this -

someone knowledgeable. Which would just about have to be her Mom. I agree 100 percent. These people in the drawings simply cannot be anyone but our artist and her mother, out on a hunting expedition on The Plateau. Actually, at least three expeditions if we interpret the drawings simply. I doubt seriously that Spear-Lady actually took the King-Kong spear on hunts - this is surely just artistic license, purely symbolic, meant to clearly identify the person holding the spear."

Several seconds passed in silence, until Joan said softly "Mother and daughter - alone, apparently hunting deer, with not a single human male in sight. They did it repeatedly as the kid grew up, apparently with nary a male about. Did anyone just hear an icon being oclasted? That would be the classic icon about only men doing the hunting."

Gerard said "I'll agree. Completely. I believe I hear the distant crunch of overhead glass breaking!"

A collective deep breath and Gerard led onwards, deeper into the cave. Slowly. Each person savoring, studying. Around two, three, four sharp bends. He stopped, told the group to be ready for something spectacular, the portrait gallery was around the next corner - he had only shown one vertical pair during his lecture, and although warned, nobody was prepared for the extent of the display. "Thirty pairs of profiles in FRAMES!?" was the collective exclamation. All Gerard could do was shrug. The group spread out as each person chose a separate bit of wall to study. A loud voice declared "Pairs. All profiles. Looks to me like each pair is a man and a woman - but I can't be sure. Any ideas what this is? Anyone?"

Joan chimed in: "My guess is couples. To me this seems a purely "Man-and-Woman" arrangement, and it just screams 'couples!'. I wonder if she did every couple in the colony? There aren't any children - could this be a census of adults, maybe?"

While everyone else was ruminating on couples, Gerard motioned Joan to his side. He showed her the final pair of over-size portraits, the only full-face ones in the lineup. Together they stared at the images.

Joan finally said, very quietly, "Hyper-realism. God but she's old! Look at the wrinkles. She's practically toothless, too. And, Gerard - look at what she's wearing in the picture!" The bottom edge of the portrait included the upper part of a large jawbone worked into a complex necklace. It was another detail Gerard hadn't yet noticed: he felt embarrassed, but certain he could be forgiven - after all, he HAD been both busy and gob-smacked on the one twelve-hour day he had spent with the art - the same day he discovered it.

"Jeezus!" he exclaimed, grinning from ear to ear and knowing the question was unnecessary: "You don't suppose we've seen that necklace already, somewhere else and recently, do you?"

"I'm absolutely certain of it" said Joan. "This drawing has to be Spear-Lady, as an ancient crone. We know she died at about 80 plus - this woman is certainly that old or older. Must have been painted just before she died." Then, with wonder, she said "Gerard, I can't believe it - we actually have a face now for our Spear-Lady. As an antique human, but still, to put a face to all this stuff is amazing. No, it should be simply impossible after so many thousands of years. But we've got it!"

Gerard murmured agreement, thinking privately "You want a face, Madam, wait until I introduce you to Tall Blue herself - she's just around the bend." Then as the rest of the group joined them, he pointed to the old-woman image and said "Behold our Spear-Lady, age 80, maybe even older. Look at the necklace."

Only then, with the entire group clustered at Old Woman and staring at the portrait in almost-reverent silence, did Joan focus on the two drawings attached to the upper and lower frame-lines. Her heart was thundering as she studied them. Finally, in a whisper, she said "Look, everyone! Biographical details. Attached to Old Woman's picture, we have action images of her killing a cave bear. And killing Goliath. And we've already seen pictures of her and her daughter out hunting. These two women are the glue for all this. All of our suspicions about both women, but especially about Spear-Lady, aka 'She who killed both Goliath and Cave Bears' seem to be confirmed by these two action scenes. Amazing."

Gerard and Joan shifted their focus to the final portrait, the second oversize one, attached to Old Woman. "It's only about half-

210

done. And it's the only unfinished item in the entire collection!" muttered Gerard. The whole image had been lightly sketched in, and three quarters of the face itself had been completed. It was obviously the same woman as the old-lady image, in the same view. But at a much, much younger age... no wrinkles in the forehead, mouth full instead of sunken, and good, wide-open eyes.

Joan shook her head, asked Gerald "Is this the only one that's done twice? As well as being the only incomplete?"

He said yes, it was. Then, idly, he asked the air: "Why in the world would Tall Blue have done this one, and only this one, twice? And then she never came back to finish it. Did she die mid-portrait? Or did she get tired of all this work? Or perhaps the cave entrance got sealed by a rock-fall before she finished? Huh?"

Anton laughed, which caught everyone's attention. "Here's my guess. I'm going to extrapolate like crazy. Blue did this portrait of her Mother, that is, Spear-Lady, when Mom was an old woman. A very, very old woman. Blue did a wonderfully realistic job. Why do another right beside it, but show her so much younger? Because Blue brought Mama in here -which explains the three-pair hunting scene- and Mama had never really seen herself at all, much less as a seriously ancient person. I'm guessing that we're being treated to pure vanity, folks. Spear-Lady just wanted to be shown as young and pretty. We all know that nothing like that ever happens in our modern society. Not much. I'm sure Spear-Lady must have come here for a visit when she was old - why else would Blue have gone to the trouble of drawing the two obviously-different women hunting in the landscape? Two women who could easily and accurately be identified and told apart, and whose roles change as we read the drawings? Why do all that unless somebody was going to see the pictures? Someone who would understand. My bet is that Spear-Lady came here as a very old woman, complained about her "old-age" portrait, and Blue got cracking on number two to please Mommy."

He stopped, snorted at himself: "Is that enough speculation for you all?"

While the rest of the group discussed Anton's ideas, Gerard

211

tapped Joan and Anton, silently led them away, deeper into the passage. Around one more angle, and the pulpit or altar was in front of them, topped with the stark-white bear skull. Beside it lay two slender light-weight bones. "Ye gods!" said Anton, instantly fascinated by the skull. "What a freaking monster!"

Gerard agreed, said "Look from this side." He carefully stuck his finger into the left eye socket - it went all the way into the cranial cavity. The three of them looked at one another. "Somebody speared this sucker squarely in the eyeball. What an incredible throw. Or jab, even. And what a set of cojones it took to get close enough to do this!"

Anton sighed. "Hey, folks - seriously now, we already know who threw the spear that did this to Mister Bear. Remember Sherlock's maxim - when you eliminate the impossible, then the answer is whatever remains, however improbable. Who do we know who is (a) good with a spear, and (b) wears a necklace made of a bear mandible plus bear canines plus bear claws? The spear-wielder must have been Old Woman herself, aka Spear-Lady, aka Woman Who Kills Big Nasty Critters - although undoubtedly she did all that at a much lower age than in the portrait! For sure it was her. And 'cojones' is still the wrong word."

Anton paused: the other two listened silently. "Right... good question. What IS the feminine version of "cojones", anyway? It's not 'ovaries'. Since there doesn't seem to be such a word for women, I propose 'balls' as a gender-neutral term for our use here!"

Then he finished up: "The kicker, folks, is this. Look at this skull! What do you see that's important, other than the spear-in-the-eye?"

Joan understood at once. "This skull's got no upper canine teeth!" she exclaimed. "Plus, of course, no mandible!"

Gerard's penny dropped next, and he announced "I'm betting that the canines from this skull - from THIS skull! - are already back in the lab - they must be part of Spear-Lady's necklace. I'll just bet that the loose canines from her necklace will fit this skull perfectly. Bet you, bet you, bet you!"

"The jawbone will fit the skull, too... I'll bet on that as well" said Anton. Then he laughed. "Know what? We now have one woman, that would be Spear-Lady, all one hundred and fifty centimetres of her, who killed Goliath, and who also killed this cave bear. Not just any old bear, but THIS VERY ONE! Jeezus Keerist, what a life that woman led - both she and the daughter she produced! With a few more bits of information, someone could write a book! At least a partial biography."

Anton reached out and tapped lightly on the two slender bird-bones lying beside the skull. "Flutes! Look at the finger-holes. I wonder if Mom and Daughter played duets? Hell, we could move UP's School of Fine Arts out here - it'd fit right in. At the rate we're going today we should keep an eye out for the world's first musical score - must be around here somewhere!" Then "I'd love to mark the skull's position and take it home with us today, just to see if our ideas are right."

The three of them were now alone, having moved -laying string all the while- a few tens of metres ahead of the gaggle. "Over here, now..." Gerard pointed to the slit-door leading to the Portrait. "Inside is the piece de resistance. Believe me." He was choking up. Joan patted his shoulder: he took a deep breath, said "Go slow, follow me - there's room for all three of us."

As they stood there in the portrait chamber, stunned into silence, Gerard said "Tall Blue, meet my friends. Anton, Joan, meet Tall Blue. In her prime! NOW we have a second face, by god, to go with everything else we've learned. Mother and daughter. We have them BOTH! In our business, it certainly is luck over skill most of the time."

Nobody said another word for several minutes. Finally Joan breathed "She is beautiful! It's not just that it's a beautiful painting, but as an individual human she is simply gorgeous. And look how the eyes are focused on the viewer! How the hell did she do that? This lady had talent by the bucketful."

A very long pause, ended by Anton: "Yes, she was. Or rather, she IS a genuine beauty. I do wish we could all have met in person."

Gerard coughed lightly, and when the others looked at him, he grinned, shined his flashlight upwards on this face, and said "We're

213

related, Tall Blue and I. Which means that Spear-Lady and I are also related. They are FAMILY to me! Directly, I mean. Genetically. It's the blue eyes. They're due to a single point mutation in _Homo sapiens_. Every blue-eyed human goes straight back to one person, so Blue and I are relatives. Blue's mom had the blue recessive, so she and I are also related. And of course, all of today's blue-eyes are related to Goliath as well - we get villains with our heroines, I guess. Wow!"

Then he carefully walked them through the contents of Tall Blue's personal space. Bark-paper with sketches. Brushes. Pigments. The folder.

Serious mental overload all around.

After everyone in the group had had personal time with Tall Blue's portrait, Gerard led the way back to the outer world, where they carefully re-sealed and hid the entrance, then sat down for a much-delayed lunch. Silence for a long time. Then Joan spoke. "Everybody, this location MUST be kept a secret until we can get a proper entry-way guard. We're going to need a steel cage over the entry, and real human guards 24-7. I know the politics and bureaucracy: I can make it happen really, really fast. It'll be in place within three days. Believe me. Meanwhile, absolute secrecy as to the location. Not the slightest hint to anyone until I give the okay. Are we agreed?" They agreed.

58 - VEEJR'S ART IN MEN'S-CAVE
Uncle, Medicine Man, and Chys accompanied Veejr on her first painting trip to the Men's-Cave. All she took were a bag of miscellaneous charcoal bits and sticks, and a small bag of powdered red ocher she had spotted in another trader's back-pack and insisted on owning. Mother and daughter had supplied two gazelles as the purchase price. Both parties thought they had enormously out-bargained the opposition - a perfect trade.

With four lamps and four torches burning, the painting party sat in front of the final and best existing painting - a bison, entire. Veejr studied it: her audience waited patiently. A mild debate - what animal to begin with? Decision - another bison. That way they could compare hers with the earlier one. A competition! She agreed, stood up and said, very analytically, "This is going to be hard. I need to do a big picture, like this one, but I've only done little ones on bark."

She brought up her mental images of bison, studied them, picked one to begin with, compared her mind's picture with the existing art. Although the old painting was quite detailed, it had almost nothing exactly right - but even so, it was definitely a bison, nothing else. And it was also attractive, as art. Every detail was wrong, yet the outcome, the overall image, was good. Weird. A lesson it would take her months to fully assimilate.

Doing her drawing was indeed difficult - much more frustrating than she had expected. Just like working on bark, the first important thing was to PLAN way ahead, and second - having planned, to take a deep breath and just START. She closed her eyes to get the mental picture right, gripped her charcoal-twig brush, opened her eyes, and began. Just like on bark, but BIGGER. The surface was smooth, not as rough as the boulders outside the home cave - it took the charcoal well without gobbling up the brush. That was nice. She forced herself to NOT think about the line she was laying down. Always, when her drawing was really working well, it was like there was a direct connection between her mental picture and the line being placed on the bark, without any thinking in between. After a few seconds, she got that feeling. In fact, doing a big drawing felt rather nice, especially being able to use the larger muscles of her arm and shoulder instead of just making tiny fingertip motions. The outline went onto the wall as if by magic. In another time and place, her abilities would have rated the epithet "prodigy".

After perhaps five minutes of fast, smooth work she paused, stepped back and studied it. NOT satisfactory. Weird - here, in a reverse of the old drawing's problem, she had gotten the details correct, yet the overall picture was ugly, all wrong. Veejr's lesson-in-drawing #2 from the day's exercise.

The audience thought otherwise. But her standards were not the same as theirs - hers were much stiffer. Medicine Man patted her shoulder and said, admiringly, "Very good! Your first wall painting and it's going to be better than the best old drawing - we can see

215

that!" Veejr disagreed, went back to work, got more and more frustrated. She learned in the next five minutes that the calcite surface was lovely but unforgiving - charcoal laid on it was almost uncorrectable - she would have to be much more careful.

She abruptly took her largest charcoal and made a huge X through the work before anyone could stop her. The adults remonstrated: she replied, very much in command now, "Because it's my own drawing, I get to decide if it's good or not. Or if it's something to keep. Sit down again and I'll do another one. Now I know what I need to do to make it come out right!"

They sat, as ordered.

The second version, outlined, shaded, detailed, took two hours to complete. Her companions sat quietly, assisted her by keeping the wall well-lit, and watched in awe as the animal emerged from nothingness. They quickly realized that she had been correct - her first and second iterations were light-years apart. When she finished and stepped back to study the image, they said nothing, simply stood and contemplated it with her. She nodded, grinned at them and said "This one is better. We can keep it."

Then she reached for her bag of red ocher, dipped three fingertips in it, and down in the corner she carefully traced the same triple-S mark she had developed working with her clay slate. Done, she looked up again and said "That means I made this painting. Veejr did it. Not someone else. I won't put my mark on a bad painting! Never!" She was entitled to her artist's ego.

Medicine Man and Uncle told her "Now you need to do a lot of drawings here - several of each kind of big-game animal. Maybe you can do a little bunch of simple drawings for the animals that live in herds? Lots of drawings. Then we'll see if the hunting improves!"

With that goal, over the next several months, she did a good many paintings. And both her art and the Tribe's hunting did improve. The men were ecstatic - their theories were vindicated (at least, when they carefully chose their memories, and somewhat rewrote their thoughts, all for post-hoc consumption). The men were of course wrong about the cause of the improvement in hunting re-

sults - how could anyone have known that the Tribe was just beginning to ride a short-lived, climate-driven upwards trend in prey population density and that they were attributing the Tribe's blind good
luck to Veejr's work? Which (regardless of causality) garnered her a
huge amount of respect, verging on worship. Odd though she might
be in terms of eyes and height, she could thereafter do entirely as
she pleased - a truly wonderful thing for any artist.

Veejr's twice-weekly all-day disappearances into the Men's-
Cave became part of the community routine, and under orders from
her and Medicine Man, nobody ever followed her to see where she
was going and what she was doing. Nevertheless, the existence and
nature of her work had slowly but inevitably become accurately
suspected by most. Once the improvements in both art and hunting
had been going on for a considerable time, Veejr prevailed on Medicine Man and Uncle to show the Men's-Cave and its art to the entire
Tribe. The fact that she and Chys had been in the cave so much
surely debunked the "Men Only" taboo. Especially so because in
spite of women-in-the-cave, Tribal hunting had improved. When the
men eventually agreed and opened the cave to all, Veejr's reputation
immediately rose another step.

59 - MEDICINE WOMAN

Veejr and the much older Medicine Man turned out to be kin-
dred souls, intellectually. They got along famously. Veejr once
joked with both Uncle and Medicine Man that maybe it was finally
letting women into the Men's-Cave, rather than the new Veejr-art,
that was the key to good hunting. Uncle was not amused, but Medicine Man took note of the comment - it was evidence that just maybe Veejr might share his unease at how most people intermingled or
confused two concepts he was having great trouble articulating and
dealing with in his practice - today's terms are 'causation' and
'correlation'. When Medicine Man once opened that subject, he and
Veejr agreed - just because something came after something else,
did not mean that the first caused the second. Nobody else in the
Tribe was interested in pursuing this interesting and difficult propo-

sition.

Medicine Man was getting old, and he could see the process accelerating. This posed problems. Connected with the position itself, every tribe's Medicine Man had two major "administrative" tasks (as opposed to caring for patients). First, to preserve Tribal medical knowledge and pass it along to the next generation. Second, to expand that knowledge as much as possible.

The second involved an occasional sabbatical leave - each tribe's Medicine Man would leave home, alone, for some months. He would travel under a right of peaceful conduct to another tribe, the more distant the better, where he and the resident Medicine Man or Woman would exchange knowledge and work together. The Tribal medico would return with expanded knowledge and experience, and occasionally something more concrete - for example, a new wife/husband (genetically a good thing!), or some special rare or useful material goods, and, in particular, occasional new medicines.

The first task was more complicated. Medicine Man could not just run off and leave the Tribe defenseless: he must have a respectable, well-trained and responsible alternate. This posed a dilemma - for many years, Medicine Man had been watching Tribal children as they matured, seeking a good candidate to be his understudy and eventual successor. During the whole past decade, the only serious candidate was Veejr - whom he had personally helped sidetrack into cave painting. But she was by far and away the most intelligent child he had ever encountered... a bit spoilt in some ways, but thoughtful, quick and logical. Her being female was, for a change, not an impediment. Tribal medical business was largely gender neutral. Medicine Man had met several Medicine Women during his travels. In some ways women medics were preferred over men - they handled patients better (the patients being mostly men, and such injured/sick men behaving so much like small children), and once past child-bearing age they lived a good deal longer than did men, which made them much better long-term repositories of knowledge.

After much internal mulling-over, Medicine Man broached

218

the topic of Veejr becoming his student, first with Uncle, then with Chys. Medicine Man made a big point of admiring Veejr's artistic abilities and contributions to the Tribe. But, he said, she didn't do art ALL the time - she had plenty of free time that could be dedicated to something else. And because that free time resulted from Tribal subsidies, why shouldn't it be something of importance to the entire Tribe? On top of that, she had those incredible blue eyes that should enhance any medical abilities she had or could develop. Plus of course, she and he got along. Medicine Man would be very, very happy to have her as his understudy.

Would Veejr be interested? It was a lifetime commitment if so. After considerable thought, Chys agreed: Medicine Man could approach the child with the notion. But it would be Veejr's decision, not Chys's and certainly not the men's.

The proposition intrigued Veejr instantly. She wasn't at all bored with her art, never would be, but it certainly would be nice to have something else to do in addition, especially something as prestigious as being Tribal Medicine Woman Trainee-Designate. She agreed.

A year into her training, she was soaking up knowledge like a sponge, continually amazing her mentor with both memory and understanding - especially with her ability to see connections where he had seen none, and to detect causal relationships between actions taken and results observed. Once told to her, new "outside" information was instantly learned and integrated into the Tribal storehouse of medical knowledge. Medicine Man was exceedingly pleased with his choice: she would soon outstrip him, which was fine - he was neither a possessive nor a jealous person. The job, well done, was the only important thing. Every Medicine Man or Woman was a receptacle, a diagnostician and a dispenser - sometimes also an experimenter - but never the 'owner' - of medical information. Locally, ownership lay with the Tribe - but with the mixmaster system of sabbaticals, ownership ultimately resided in the entire species, not any smaller portion of it. Once learned and disseminated (via the medical network) into this early version of distributed memory and processing, medical knowledge was nearly immune from species-wide loss.

In Tribal culture there was no feeling that medicine was particularly magical - most injuries, and many common conditions or illnesses, were natural - readily explainable by cause-and-effect reasoning that could be checked, verified. If there was anything curative to be done, the medicines and treatments were also perfectly understandable - juices and extracts and salves and special dietary items, re-aligning broken bones, covering a wound to prevent further injury. Demonic possession and some form of investment of the body by ethereal spirits were seldom invoked either as explanations or cures - and then only weakly. Ignorance was widespread on many important topics: everyone was used to that, to simply getting on about life despite all of its unknowns. Ignorance was to be fixed if and when possible, but not feared in and of itself.

Much medicine in fact involved only self-diagnosis and self-treatment, then as now. To do that well required public medical knowledge, of which there was a great deal, although often confusing, conflicting, and widely scattered. Veejr of course had recall capabilities adequate to the topic, but most people did not. Most people needed some sort of memory aid or augmentation.

Like many who would follow her into the medical professions, Veejr was inundated with routine near-trivial requests for help and information. The 'trivialities' were not trivial to the holder, hence those requests did have to be dealt with. It didn't take long for her to combine this incoming flood of knowledge, and the public's need, with her art. Seeking some respite from the hubbub of low-level care, she produced, in an unused part of the Men's-Cave, a unique and inventive system for storing and dispensing medical knowledge.

60 - PHARMACOPEIA

Even Joan's most responsible graduate students occasionally took holidays from the basic rules. A common holiday was casually to step beyond the currently-set boundaries of exploration and study, to have "just a quick peek" around the next corner of the Men's-Cave, into unexplored space.

The previous weekend, third-year student Sherry had taken

just such a holiday, solo (doubly against the rules!) and was now having to own up to it. She could not in good conscience fail to report the new art she had found. Or not-exactly-art. She was sure she had figured it out already despite the works being utterly unique, and that increased her excitement.

She went to confess her sins to Joan, who at once reassured her about the transgression: "You wouldn't belong in the program if you could always resist temptation!" Then, "Before you get started describing things, STOP! I love surprises. Let's just you and me and Gerard go together, and you can introduce us to your find - that way we two will arrive on-site with no preconceptions whatever."

About two hundred meters deeper in the cave than the current yellow-tape rules allowed, the three stood before the first section of Sherry's find. Just scanning their powerful lights down the wall made it clear that this was utterly different from "routine" art.

Three-centimetre-wide vertical charcoal stripes divided the wall space into sections, each over two metres across. No, the term had to be "PAGE", not section. There was nothing else to call the units marching off into the umbra except "pages". As in book. The mere fact of pagination itself was startling - utterly unique. And upon even the most cursory examination, no thought required, it was obvious that all the pages followed a consistent format.

The trio stood spellbound, contemplating the first page. At eye-level on the left, a quick outline of a human head, in right profile. Three zigzag lines emanated from the head: a horizontal from the temple, a downwards-diagonal at the occiput, vertical at the crown. Then on the right side, several 50 cm tall drawings of plants, one above the other on the page. Each plant rated two meticulous drawings: one of the entire plant, the second a magnified version of some particular part. Beside each plant was drawn one zigzag, oriented to mimic one image from the profile. In the uppermost left corner, the red-ocher print of a single finger. Down in the lower right corner, the now classic SSS signature.

"Good god, here she is again!" said Gerard; "Isn't there ANYthing our Tall Blue doesn't do?"

Page two was a pair of flat-art profiles, one left-side, the other right. Almost schematic, with the mouths open un-naturally wide, corners of the cheeks pulled impossibly far back to show all the teeth: the molars were quite different from the other teeth. Zigzag ending at one specific tooth. Plant, with roots. The point of another zigzag touching the plant's roots. In the same loci as in the first page there were two red fingerprints, and another signature.

"Page numbers!" - Joan said, excitedly. "Who was worried about these folks' mental abilities, anyhow? Look here… we have counting symbols used as page numbers!" She was practically hy-perventilating. Laughing aloud, she leaned forward, extended a fin-gertip to almost touch the wall, gleefully counted teeth - "In this oral quadrant, lower left, we have one, two, three, four, five, six, seven, eight. Times four is 32. That's the correct number of teeth in a hu-man - she's BETTER than Mister ARISTOTLE - he got the number wrong!" Then, under her breath, "Plus I'll just bet you he had no idea whatever how to treat a toothache! That should make the score Aristotle nil, versus our gal's two! Tall Blue rules! You GO, Girl!"

Page three, a profiled skinny woman to the right of a heav-ily-pregnant woman. Beside the pair, another lovely plant, a differ-ent species. With details - the flowers and buds, but no leaves, stems, or roots. Three fingerprints.

Page four the same as three, but with the figures reversed left to right. A different plant - details of both roots and leaves.

When she'd first glimpsed the work the other day, Sherry had instantly understood the purpose and content of every page. Now, unable to restrain herself, she sputtered, voice unsteady and overloud, "Hey, guys! Lookit! ITS A NEOLITHIC MEDICAL TEXTBOOK WITHOUT WORDS OR GRAMMAR! Each page covers a condition or complaint. Who wouldn't recognize lightning bolts as meaning pain? Three different pain loci for headaches. Three different plants to treat the three different loci. Differential diagnosis, differential treatment! Drawings of whole plants to guide the unwashed amateur, then details about what part of the plant to use! It's a medical encyclopedia, a reference text! And the pages are numbered. You could tell a patient 'Got the cramps, Girl? Go to the cave, check out number seventeen, that'll fix you right up!' Then leave it up to the patient to go find the plant and use it. I wonder where are the detailed instructions for use? Make tea, chew and spit, chew and swallow? The instructions must be here somewhere! This absolutely has to be the world's first illustrated pharmacopeia!" Then, in a harsh stage-whisper, "NOBODY IS GOING TO EVER BELIEVE THIS!"

Nonetheless, she kept on going. "So - page two covers toothache! Then how about pages three and four? Page three is before-and-after views, going from really heavily preggers to not-at-all-preggers. Abortifacients! Next, on page four, the treatment is going the other way, from not pregnant to full-term pregnant. Fertility drugs!"

Then, more calmly, "We need a botanist, STAT, to see if these plants are identifiable, find out if they still grow around here... and whether they actually do work as advertized! Sheesh! Now we're into drug research!"

Joan nodded, then pointed to page five: it showed an arm with a serious slice-wound, dripping red-ocher blood. Painted beside it was a needle with coarse thread. Black stitches drawn across the wound over the ocher. A plant, yet again a different species."Surgical repairs of wounds! I wonder - is the plant a coagulant, an antiseptic, antibiotic, or whatever? You're right, we've got to ID these plants and find out." The pagination was a full five-fingered handprint.

Next page, a head in profile, bent forward, vomiting copiously. Another plant and detail. Just use the roots, nothing else. Joan thought to herself that the ancient author had needed an editor - the intent was unclear. Were these instructions for inducing vomiting, or for curing it? A full hand plus one finger - page six. And counting in base five. None of the old "One, Two, ... Many" for our Tribe!

There were over twenty such pages, all numbered by simple base-five integer counting, all carrying in the lower right-hand corner the well-known SSS.

Gerard tapped a fingertip beside one of the signatures and wondered aloud "Is she just the artist? Or is she the person knowledgeable in the healing arts? The Tribal medicine-woman? As well as being the Tribal artist-of-record? What the HELL do we have here - a neolithic renaissance woman, an early daVinci?"

That proved to be a very difficult question to answer. Still is.

61 - VEEJR'S PARTNER AND KIDS

Veejr kept working to improve her art as she matured. Over the next few years, she developed a distinctive style - one could see it evolving if one studied the long procession of her works in the Men's-Cave - and only two other paintings had been canceled, false starts that were "officially" stricken by being denied her signature.

By fourteen she was an attractive girl, verging on maturity, a full head taller than anyone else in the Tribe, and still growing. Combined with her blue eyes, that made her a bit of an outsider. As a pretty, intelligent young woman, she'd quickly become sexually active: the pace of those activities accelerated rapidly and they culminated in her first pregnancy late in her fifteenth year. Pregnant by the black-eyed father of the Tribe's Blue-Eyed Baby#2, recently rendered wife-less by a treacherous riverbank. He was significantly older than Veejr, but such an age gap was routine in the Tribe. Much more importantly, he was utterly undeterred by either her eyes or height. His own baby's eyes had been a total surprise - both parents were dark-eyed, but both - obviously - carried the blue recessive. Veejr had paved the way for Blue-Eye#2, so there had been no uproar, no talk of instant infanticide. The eye-color shared by Veejr and Blue#2 had been a strong attractant between him and Veejr. Veejr's second pregnancy a mere two years later confounded everyone - a blue-eyed boy twinned with a black-eyed girl. Her third and final pregnancy produced a single blue-eyed girl.

62 – MUSINGS ON HEREDITY AND GENETICS

Because of Veejr and her crazy blue eyes - which everyone agreed HAD to have come, somehow, from Monster - Chys pondered for months, ultimately years, some questions of what would eventually be called "genetics." Specifically, about parents' contributions to their children; to how kids turned out both physically and behaviorally; the overarching rule of thumb being "Like mom/dad, like child".

Chys, and the human race generally, didn't yet have the vocabulary and conceptual base for dealing readily with such abstract questions - but we humans are capable of logic and we are fine observers, and the two traits together make a powerful puzzle-solving combination. It was very complicated, confusing stuff to think about and doing so often made her head hurt. She really needed a way to record her thoughts so that she didn't have to continually re-build the logic-chain, but no such recording process existed. For her artwork Veejr had invented two media that would have served for recording Chys's thoughts, namely bark paper and clay tablets - but writing wasn't yet even a gleam in the eye of any of its eventual inventors. Not for many millennia yet. And unfortunately, her thinking left no physical traces to amuse or confound or instruct future generations.

Chys had a lot of information to use in thinking about the problems. Blue eyes in Monster. Her own black eyes. Her parents had both been black-eyed. Her and Monster's child (Veejr) having blue eyes. Then along came the unrelated Blue-Eyed Baby#2... out of two black-eyed parents! The event astounded everyone. For sure there had never been a blue-eyed male in the Tribal settlement, not even as a visitor, and Chys knew that the mother, a good friend, hadn't mated with such a man in the bushes. No, Blue-Eyed Baby#2 had come from two black-eyed parents, without any outside help. One could understand Veejr's blue eyes, which had an obvious if not completely understood source. But black plus black giving BLUE?

Headache! But Chys kept trying.

She began with the common knowledge, entirely obvious to even a casual observer, that babies tended to get a mixture of parental characteristics. Setting aside the blue-eye problem for a moment, thought Chys for the Nth time, a baby might, say, have its mother's wide high cheekbones, plus Daddy's chin-dimple and flat nose. As, for example, did Blue-Eyed Baby#2. Clearly then, babies were mixtures, and contributions came to every baby from both mother and father. Always. No father, no baby. If this passing-on of physical

225

traits worked for noses and chins and cheekbones and others such as birthmarks, why not also for eye color? The eyes themselves were known to work perfectly fine whether blue or black, so color didn't seem to be terribly important functionally, just a curiosity.

"So", Chys told herself, "...consider Blue-Eyed Baby#2." That baby, like every baby, got half of each of its traits from Mom and half from Dad, both of whom were black-eyed. Blue-Eyed Baby#2 had to have gotten some eye-color stuff from both Mom and Dad, just the way she received stuff for facial structure. Which meant that both Mom and Dad had to have given some BLUE eye-color stuff to Blue-Eyed Baby#2. Even if you could not see from the outside that the parents had any blue stuff, it must have been there, hidden somehow, and it had to be present in BOTH parents.

Hmmm.

But she knew a lot more about Blue-Eyed Baby#2's parents - they had produced two other kids, both of whom had black eyes, not a trace of blue. That meant that two parents with black eyes could produce EITHER a black-eyed OR a blue-eyed baby. Nothing seemed to be mandatory about eye color and parentage.

Hmmmm again. And once again her head hurt.

More data. What about herself and Monster? Monster couldn't have had any black-eye in him - to have blue eyes he had to have gotten blue from both parents. And the fact that Monster and her own black-eyed self had produced blue-eyed Veejr meant that SHE HERSELF had contributed blue to Veejr! Which meant Chys had to have gotten it from her own black-eyed parents. More hidden blueness!

Which led to the question, where the HELL did her own blue come from? It was hidden for sure - her own eyes were black, black, BLACK.

Once or twice the thought flickered past that perhaps - just maybe - the old wives' tales of a long-ago Tribal encounter with blue-eyed visitors had been accurate. One such man could, possibly, have put some blue-eye stuff into the Tribe - hidden blue - and eventually it somehow magically got passed along to Chys herself without anyone ever seeing it simply because many parents in the chain had carried the blue, but always with it hidden under black. Then, the result of Chys's hidden blue plus Monster's pure blue had been Veejr. That seemed too fanciful to countenance: after all, until Veejr there had been no blue-eyed babies whatever in the Tribe. So that was where she dropped it. And work the puzzle as she might all through her life, she never knew that she had, in fact, solved it. Unfortunately, from then unto the time of writing, every generation would have to wrestle with the puzzle -if it chose to do so- from the ground floor. And occasionally there were individuals interested in such esoteric things.

63 - GERARD AND MITOCHONDRIAL DNA

Gerard was doing well in his graduate work, but internally he was increasingly unsettled - for no good logical reason, just a need, a feeling that he was going to have to pursue a personal research avenue. And soon - the itch was intensifying. Normally the calmest and most logical of scientists, he'd been powerfully rattled, emotionally, by a series of findings. First, Tall Blue's self-portrait, with which he'd almost literally fallen in love, much to his puzzlement and dismay. He'd even gone so far as to kiss the picture, gently, once only, before she was introduced to the rest of the world. The kiss was, obviously, an event never to happen again. Second, the specific realization that he and Tall Blue were genetically related, at least marginally - she and he both had blue eyes, and all blue-eyed humans could be traced back to one individual with a single-point mutation. Third, a profound and growing admiration for the body of work Tall Blue had produced - in his mind, the more one learned about that woman, the more he thought of her as a neolithic Leonardo... and not just in terms of her art. He deeply wanted to know more about her. A short course in "genetics as a research tool" opened an interesting possibility.

For both La Fond and UP, all genetic analyses of DNA were done on La Fond's machinery and computers. Gerard made an appointment with Carlo, the lead DNA technician, pumped him gently for information. Yes, the lab could, and routinely did, analyze samples for mitochondrial DNA - the DNA that is specifically inside subcellular organelles called mitochondria, and NOT in the nucleus. Since mtDNA is not in the nucleus, it gets passed from generation to generation only by being carried in the egg - there is no confusing male contribution to mtDNA in the next generation. mtDNA had been shown to be extremely stable across many hundreds, even many thousands of generations. Analyses of mtDNA yielded the discovery that apparently all modern humans can trace their ancestry to a single UR-woman several hundred thousand years ago. Since that time, occasional minor changes in mtDNA have appeared: comparison of modern mtDNA with historical samples and other data can show how closely-linked two modern individuals are (or are not). The closer to a perfect match between two people's mtDNA, the more closely they are related. Anthropological gold, such data.

Gerard had a simple idea that occasioned two simple questions. First, had an mtDNA analysis been run yet on Tall Blue? He was in luck - the answer was "Of course". The second, presented with some hemming and blushing, was "Could the lab do one on ME?" Carlo was surprised, but only mildly - he'd had many requests for such analyses in his years at La Fond, mostly from people emotionally desperate to establish who was or was not someone's actual parent (marriages, birth certificates and other such trivia aside). 'Could X be my birth-mother?' often came from adoptees. Questions of illegitimacy came from both parents and offspring. Carlo always referred such requests to La Fond's mucky-mucks and ethics folks: the usual answer was a gentle "This can be done commercially - here's a phone number."

Carlo probed tactfully, and quickly found that Gerard's interest was quite different... a powerful curiosity as to how closely he was related to Tall Blue, other than merely by having blue eyes. Carlo then suggested they take the idea upstairs. Gerard managed to present the project as an interesting side-issue within the larger context of Tall Blue research - without actually hiding his own interest. When that interest was discussed, it actually spoke in his favor. The upshot was "okay", but that he would have to pay half the cost of the analysis, since some fraction of the work was being done on his personal behalf. No cash needed - he could work it off just by learning how to do the analysis himself, and then doing it under Carlo's watchful eye - a wonderful learning experience. "Scientific purposes" aside, everyone admitted to being simply curious.

Gerard provided the necessary cheek-swab sample. The actual chemical reactions and extractions were entirely automated, took a weekend. Carlo and Director Joan had taken a personal interest in the modern vs. ancient comparison. Over coffee they had discussed the interesting idea of any close relationship between Gerard and Tall Blue - largely in joking terms centered around what sort of legal claims Gerard might bring - say, towards ownership of grave goods or even of signed wall-art- if he and Tall Blue happened to be closely related.

Carlo ran Gerard's data on the computer first thing Monday morning. He stared at the results, set up a meeting with Joan in her office, slipped the single-page machine-generated report into a manila envelope, and went to find Gerard. Carlo refused to answer any questions, insisted that they should go visit with Joan in her office.

Joan waited until everyone had coffee in hand. Finally, watching the rather obvious rising tide of anticipation in Gerard (he was squirming in his seat like a five year old!), she turned to Carlo and asked "SO?"

Carlo opened the envelope and pulled out the sheet, handed it to Joan. She scanned it, found the relevant number in bold at the bottom, almost choked. "Jeez!" she said, and handed it to Gerard.

98.2% match.

As close to a perfect match as today's machinery and protocols allow. Three runs each for Tall Blue and Gerard, almost identical results both within and between.

Gerard was stunned. From nowhere, his eyes brimmed, and though he tried, he couldn't speak for nearly half a minute. The others all waited politely.

When sounds would come, he managed to say "Damn! I think, from what I've learned lately, that that means direct lineal descendant. The one point eight non-agreement is even smaller than the usual noise! Nothing's broken the string, anywhere, across all this time!"

He looked back and forth between Joan and Carlo, took a deep, shivery breath, and said "You know, this is NOT what I expected.... I was just curious, the whole question came up just because both I and Tall Blue have blue eyes. I really, truly did NOT expect this! Jeez, indeed!"

Carlo laughed, patted him on the shoulder, and said "You now have, I'm quite sure, by far the oldest documented personal pedigree on this planet! Forty thousand years more or less, at about twenty per generation, makes Tall Blue something like your two-thousandth Great Grandmother. And Killer of Goliath and Bears is therefore your two-thousand-and-first. That's quite a family history regardless of anything in the intervening few years! You're a direct lineal descendent of both Spear Lady and Tall Blue. It does seem right, somehow, that it was YOU who found her art. And to top it off, you have real portraits of two of the women in your direct line-age, from forty thousand years ago! Congratulations! "

Although the mtDNA results quickly made anthropological headlines within the community, the most immediate result was the finest graduate-student party of the year, dedicated to the honor of Gerard's long-lost and unsuspected relatives, found at last.

64 - FOUNDING VEEJR'S GALLERY

Dealing with her new family slowed but did not stop both Veejr's Men's-Cave art and her medical activities. When her young-est daughter was weaned, Veejr, like Chys before her, went back to previous activities: lots of work in the Men's-Cave, lots of miscella-neous drawings on bark. But she was, finally, getting somewhat bored. After all, the Men's-Cave work was commissioned and she had no freedom to really just play. The art on bark was almost liter-ally "disposable". Both were unsatisfying.

Then one day her partner, call him Husband, told her that he'd found a new cave not too far away - there was no sign any other humans had ever gotten into it, and there were no animal spoor ei-ther. Lots and lots of smooth blank white wall. Would she like to see it?

Chys, now well into middle-age, volunteered to handle the children, no questions asked. Veejr and Husband got the needed lamps and set off.

It was a huge cave - magnificent, complex, deep, dry, with a single known small entrance, which could readily be blocked and hidden with a small slab.

At medium-depth inside, there were hundreds of metres of high white walls, unusually smooth, perfect for art-work. Veejr's juices flowed. Never had she encountered so much lovely, usable virgin space so ripe for charcoal and paint. The biggest piece of white bark in the entire world! A literal, genuine 'tabula rasa' - and of heroic size. It cried out for art - not pragmatic pictures aimed at improving hunters' luck, but just for decoration - art for art's sake, purely to satisfy herself.

By the time they had **explored** to the limit of their lights, Veejr had a plan. She explained it to Husband, swore him to secrecy. If he agreed, this could be HER cave. Private property. Secret. A personal place where she could do whatever she wanted to in the way of art, for her own purposes, at her own speed. Very different from the purpose-driven 'top-down' work in the Men's-Cave.

Husband was no dummy - he had no desire to be anything but a hero to his lady. Besides, he really liked her art, and admired her for it. He readily swore himself to secrecy about the existence of this cave - and volunteered to help however he could. At the very least, he would provide all the lamps and charcoal she needed.

A week later they returned, laden with torches and lamps and art supplies. She made a little cache of them just inside the entrance, then took out a deer-bladder full of red ocher grease-paint. Stretching far up the wall (she was by far the tallest person in the Tribe), she used three fingers to make her SSS signature, strong and clear. She laughed when she finished, told Husband "Now that my mark is on it, this cave belongs to ME! Nobody else. Never!"

For small bits of personal property, the concept of ownership, of "mine!", was well developed. Also well-developed was the concept of "ours" - Tribes had forever laid collective claim to hunting rights on specific territory. But the idea hadn't arisen of claiming ownership of the land itself. Which likely made Veejr's statement that day the first-ever claim by an individual to permanent, personal ownership of a piece of real estate.

Very much like Gerard would do far in the future, and walking the exact same underground pathways, Veejr spent weeks exploring the cave, carefully building a mental map, re-checking it. The Men's-Cave work had been a very useful training exercise in so many ways!

Over the next several decades, for her own purposes, she would paint hundreds of animals as individuals and in herds, going about their business of grazing, fighting, mating. And also being stamped-ed, killed, and butchered. People too, of course. Quickly she evolved from picturing mere objects to picturing events. When she began to tire of re-inspecting her eidetic memories, she gradually changed her artistic approach - her paintings became more stylized and formal, much less naturalistic. The entire transformation was documented up and down the passageways of her cave. Gerard's Gallery.

65 - STARTING AN ARTISTIC DYNASTY

When Veejr's youngest daughter, named 'Zachs', was about five, the girl showed an interest in Mom's art: she was happily en-couraged by Veejr and Husband. Her interest seemed solid - at least it didn't evaporate overnight. She showed some aptitude, and with Mom's help she made significant progress rather quickly. Veejr took her to the Men's-Cave occasionally, just a few little "workday at Mom's office" expeditions. Zachs thought the trips great fun. After a few months of watching the kid generate increasingly complex doodles in the Men's-Cave, Veejr was quite pleased to be asked by her, one afternoon, how to draw a tree. Veejr found it easy to demonstrate and explain: the lessons escalated rapidly, and Zachs quickly blossomed into a junior version of Mom.

After just a few months, Veejr took Zachs to her new, secret cave. Once inside, Veejr had her own tasks for the day, but wanted to see what the kid might do, and also to be available to teach if asked. The big problem was the logistics of light - solved when Veejr drew a horizontal charcoal line at about her waist height, then gave the space below the line to Zachs. Veejr would work in the space above the line - that way they could share the light from several clamshell lamps.

Eventually a bright graduate student would figure out the correct reason for the odd horizontal line and the two wildly contrasting abilities it separated - but only after extensive debate fueled by large quantities of beer.

66 - EYE-STONES

Some considerable time later, deep in her own cave, Veejr was working on a magnum opus. She had been fascinated with mirror imagery ever since first seeing herself reflected in a riverbank puddle. By now she was an accomplished artist with a great deal of experience - including many successful small charcoal-on-bark and charcoal-on-limestone portraits in profile, full-face, and even a few in 3/4 view. The 3/4 were far and away the best - and also hardest to do. She had decided some time ago that she wanted to do a self-portrait, the idea coming from seeing herself in puddle-mirrors. She'd found the perfect place for it, far back in her private cave, many metres beyond the current terminus of her portraits and other art. A small, isolated, perfectly white closet-sized room, with a narrow vertical slit-like entry. It had a wonderful wall for such a project, unusually smooth, not quite flat, with gentle curves and bulges she was sure she could use to advantage. This would be a project for the ages - consciously so. She was certain that her paintings would vastly outlast herself, and also everyone alive today. She wanted people in the future to see her art, to see herself, to know her. This was the vehicle for those hopes and aspirations.

Veejr had worked, now, for weeks on the three-quarter frontal image, using her eidetic memory of various views of herself in reflecting pools. She had worried that she couldn't do a decent three-quarter-face without knowing the view from the sides as well, and in a puddle-mirror anything save full-frontal verged on the impossible. Nevertheless, she had used reflections to make test drawings in charcoal, about one-third size: full face, plus her best shot at rough left and right 3/4-views.

The Portrait was nearly done - herself, nude, from navel to the top of her head, her body squarely full-frontal and face at 3/4, with hair in braids, the ends fastened with bow-tied leather thongs. She had used the contoured wall surface very thoughtfully, with subtle wall-bulges for cheeks and chin and forehead. She'd left the proper areas of white for the eyes - shades of her drawing rabbits decades ago!

Altogether, it was a fine, fine job - and she knew it. So far, so good.

But Veejr finally had to face a central problem in the grand design of her portrait. She really wanted to put in blue eyes, clearly her own most striking facial feature: unfortunately, as far as she knew, no such thing as blue paint existed. But she was used to thinking her way through problems, and a possibility suggested itself. Years ago, on their first expedition to view big-game, she and Mother Chys had encountered an upper-plains trader, to whom they had sold two Veejr drawings, receiving as partial payment ten small pieces of cut and shaped turquoise. The pieces were circular, a little bigger than the nail on a pointer-finger. They were approximately cabochon-cut - each had one flat side, with the obverse gently rounded, each stone was pierced dead-center for a good-sized thong. They were intended for making body-ornaments - as beads for use in necklaces and bracelets. Neither Veejr nor Chys had thought to ask if the stones were simply found that way naturally, or whether some human had produced them - and if the latter, then HOW?

Chys, at Veejr's insistence, had carefully chosen stones to match Veejr's eye color - which to Veejr was the point of the exercise. They were her only way of knowing that important part of herself. The stones had been her secret treasure, never displayed or mentioned, never strung for wearing. Hidden away and almost forgotten. Almost.

Veejr got them out of hiding, studied each in the bright afternoon sunshine. She was a superb observer and knew that in a live

234

person the front of the eye is quite curved, most sharply in the area over the iris. Could she somehow shape and re-size these blue beads, using their existing curvature to advantage, to resemble blue irises? And if she could do that, could she then figure out how to attach the stones to the portrait?

She considered and rejected the idea of grinding a bead or two into ocher-like consistency, mostly because she had no idea how to turn ground blue-rock into a pigment that would permanently bond with the calcite. She abandoned the idea of making blue pigment, without having solved the problem of making whatever she came up with really STICK - the solution had to provide truly permanent attachment. Some sort of glue, probably. She would deal with that problem later, knowing that if she DIDN'T concentrate on that problem, her unconscious mind would go ahead and work on it while she was busy elsewhere.

So she decided to address the problem of getting the final shape, size and curvature that she needed. While she did that, her brain would work on the attachment problem - there HAD to be a solution.

When it came to shaping stone, she was a highly skilled knapper, but had only worked obsidian and flint, and nothing this small. Here, she was thinking about doing something exquisitely finely detailed, and in what she came to think of as 'bluestone' - an unknown material. The necessary experiments would inevitably waste some of her small stock, but there was no real alternative. She visualized what she hoped to accomplish with the portrait, then set aside the three best stones as potential irises - nearly identical shapes, and all of them the same lovely bright blue.

She chose the most irregular, least valuable remaining bead as her experimental object. Rubbing it on rough limestone wouldn't work to reshape the bluestone - the bead wore a little groove in the limestone. The hardnesses were the reverse of what she needed. She tapped and poked, and listened to the bluestone ring - it was very nearly as hard as glass. Neither flint nor obsidian would scratch it. Perhaps, she thought, it could be worked by knapping? It certainly seemed hard enough and glassy enough to yield flakes.

She donned her knapping-goggles: eyesight was too precious for taking chances, and even the tiniest of flakes could destroy an eye literally in a blink. Then she put in several hours of experimentation interspersed with tool-making. Bluestone was a slippery, difficult beast, almost impossible to hold tightly enough to work. Finally, encouraged by having managed to punch a tiny flake off the slippery, smooth surface, and simultaneously frustrated by not being able to get a purchase, she inserted the pebble into a carefully-prepared split stick and lashed it down like a miniature stone ax-head. Now she could hold the stick in the bend of her knee, and place the bead against the hard surface of a flint nodule, properly oriented for a series of carefully-orchestrated gentle taps.

Success!

Working carefully and slowly, she explored the blue-stone's characteristics. Yes, she discovered, the stone could be worked rather like flint. Gentle, properly-directed tapping would remove fairly predictable tiny flakes. Encouraged, she set to work on the real thing. One of her three chosen iris-beads was larger in diameter than the others, needed to be cut down. A good place to begin. Several hours of work, of steady careful tapping with a continually re-sharpened tool, ultimately yielded a nicely circular domed and pierced stone, with its original flat side intact. She was quite happy with the result. She was also developing a fierce headache from the eyestrain and physical tensions of doing such fine work.

Next day she worked on iris number two. Half-way through, with the work progressing nicely, the stone unexpectedly shattered. That was just part of every knapper's life. Undismayed, she proceeded to number three, which behaved itself quite well. By day's end, she had two finished irises, almost identical - especially from viewing distance. She was quite happy with the result so far. She stowed the completed stones in a leather pouch, and turned her thoughts to the next puzzlement, namely how to mount them. It was a first-class problem. The only reasonably effective glue she knew of was pine resin. Everyone used it -and thongs- to attach spear-points to shafts, and knife-blades to handles. Sometimes even leather to leather. But it eventually dried up and flaked off, at least thin coatings did. It was invariably brittle and crumbly on old spears, whereas she wanted real permanence.

Nevertheless she experimented, knowing that data was more useful than opinion, guesses, and speculation. A few drops of gooey fresh resin from a half-burnt pine torch let her try sticking an unused bead to a limestone wall near home. It was quickly obvious this idea wasn't going to work. The resin adhered just fine to the limestone but really didn't stick well to bluestone. Plus, gravity dragged the bead downwards -slowly- until it ran out of resin and fell off. Even the resin itself refused to stay put on a vertical surface.

Then, her subconscious problem-solver suddenly presented her with another, and radically different, possibility. "Ideas comes from such odd directions!" she thought. She had spent a great deal of time at the riverbank as a child, and had noticed little agglomerations of pebbles in mud, with some half-buried pebbles poking up above the mud like frog's eyes. She had once taken a twig and used it to pop some of the pebbles free: they left perfectly nice holes in the mud, each hole the exact shape of the pebble that created it. It had taken considerable force with her stick to pop each half-buried pebble from its socket. Veejr wondered if perhaps she could imitate nature, but in reverse. Maybe she could make holes in the calcite for the iris-stones? The holes would have to fit the stones tightly - but why not?

Hmmmmm.

That would be pretty delicate work, and she didn't know any-one who had ever tried to work limestone that way - or at all, actual-ly. Limestone was far too soft for tool-making, and what else would you work a rock for? She smiled at that thought - how dumb! After all, she herself, right now, was certainly working rock for "some-thing else"!

Thinking-time. She had already proved that bluestones were harder than limestone, and that flint and bluestones were nearly the same hardness. That meant she should be able to make a hole in limestone, using flint as the cutter.

She stepped over to where she did her knapping and rummaged on the ground for a sturdy piece of flint scrap, with a properly-tiny tip. With the scrap and her knapping hammer she tried the process on the nearest limestone boulder. The first few gentle taps convinced her that yes, with great care and patience, she might very well excavate a hole. Ten taps and her tool's tip broke. The idea seemed to be feasible - but it was going to be deadly slow! She was going to use up a great many punches. Oh well.

All the next day she practiced and experimented, first figuring out how to mark accurately the hole she needed, then delicately chipping away tiny dust-like flakes of limestone. As she worked, she got better, and faster. Sooner than she expected, she was having to check the depth and shape of the hole. She decided that the holes to hold the bluestones had to be just the tiniest bit smaller in diameter than the finished iris, so that the stone could be tapped into place - each must be gripped by the sides of its hole, but not so tightly as to break the stone when it was being set. And she would get exactly one chance with each stone and hole!

It took hours of delicate work to finish the test hole, using bead #3 as a model. Then, to study the effect, she slightly enlarged the hole so #3 could easily be inserted and removed. It worked beautifully both mechanically and artistically - the curve of the bead made a lovely natural-looking cornea. And when filled with charcoal, the thong-hole made an excellent pupil. She filled the holes of both stones by driving in charcoaled small twigs and then snapping them off flush with the surface - the result was remarkably realistic. She held the irises up to the wall at the correct eyeball-separation distance. Neither pupil was perfectly centered in its stone. If she rotated them, it first gave the impression of two wall-eyes, then a flat unfocused stare, then the oddity of cross-eyes. But finally - wonder of wonders - the asymmetry could be used to produce a pair of eyes focused on her own! Using her well-developed imagination, she could visualize the result in her portrait - the portrait would be ALIVE, with its gaze focused on the viewer! A completely unexpected, and wonderful, result.

The following day she began eye-work on the portrait itself, carefully locating and then excavating the holes. Dim light and fanatical care slowed the process enormously, but all went smoothly and in a couple of days she was ready to do the installation. She had decided it would be a good idea to cover all bets: she put a dab of fresh, runny pine resin in each iris-hole just as added insurance. Besides, as she pushed the bluestones into their sockets with her thumb, the resin would act as lubricant as well as glue. And when it eventually dried out, the mechanical fit would hold the bluestone, regardless of the fate of the glue.

She adjusted the stones for the best focusing effect, marked the wall and the stones. She was extremely nervous, but the installation went perfectly. With just moderate pressure, each stone went into place with a tiny 'pop' - the bottoming out was easy to feel. The fit, the mounting, was excellent, the irises un-wiggle-able.

The finished eyes were eerily realistic. And the transformation of the Portrait from "OK-lifelike" to "Oh my god it's YOU!" was instantaneous. Not to mention gratifying.

67 - LEFT TO WRITE: NOUNS? VERBS?

For the next three years, as Zachs grew, she studied with her mother. About half-way through the first year, Zachs began to produce recognizable images. She decided to imitate Mother, and invented her own signature - a simple five-pointed star. The day she invented it, she did an entire field of them on the wall, ten by ten seemed reasonable, one for each finger, in two orthogonal directions. Good practice, and it made a pretty pattern, with no deeper significance - but it would puzzle generations of graduate students. Then, Veejr-like, she began signing her paintings with the star. As she grew taller and as her art improved, her drawings gradually rose farther and farther above floor level. When she began to encroach on Mother's space, Veejr gave in to Zachs's enthusiasm and allocated to her one entire section of a long wall. Exclusively hers.

Later, Zachs would sign drawings on that wall with not just her star, but also her two-part "chain of signatures" - hers plus Veejr's together. That combination, too, would mystify anthropologists of Gerard's time. The combination signature came about when Veejr and Zachs were talking one evening whilst dinner cooked. Brother was asleep as usual. Zachs was idle, doodling, drawing in the dirt

239

with a stick. She drew Veejr's SSS, and said, "This means YOU. Everyone knows who did a painting if it has this mark on it. I'm marking my own pictures with my star. That way people will know those drawings are MINE. The star means ME. Zachs. Nobody else."

Thus began the first of a great many serious conversations between them.

Zachs paused only a moment to gather her thoughts: she had been pondering all afternoon, and launched as if into an ongoing conversation - a propensity that the whole Tribe thought peculiar. "I learned from YOU! You taught me."

Veejr smiled, said "I'm not sure about that. Learning and teaching are different things."

"What do you mean, Mom?"

Veejr pondered: there was a hole in her concept-space, and she was going to have to fill it. Mental work, pushups. Finally she said "Suppose you are trying to do something and can't do it, so you ask me for help. Or you ask Uncle. If we help you to do that thing because we already know how to do it, then we are teaching you something. And you are learning from us. But suppose you are walking along a trail and finding signs of a gazelle. You are learning something - you're learning about that gazelle and maybe about the path you both are taking, but neither the gazelle nor the path are TEACHING you anything. You are learning but there isn't any teaching happening. When I was your age I taught myself to draw - nobody helped me so there wasn't any teaching unless I did it for myself. "

Veejr found herself surprisingly exhausted by all this abstract thought. She shrugged as if making fun of herself and asked, "Does that make any sense?"

Zachs had followed Mom's reasoning easily. "Yes." It was fun, using in new ways her ability to think.

Zachs erased the marks and drew again. "If you teach me, then you are first and I am second, like this." She first drew Veejr's SSS: then farther to the right and next to the SSS, she drew her own star:

SSS ☆

She stared at the paired symbols, then said "I'm behind you. That could mean you are number one for painting, and I am number two. But it could also mean you are number one in going along a path, and I'm just following." Another long pause. "Or it could even mean you were born first and me later. Or that your paintings are better than mine." In a very few seconds, she'd run through - invented, really - the need for abstract symbols for quality, sequential ordering, and timeline.

Veejr understood, nodded agreement, then got distracted by caring for the roasting meat.

Zachs was frowning, deep in thought. Veejr got the roast properly adjusted, returned her attention to the conversation, waited for her daughter to speak.

Finally Zachs said "Mom, it can mean too many things. Just with two marks! But I have an idea. Watch me this time." She erased the marks. "When you're teaching me, you're usually talking to me. That's part of teaching. So your mouth is open a lot of the time. An open mouth looks like this:"

<

"If you teach me something, your mouth opens and you talk. I hear you, so I learn something from you. Like this."

She drew

SSS < ☆

"See?! That means YOU opened your mouth and taught ME something. I should put THIS on my drawings, both of our marks and the 'taught' mark, because you taught me how to draw."

Veejr understood perfectly, and despite her little headache, stayed in the game. She took the stick and said "After I teach YOU, then suppose you learn something else and you get to teach ME, then it would be like this:"

SSS < ☆ < SSS

They were suddenly working at a level of abstraction new to both themselves and their species in general. For the first time ever in human thought, both writing and time moved from left to right. And the symbol "<" was behaving suspiciously like a verb.

Zachs laughed delightedly - the ideas, and the marks meant to

241

represent them, made perfect sense. But so what? She realized with a start that even more was needed. And also that this was a dangerous path - there might never be an end to it. She felt the need to carry on, however, and said "Mom, suppose I'm just learning, like you said, from a path or trail. From something that can't teach because it doesn't talk or move. That wouldn't work with these marks because a path doesn't have a mouth and so it can't teach. At least, not by speaking. That means we can't use "<" because it already means 'teach-by-speaking'. We need something else. A path has two sides, like this "∥". And I can learn from the path, so it's almost as if there is teaching going on. So we need a mark that means teaching without talking. That mark could be "=". Maybe me just learning from a path, but without anyone teaching, would be drawn like this:

$$\| = ☆$$

Veejr's headache, and dinner, put a stop to the exercise, at least for the moment. But a bug had been planted in both women's brains, and over many years the two returned to the idea over and over again. It became their private mother-daughter game. Conversations would generate new concepts that needed new symbols: new concepts required new operators to connect them to express more complex thoughts, as did gradations in a single concept. Very early on, they began to keep a list of symbols and examples of how they were meant to be used, all written on sheets of Veejr's bark paper. No trace of which has survived. But late in life Veejr would transcribe most of the symbols, well over a hundred of them, onto the wall of yet another nearby cave, a secondary cave in which she continued her art after The Gallery was closed by a rock fall - a cave not yet found by anthropologists, for whom Lady Luck is still very much in charge.

The immediate, long-lasting result, implemented the very next day, was that Veejr began signing her work **SSS** < ☆ --- and it became a lifelong habit.

68 - RE-ASSEMBLING PANCAKES

Breakfast coffee and croissants on the porch, with a delightful early-summer breeze. Joan, now Directrix of La Fond, turned to Anton, seemed about to speak but didn't. He eyed her over his coffee, grinned, and said "Out with it! You have a question or a proposition. What is it?"

She shrugged. "I'm almost afraid to ask."

He said nothing, just waited.

She sighed: "I need your help. In fact, the whole team working on the Spear-Lady plus Goliath plus Tall Blue business --- we all need your help. Care to guess on what?"

Anton's turn to sigh. "Bet you it's those heaps of busted fired-clay tablets, isn't it? You said six months ago that they might be really important, and you made quite a point that nobody seemed able to make much headway on piecing them back together. And you haven't mentioned them since - probably because I didn't respond very positively back then. But I was busy, setting up my winter courses. Not so busy at the moment. Am I right?"

She nodded, flushing a bit. "You're cute when you get caught!" he said. "What do you need me to do? Put the damned tablets together? Using my extraordinary world-championship jigsaw-puzzle talents, of course!" He was now twice-over world champion jig-sawyer.

Joan admitted it: "Bingo. None of our team can do it - the stuff is mostly pretty badly shattered. All the pieces are scrambled together, and besides there is so darned much of it. We can't automate the work, either - no computer image-analysis program exists that can help much. The tablets could be really important if the markings turn out to be some sort of alphabetic or numeric script. In fact, any type of script whatever would do just fine! We'd all be famous forever. But to figure that out, we need the stuff reassembled. All of it, from both Spear-Lady's and Tall Blue's graves. So weird, the two graves having nearly identical piles of such an oddball material. Everyone else is worrying about "Is it writing?" - but I personally think there's a much bigger mystery buried in those two piles of shards. Maybe figuring out THAT would make the task a bit more exciting for you, Herr Doktor Professor of the Murder-Mystery?" Joan sighed again. "You, frankly, are our only hope for getting the fragments reassembled in this decade. But it's probably a week's work. Maybe a month, who knows? But it has to get done, and sooner is better, if possible."

He interjected "How sharper than a serpent's tooth, to be her only hope!"

She paused, then laughed and said "Good point! But you don't have any summer salary this year, and I have discretionary funds. If you'd like, La Fond could pay you as a consultant. I could clear it beforehand, be sure there's no conflict of interest. Maybe get our benefactor to pay you directly or something."

Anton smiled, shook his head, said "Nice idea, but not necessary. Actually, I've been waiting for you to ask - almost volunteered last week. I like doing anthro puzzles with you and your team, and I'm free for the summer now. I understand the mystery and why the tablets could be so important, and I'd be happy to help. Of course, you'll have to turn the stuff loose into my care - which goes against the grain for every known anthropologist! It was a hoot working with your team on the research, and on writing the papers we've published. So all I'd ask is the same arrangement - just co-authorship. Okay?"

It was okay.

The arrangements were straightforward. Spear-Lady's grave had been frozen whilst still in the ground, then excised and taken bodily -intact- into UP's facilities. The same had been done with Tall Blue's adjacent grave. Both heaps of shards had been left in-situ in their graves - only superficial cleaning of readily-exposable surfaces had been done to date, and it was the cleaned surfaces of a few partly-exposed intact tablets that were fueling the "Is this stuff writing?" ruckus. Anton would need to completely disassemble both piles of shards, then reassemble the individual tablets. A complex jigsaw. With detailed photography of the entire process, of course - perhaps even a running video of all the work. That bothered him not at all. But he refused to do the work at the UP campus nearly two hundred kilometres away from home, even though UP had research jurisdiction over the graves of both women.

His was a wonderfully strong position, an unpaid volunteer

who was critical to the work. He imposed only one minor condition - "I'm going to disassemble the heaps anyhow, before I can reassemble anything, and it shouldn't matter a bit where that's done. Let's take both complete heaps out of the graves and send them to La Fond - since you and I live next door to that institution. They have fine facilities... which I doubt I will need on this project. Baked clay isn't that bloody fragile! All I need is a comfortable work-place near home, good lighting, a couple of probes and some brushes."

Given the real need for his talents, he won easily.

The two heaps were extracted intact from their graves and brought - carefully packaged- to his newly-assigned workroom in La Fond's lab. Two black-draped roll-about work tables, each with a block of dirt topped with a pile of shards tightly interlocked in sandy matrix. He went through a short, informal course in the necessary simple micro-excavation techniques, got the camera and monitor setup functioning, and then sat down to study Spear-Lady's heap, from all angles.

The first thing was to disassemble the pile completely. For pieces large enough, he would number them in situ, so that the photos could enable reconstruction of relative positions. But the more he looked, the less complex the puzzle seemed. A long look at Tall Blue's pile gave the same impression. The reassembly wasn't going to be nearly as onerous as he'd suspected.

He began the routine - first, use a Rapidograph #0000 pen and Higgins Eternal Ink to put minuscule numbers on the shard of interest. Record all pertinent information in a written log. Take lots of photos. Then clean and pry gently with a blunt steel toothpick on a stick, plus toothbrush and soft paintbrush. Nothing difficult or complex about this - complexities would be expected in the reassembly. All removed matrix -mostly sand- went into a carefully labeled container - who could say what information some future technique might extract from it?

The first shards were easy. He laid the bits out on the black cloth. The pile seemed to be nothing but shards and matrix - no other artifacts mixed in, and that made things easier still. At the end of his first morning's work, he had the Spear-Lady's pile one quarter untangled, but nothing reassembled - just several hundred loose, cleaned bits. Already his mind had fitted a few together, during un-occupied moments - but he was going to wait until the pile was completely disassembled before actively working on reassembly.

He disliked calling them "tablets" - they were not the right shape, or regularity, or massiveness. A "tablet", he thought, ought to be hefty, thick, quite un-fragile, maybe with rounded corners, rather book-shaped, probably mass-produced. Like the Mesopotamian or Babylonian and even Roman stuff. He'd immediately taken to call-ing them "pancakes" - and the name was picked up by others in the lab. It stuck.

Joan arrived with lunch-for-two. She was duly impressed at his progress - especially when he showed her the two intact pancakes he'd uncovered.

"Look at the markings!" he told her, proffering one of them. "They were obviously made with some sort of a sharpened stylus, and whoever did them was pretty good with their implements. Lots of almost identical loops and circles and hatchings. But I'll be damned if there's anything here that looks to me like writing or numbers. More like doodles, or the cursive handwriting exercises I had to do - whole notebooks full of them - when I was in grade school in Mexico. I think peoples' idea that this might be actual writing is crap. Somebody may have had fun making these marks, and the pancakes may have had some sort of significance for the people or their society, but writing it ain't. Not in the modern sense anyhow. Too bad. That would have been fun. Doesn't really matter, though - our next journal article is right here, a negative one, de-bunking the 'primordial writing' hypothesis!" He grinned at her.

While they were eating lunch, using the lab roll-about as their table, Anton twiddled idly with a few of the loosened shards. He mused aloud - Joan listened sagely to the ramble, nodding intelli-gently. Each shard had a smooth side and a much rougher side. The smooth side had a slightly uneven surface, and looked like it had been rubbed down with fingers. Overall, the intact shards reminded him vaguely of the drying surfaces of mud-puddles, cracked into polygons, their edges curling up, tops slick-smooth and bottoms sandpapery rough.

After some thought Joan said "Anton, that's all well and good, and you're undoubtedly right - but the real 64-Euro question is, '**WHY** are these pancakes in the two graves?' We've never found anything like this elsewhere. NOBODY has! Why are they here? What is their significance?"

She paused as he said "Whoops! Hold for a second..." He picked four shards, apparently at random, from the field of bits he'd cleaned. He fitted them neatly together. Joan just shook her head in wonder. He apologized: "My brain is on puzzle autopilot... sorry -- disappearing like that was rude of me."

Joan leaned over and kissed him: "You can be rude all you want for as long as it takes to put this stuff together. Besides, you can always make it up to me tonight. I'll be back a little before five to pick you up. Thanks again for volunteering. Cheerio!"

Anton worked his way around Lady's pile, loosening, cleaning. With the top several layers removed, he was getting close to extracting another apparently unbroken pancake, a bit larger than the other intact specimens and with its smooth "writing" surface already partly exposed. He worried loose several interlocking pieces, leaving the candidate for intactness overlain by just three finger-sized shards. Its curled edges and smooth side faced upwards, but there were still no markings in view. He thought that odd because every significant shard so far bore at least SOME markings.

He was proud of his new-found ability to write tiny, clear numbers: he marked and inventoried the three covering pieces, then loosened them and set them aside. He took his brush to the two or three millimetres of matrix remaining on the intact pancake, wondering what he had here.

The first stroke with the brush brought him up short. Surprises like this were, really, what the whole of anthropology was about!

A perfect right hand-print. Intact, complete, from heel to fingertips, fingers widely spread.

Far, far too small to be an adult's. The hand of a youngster. A child! Every line and wrinkle, even the ridges of the fingerprints, were absolutely perfect, and as clear as if taken yesterday by the FBI. He found it hard to breathe for some seconds. Then another swipe with the brush uncovered a small incised character squarely in the center of the palm.

Three parallel esses, very neatly and carefully done.

The hairs of his shoulders and neck and arms all stood up and prickled icily.

He'd seen that symbol before!

And not just once. It was on all the artwork in the Portrait Gallery. It was on the wall of the entry-hall for the Gallery. It was on the body-covering slab from inside Spear-Lady's grave. It was EVERYWHERE in this territory. Deep in caves. In cave entranceways. On a gravestone and on so many paintings. Now on these 'semi-pottery' shards by the literal bucketful.

Every-bloody-where. SSS.

His mind whirled. If it was a signature in those other locations - and everyone who'd ever seen it agreed it was a signature - well, then, it probably had to be a signature here, as well. And almost surely it was the signature of whoever had made this palm-print - and also made the pancakes. And a child had made the print. Guaranteed. No hypothetical midgets allowed. And if THAT was correct, then this pile of shards, these busted pancakes, were childhood productions of the best cave artist on record. Tall Blue. Which meant what? She made these pancakes when she was a kid, then stored them (?why?) for a long time. How long? If Mom were say 20 when TB was born, then her Mom was about 25-30 when TB produced these SSS pancakes. Mom died aged about 80, so the storage time for the pancakes found in Spear-Lady's grave was about fifty years! If all the pancakes for both graves were produced at the same time, the storage time for the half of them found in TB's grave was more like 80+ years. A kid's project being preserved for eighty years? If nothing else, that surely implied strong long-term social stability.

It must be the case that The Kid had made these pancakes and stored them. But why would she have done that? And these two graves were twenty or thirty kilometres from the SSS-Gallery! So, why WHY **WHY** were these pancakes buried HERE, with Spear-

Lady? And with Tall Blue, herself... buried half with their creator, half with that creator's own Mother! More damned puzzles, everywhere one looked! A trivial question popped up straight from his intuition - Would there be at least one similar hand-print pancake in Tall Blue's pile? He would bet anything he owned on "YES!"

Mind-churning.

Obeying his own version of Ockham's razor, and avoiding overt invention, the best story - call it an hypothesis - that Anton could come up with was "These pancakes are a kid's project. The marks aren't writing, but just a child playing around - very thoughtful, very sophisticated, but playing around nonetheless. Doodles. Baked doodles, from forty thousand years ago. And then 'The Kid's' play-toys, the pancakes, had been deposited in these two graves. One of which held the adult artist whom the pancake-making child became. The other of which held that artist's mother. A most interesting family!"

He stared for a minute, then draped a towel over the pile, pushed his chair back, and went in search of Joan. He was going way too fast, needed a break and sanity-check.

Joan was more boggled than Anton. They showed the handprint to the students in the lab, had a half-hour collective gabfest that resolved nothing whatever. They agreed, however, with Anton's plan - no jumping ahead, no outrunning the data! Anton would finish Spear-Lady's materials before moving to Tall Blue's pile. Anton did make a prediction out loud and in public - not only would there be a handprint pancake in TB's pile, but it would be a matching LEFT handprint. Joan didn't argue.

Surprises were part of the routine, it seemed. As Anton approached the bottom of Spear-Lady's heap of shards, he encountered something deeply buried and distinctly non-pancake. Roundish, very hard, his probing eventually suggested two large pebble-like objects. Intensely curious, he stopped worrying about pancakes and paid special attention to freeing the oddities. Out they finally came. A bit of clean-up with a toothbrush, and he could hardly conceal his delight - a smooth, thumb-sized gray pebble of extraordinarily high density, and a chunk of common iron pyrite. From his scouting days, he understood at once, called the group over to see. A small solid-iron meteorite. It plus the pyrites were the ultimate, foolproof, last-forever fire-making kit. This, he suspected and said out loud, was quite likely Spear-Lady's most valuable possession. And someone had tucked it into her heap of pancakes. He would bet the daughter had done it - Mother might well need fire on her afterlife trip. Or maybe Tall Blue was just being sentimental? Maybe that sentimentality was the only explanation needed for the 50/50 division of the pancakes between mother and daughter - why invent fancier explanations without need or support? Anton guessed that the meteorite had been Mother's property, likely devolving onto Tall Blue, who perhaps in a fit of mourning had given it back. A good story, anyhow.

But just where the hell had Spear-Lady gotten a meteorite?

Later, while nobody was nearby, Anton gave in to the urge to try striking sparks - he was hugely satisfied, and genuinely surprised, at the shower of long-lasting sparks he got from a single stroke. It made him realize just how valuable these rocks - especially the meteorite - must have been back in Spear-Lady's day. The ultimate in neolithic high-tech and survival gear. Timeless, too - the identical basic technique is still taught to scouts and military and others, world-wide.

Two days more, and Anton had Spear-Lady's pancake-reassembly done as well as he could. Thirty six pancakes, four of them intact, plus the intact handprint. Lots of woman-made marks, but little doubt remained that they contained no hidden meaning,. They were not "writing". Kid doodles. Too bad, but still interesting.

On day four, Anton moved to Tall Blue's materials. Knowing what to expect sped up the process. It wasn't until two-thirds down Tall Blue's pile that a large shard emerged, carrying the full-length imprints of four fingers. Twenty minutes later, three major pieces fitted together and Anton had the complete hand-print. Left hand. With the SSS signature in the palm. If the Kid were still alive, they could get the FBI forensics people to identify her by fingerprints, no problem. And just as with Spear-Lady's materials, there appeared to be no meaning in the stylus-scribbles on the pancakes.

As soon as he'd finished, Anton called Joan to come and have a look, pointed out one other oddity - each grave had originally contained exactly 36 pancakes - his reconstructions proved that conclusively. And each had a single full-hand-print cake. Precise equality. Except for the left-right handprints.

Queries - why the pancakes in the graves, and why the equality? He speculated aloud for his own and Joan's benefit. Tall Blue's and Spear-Lady's burials were closely related. For some reason the 72+2 pancakes had been of interest or importance to them both. In death the cakes had been portioned out carefully, no favoritism. Why a left-handprint in one grave, and a right-handprint in the other? Maybe the whole pile of 72+2 had been made at one time - but surely not for burial services? Any kid making pancakes would probably have made just one each of left and right - he could imagine the process clearly. If the cakes had been made with burial services in mind, or with the initial idea of an equal division, then to preserve equality the cake-maker would have made both left and right handprint cakes for each pile, a matched pair for each half of The Kid's production run. Ergo the cakes had been made well in advance of their use in the burials. But not made with burials in mind - nor with the idea of dividing them up into two equal parts. When needed for the burials, the maker-kid hadn't gone back and made another set of L+R to establish perfect equality. If the kid didn't do so, it was probably because by the time of the burials it was impossible to get equality. Why would that be? Because the owner/maker of the prints was grown up (or even dead?!) by the time of the first burial. No way a pair of kiddie-prints and a new pair of the same hands (but adult-sized) could be separated into identical piles except by discarding the handprints – hardly a likely solution given that the entire set of pancakes had been stored somewhere for decades before the burials! And the experts had determined that the two ladies' burials were not contemporaneous, they were separated by at least a couple of decades. Someone had placed half of the cakes in Lady's grave, then much later the other half went into the second grave, namely Tall Blue's.

Good grief! His turn to have a headache.

69 - CHYS VISITS THE GALLERY

By the time Veejr arrived at formal adulthood, say fifteen, per-haps sixteen, she'd been doing her art for over ten years and was quite good, and still steadily improving.

For several years she'd been routinely adding pictures to the Men's-Cave -always of big game. A few years past she and Chys (who at the time were still the only two women allowed into the Men's-Cave) had argued that there was nothing "male-sacrosanct" about that cave's artworks - that the cave should be open to every-one's view. This was because the artwork was intended to benefit the entire Tribe by abetting the ongoing quest for big game. The art was also in a real sense "paid for" by the entire community, in the form of food and other necessities, subsidies, given to Veejr and Chys by the whole Tribe to compensate for their loss of time for food gathering and other activities. And if that wasn't reason enough to open the cave, well, the two of THEM were certainly women and had been INVITED into the cave, so any taboo was long-ago moot - broken and proven inconsequential, because nothing bad had result-ed. Men not liking to lose any "male only" prerogatives (even silly ones), the arguments about general-public access to the art were long and even occasionally nasty, but eventually the women's logic prevailed, perhaps aided by Veejr's thinly-veiled threats to stop painting unless a certain decision was reached.

In the Men's-Cave, Veejr now painted only to order - the Tribal council would declare which species needed special attention, she would execute the next paintings in the growing series, and the en-tire Tribe - her public - would be invited in for a viewing. In study-ing the art on the walls, the first thing one saw was, nearest the en-trance, the original art by an unknown hand, in all its crudity. Then Veejr's art took over: it was enormously better, right from its first appearance. One could also track her steady improvement.

A publicly-supported art museum, a wee bit ahead of its time. A museum with just a tinge of 'place-of-worship' about it. A muse-um with two artists-in-residence. A good young artist in her own right, Zachs was not merely Veejr's daughter - she was her student, her protégé. Even as a youngster she had her own walls in the

252

Men's-Cave, where Mother and daughter often worked back to back: together they burned up a great deal of animal fat, sometimes having upwards of a dozen lamps going simultaneously. The myth remained intact that it was due to their artwork that big game (with its abundant lantern-fat) was so seldom in short supply.

Meanwhile, Veejr had also been working continually in her private cave, the Gallery. The only people who had ever visited it were Husband and their blue-eyed daughter Zachs, both sworn to complete secrecy. Nobody else –including Chys- knew of it, much less had ever visited it. With completion of her consummate blue-eyed self-portrait and one other big charcoal full-face portrait, Veejr had reached a turning point. It was time to show off her many years of privately-held work. To someone important.

Mother Chys was by now a genuine Ancient, verging on being a female Methuselah, and beginning to age more and more quickly. She had once long ago promised never to ask about Veejr's day-long disappearances, and had kept the promise for all these many years. She was certain the secrecy had to do with Veejr's art, even suspected a private cave, but never asked. Not her business!

Chys was therefore totally flabbergasted and quite deeply pleased one day when asked whether she felt up to an hour's slow hike. In the invitation, Veejr 'officially' revealed, finally, to her mother only, that she had a private cave full of her own art. It was time for Chys to see it. If she wished. Veejr insisted that the hike really wasn't difficult nor was getting into the cave.

Chys did wish. She had visited the Men's-Cave many times, hence was familiar with Veejr's and Zachs's cave-art work, the big socially-important stuff, but this sounded altogether different - a private collection! Of course she wanted to go!

Standing in the undecorated, naked-white Gallery antechamber, Chys was awed just by the size of the cave. Veejr led her through the initial twists and turns, brought her to the first long wall of paintings. There were many walls, and hundreds of paintings. To see them well, each woman carried a lamp in each hand. Plus a shoulder-bag of extras.

Chys gaped, thunderstruck, as Veejr walked her slowly down

the long, long rows of drawings. Gazelles, rhinos, vultures, bison, horses - in profusion. Pictures of actions, of events. Veejr pointed out how her work got better and better the deeper they moved into the cave.

Although Chys had decades of experience studying and understanding Veejr's work, it took her a full minute of examining the big landscape of The Plateau to make it comprehensible. Veejr watched recognition suddenly dawn, just as it had decades ago with her first face, the one she'd drawn on her thigh. Veejr then pointed to three pairs of small female figures in a lower corner, said "This is you and me on our trips to see the big animals up on the plateau! That was a long time ago, and so much fun! The men were sure we'd get lost or killed. Dummies!"

Chys leaned in with her lamp, studying: the three-pair scene was understandable at a glance. Chys reached out, gingerly touched the figures of herself, then sighed and turned to Veejr. "Thank you, daughter. This is very special. Thank you."

Veejr next guided her to the long double row of profiles in frames. Chys held her lamp close to the art, studying the pictures. Another "Aha!" - with one finger she tapped the end pair and named them - man, woman - a couple, both of whom she knew well. Likewise the next vertical pair. Every image was identifiable. All were adults, all in husband/wife pairings. Several individuals were long dead, but Chys recognized them instantly. The realization that she could again see someone whom she'd helped bury many years ago floored her.

Knowing what was coming next, Veejr was getting antsy as they worked their way to the far end of the rows. Anticipating this visit, Veejr had recently spent a day adding two small scenes of human figures, one above and one below the Old Woman's circular portrait. The upper new drawing was of the infinitely retold tale of Chys and the cave bear, complete with her spear in the bear's eye, and three men with broken spears. The lower was a sharp, clear depiction of a woman standing in a high crouch behind a bush, holding a huge spear angled upwards, with its butt anchored to the earth beneath her right foot. On that spear, impaled through the chest and spraying ocher-blood, was a male figure twice the spear-woman's size. Both images accurately portrayed what Veejr had learned from Chys about the two incidents, on those memory-hunts so long ago.

Chys stared briefly at the Old-Woman portrait, then reached out to touch the images of herself in the two small, newly-added action scenes and murmured "Your art is magic, daughter." She grinned: "How wonderful! My bear is alive again!" Then she tapped the image of Monster transfixed by his own spear: she sighed almost wistfully, squeezed Veejr very tightly again, and said in a low whisper "I've always sort of wished he and I had met some other way! I don't think he was really a bad man - after all, he could have killed me and didn't, even though his companions all thought he should. And he fed me. Maybe he and I could have made more blue-eyed babies. Like YOU!"

Veejr grinned: "Mother, one of me was probably more than enough!"

Chys shifted her attention to the final, oversize portrait itself, a full-face view of an old, old woman. Together they stared at it, silently. Finally Chys asked, very softly, "Why is this one so big? And from the front, not from the side like all the others?"

Veejr said nothing for a few seconds, then "You recognized all those other pictures, the couples. And the two little pictures that go with this one. Don't you know who this is?"

"I think so..." Chys said. She turned to face her daughter. "This is ME, isn't it?"

Veejr grinned and nodded. Mother turned back to the portrait, studied it intently for a few seconds. Then she reached out and tapped the image on the forehead with her fingertip, delivered her critique. "This woman is OLD!" she said. "Look at the wrinkles! And her eyes are closed. Is she supposed to be DEAD? I'm not dead, not yet!"

Mama – Veejr's very own personal life-long art critic!

Mama wasn't angry, Veejr realized - just clearly upset over something about the portrait. Veejr was nonplussed, didn't quite know what to say. It was a very, very good likeness, one of her best ever, and yes, Mother WAS now an old woman covered with wrin-

255

kles, no argument possible. But DEAD? Veejr disagreed: she said nothing, waited.

Chys finally cracked a little smile, shrugged, hugged her daughter again. The tension evaporated. "Well, I suppose I have to agree that I'm an old woman now. Going to die sometime soon, I expect. One thing I am sure of is that your paintings and drawings of people are always accurate. So I suppose this is how I really do look. Maybe living long enough to get this wrinkled is a mark of honor for a woman, like men and their bear-claw scars?"

Then she giggled, an odd sound coming from such an ancient face. She tapped the portrait on the chest: "Good job with my fancy bear-jaw necklace! Remember, you have to bury it with me." She paused to think, then went on quite vehemently: "This picture may be accurate, but it is NOT how I feel inside." She tapped her own forehead. "In here, I'm only about as old as when you were born."

After a deep thoughtful breath she continued: "No woman likes to think she has lost her beauty, daughter! **DON'T FORGET THAT EVERY OLD WOMAN WAS ONCE YOUNG!** And we all want to stay that way forever! You will, too, believe me!" Almost coyly she continued: "You have a good imagination, and with your crazy memory I know you can remember what I looked like when you were a small child. Can you do another picture of me, right here beside this one, and show me when I was a beautiful young woman? A woman who wasn't chased as much by men as she would have liked --- mostly because she had a crazy blue-eyed daughter? Can you do that for me?"

Veejr was strongly moved - Chys had never, ever asked Veejr for an artistic favor, not so much as a thumbnail sketch.

Then, softly, "Veejr, I know this is what I really look like today. It's a very good painting and I like it very much even if I'm complaining. It's so different from all the others! That, and the bear and Monster drawings, make me feel special. My complaints are mostly in fun. But I really would like another, too - the young me. That way if anyone in the future ever sees the picture, they can see me the way I want them to! I've BEEN both of these two people, both young and old, so anyone who does see all this art ought to have BOTH pictures to look at, so they can know ALL of me." She sighed, squeezed Veejr's hand: "Does that make sense to you? It sounded pretty good to me, but then, I'm a very old woman and maybe I'm not thinking clearly nowadays."

Veejr hugged her and said "Makes perfectly good sense to me! Of course I'll do another picture, just like you want it. I promise."

Only then did an understanding of the entire visit come to Chys with a heart-clutching jolt - her daughter had drawn the three small scenes to tell something of Chys's personal history, major happenings in her own life story, permanently on the wall. Perhaps forever? In Veejr's own private collection. Veejr felt her mother's reaction, understood it, squeezed her in an embrace radically different from any previous hug.

Finally Veejr led Chys to the self-portrait room, with the door-slit guarded by the skull of the cave bear Chys had killed so long ago. Chys recognized it instantly. "So this is where the skull went!" she said: "...and such a good place for it!" She paused to stare closely at it, remembering how she had forced herself to swallow her absolute terror as she aimed her puny spear, the relief flooding her as it landed in the bear's eye, the secondary terror of trying (and failing) to get clear of the falling animal. And of course quickly reliving the ceremony where the men awarded her that fancy, scary chunk of bone. She still wore the jawbone-necklace on important occasions, and had long ago decreed that she would wear it in her grave as well. She reached out and tilted the skull, held the lamp closer, stuck an index finger into the left eye-socket just as Gerard and others would someday do. She looked into Veejr's eyes with almost a smug expression - "I was pretty good with my toy spears, daughter! This isn't very much of a target, but I hit it! I think this is a good place for the skull. Just be sure to give it to your own daughter someday."

Veejr stepped to the slit, said "This is awkward, but you can get through ok. Inside is my best work. Come on!" She took Chys's hand and helped her wriggle slowly through the entryway.

Chys's response to Veejr's blue-eyed self portrait was almost identical to Gerard's forty thousand years later. She had to lean

257

against the wall and catch her breath. The reaction completely satisfied Veejr... well worth the long wait and all the work!

When she could speak, Chys said, pointing, "This painting is ALIVE! It's impossible, but there you are, trapped on the wall while you're still walking about! You are amazing!" She touched the blue eyes, grinned, and said "I know where you got the eyes! From the trader on The Plateau. I have wondered many times where those stones went. This is a fine way to use them!"

Together they silently studied the portrait for a couple of minutes. Then out of an introspective fugue, Chys said "Veejr... the paintings in this cave, this picture of you, the picture of me... they won't go away quickly like your marks in the clay at the river. How long will they last?"

There was another hole in the Tribal conceptual toolkit, a hole having to do with timelines and their absoluteness mixed with indefiniteness, their essentially limitless extension fore and aft, moving smoothly forward yet unable to go back, moving smoothly yet broken up into discrete segments like heartbeats, breaths, days, moons, seasons, years, generations. Many people in the Tribe and elsewhere had worried over bits and pieces of the problem of time. Nobody had solved it then - nor has anyone in Gerard's day.

Veejr shrugged and said "A long, long time. Longer than your life and my life and Zach's life all put together, I'm sure. How long? I don't know. Probably longer than we can imagine. I hope so!"

Chys nodded agreement. "I hope so too. I'm sure you're right." Then, with a strange look, she muttered "Veejr, because of you and your art, we - you, me, the couples, the animals - we will all live forever. So please, do my pretty picture. Then when you bury me, I will still be here. Just like the people in the long rows of pictures. Someday some of your and my children's kids many times over - they will see us again. We will still be alive. Forever!"

70 - DEATH

Chys knew she was dying. She knew because she had seen many people, over her decades, going through what was now happening to her. The concept of death and dying didn't worry her: besides, what could she do about it? She had no complaints. Her body was worn out, most systems were actively failing now, all except her mind. But the machinery had served her well throughout an adventuresome life. She had experienced and survived things most people could not imagine if they tried. She was over eighty. Way more than twice the average lifespan. By far the oldest person in the Tribe, older than any person ever even rumored to have been. Her eldest daughter Veejr, at well over fifty, was already regarded as nearly ancient.

Nobody was certain of Chys's actual age: number of years hadn't yet taken on the mystical aura it would in later times, and no accurate calendar yet existed. Not that the society couldn't count that high, it was simply that there was no need for the number when applied to peoples' ages. Such large numbers could be useful in dividing up resources, yes - discussing or evaluating people's ages, no. Hence nobody kept count. Individuals with good memories could walk audiences backwards through years tied to seasons or events, but two parallel recountings might differ radically - which bothered no-one. The rigid silliness of human-time had not yet imposed itself on human affairs.

In fact, Chys had outlived all her children save Veejr-the-Artist who was also Veejr-the-Medicine-Woman, with whom she had been living now for several years, growing increasingly frail whilst waxing god-like to the rest of the Tribe. The stories about her youthful exploits were very much the stuff of local legends. "She who kills Monsters and Cave Bears" would live on beyond her death both in story and in her portraits in Veejr's private cave. Chys found that knowledge oddly satisfying. She even found it amusing to wonder who would ever see her portraits. Veejr had assured her that the "younger" portrait - as requested by Chys when faced with a realistic painting of herself as an old, old woman - was almost finished. Chys knew she would never see it in person - she could barely walk at all now, so no more hikes to the Gallery. But SOMEONE, SOMEDAY, she was certain, would see the works. She hoped those future viewers would like them, would understand the meanings and the stories.

Chys and Veejr and Veejr's daughter Zachs had for years discussed the interesting but not very critical questions of death and burial. Not critical because there was little uncertainty about the whole process, and no very clear concept of an afterlife. The simple facts were that everyone died, everyone had to be buried, unless of course they got themselves eaten, or disappeared by drowning. Or, occasionally, simply vanished due to unknown other causes. Why it was necessary to bury the dead was something they never explored - it was a fundamental unspoken assumption that burial would happen, that it was absolutely necessary (else why had the Tribe taken the trouble to bury Monster so long ago?) - but WHY it was necessary, that they could not intelligently discuss. It was like the sun coming up in the east - it just WAS.

Death was certainly a major event, a turning point in every human's existence - but not overly complex. Usually, one got old (if you were lucky!) and sick and then stopped moving, including breathing and talking. Left alone long enough after that, one began to swell and then to stink. Just like any big dead animal. All understood that the body was going to decay - buried or not.

Although there was no well-developed theory of an after-life, there was certainly an acknowledged and much discussed feeling that there was something inside each person that rendered the body human, in the sense of different from other life-forms, and that the "something" went away at death. The person inside was the important part of every human - and at death it got up and left. Gone, nobody knew where - and it never came back. Ever.

The concept of nothingness wasn't yet available, so because the dead had obviously gone SOMEWHERE, the most basic and difficult question was, "Where does the person go when they head off on that journey?" Which was unanswerable: because nobody had ever gone and returned to tell, debating about it was pointless.

For those of the dying who had time to plan such things, the addressable questions were simple - where to site their grave? Who would handle the body? What goods should go into the grave? What property should be left to whom amongst the still-living?

To those folks staying behind, the next logical question was "What will my dead relative need on their journey?" Certain critical objects were obvious - life without a knife, or a spear, or fire-rocks, even some favorite personal adornment, seemed to be a poor way to go, so those were routinely interred with a person's body. Sending a relative off on such a journey also seemed a good time to give personal gifts, both useful and sentimental. And wherever the person was going, any symbol of power couldn't hurt. If the deceased owned such things, making the items available to them post-mortem was clearly a reasonable idea.

For over a year the three women had talked about where Chys should be buried, and exactly what should go into the grave with her. Chys was adamant about a few things. First, location: she knew exactly where she wanted her grave-site - a difficult spot, hidden well back under the huge overhang that protected the major settlement. The very driest possible location. She was sorry it would be difficult digging, but that was what she wanted. Veejr agreed, and as Chys's oldest and nearest relative, she would be in charge.

Woman Who Kills Monsters and Bears got her way. As usual.

Secondly, Chys wanted to be buried with her two major power symbols, her bear-mandible necklace, and the huge spear she had taken from Monster. But she vehemently did NOT want the big spear broken up, as the Tribe had done with Monster's other spear when they'd buried him. It must go with her, intact - if it were broken, who could say what would happen to its power? Certainly nothing good! She wanted a few specific items in her grave - knives, her cowrie bracelet, a nodule of good flint and her knapping hammer and goggles, plus other miscellany. Nothing grandiose, nothing she couldn't carry with her in this upcoming journey, no matter what form the journey might take. And there was the matter of the skull of Chys's cave bear - which she had given to Veejr, who carried it to her private cave to act as guard over the art-work, especially the self-portrait. Chys thought it a good idea, but not a requirement, that Veejr eventually pass the skull along to Zachs. If she wished. No pressure.

To deal with the Monster Spear they would simply have to dig

261

the grave a bit differently from the usual simple pit. Having learned the rudiments of sketching from her daughter, Chys drew an outline in the dirt: a bathtub-shaped grave, with a long narrow trench paralleling how her own body would lie. It was functionally something between a concept drawing and a blueprint: the intellectual stretch and reach needed to produce a such a pictorial plan for future action, for future construction, was something that would have entranced Gerard's generation, had anything been left of the plan for them to see. The trench was for the intact Monster Spear. Daughter and grand-daughter agreed. Plans were reviewed in detail several times, finally declared complete. Just in time.

Not long thereafter, Chys simply stopped breathing in the middle of the night: she was stone cold when Veejr came to feed her breakfast.

That day Veejr and Zachs recruited all their male relatives, plus many volunteers, to dig the grave - tradition was that a body must be buried by the second sundown post-mortem. There was no grumbling when Veejr laid the Monster spear in position grave-side, to mark the extra long, narrow slit-trench needed to accommodate it. All agreed on its power, and that the power was peculiar to Chys alone - obviously the spear MUST go with her, and unbroken, per her instructions.

In retrieving the Monster's spear from the depths of the cave, Veejr found beside it her long-forgotten cache of fired clay pancakes. Waxing nostalgic, she impulsively divided them into two equal stacks - which left the paired left-right full hand-print pancakes. She made up two bundles of thirty-six. It seemed right to her that if Mother got to keep, in death, half of the pair of cowrie bracelets, then it must be appropriate to give her half the pancakes. Each bundle got one of the handprints, too. While helping to lay out the body and goods, Veejr tucked one bundle into the space just in front of Chys's shins.

Veejr would eventually get for herself the other half of both the pancakes and the cowries - she already intended to have Zachs put the other bracelet, and the other bundle, into Veejr's own grave.

Before starting to dig, Veejr told the assembled workers that she had another special idea for this special grave... if they would help, it would be an extra honor to Chys, but a good deal of extra work. Nobody was about to refuse - after all, Veejr was now both the Tribe's Medicine Woman and its Artist, in addition to being its eldest citizen. Plus she had the power of being the original blue-eyed Tribal member. Not even to mention being responsible, through her art in the Men's-Cave, for the Tribe's ongoing luck in hunting big game. She explained the idea - the workers agreed to it, and she led a smaller party, armed with heavy choppers and ham-mer-hatchets, into an unused passage in the Men's-Cave. She showed them a floor-to-ceiling free-standing curtain of calcite, some ten centimetres thick and a metre wide. With care and considerable exertion, they broke free a slab a metre and a half long. After widen-ing the entrance a bit they manhandled the slab out of the cave, then carried it, using slings, back to the burial site.

The plan, she explained, was to cover Chys with this rock - the grave would have to be enlarged slightly to make things fit. The idea was extra protection for the body. They would just barely bury her, then fit the slab over the body like a below-surface lid, and fi-nally fill the grave to the top as usual. The Chief thought it a good, if weird, idea - but insisted that if the slab was to do its job properly it must not simply rest on the just-buried body. That would never do, the unsupported weight might possibly pin her down and pre-vent her departure. He volunteered from communal supplies six large intact flint nodules - valuable gifts indeed, and an honor to her from the entire Tribe. They would be set in the main grave to sup-port the slab, so as to keep its weight off the body.

In the grave, the body - suddenly tiny and vaguely birdlike, weighing almost nothing - was arranged by Veejr herself: it was she who carefully wrapped Chys's hand around the carved checkering of the Monster Spear and then packed the dirt to hold the hand in place - that way Chys would be forever ready for whatever might happen. Chys's two hunting spears, long disused, went into the main part of the grave with her. As did her broken-pointed cave-bear spear. Chys had always felt, but confided it only to Veejr, that the smaller, bro-ken spear was the more potent, had accomplished a much more dif-

263

ficult job than had her big souvenir. The intact giant spear was symbolic but unblooded, whereas the broken "child's toy" had done its duty, given its all to save the owner. But the bear-spear certainly lost out in visual impressiveness!

The funeral itself, if it could be so called, consisted of each person standing over the still open grave, stating his or her relationship to Chys, and simply saying goodbye. After goodbyes, the six flints were properly set, and with great huffing and grunting the slab was settled successfully into place. Just before the workers began to fill the grave, Veejr brought out a clamshell of red-ocher paint. She dipped three fingers into it, and wrote her signature on the slab, directly above Chys's head. Then she looked at Zachs, handed her the shell. Zachs used one finger to make her own signature below Veejr's - her five-pointed star.

As was proper, the grave was quickly filled, the dirt packed tight, and all traces of burial activities erased. That evening there would be a prolonged story-telling session with Chys and her exploits as its theme. With plentiful liquor made from fermented catail roots for all. And life would go on.

71 - SLABFALL

Chys died without Veejr ever finishing her "younger self" portrait - a failure that was no fault of Veejr's. Before she could return to the Gallery to finish it, the area got a most unusual prolonged period of torrential rainfall. Groundwater is a fine geological lubricant. It is amazing how quietly a million or more tons of limestone can lose its grip and exchange potential energy for kinetic. The midnight rock fall didn't even waken anybody in the Tribe. But it obliterated the only known entrance to Veejr's Gallery.

The event wasn't noticed for several days, until a hunting party following the base of The Rampart found its traditional path buried metres deep in freshly-broken limestone. From the party's descriptions of the locale, Veejr suspected the worst.

Next day she took a small party to explore: she could place the entrance roughly, using remaining un-affected features, but within an hour she was certain there was no access. The Gallery was sealed, the 'pretty-woman' portrait of Chys would remain unfinished - that bothered her more than the rest of the loss altogether. She consoled herself somewhat with the knowledge that almost certainly the fall hadn't done any damage deep inside the cave. Her art still existed, there was probably no destruction - the work was in fact quite safe - just inaccessible. Someday, who knew when, another rock fall would most likely re-open the cave. But there was nothing useful to be done here and now. She was upset about losing access to so much of her art, but also philosophical - there was nothing she could have done to prevent the rock fall... that fall was inevitable, everyone knew that it was a commonplace occurrence for caves to open and close, anything but supernatural. And short of finding or making a new entrance, there was precious little a person could do about the process. She wanted to be angry about the loss, but couldn't figure out who or what to be angry at (rather like dealing with death) - so she threw herself into displacement medical artwork in the Men's-Cave.

Then, a few weeks later, her Husband (who had found the Gallery cave for her so long ago) brought news he hoped would brighten things a bit - whilst hunting small game, he and his companions had found another cave, apparently just recently opened by a minor rock fall, perhaps simultaneous with the Gallery fall. They had explored it a bit - it had walls adequate for her work, and seemed to be completely unused. They would be happy to show it to her if she'd like to start another gallery, or at least have a place to paint. But not secret like the first - too many people already knew of it.

Hers for the taking. A present.

She took it. And used it extensively. Then, long after her death, it, too, was sealed by rock fall - and has yet to be rediscovered.

72 - DEATH AGAIN

Veejr lived on to nearly her mother's age, being cared for by daughter Zachs and family. Old age and pneumonia killed her at the end, but in her last day of coherence, she insisted to Zachs that she should be buried as close as possible to Mother Chys. From a distance of over twenty years, Zachs could remember reasonably well where Grandma's unmarked grave was located - but not perfectly. When laying out the new grave, she was off by a couple of metres, and it just nicked Chys's grave - such a minor incursion that it wasn't noticed. At least, not at the time - in fact, not for nearly 40,000 years.

Into Veejr's grave, as had been pre-arranged with Zachs, went grave goods relevant to her dual roles in the Tribe - Artist and Medicine Woman. First the body and her art supplies - clamshells full of valuable pigments, the remainder of her blue beads, her cowrie bracelet, and the package of 36 clay pancakes, complete with right-hand print. Plus knives and brushes and other miscellany, including a thong-tied bundle of dozens of blank sheets of bark, made up into a rectangular package ten centimetres thick by twenty by twenty. One never knew - perhaps each person's after-life journey was unique: as the Tribal Artist, she might very well need all those pigments and charcoal - and if so, then she would surely need paper as well. The squares were not quite dimensionally identical: the bundle had on all of its four narrow edge-faces rather the appearance of a modern deckle-edged book. This particular artifact, far more than any other in either woman's grave, would drive future generations to distraction.

After the art supplies had been loaded, the burial team partly filled the grave, packing and smoothing the dirt until the body was out of sight. Then they laid down a layer of small bundles of various freshly-cut important medicinal plants used by Veejr and her trainees. The new Medicine Woman, having just that day taken over from her dead mentor, decided purely on a whim that the bouquets should be laid down in the same sequence as they were shown in Veejr's Men's-Cave pharmacopeia, which sequence was utterly random. The parallel sequences would eventually be noted by a young anthropology graduate student, and would form the basis for a 300 page doctoral dissertation, the speculations in which would have amused Veejr no end.

Zachs thought seriously about trying to cut a Chys-style calcite slab for Veejr, but quickly gave up on the idea. It would be far too much work, and the original curtain of calcite hadn't enough remaining material for a second slab anyhow. And for Veejr there didn't exist the superstitious forces that had driven the idea for Chys - Chys's having killed both Monster and Mister Bear were far more potent doings than Veejr's "merely" being an Artist and Medicine Woman. This anything-but-simple burial next to Chys would more than suffice, even without a lid.

73 - COWRIES

Anton came home from the store to find Joan sitting at their dining table with a bemused, but happy, expression. He stooped to kiss her, then sat and asked "OKAY, lady-love, what happened to YOU between the time I left and just now? Give!"

She smiled at him: "You want more hard data for our little anthropological real-world mystery? And maybe we should talk, seriously, about "Exactly what is the mystery?" anyhow! "

"Sure! What's the new data? And, Joan... I think the 'mystery' is the fitting together of all this information we keep finding that relates -centrally relates- to the Portraitist, Miss Triple-ess. From a hell of a temporal distance, we seem to be assembling almost a biography! The "mystery" is just this - "Working logically, how complete a story can we assemble?" And with what degree of confidence in its accuracy? This whole business is a serious multidimensional jigsaw puzzle - one with almost all the pieces missing."

"That sounds good. I'll buy it for now" said Joan. Then, "One of the students working on Tall Blue just called. They uncovered and freed the left arm-bones today. Guess what they found?"

Anton thought, then said "No idea. Could be anything, but obviously it has your attention. Theirs too, or they wouldn't have called."

"Cowries. All found at her left wrist. A bracelet. She was right-handed - we know that from her art, and believe me, if I had to throw a spear right-handed, then for sure I would wear a bracelet only on my non-dominant wrist. In precisely the style of these two ladies."

Anton looked startled, then laughed delightedly. "Wait... let me guess. There are twenty-two of them, that is, cowrie shells. Right?"

Joan nodded - he was quick today!

"Wunderbar!" he said. "Now we have two women, mother/daughter, in two adjacent graves, buried twenty years apart, and wearing identical bracelets! From forty thousand years ago!" Then "And each woman got one full handprint on a grave-pancake. Both handprint pancakes are signed. Signed by the same person - a child - who when she grew up used the same signature mark as the Portrait Artist. The Artist, miss Esses, used this sign as a kid, as an adult on her art, and finally on her Mother's gravestone!"

Joan nodded: "And her art implies strongly that women went on repeated big-game hunts without men. Not to mention that she was fully capable of male-style heroic deeds." She shrugged, grinning from ear to ear. "You know, don't you, that we're probably going to spend the rest of our lives figuring all this out!? And of course, we'll be getting most of it wrong, too!"

74 - EMITTING A TRIBAL PROPAGULE

Chys's and Veejr's Tribe was quite successful - over several hundred generations its population grew steadily. But there was (and still is) a maximum size which the social and ecological systems could maintain, approximately 100 to 125 individuals. Growth beyond that made everybody uncomfortable, and began to impinge in readily detectable ways on the surrounding ecological support structure. Hence the Tribe, being successful, experienced a gradually intensifying cyclic pressure to emit propagules – to send off small groups to colonize elsewhere. The process also served to lower the local population pressures. But any action to the benefit of the Tribe must, necessarily, consist of actions taken by individuals, and for humans that usually means (paradoxically) actions taken with the aim of self-betterment by the emigrants. Over the many centuries, the process recurred every generation or two. The same, of course, was happening elsewhere, in other successful societies - the whole process generating genetic variability and mixing. And an ever-expanding total range and population for our species.

Pressures were always the most intense on young males, who universally suffered physiologically from elevated testosterone levels, and socially from a constricted range of options and limited chances for moving up in the local social structure. And often from a shortage of available females as well.

Came a day when a relatively nearby settlement launched a trio of young men - strapping lads, intelligent, experienced hunters all, lifelong friends, tired of local constraints, consumed by the human teenagers' lust for adventure and exploration. Not only was their own settlement under population pressures caused by success, but from the lads' point of view there were, locally, very few viable mate-candidates.

The three young men got tribal permission or blessing - not that they actually needed it - to leave. The first goal was simply getting away from the known. Goal #2 was to find mates - after all, three men do not a viable human propagule make! For mates, they would have to go to other settlements, other tribes. If they could be found, mates were not a purchasable item - they would have to be convinced to come freely. The third goal was to satisfy simple human wanderlust, the need to travel far away, to find a place to settle and develop a new home and society of their own, without the old place's "mature settlement" constrictions.

The trio took several weeks to cover the few hundred kilometres to the Tribe's location. After making themselves known, they were allowed into the settlement as a curiosity - but everyone knew what the true goal was. Knew it, understood it, and agreed with it. In fact, from the beginning the visitors made clear their intent to obtain mates if possible, and then to leave, traveling far in search of unoccupied hospitable territory.

There were an unusual number of eligible young Tribal women available at the moment, and no eligible bachelors. An altogether favorable combination insofar as the trio was concerned. The young men were personable; their language was related to the Tribe's, which helped with communication. And of course both factors helped with the courtships that sprang up almost instantly. The visitors volunteered to participate in a Tribal hunting party - one way of proving their personal worth. They performed very well indeed. They were motivated.

Hormones and proximity did their magic: in less than three weeks, three pairs had self-assembled. One pair included Veejr's blue-eyed grand-daughter Zixx (out of Zachs), the lineage's third generation of blue-eyed women artists. She was totally smitten by one of the newbies who, when introduced up close, had been utterly fascinated by her eyes, and who told her in no uncertain terms that they were beautiful so far as he was concerned and to hell with any-one else's opinion. Zixx was fourteen and nearly full grown - and (courtesy of Monster/Goliath's genes) considerably taller than any of the three potential suitors. Her particular man was equally favor-ably taken with her height - no dummy, he had peered ahead a gen-eration and visualized the children they might produce - with his powerful musculature and her height, they would have a serious edge over their peers. Her artistic bent he didn't understand, but when she explained and then demanded that he promise to help her maintain the habit, he readily agreed.

In short, Zixx faced a devastating combination - raging hor-mones both male and female, population pressures on the communi-ty; a handsome available man known to be a good hunter, and one who LIKED the two controversial aspects of her physiognomy. She was head-over-heels in days if not hours.

Veejr and Zachs immediately knew what was going to happen - it was time for Zixx to leave the Tribe, a normal if wrenching thing. Objectively, the girl could not have picked a better person or group or time. Everyone knew that the chances of ever seeing one another again were vanishingly small. But the urge and need to leave were irresistible.

The three couples soon announced to the whole Tribe their de-cision to leave as a unit. They would travel downstream, following the river as far as possible. There were persistent rumors, sometimes quite detailed hence believable, that the river eventually emptied into a body of water far, far larger than even the great Plateau atop The Rampart - water that could not be drunk - far too salty - but which was full of the most amazing fish, easily caught and delicious either fresh or smoked.

A week later, the Tribe had a departure party for the six. Tribal women prepared for each female emigrant a large knapsack, half-filled, not-too-heavily, with what amounted to a dowry - utensils, supplies, food, knives and spear-points, thong and fire-rocks. In her own pack, Zixx insisted on including a small sampling of art supplies. Red ocher, a few charcoal brushes, half a dozen sheets of bark - all those things could and would be found elsewhere, the emigrants were certain, but it would be nice to at least start out on this journey into the unknown carrying traces of the old homestead and relatives and memories. Both Veejr and Zachs asked Zixx and the trio of young men to make them two promises. First, that Zixx would insist on settling only in some place where she could continue the family line of art-work. To this the three young men readily agreed. And second, that Zixx would teach her own daughter to paint as she had been taught herself. Everyone simply assumed that such a daughter would eventually materialize. Zachs and the men found those promises easy to make. After all, the whole party understood the purpose of the Men's-Cave art, and the group would certainly welcome a continuation of the tradition in their new home, wherever that might turn out to be. Never, ever turn down a potentially lucky thing!

The blue recessive was strongly present in this propagule - Zixx was homozygous, and one of the other two girls carried the blue recessive masked by black. Three female blues out of six possibles - fifty percent! A major inroad by the sneaky gene.

Moving many hundreds of kilometres downstream took the sextet some months, seeing that travel had to be interspersed with exploration and with simply finding each day's food. But eventually the river did bring them to the rumored infinite body of non-potable water.

The seacoast was, from the first, a good place. They had seen no sign whatever of other humans for the last couple of hundred kilometres - no competition, no worries about neighbors friendly or otherwise. Food from the ocean was easy - there were endless coastal swamps full of tasty birds totally unafraid of humans, tide-

271

pools full of edibles free for the taking, fish that could be seen and speared (after some practice) from the surf-zone rocks. An endless supply of shellfish, for the taking. The three men had all learned to swim as children, which helped greatly with the food supply. A few day's travel south along the shore they encountered another river, which they followed upstream a very few kilometres - where they found a lovely cliff, a mini Rampart of yellow sand and hard lime-stone. Situated well above both sea-level and the river at flood, with a huge flood-plain supporting abundant edible plants and their in-digenous herbivores, the cliffs were honeycombed with usable cav-erns that contained not the slightest trace of bears.

The cave complex became their permanent home: their new settlement had become a successful propagule.

Having gone forth with a vengeance, they turned immediately to multiplication. They had been on the road for over six months, and already all three women were well into their first pregnancies. One had been taught the rudiments of midwifery, a purely "see one, do one, teach one" education. Fortunately she was the last to deliver, hence was available to help in the other two births, training the other women to aid in her own confinement. All three children were healthy and black-eyed. But the sneaky blue-eye gene was present, hidden, in every child Zixx produced, and as insurance, in half the children of the other "recessive" woman. Zixx was both fecund and lucky: not only did she have several kids, but all save one reached adulthood safely and had children of their own. By which time blue eyes were no longer remarkable in the new settlement.

Zixx's eldest was a daughter. Even whilst caring for the child, named Lyss, Zixx was searching nearby for an appropriate cave for art - she was addicted, she had promised her mother and grand-mother, and besides, the understanding in the Tribe had always been that her family's art brought good luck in the hunt. Therefore she'd better get cracking! The search didn't take long. With torch and holder and charcoal, and with baby Lyss on her hip, she began a whole new cave.

The artistic tradition from generation to generation held true. At age five, Lyss was in the cave with her personal charcoal twigs, tagging along with and imitating Mother. At age seven, by then capable of drawing, sketchily, a few recognizable animals, wanting to imitate Mother in everything, she chose a signature for her own work, thusly

^^

Back during her apprenticeship with Veejr, Zachs had developed her own signature, a simple five-pointed star. However, she habitually signed her work with a complex symbol incorporating both her personal symbol and Veejr's, the two linked by yet another symbol invented by themselves, meaning "taught". This she did to honor and thank her mother/teacher. Zachs had worked in both the Men's-Cave and Veejr's Gallery, and a good number of paintings carried the compound symbol, which she regarded as her normal mature signature. The linkage was thus

SSS<☆

meaning "Veejr [spoke to] [taught] Zachs, and Zachs did this painting".

Both parental and artistic lineages were now matrilineal in the Tribe. Zachs had in turn found a very apt and enthusiastic pupil in her own daughter Zixx, the third artistic generation. A tradition was building. Veejr was slowing with age, and the Zachs/Zixx pair regularly worked together (both individually and collaboratively) on the art required in the Men's-Cave. As a youngster, an apprentice following her forebears, Zixx invented her own signature symbol, "**&**". When she felt that she had gotten good enough, she began signing her own works with the more complex full lineage

SSS<☆<&

meaning Veejr taught Zachs, who taught Zixx, and Zixx painted this.

Zixx took the entire signature-tradition with her when she left as part of the three-couple propagule.

That ultimately produced the magnificent signature-chain

SSS<☆<&<^^

Meaning, of course, Veejr taught Zachs, who taught Zixx, who taught Lyss, who made this painting.

Which, Lyss quickly decided after writing it a few times, was entirely too long and complex. But what was she to do about it?

Starting at about age 4, Lyss talked extensively with her mother about the family lineage, about who great-grandmother Veejr and second-great grandmother Chys actually were, as real people. While the concept of 'mother' worked for Lyss, the idea of 'grandmother' was a bit difficult (having never seen such a person herself), and that of great-grandmother was simply too abstract to comprehend. GtGt Grandmother Chys surely must have existed and may have been important - so said Mother Zixx and who was Lyss to argue with her?- but even a Gt Grandmother named Veejr, who used the signature SSS, had no reality for Lyss. Hence very early on, at age nine or so, she simply dropped the to-her-meaningless "SSS" from her signature. Thenceforward her work bore only the simplified

☆<&<^^

Her mother, of course, remained

SSS<☆<&.

One day early in Lyss's "apprenticeship", whilst enroute to the cave, she asked how her mother had learned to draw. Instead of heading into the cave at once, Lyss and Zixx sat down outside and Zixx did her best to explain again, particularly about the line of ancestors leading down to themselves. The whole concept of previously-existing but now gone versions of "mother" had become less confusing by this time. Zixx was able to relate the names in proper order back to Chys, having learnt the sequence from her own mother, but she was unable to put much reality into her descriptions, having not known personally the earlier members of the sequence.

It was an exercise both edifying and frustrating, leaving Lyss less confused but hardly satisfied. Eventually they picked up their supplies and headed into the cave. Not far inside the entrance Zixx stopped, said to her daughter "Sit here, watch. I think I can draw something that might help."

On a short bit of unused smooth wall, at shoulder height, she wrote with quick practiced strokes the chain of name-symbols, in order stepping backwards, narrating and commenting as she went -

"Lyss is ^^ --- This mark means YOU!"

"Zixx is & --- This mark means ME! I am your mother."

"Zachs is ☆ --- This mark means Zachs, my mother, who was your Grandmother. I knew her well, of course... she raised me. I left her home when I was a very young woman, to come here. Where you were born."

"Veejr is SSS --- This mark means Veejr. She was my mother's mother, so she is my Grandmother. She was the first person in our old Tribe ever to have blue eyes, and all the blue-eyed people in our Tribe today got their blue from Veejr. She is your Great Grand-mother - I knew her, just a little bit. Veejr was the Tribe's Artist - she used her drawings to help the men succeed in hunting, just like we will do here, you and I together. Veejr invented putting our own marks on pictures. And she was also a powerful Medicine Woman."

She went silent for a moment, and Lyss asked "What about Veejr's own mother? You've told us stories about her. But you said you didn't ever know her."

Zixx nodded: "That's right, her name was Chys and she died before I was born. She was Veejr's mother and Veejr was the first artist. Chys was a hunter, a very fine one, and quite brave and lucky. She killed a huge man, and a cave bear, all by herself! She is the first woman hunter I ever heard of, but she was not a painter, so she never invented a mark for herself." She paused, frowning, then said "We need a mark for HER, in this list, or the list will be incomplete. Because she was so important and famous, it should be a strong mark. Maybe like this:"

She took a wider brush and drew

A

She looked at Lyss, who nodded, eyed the mark, and said "It's very strong, like the frame of a tent. I like it. Now we can have a complete list!"

Zixx smiled, said "Remember - Chys's Tribal hunting name was Woman who kills Monsters and Bears. Let me show you what she did to get that name."

Despite never having met Chys, Zixx knew in detail the stories of her exploits. She took a charcoal stick and drew two quick sketches, one on each side of the new symbol. One was a set of three stylized men, not quite stick figures, each holding a broken spear, the trio facing a huge and evil-looking animal much taller than themselves. Off to the side she sketched a smaller female figure, arm raised for spear throwing. The spear was lodged in the bear's head. Zixx turned to Lyss and said "The big animal is called a bear, they live in caves back where I came from, and they kill a lot of people. They are the most dangerous and ferocious animal in the world - we are very lucky not to have to deal with such animals here. Even though women were not supposed to go hunting, Chys did. All by herself Chys killed one huge cave bear and saved three men's lives. She was very brave and very good with her spear."

Lyss's eyes were round - she'd heard fireside tales of bears, but never this story.

Next Zixx drew a pair of outline figures, mere quick-sketches, showing a huge man impaled on a large spear, the spear held and controlled by a woman half his size. "This man attacked Chys and she took his spear away and killed him with it - he is the "Giant" in her hunting name. And he was Veejr's father, too. Like I said, Chys was a very brave and powerful woman who really deserved her hunting name. Our mother many generations ago. We should be proud."

Zixx contemplated the list and the two drawings, grinned, drew a quick little bundle of plants, with leaves and flowers, beside Veejr's symbol and said "There! That shows she was also a Medicine Woman as well as an artist." Then "Later, if you want, you can figure out what to put beside all the other names. Now - let's go do some good work today!"

Unfortunately for anthropology, Lyss never did add details to the genealogy.

Both Zixx and Lyss were prolific with their art. It seemed to work its traditional magic on big game, and with that help, plus considerable other talent and lots of hard work, the new settlement thrived mightily.

And as both had expected, Zixx and Zachs never heard from or saw one another again.

75 - SOMETHING NEW

Joan eagerly took the call - it was from Gerard, her very first grad student, who had finished his PhD some twenty years ago. Both of them were now in their professional prime: they still shared a deep interest in everything that had been, or would be, found out about the specimens and sites that had made their careers. No, she always thought, it wasn't right or fair to call their ancient human subjects "specimens" - she and others had over the years pieced together too much information about the actual individuals - they were PEOPLE, not specimens. And they had names - Spear-Lady (aka "Woman Who Killed Cave Bears and Goliath"), her daughter Tall Blue, Spear-Lady's victim nicknamed Goliath - who was also Tall Blue's father. The recovered or reconstructed people had quite individual personalities, at least for her and Anton and Gerard - and for several full five-year generations of grad students as well.

She hadn't heard from Gerard for nearly a year - he had, she knew, taken a fine new position at a distant university, and was very active in research, publishing regularly. In fact, he'd just recently done an initial report on a new cliff-cave complex down south, near but not on the ocean. A remote site, large and apparently undisturbed. Promising.

It was a cell phone call. "That's odd", she thought. It was midsummer, Gerard would surely be on-site, which meant far from cell facilities. He didn't like telephones in general, cells in particular. Maybe he had actually reformed and sprung for a satellite phone?

There was no social chitchat and nonsense from Gerard when on a phone-call. "Hi!" he said - "Sorry to interrupt but I have something you need to see. Right now, immediately. I just sent you three pictures from the new site. As email attachments - poor images, from my phone's camera. They will have to do for the moment. Better pictures will be coming soon, I promise. Get your email up, I'll just hang here and wait. Open #1 first."

The connection and logon always took about twenty seconds. Meanwhile, as the system ground along, she could feel the familiar rise of the hairs on the back of her neck - something she hadn't felt for far too long. "Old and blasé...", she thought - "...that's what I'm getting to be." But she knew to trust her instincts - Gerard wouldn't have called at all without something truly significant and interesting to report. What would it be this time?

The email program finished loading, connected - his message was topmost.

"Here we go...." she said into the phone, and clicked on attachment #1. A full-frame close-up photo appeared:

☆<&<^^

A long, long wordless pause. Then, under her breath, "Great god almighty, Gerard... is it really what it looks like?"

"Go to number two" he said.

She could almost feel the grin in his voice!

Breathing momentarily suspended, she opened attachment number two:

SSS<☆<&<^^

"Jeez, Gerard!" was all she could manage: her chest and throat were constricted. Finally getting her voice going, she said softly "Gerard, it looks like our gaggle of women artists is going to haunt us forever!" Then, "How nice!" A pause. "Fifteen hundred kilometres apart!"

He chuckled briefly into the phone. "Yep. Tall Blue, our Lady of the Self-Portrait, her unregistered trademark being SSS - she is at far left in number two. Then comes her daughter connected to her with what has to be a verb meaning something like "gave birth to" or "taught" or "spoke to".

That's a WRITTEN _VERB_, Joan! That is to say, 'verb' in bold underlined italic and all-caps, if you please!"

Gerard paused, then said slowly and forcefully, "I'm no professional linguist, but here we by god have abstract symbols for known individuals. In other words, NAMES! Written names. Connected by a written verb."

Another pause, then "In some circles that's called communication by writing. A.k.a. literacy – at some level."

Joan managed to sputter her agreement.

Gerard started again. "Joan, just THINK how close we are to finding writing, a real written language! Right here! You can almost

TASTE it! The writing process had to start somewhere - maybe it started independently at fifty different times and locations, maybe they all failed, but we're so damned close! We even have a couple of the most primitive steps documented. Who knows what we'll find here!"

"Plus, these signatures absolutely link our new site with the original Spear-Lady site, and directly link people HERE with their relatives THERE, meaning at The Rampart. Linkages with specific individuals about whom we know a hell of a lot. And like you said, these newest signatures are separated from The Rampart sites by 1500 kilometres. But it all includes the same artists we know and love! Actually, we have a lineage fully documented right here - and my guess is that the only rational interpretation will turn out to be that Tall Blue's kid or maybe grandkid left The Rampart settlement, emigrated to our new site, and took up her art again. And SHE then taught her own kid to draw - the Kid would be the artist who is sign-ing art with a double caret. We've found and documented an honest-to-goodness dynasty in the making, Madam! In a society that is on the verge of writing, that understands medicine, and which perma-nently documents their medical knowledge in written and picto-graphic forms. And it has spread territorially, in one generation, some 1500 kilometres. That's one hell of an expansion."

"Given all that, who else would one expect to be the next add-on to the signature chain? The next generation, and that would al-most certainly be a mother-to-daughter thing, not bringing in some outsider or some male! It's an artistic chain and it's genetic as well, I bet."

A prolonged silent pause.

"Joan, the whole layout down here is eerie because it's so much like the Gallery in lots of ways. The two complex symbols, the 'signatures', of attachment #1 and #2 both occur in the same mess of gradually improving little-kid's work in the main cave. Where most of the good stuff has the signature in attachment #3 - take a look!"

Joan brought it up onscreen:

☆<&<^^

She thought, then sighed deeply and said "Gerard, signature

number three almost certainly reads "...from Tall Blue's daughter, thence to Tall's grand-daughter, thence to great granddaughter". She paused, anticipated a protest that did not materialize, and then went on: "I know, I know - we don't know the genders of those new artists. Not yet! But I'm inclined to bet on their being females! We have no nicknames for daughter and grand-daughter. Or for the next generation either -- that being the person using this two-caret signature. Let's call this symbol's person "TwoHat". TwoHat must be Tall Blue's great-grand-kid, which means TwoHat is Spear-Lady's great-great grandkid!" She laughed, muttered "In accordance with my intuition about gender, those should not be "kid' but "daughter."

"I'm going to predict something, Gerard. I'll bet you that the full-length four person signatures only occur in the artwork where the youngest, the kid, was just learning to sign stuff at all - bet you that she got tired of it being so cumbersome, and shortened it by dropping Great-Great Grandma off the left-hand end. She almost certainly never knew the woman anyhow. Nonetheless, we have perfect overlap of symbology, rather like tree-ring analysis. The name-chains even read left to right! They were all right-handed, Gerald. Even the cowrie bracelets say so. Right handed and I'll bet mostly if not all blue-eyed. I do hope we can someday find materials to check on the blue-eyedness. Maybe we'll be able to scrape up a bit more information on your personal genetic linkage to our Tribe! I expect there will be plenty of bodies in the graveyard for more mtDNA analyses. We've been ungodly lucky throughout this work, it's possible we haven't ridden our streak into the ground yet!"

76 - CONTINUATION
A very long pause indeed - they could hear one another breathing. Then Gerard broke the silence:

"You're just as fast as ever, Madam. I agree - that's what we have, exactly."

Gerard wasn't quite done. "One added small detail, Joan. We have our own ground-penetrating radar on-site. We think we've located well over twenty graves already, but we haven't excavated even one yet. Some of them are loaded with small echoes. This should be fun. After all, you and I both believe we're not yet at the end of this saga."

Another long pause, during which Joan somehow felt like she was waiting for the other shoe.

It came.

"Oh, I almost forgot - one last little teaser for you, Joan. I just pushed SEND on another email. Open the attachment... it's a shot of some rather quick-and-dirty sketching we found just inside the main new art cave. I think the drawings' scenario is sort of incomplete and informal. Feels to me like they were done to illustrate a story some-one was telling. The pictures aren't really up to the ladies' standards as 'formal art' – they look a lot more like my scribbled blackboard diagrams made during a lecture!"

Joan stared at the screen - it was the chain of signature-marks they were all so familiar with, but with the "A" preceding "SSS" --- and with the three simple sketches Zixx had done for Lyss.

"Migawd...." she breathed into the phone. "They've assigned a written symbol to Spear Lady! They are writing a HISTORY, Gerard, not just chanting a lineage! This is LITERATURE! The lit-tle sketches with the symbol establish A's identity without a doubt. And her descendents got the essence of her exploits correct. Across several generations. They even have plants associated with Tall-Blue-Medicine-Woman! Fifteen hundred kilometres, someone moved away that far, and commemorated the entire lineage. Down to the detail of broken spears several generations back. I can't be-lieve I'm still breathing."

Gerard was grinning - she was sure of it, could feel it coming through the phone. "So - here's a proposition" he said. "In my re-search budget there are uncommitted travel funds for a few un-specified co-investigators. How about you and Anton get your butts down here for a week, starting next Monday - my assistant can make all the arrangements. God only knows what we may find in this cave - so far we've only gone in a hundred metres but the art just seems to keep on going. We really do need to work together on this one. That's two varieties of the royal WE. To wit, "WE the institutions" and also "WE Joan, Anton, and Gerard". Bet you there's at least a few more years' work to do! Who knows what we may find around the next corner? Hell's bells! - Tall Blue wrote her pharmacopeia, maybe she really DID write a book?! Or maybe her offspring did. Somebody had to start! Let's go see."

POST SCRIPT

On our recent ancestors' intelligence

There is a debate about when modern man's direct ancestors achieved the present level of human intelligence. Many seem to believe that relatively recently (say, 40-80 k years ago) there was an abrupt change or 'step function' in intelligence. That, for instance, a 'pre-step' person from 60k years ago might be our physical, but certainly not our mental, equal. An interesting "thought-experiment" would be a living Turing Test, thusly: take a newborn from 60k years ago, time-transport her to today, and at age 25 see if one could definitively tell her from her modern compadres, all participants having been brought up in all respects as modern children. I expect she could not be told apart. That is why I wrote this story. It seems to me quite likely that any feeling of 'present-day quantitative or qualitative superiority' is purely a function of the paucity and fragmentation of physical evidence.

Why do I feel this way? For two reasons. First, the idea of a sudden large "step" is illogical, because evolution seldom (if ever) proceeds in large jumps - it seems almost inevitable that apparently-large jumps eventually can be (read "are always eventually") resolvable into a series of small (although possibly rapid) steps. The converse is never seen. The apparent suddenness of many striking and undoubtedly-real changes usually proves to be due to fragmentary data or poor analysis. The usual evolutionary series of minor changes is far more likely - and much harder to document - than some merely postulated major step. Second, because I think the proponents of the "step" theory take the wrong option in evaluating our forebears' intelligence - they choose the low end (based on weak evidence) rather than the high end (and our own existence today should be a powerful argument in favor of "high end" estimates).

In light of our ancestors' proven abilities to solve complex problems (QED - after all, here we stand!) plus the paucity of physical evidence available to us, the default position should be in favor of HIGH intellectual capabilities - at the far end of the spectrum of the interpretation of any data. Our ancestors were superb problem-solvers: to survive and prosper they solved untold problems, most of which we will never know - neither the problems nor their solutions. At every turn, those ancestors deserve MORE credit than suggested by the available direct evidence, not less!

Our forebears predating any postulated "step" clearly were capable of high-level abstraction and logic, for without those mental tools (which are surely a powerful correlate of 'intelligence' however defined!?) they could not have survived and succeeded as they did. Looking just at the known problems encountered and solved by humans from our time-traveler's "home era" and before, I find it hard to believe that those "pre-big-step" people were any less intellectually capable than my own generation.

What they did NOT YET HAVE back then is the benefit of our species' slow accumulation of thousands of generations of cultural development and cultural evolution. Those folk back then were PARTICIPATING in the grand "*Homo sapiens*" experiment, and should not be criticized for not having in hand the usable results! We, today, are the beneficiaries of a cultural learning curve that has suddenly gone vertical, a curve whose foundations our ancestors built for us but the results of which they did not have available.

I premise this story on my belief that people quite far back in time, who were undoubtedly anatomically *H. sapiens*, thought about and intelligently discussed topics, and handled problems, that even today we 'modern' humans find difficult. It was in that process that they gradually developed the conceptual and knowledge frameworks within which we exist today. Some current, very recent capabilities (e.g. writing) may greatly facilitate today's handling of difficult questions, but the lack of those advanced capabilities should not have prevented earlier generations from being aware of and concerned about those questions, or from intelligently and logically dealing with them. After all, as shown in detailed written records, humans wrestled intelligently with the structure of matter and the rules for its behavior, long before quantum theory.

Problems in uncovering, inventing, interpreting "history"

It is questionable whether 'history' is, or even can be,

'science'. In science there are only two fundamental questions. They must be posed in this order:

(1) What exists out there, in nature? and

(2) Why is it that way instead of some other?

Those amount to (1) description and (2) understanding. Doing #2 before #1 is philosophy, or theology, or bullshit.

For "history", on many scales, both of the fundamental scientific questions may be unanswerable both practically and in principle. Certainly, on the theoretical and atomic levels, it is literally impossible to have perfect agreement between two observers as to "What happened at locus (X, Y, Z) at time T?". There is no reason to prefer one observer's view over the other: neither is "correct" - or, alternatively, both are. Although we would like it not to be so, the macroscopic world of "history" seems also to possess this property, namely indeterminacy, in abundance.

There are many who would argue that there is, therefore, no such thing as "**THE HISTORY**" of a phenomenon. I tend to agree. However, I do not agree that there is never a preference to be raised between competing (or, better, 'parallel') views; obviously some are more rational than others, and I generally prefer more rationality over less.

On the macroscopic scales important for historians, anthropologists, archaeologists, anthropologists and the like, the study, writing and interpretation of history - the "What happened, when, where, to whom, and why?" - is plagued with huge problems of scarce data and great uncertainty. The skimpier the data, the more difficult are the problems of both description and understanding. There will always be multiple possible descriptions and explanations... some more likely than others.

Especially for our species' early history the recoverables are both monumentally fragmentary, and widely scattered. Such large-scale uncertainty poses not merely a type of 'winners write the history' problem - it also exposes the much larger problem that MOST of what occurred in the past is quite irrecoverable - we not only cannot know how the pieces fit together, we cannot even know that most of the pieces exist(ed). Atop which is the problem of variable interpretation of such fragments as do survive. Ten equally well-trained individuals given the same data will often arrive at fifteen answers to question #1- "WHAT happened?" - without even attempting the much more interesting question #2 - "WHY?" Given such evidence, one can seldom make positive 'historical' statements such as 'X happened because of Y'. Rather, the best outcome of an investigation is often a rather wimpy "We can for the moment eliminate Z from the universe of possible explanations for our observations" - a slow and painful way of making progress.

Trying to assemble a coherent picture of the past and of the temporal evolution of inferable past phenomena, and especially trying to establish both the reality of changes (inferred or observed) and causality for those changes, is incredibly difficult. Observationally, it is as if one is peering from the air at something quite complex, occurring in the ocean's depths. Peering at random times through the heaving, random surface, at something which is usually almost completely obscured. One can get only isolated, disconnected fragmentary views of bits of the phenomenon, which is itself almost certainly changing in all four dimensions even as one looks.

That is just the observational problem - then comes the "WHY".

Furthermore, one almost never has anything even vaguely resembling a set of replicated observations - the *sine qua non* for modern science. Only a few often tiny and often apparently random physical artifacts and other information persist for any significant time and become (equally randomly) available to us as we try to understand human evolution. Seldom are the bits more than crudely correlated: causality is out of reach.

Because information about our species long ago comes to us often in disguise, usually at random, and in multitudinous forms, to produce an accurate description of, or causal explanation for, observations about human history or evolution, requires not just hard work, but lots of dumb luck. Social evolution, wherein much of critical importance is not physical, leaves neither skeletons nor imprints in the mud. Attitudes and beliefs seldom leave shards. The utterly fortuitous concatenation of rare or even wildly improbable events seems to be required for progress in understanding to break through the 40,000 year barrier. The "correct" minds must encounter one another, however indirectly, across vast gulfs of time and space. We need the lucky happenstance of those minds being focused in some way on the same thing despite huge temporal gaps.

Problems of developing and retaining complex culture

One needs a goodly bunch of people to insure against random losses of knowledge - such loss can kill development. It is a curious, perhaps unfortunate, coincidence that the rough **maximum** size for a hunting-gathering community (100-125) dances around the estimated **minimum** number of people required to maintain and transmit complex culture (300 and up). With complexity come difficulties of maintenance - demanding redundancy. Specific bits of knowledge must reside in more than one person, lest the knowledge die with the individual and be lost to society. This is why tribal elders are so important worldwide - they are every pre-literate society's research libraries and repositories of accumulated experience.

The unfortunate equivalence of the two sizes means that just about when a group gets to the requisite number to maintain complexity, it runs headlong into the ecological limits on group size. Somewhere, probably a few times, due to extremely lucky conditions, groups of humans recently managed to punch through that barrier (e.g., by developing agriculture) and then to create complex societies that were sustainable for long periods. Our neolithic protagonists seem to be dancing along that edge.

Structure of this story: making the reader work a little bit!

The distant past reveals itself piecemeal and seldom in any overall coherent temporal order. Different pieces become available at various times, for various reasons. We may well know details about an event forty thousand years ago before we know about events twelve hundred years ago. Getting the historical time-line sorted out is a major task. In the text, events for the story's two lines of protagonists are presented roughly in chronological sequence. But not perfectly so. And cross-referencing is even less perfect. That is all intentional: it imposes on you, the reader, a very mild version of the historians' and anthropologists' task.

This novel is about such difficulties, and also about the existence of unexpectedly multi-talented individuals at the right time and place both then and now, doing the right sort of things in the right sort of circumstances. Almost certainly there are aspects of both the 'great man' and 'pressure of events' theories at work. Strikingly potent individuals occur even today, and many events ("progress") seem to pivot on those folks' existence (Newton? Aristotle?). Likewise societal evolution seem to make some events foregone, with the need generating the individual (Edison? Tesla?).

The story stresses the absolutely critical role of simple 'luck of the draw' in the ongoing development of what we almost laughingly can call

"A [**not THE**] [hi]story of our species."

We follow two groups along parallel paths of human experience. They are separated by forty thousand years but occur in the same physical location. Path #1 includes half of the protagonists: they exist within a human Tribe somewhere near the ***sapiens vs. neanderthal*** finale. Paleontologically, the Tribe is definitely *H. sapiens* (modern), and situated near the postulated "step function in intelligence", but it is unclear which side of the so-called step they occupy. Path #2 is that of a group of anthropologists in today's academic world, studying those Tribal peoples' unusually extensive artifacts (luck of the draw being very much on the moderns' side for once!), interpreting them as best they can, trying to identify and understand big trends and major events, whilst also trying to address small-scale aspects of individuals' daily lives, seeking to get some sense of the PERSONS behind the artifacts, even at a 40,000 year remove. The interpretations are often off-target and wildly mistaken, and sometimes remarkably accurate. With our intermittent God's-Eye view, we readers are occasionally privileged to be able to determine which.

We follow the Tribal members in considerable detail, to show how perfectly reasonable, human-driven chains of events (individually unlikely, but collectively highly likely to occur SOMEwhere and SOMEtime) can work together at both ends of the time-gap, to enable us today (given both great skill and luck) to make connections with, and understand aspects of, our societal forbears. I try not to let the characters know things, and engage in behaviors, that would be illogical or unseemly for their stage of social and knowledge development. Note that I did NOT just write "illogical or unseemly for their intelligence, or stage of intellectual development."

Final comments

In light of our ancestors' successes, we should be happy to grant them more credit than will ever be documentable with "hard evidence" - our species' success to date is, itself, incontrovertible evidence that they deserve such treatment.

www.ingramcontent.com/pod-product-compliance
Lightning Source LLC
Chambersburg PA
CBHW021950170626
46808CB00001B/88

* 9 7 8 0 6 9 2 6 5 8 6 9 7 *